P9-CEQ-762

CLOSING COSTS

ALSO BY BRACKEN MacLEOD

Novels

Mountain Home

Stranded

Come to Dust

Collections

White Knight and Other Pawns

13 Views of the Suicide Woods

CLOSING COSTS

BRACKEN MacLEOD

Houghton Mifflin Harcourt
Boston New York
2021

hmhbooks.com

Library of Congress Cataloging-in-Publication Data
Names: MacLeod, Bracken, author.
Title: Closing costs / Bracken MacLeod.
Description: Boston : Houghton Mifflin Harcourt, 2021.
Identifiers: LCCN 2020034159 (print) | LCCN 2020034160 (ebook) |
ISBN 9780358334736 (hardcover) | ISBN 9780358540137 |
ISBN 9780358540205 | ISBN 9780358335764 (ebook)
Subjects: GSAFD: Suspense fiction.
Classification: LCC PS3613.A27395 C58 2021 (print) | LCC PS3613.A27395
(ebook) | DDC 813/.6—dc23
LC record available at https://lccn.loc.gov/2020034159
LC ebook record available at https://lccn.loc.gov/2020034160

Book design by Chrissy Kurpeski
Typeset in Garamond Premier Pro

Printed in the United States of America

1 2021

4500827501

for Dallas Mayr

When I was at home, I was in a better place.

— WILLIAM SHAKESPEARE, *AS YOU LIKE IT*

No one is more arrogant toward women, more aggressive
or scornful, than the man who is anxious about his virility.

— SIMONE DE BEAUVOIR, *THE SECOND SEX*

Where it went was to the basement.

— JACK KETCHUM, *THE GIRL NEXT DOOR*

CLOSING COSTS

I

◆

NELLE

1

TWELVE WEEKS AFTER CLOSING

Home.

It was nice to be home. Nelle Pereira had been looking forward to this long weekend for a while. Work lately had been hard, and she felt like the stress was piling up, ever mounting, until the smallest upsets left her feeling raw and depleted. A mere two days off was not enough to reset her mental reserves. She hadn't worked up the nerve yet to quit, but was nearly there. Maybe Monday she'd tell Tony she was leaving. Give him enough time to find her replacement; he'd been kind to her, and she didn't want to leave him in the lurch. And then she could spend more time with her husband doing the things they'd always put off because there was never enough time with school and then work. Never enough money. They could try again to expand their family. They could afford it now. And they owned a home.

Home. The word wasn't onomatopoetic, but sounded like it could be. The long *oh* and a soft *mmm* at the end, both preceded by an exhalation. It sounded like the kind of contented moan a person would make during a lingering, comforting embrace. The word was warm and safe and all the things she adored about being in the house she and Evan had bought just over three months ago.

It was nice to be *home.*

She lost herself in the sound of the showerhead above and behind her, the rushing patter of water against her skin and the tub and curtain beside. Steaming hot water beat against her shoulders and cascaded down her back as she stood, letting the spray massage her. An unhurried, hot shower was a decadence. But April in Massachusetts could be eighty degrees one day, and forty and snowing the next, and the nights were usually cool. Though today was forecast to be a warm one, Nelle was a summer creature. She soaked in the heat to ward off the chill of the night before and the one to come.

After she shut the water off and pulled back the curtain to grab her towel, she looked at her dripping hands and water-wrinkled fingertips. *How long do you have to shower to get pruney fingers?* Nelle dried off, stepped out of the tub, and called to her husband, "Sor-ry, bebê! I'm done." Evan had promised to have breakfast on the table when she got out, but he was used to her Saturday morning hedonism.

She finished blotting her hair and dropped the towel on the floor. Seeing only the hazy silhouette of her body in the foggy mirror, she smiled. She felt good. A little *more* than good, actually. Her muscles were loose and warm, and she felt pleasantly relaxed from head to toe. She opened the door and peeked out, intending to give Evan an incentive to abandon breakfast for the bedroom.

He wasn't where she expected him to be, just around the corner in the kitchen by the stove or the fridge. The bright room was empty, sunlight from the window glinting off brushed steel appliances.

She padded upstairs toward the bedroom, careful not to slip with still-damp feet on the hardwood floors. A concussion would not be conducive to seduction. Evan teased her about tracking water all over the house, showering downstairs when there was an en-suite full bath off their bedroom, but the showerhead upstairs was one of those low-water types, so the pressure was weak. On weekends and after exercise, she needed the stronger nozzle from the first floor, and told him that until he replaced the showerhead in the master bath, she'd be taking her indulgence on the first floor, thank you very much.

She peeked into their bedroom. The bed was made, and the room, as empty as it was quiet. Across the hall in the guest room, the setting was the same. Unused bed, unopened curtains, and no life except for the Devil's ivy plant on the dresser that desperately needed watering. She turned out the light and stepped out into the hall, peeking into the upstairs bath, thinking maybe he'd ducked in there. But then, Evan wasn't shy about peeing in the same bathroom where she was showering—or doing her makeup, or brushing her teeth—and if he was sitting, the door would be closed.

He wasn't upstairs at all. "Evaaaaan. Where aaaaare you?" She went back downstairs and checked the guest rooms down the hall at the south end of the house—still filled with packed boxes, three months after their move. Not there. She searched for him in the dining room. Empty. "Hey, bebê! Where'd you go?" Her voice echoed in the narrow, high-ceilinged room. She listened, hoping to hear him poking around somewhere. Maybe a rustle of packing boxes or the record player needle dropping into a groove. But, nothing. The kitchen, dining room, and family room were all open floor plan. If she couldn't see him in the kitchen, he wasn't in any of those places.

She crossed back through the kitchen and opened the basement door, the only place she hadn't checked. He could be doing a load of laundry, right? On a Saturday morning. Of a long weekend. Unlikely, still . . . "You down there?" She listened, but got no reply. She shut the door and returned to the bathroom.

He must be outside.

She dressed in the old camisole top and baggy cutoff sweats she wore to lounge in on weekends. While their house was on the outskirts of town, it wasn't *that* remote and there was a limit to her exhibitionism. She didn't need to give an eyeful to the mailman or some other delivery person she might meet on the front step.

Sure, I can sign for that package. Huh! I don't seem to have a pen on me.

The morning outside was cool but not cold. Not bad. It had rained overnight, and the air was rich with the smell of earth. The petrichor out in their suburban paradise was different than in the city; there was no bus exhaust or hot asphalt competing with the smell from the patchy grass in people's postage stamp yards. Here, they lived on the border of a forest reservation, redolent of wet woods and soil. It had been alien at first, but now it smelled to her like life. She took a deep breath and held it. It was nice. Exactly why they'd moved out of Cambridge . . . well, *one* of the reasons why.

She let her breath out and resumed the search for her husband. His unannounced absence filled her with a creeping unease she knew was irrational, but grew in her gut nevertheless.

She wandered around the side of the house on the forested side of the property, her freshly washed feet getting dirty in the dewy lawn. It felt nice. Who needed shoes out here?

Evan's car was gone. *He must've run to the store.* Yeah, that was it.

She walked back to the front door, pausing to wipe her feet on the mat before going inside. They were still damp, and she didn't want to track mud and grass all over the floors.

She strode through the house into the dining room. At the far end, she picked her phone up off of the charging mat on the desk tucked in the small nook and started tapping out a text.

grab some champers while you're @ the store

After a second, she sent a follow-up.

PLEASE XXOO :^*

She hit SEND and waited. A couple of seconds later, a short blast of music echoed from the kitchen. She followed the sound and found Evan's smartphone on top of the coffeepot, where he liked to set it when he was cooking. When it went off a second time, she looked at the device like it was a bomb. *He takes it with him to the bathroom!*

She set her own mobile down and picked his up. Where would he have gone with the car, but without his phone? They were walking distance from the only neighbor they knew, and *they* were out of town. She tried to recall when Juanita had said she and Colin were headed off for the long weekend. They'd been gone a couple of days at least already. After three months, she and Evan still hadn't really gotten to know anybody else nearby yet. They'd picked the house for its seclusion. When she and Evan first moved in together, they'd alternately joked and promised each other they'd never move to the country. City people forever. That's where life is. *Never say never.* They'd rented in Cambridge long enough that the little forgivable quirks of a first-floor apartment in a "triple-decker" started to become annoyances, and then intolerable drains on their patience and happiness.

Evan *had* to be at the store. *Unless something happened,* said the unsteady feeling in her belly.

She entered his unlock code and looked at his texts. *Maybe it was his mom?* She was recovering from a broken hip and insisted on staying in her house alone, even though she was still unsteady on her feet and using a walker. Her mother-in-law was the kind of person who'd call her son before she dialed 911, even though it'd take him over an hour to get to her place up in Salem. Evan was levelheaded. He'd send an ambulance and *then* follow them to the hospital. And he definitely wouldn't have gone without being sure she knew what was happening.

The messages Nelle sent him just a moment ago were top of the list. The next texts came two days ago from their friends, Gen and Jun, about getting together for dinner soon. The most recent message from his mom was days ago. So, Inês was just fine and probably sitting in her BarcaLounger watching serial killer documentaries on the Discovery ID channel. No phone emergency.

No news was good news, but it didn't help settle her nerves. She set Evan's phone down and went to the kitchen window to look in the back yard. The view of the tree line and the forest beyond the back yard was nice; she tried to focus on it instead of his absence. Her husband slipping out for a few minutes was *not* the end of the world. There were a million reasons why he might disappear for a bit. It had to be the store—he'd run out of eggs or lemon juice for the Hollandaise sauce. Since he couldn't be quaintly neighborly and go next door to "borrow" something with the Darnielles out of town, he'd had to drive to the store.

Anxiety was a plague. With unpleasant regularity, Nelle's imagination darkened banal incidents into sinister preludes of catastrophe. She wished her mind didn't work like that, but it was what a guilty conscience did. It made you wary of trusted people, apprehensive of variations from routine. It always reminded you that, somewhere, accountability might be lurking.

With nothing else to do but await Evan's return and the normality he'd bring, she opted to sit down with a novel. Maybe she could sink into something fantastical with a witchy monster hunter.

She turned to grab a book off the pile on the end table in the living room and caught sight of her husband's gray silhouette reflected in the clearing bathroom mirror. He was in the shadows of the hallway by the guest bedroom. How had he sneaked past her? Why hadn't she heard his car, or the front door?

"Damn it, Evan! You scared the hell out of me."

The figure disappeared from the mirror, and for a moment she thought a trick of the light and her anxiety were making her jump at shadows. But then, it wasn't a shadow. It was a reflection. And it had moved. She saw it.

And Evan didn't move like that.

The figure turned the corner. She blinked hard at the sight of him. He wasn't a monster, but a man with a receding hairline, eyes shaded under a heavy brow, and a thin mouth.

He was ordinary. And terrifying.

His face was set in a grim mask of intent that looked like the expression men wore before getting into a fight, or . . . worse. He stepped closer and she tensed, ready to run but recognizing it was too late. He'd caught her. *Who are you?* and *Why are you in my house?* passed through her mind, but she couldn't find the breath to say them out loud. He moved a step forward, and she backpedaled for the front door instinctively, reaching out blindly for the knob. He closed the distance too fast — ready for the sprint while she was still playing catch-up with her own reactions. She screamed, "No!" as she felt his hand on her shoulder. She spun and jammed her fingernails at his face and dragged them down his cheek.

He pulled away, a hand pressed to his torn face, and she stood tall, feeling that this was a moment that could go her way. She could do this. And then he punched her in the stomach so hard her legs gave out. She fell to the floor, not wanting to give up, not wanting to just lie there, but unable to refuse her body's compulsion to curl up into a ball. She couldn't scream. She couldn't breathe. Her stomach cramped, and she retched.

The man leaned down and grabbed a handful of her damp hair, pulling her head up. She reached out and dug into him with her nails again. This time, his chest. He let go. As she attempted to scramble away, she kicked at him. Through the thrum of her heartbeat, she heard him curse at her, and then he stomped hard on her bare ankle. He was wearing boots. A fresh jolt of pain bloomed in her leg. Her stomach was still cramping, so she couldn't get a deep enough breath to cry out.

Her arm bumped up against the big bookshelf, and a couple of books dropped on her head. She snatched one from the floor and hurled it at the intruder, but it bounced off him. He said something hostile she couldn't make out through panic-dulled ears.

He leaned in close, and she began to kick again, hoping that one wild heel might catch him in the stomach or the balls. Give her a small interstice of time to get on her feet, get ahead, get away. Her struggles amounted to nothing as he grabbed her hair again and yanked her hard around, wrenching her neck. She felt faint. He shoved down against the side of her head, pinning it to the floor. She felt the press of something hard against her cheek. It stank like a machine — oily and mean. He said something. She didn't respond; his noises didn't mean anything to her. They sounded like the grunts of some beast — something feral that wanted to rip her open with its tusks — a wild pig snorting fury and snot.

"Shut up," he repeated. This time, the words got through. She hadn't realized she was sobbing. Not until he told her to stop. "Shut the fuck up, or I'll shoot you in the face."

Shoot me. It's a gun. He has a gun *pressed to my* face. *Ohfuckohfuckohfuck!*

He pressed the barrel of the gun harder into her cheek. She yelped and tried to twist her head away, and he bore down with his other hand. Stars exploded behind her eyes. In the moment, she saw an image of herself at work. Not standing over the body of someone she was preparing for a memorial, but *on* the embalming table. Her boss, Tony, standing over her with eyes red from crying and holding a trocar, ready to insert it into her body and drain her. He'd work diligently to repair the bullet wound in her face. The broken skull and powder burns would make it difficult, but he was a professional and would try, and cry, and she would be dead forever, never knowing what happened to her husband.

The image faded as the intruder eased up on her head. Not enough for her to move, but the pain receded somewhat. "I don't *want* to shoot you. Are you going to be a good girl?" he asked.

She didn't believe him. If he didn't want to use his gun, he wouldn't have brought it into her home. He wouldn't have shoved it in her face. Still, she went limp and quieted herself; struggling wasn't doing anything. "Y-yes."

"Good girl." He stood. "Let's go."

"Where?"

"The basement."

She wanted to scream.

2

The cellar had looked the same since the day they'd moved in. To the right of the staircase were piles of boxes that the movers had left months ago for them to sort. They kept telling themselves they needed to get that done, but always found something different to do with their weekends instead. To the left was open space where Evan had assembled a weight bench beside the water heater. The same old set of dumbbells he'd ignored in their apartment sat on the pad next to the bench, gathering dust.

The normality of it all was unsettling. Where was the dream logic that made cellar staircases lead to city parks or fold over on themselves, so she never went down, but always emerged back at the top in the same hallway she'd left? She *needed* it to be a dream. If the cellar transformed into a forest, she could pretend she wasn't marching down to her death ahead of a man with a gun. But she was aware of the ache in her ankle and stomach and face, her hand gripping the rail so she wouldn't fall and break her neck if her wounded ankle gave out. *Huh.* There was a man behind her with a gun, and she was worried about falling down a few stairs.

She was still in her comfies and barefoot and smelled like lavender soap and tea tree oil shampoo. Everything was bright and clear and not at all a dream. It had no goddamned business being that way.

The man jabbed her back with his pistol when she hesitated at the bottom of the stairs. She didn't know which way he wanted her to go.

He grunted and shoved her to the left toward the weight bench. For a second, she wondered whether she could reach a dumbbell and swing it at him before he could shoot her. But if she lurched ahead a step, maybe two, he'd pull the trigger and his bullet would rip through her like paper before she had the chance to reach for a weapon.

She stopped in the center of the space and turned hesitantly, peeking at him through a flinch. He stared at her with a look of ... She wasn't sure what it was a look of. Despite the long red scratches down the left side of his face, the man appeared calm. It was a far more frightening look than if he'd worn an expression of rage or contempt. He'd beaten her up and threatened to kill her — he was *still* threatening her — and it didn't seem to bother him. His face made her think of a clown, but with no makeup, no fake smile painted on. The *real* look of vicious indifference underneath. The reason people thought clowns were frightening. And she was frightened.

She couldn't bring herself to face him squarely. Her body wanted to be small and not to present him with a full target. The urge to try to slip behind the water heater or the furnace for cover and comfort was overwhelming. Something big and metal that might stop bullets. That could block his gaze. She stood still instead.

A hot swell of anger at her husband rose in her belly. The part of her mind that was panicked and angry said it was *his* fault the man was in their house. Evan had gone out to get whatever the fuck it was he needed from the store and left the goddamned door unlocked. The man — the intruder — had been watching — watched him leave — and, while she was in the shower, walked right in like he lived there.

Leaving doors unlocked was what normal people did, though. *Normal* people who left to run short errands didn't lock their doors, because it was morning and someone was home and who thinks that anyone would ever break into a house in the morning? No one, that's who. *I'll just be gone a minute. No need to lock up or even take my phone.* Except, *we're far from normal people. No. No one is to blame but* this *man.*

She thought about what happened to people whose houses were invaded. *You're going to die. He's going to kill you because that's what men who break into other people's homes do. They* murder *them. He'll wait for Evan to come home and ...*

She didn't want to think of "and." But it stayed there, haunting her, existing at the edges of her mind, just out of reach.

The man nodded behind her. "Take a seat." When she didn't look where he was motioning, he did it again, exhibiting less patience. His brow furrowed. But she didn't want to take her eyes off of him, the danger in the room. The man motioned at her with his gun and repeated his command. "Sit." She glanced over her shoulder. Behind her were their spare dining chairs, side by side like a pair of IKEA tombstones. Sitting was the beginning of the end—a kind of giving up of the ability to run away or fight back. Sitting was surrender. She didn't move. He jerked the gun again and shouted, "Get in the fucking chair!"

She flinched. His voice echoed off the concrete walls. In their old place, if Evan played his music too loudly or they got too boisterous while friends were over, the neighbors were right there pounding on the door, demanding they keep it down. Here, theirs was the last house on the road before state forest land, and the only neighbors were out of town. The isolation settled on her shoulders like a weight. Not even a gunshot would draw anyone's attention. That was what they'd paid for—solitude.

With effort, she did as he commanded and took a step toward the chair. The first was almost impossible. The second was difficult. And then after a third, she was more than halfway there. Another two steps and she stood in front of a seat one of their friends had sat in only a few weeks ago at their housewarming, drinking and laughing while Evan played music on the record player and she told stories about her experiences in the funeral home.

"Sit." He gave the command like she was a dog. *Sit. Beg!* She did as she was told. "Don't try anything," he said as he picked up a roll of tape from the shelf beside him and stepped toward her. *That's not where Evan keeps the tape,* she thought, alarmed.

Nelle's hands rose into a defensive posture on their own, as if they might escape without her. "Hands down," he told her. They stayed up. He barked his command again, and she had to force them into her lap.

"Don't hurt me."

"Don't *make* me hurt you. Now, give me your right arm. I won't ask twice."

She straightened her right arm. He grabbed it and pulled it back.

Her shoulder popped, and she gasped at the pain. He snorted as if it was a personal failing to complain about being tied up. Fresh tears spilled out of her eyes as she felt him wrap the tape tightly around her wrist. The sharp corner of the chair leg bit into her skin as he secured her to it.

"Other arm."

She surrendered her other arm, giving up her last chance at freedom. Without her arms, the best she could do was kick at him, and she knew her ankles were next. As expected, he moved to her legs before binding her around the stomach, over her arms, and around the back of the chair. He stood and moved around in front of her, surveying his work.

The strip of tape tightly wound around her midsection made it hard to breathe. The irrational part of her was self-conscious because she wasn't wearing a bra. He stared at her, his gaze resting on her breasts before moving up to her eyes. She wanted to stab his out. There were so many things she wanted in that moment; a bra was the least of them. His eyes had that too-familiar look behind them. To him, she wasn't any more than an assemblage of parts. Tits and ass and cunt. Some bits worth more than others.

"Who are you? What do you want?" she asked. Her mouth was dry, her tongue felt foreign.

The man looked around for a moment and then walked past her to the washer and dryer. Nelle tried to turn her head to see what he was doing, but he'd bound her too tightly to the chair, so she couldn't crane far enough around to see. She heard the sound of the dryer door cracking open and then the low *flump* of her clean clothes flopping softly on the dirty floor. He reappeared behind her and stuffed something in her mouth. She shook her head, but he held her by the jaw and forced it in anyway, his fingers big and hard enough she was scared he'd break her teeth. He stuffed it in until she gagged, and before she could spit it out, he pulled another length of tape off the roll and stuck it over her lips and cheeks.

She began to breathe through her nose quickly, panicking. Though her nostrils were uncovered, the sensation of having her mouth taped shut felt like suffocating. She grew light-headed. She couldn't help imagining if he punched her in the nose, or even if just the musty atmosphere in the cellar stuffed her up. *I could asphyxiate. I could die!*

The man looked back at her, and she opened her wet eyes wide, pleading with him. He stared at her chest some more and tossed the tape on the floor. "That's better," he said. "I'll be back in a minute." He turned and stomped up the stairs.

Take your time, fucker.

3

The **man's footsteps thudded** above Nelle's head. Her heart pounded at least as hard as he stomped, and blood rushed into her face, making her feel hot and faint. She panted through her nose and pushed against the chair. All these things dulled her hearing, made her feel dizzy and disoriented. She had to get herself under control.

People talked about how they'd have a clear head in an emergency. About how they'd respond if a man started shooting in a movie theater or on a playground. They fantasized about heroism, talking about rushing their attacker or firing back, but she knew no one ever really knows if they'd freeze or cower or fight. Not until it happens to them. There was a small measure of comfort in knowing that she'd had it in her to start off fighting. She'd try again, if she could just keep the urge to freeze at bay.

She tried to calm her breathing so she could slow her heart rate like she'd read about people doing with meditation. But then, those people were sitting on cushions, crisscross applesauce, thinking of calm lakes and blue skies. They weren't tied up waiting for a man to come back down into a dark cellar to kill them.

Focus. Breathe slowly.

It wasn't as easy as it sounded; still, she tried. A labored breath in through her nose. A shuddering breath out. Snot spilled out of her nostrils. She breathed evenly and deeply again. But it wasn't slowing her heart. At thirty-four, she was too young to die of a heart attack, right?

No. No one's *ever* too young to die of anything. Your end comes at the hand of what kills you, and there's no "right time" or deferment for fairness' sake. Sometimes infants die of heart failure and people who do all the wrong things live for so much longer than they ever should. And somewhere in the middle . . . was her.

She thought she heard something in the corner. A small shift like a breath or a sigh. She closed her eyes and tried to focus. Her head was beginning to throb — the result of her body coming down from the adrenaline in her blood and lactic acid in her muscles. The chemicals her body released to help her confront and escape danger were now making her tired and headachy, disorienting her more than the terror of the intruder. Her own body was going to get her killed unless she got *herself* under control. And that started with breathing.

I can do this.

Breathe in. Slow breath out. The best she could find in herself was a somewhat less agitated state of panic. Like bringing a rolling boil down to a simmer.

Another shift in the darkness of the corner. She looked, thought she saw . . .

The sound of the man returning to the top of the stairs made her lose focus. Rekindled fear surged with full force, and she felt herself become dizzy. At the bottom of the stairs, he stopped and stared at her for an uncomfortably long moment. His eyes hard, but a small cruel smile playing at the edges of his mouth. She didn't want to think about what was running through his head, but she knew the look. She'd watched plenty of men size her up like something they could order off a menu. A thing to be consumed. And she'd do that thing all women did when they didn't want to make a man angry; she'd lower her eyes, try to pretend she was looking at something on this table over here or check her phone and wait for him to glide away to some other object of attention. Except, that morning, there was nothing to hide behind. Just her in the chair, and the man standing there, looking at her like a leering wolf in a Warner Bros. cartoon.

Don't do that, she told herself. *Don't make him into something harmless. He's* not!

She looked down at her lap. The man let out a huff of satisfaction and stomped off behind her. She heard the screech of the aluminum cabinet doors beside the washing machine. What did he want in there?

The previous owners had left the industrial cabinet behind, and she'd put some gardening things in there. Plant food, Weed B Gon, some all-natural menthol spider killer that smelled awful but seemed to work. No tools, though. Those were in the shed out in front of the house with the lawn mower. An image of Karen Cooper with a masonry trowel appeared in her mind.

He shut the cabinet doors and moved on. She listened, trying to guess where he stopped, what he was looking at. She couldn't tell. He was quiet. For all she knew, he was standing behind her, waiting for the perfect moment to wrap his hands around her throat and squeeze. Or shoot her in the back of the head. Her eyes welled up with the anticipation of coming darkness.

She heard him take a step. And then another. Eventually, he came around back into view on the other side of the staircase by the workbench where she and Evan had piled boxes filled with papers and files they didn't want ruined if water got in. They didn't use the workbench; neither of them were handy. "Call the landlord," they used to crow together if something wasn't working. That changed to "hire a guy!" when they bought the house. They'd never been able to afford to hire someone to fix anything in the past, but the new chant had exuberantly grown along with their bank account.

The man paused at the bench and flipped open a box. He peered inside, and she felt . . . soiled. She looked at the boxes where he stood, stacked head high and mostly unopened since they'd moved into the house. Hell, most of them had remained taped shut since they'd packed them up to store in the cellar in the apartment in Cambridge a decade earlier.

A couple of years after she and Evan had moved in together, they'd agreed that any box they hadn't opened in five years or more would go in the trash. Neither of them had kept that bargain. It was difficult to let go. Her notes on Putnam's criticism of the mind-body problem or that Women's Studies independent project on Margaret Atwood's science fiction were nostalgic reminders of studying philosophy, dreaming that she would someday be one of history's great thinkers. But things didn't work out that way and she hadn't thought about, much less *read* a single sheet of paper in those boxes in a decade. Still, her connection to them felt strong. Not that they were worth a shit to her now—there wasn't a single piece of paper over there that could save her. She stared at the boxes, imagining what was inside each one, because it was less terrifying than looking at the man making his circuit through their past lives. She hated him for opening up that past and peering inside as if he had a right to know anything about her or Evan and their lives together.

Nelle watched him out of the corner of her eye, worried that if he looked over he'd see her contempt. The man stepped around in front of the staircase leading up to the main floor of the house and paused. He stared at Nelle for a long time again. She kept her eyes down, appropriately submissive. He snapped at her. "Over here!"

She looked up from her lap. He reached down to his waist and drew a long folding knife from his front jeans pocket. Nelle's mouth went dry again. He admired it for a second before setting it down on a plastic box next to the staircase. On the side of the box was a strip of masking tape she'd labeled PAPERBACKS with a Sharpie marker. She'd intended to donate those books to the Ripton Public Library when she felt ready to part with them. He spoke again. "You do what I say, when I say it, and I won't use this. Understand?" His voice was familiar, though she couldn't place from where, exactly. She'd heard it before, or it seemed like she had. "Understand?" he repeated. She nodded. "Good. Now, you're going to tell me where your cell phone is. I could go looking for it, but it'd be better if you just told me."

Nelle grunted, pushing against the cotton fabric bunched in her mouth with her tongue. She raised her eyebrows, silently signaling her willingness to cooperate if it weren't for the obvious impediment. She'd rather he stayed over there anyway, but it was a cruel taunt to ask her questions and expect a reply when he knew she couldn't answer.

"Is it in your bedroom?" he asked.

Nelle shook her head. She tried to remember where she'd left it. Her memory of only a few minutes ago — at least it *felt* like only a few minutes ago — was more than clouded.

"In the kitchen?" His brow furrowed.

Nelle shook her head again. Her eyes blurred with tears. What would he do if she couldn't lead him through his guessing game? Pick up the knife? She jerked her head backwards, trying to communicate.

"The bathroom?"

No.

He guessed again, his face beginning to turn red. "The dining room?"

She nodded. She was sure she'd left her phone on the charging mat in the reading nook at the end of the dining room. She'd texted Evan with it over there. The previous owners had a china hutch in the alcove at the end of the long, narrow room — formerly a breezeway, the real estate agent had said — but she and Evan didn't own fine china. Just plates that went in the cupboard. Instead, they put a small rolltop secretary in that nook and beside it, a chaise longue. It was her favorite place in the house. She could sit and read while Evan was in the kitchen cooking. He'd put on a record in the living room that'd play through the big French doors at the other end of the dining room, and they'd be together in a way that they hadn't been able to be in their cut-up apartment in Cambridge. This house's open layout had been one of the biggest factors that had motivated them to buy it. It let them be together even when apart.

She jerked her head upstairs again, thinking of the reading nook.

"Don't go anywhere." If he thought his bon mot was funny, he didn't laugh or even smile. He stomped off toward the dining room. He paused, then she heard him turn back for the cellar door. He pounded down the stairs and faced her, eyes wide and wild. "Don't fuck around with me! You said the phone was in the fucking dining room."

She nodded and jerked her head in the direction she'd left it. She grunted an answer as best as she could. "Nook." It came out as a muffled, guttural sound. "OOH! OOH!"

He stood stone still and glared at her. His cheek twitched. After a moment, he seemed to get it. It looked that way, maybe. She nodded furiously, tears streaming down her cheeks as if they'd somehow shared something deep. If they could do that, they could do more.

He left her alone in the cellar again. This time he seemed to move slower, looking harder. His footsteps stopped where she guessed the kitchen might be. She hadn't ever thought about the relationship of locations upstairs to those in the cellar. Then, he stomped off toward the far end of the dining room. By the nook.

He returned, standing at the bottom of the stairs, her phone in hand. He looked at it for a long moment. His brow furrowed and his face reddened a little and he held it out and said, "What's the code?"

She grunted and shook her head to remind him of the gag preventing her from answering. "What's the code?" he repeated. She widened her eyes. *Why can't you get it? I can't fucking talk.*

He pointed at her hands, bound at her sides to the chair. "I haven't broken your fingers . . . yet." She understood and extended two fingers. Then, using both hands, seven, then four, and finally seven again. When he kept staring, she nodded to let him know that was it. Four digits. Two, seven, four, seven. He turned the device around and tapped on the screen. His face flushed deeper red, and he said in a low soft tone, "Don't lie to me." Nelle shook her head and tried signing the code with her fingers again. She didn't know whether he'd seen the right combination. Could he see both of her hands? Was he entering the numbers in order? Two, seven, four, seven. Two, seven, four, seven. She started to doubt that she was even holding out the right number of fingers; her hands were tingling from the tight tape. She was too frightened to try to look and see if they were obeying.

If she'd been able to say the numbers aloud, they wouldn't be having this moment. Speech was something she took for granted, and the inability to utter anything but animal sounds left her feeling humiliated. Like a dog.

Part of the plan.

It took concentration, and she had a hard time mustering the will to do it, but she did it again until he turned the phone around and showed her the screen with the error message on it. His face was bright red, and he took a menacing step closer. "Fucking bitch just like all of 'em," he said.

She squinted her eyes shut hard and turned her face away, waiting for him to hit her again. When nothing happened, she opened an eye and peeked at the man. He was staring at her, face still red and mouth hanging open, not with astonishment, but a kind of blankness, like he just couldn't comprehend why she was afraid of him and was trying to puzzle it out. Nelle raised her eyebrows and nodded hard, flashing the code with her fingers. Two, seven, four, seven. Two, seven, four, seven.

"Two, seven, *four,* seven. Why didn't you say so?"

Because I have a fucking gag in my fucking mouth, you fucking moron. How can I tell you anything?

She signed the code again with her fingers. He tapped it into the screen and smiled. He began scrolling through her phone. A sick feeling crept up in her stomach at the thought of him reading the private messages she and Evan sent each other. They weren't explicit—they didn't "sext" each other—but those messages were still private. *What do you want for dinner? How's your day going? I love you.* Theirs, and no one else's.

She hadn't noticed she was breathing hard again until the man looked up from her phone and said, "Calm down. I'm not looking for your nudes." He glanced again at her chest, undermining his statement.

She tried to calm herself.

"Good girl. Keep it up, and I might take your gag off for a bit," he said, as if reading her thoughts. But then, it wouldn't be too hard for anyone to tell what she was thinking at that moment. It doesn't take a mind reader to guess what desperate people want. They want to live through it.

"You'd like that, right?"

She nodded. He smiled. That expression more frightening than when he was angry. His red-faced rage was sincere, but his smile . . . He wore amusement like an ill-fitting mask. She'd seen that mask before. She knew him. Though she still couldn't make the connection.

"Yeah, me too," he said, tracing a finger down her cheek.

Gooseflesh rose on her arms. She couldn't help pulling her head away. His smile disappeared.

He turned back to her messages.

Oh, where are you, Ev?

II

◆

EVAN

4

Evan stood in line at the coffee shop feeling a little stupid for ordering a latte when there was a full pot of coffee waiting for him at home. But the clerk at the grocery store next door told him she couldn't sell a bottle of prosecco before ten a.m., and he had time to kill. He could drive home and come back later for the wine—they didn't live that far away, only a few miles—but it was unlikely he'd make it back out to the shops again once he returned home, and he really wanted mimosas to go with their eggs Benedict. He knew Nelle would too. He'd popped out while Nelle was in the shower for what was supposed to be just a trip for supplies. He'd filled a handbasket with a bottle of orange juice and three of prosecco (it was a holiday weekend, after all), along with a container of fresh raspberries and cinnamon rolls for tomorrow. Unfortunately, it was only nine forty when he got in line to check out, and the cashier wouldn't break the law—even by as little as twenty minutes—just to accommodate a bougie, boozy breakfast. He paid for the berries, rolls, and juice, stashed them in the car, and ducked over to the coffee shop to wait for ten o'clock to tick by.

"Devin? Is that you?" He turned at the sensation of a light hand on his shoulder. The woman standing behind him was familiar, but it wasn't until she said, "It's me, Brianne Maines," that he placed her. He hadn't seen her since high school, years ago, and even then, they hadn't been friends. She'd gotten older—they were *all* doing that—and a little more substantial—again, a lot of them had gained weight, but she wore her late thirties a lot better than most of their classmates. He tried to picture the girl she'd been, but the woman she was blocked his recollection.

"Evan," he said. "Not Devin."

She blushed and laughed, a little too girlishly. "I'm so sorry, *Evan.* I can't believe I did that."

"It's okay. It happens. Better than what they used to call me in school."

She furrowed her brow. "I don't remember."

"You don't remember kids calling me Evelyn?"

"They did that?"

He nodded. Their classmates had teased him unrelentingly since he preferred music and theater to football or lacrosse. He had long hair and a slight build, and the in-crowd dubbed him Evelyn half the time. He tried to remember if Brianne was part of that clique. She had that used-to-be-a-cheerleader kind of vibe.

"You live in Ripton?" he said.

"I do. I moved here about five years ago, right after my divorce. I wanted to get a fresh start, you know. Are *you* living here now too?"

He nodded and tried not to look uncomfortable at her overshare. "Just bought a place over on Wrightson Road, near Cabot Woods."

Brianne's eyes widened, and she touched a finger to his shoulder and drew it away quickly, shaking it like he was too hot to touch. "Ooh, Wrightson. Fancy."

He forced a laugh. "No, no. *That* neighborhood is down the road and around the corner from us. We're uh . . . rich adjacent."

Her expression faded from impressed to considerably less so, but still friendly. Evan thought it was his qualification about the neighborhood, but then she said, "We?"

"Me and my wife, Nelle. We moved here a few months ago from Cambridge. It's nice. Different, you know."

"Different is right. Ripton sure isn't Cambridge." Her tone changed from ebullient to pleasantly conversational.

He laughed. "For real. It's been an adjustment. We're used to taking the T or walking everywhere, and now we have to drive all over. Nelle still works in the city, so she has a heck of a commute."

At the mention of his wife, Brianne seemed thwarted, but she hadn't moved away. She continued to touch him lightly, as if to punctuate her questions with contact. *I'm here. I'm right here.* "And you? What are you doing?"

The barista saved him and called out, "Ewan."

"See what I mean? *All* the time. You'd think a name as easy as Evan . . ." He trailed off as he stepped away from Brianne to get what he assumed was his drink since everyone else ahead of them had been served.

"Are you in a hurry? Want to have a seat?" she asked.

He felt in his pocket for his phone to check the time, but it wasn't there. *Shit.* His stomach sank at the thought of it sitting in the car where someone could just come smash the window and take it. But this was Ripton, not Crimebridge. He looked at his Fitbit instead. Nine fifty-two. He kind of wanted to linger. Just for a minute. Something about the way Brianne kept touching him. The barista called out her name and she slipped past him, a little too close, to fetch her caramel macchiato or whatever the frozen beige concoction waiting for her was. His stomach tingled a little at the close encounter with her body, and when she leaned over to reach for something past the pickup table and her vest pulled up from the back of her yoga pants, the tingle became a flutter. She turned and slid a long green straw into her drink and took a sip.

"I'm sorry," he said. "I've got to get home. My wife is expecting eggs Benny and mimosas. Some other time, maybe."

Brianne's face fell, and her lips let go of the straw. "Sounds delicious. I'm jealous." She held up a finger, turned, and grabbed a pen from behind the counter. If the employees had a problem with her invading their space, they didn't let on. She scribbled on her receipt and handed him the scrap of paper. She'd written *BAM 978-555-1369*.

He said, "BAM?"

"Brianne Allie Maines. Always *three* initials. They made fun of me too." She winked. "We can trade war stories some other time. I'm always available." She smiled and took another sip of her drink.

Evan smiled back and slipped the receipt in his pocket. "It was nice to bump into you, Brianne. See you later."

He shook her hand. She held on too long and said, "I hope so."

Evan left the coffee shop quickly but without seeming obvious that he wanted to both run as fast as he could and stick around just a bit longer. It felt nice and a little dangerous to flirt with a stranger, especially one who meant it.

Who was he kidding? Danger was a thing both he and Nelle more than brushed against these days. Danger got them that nice house in a rich adjacent neighborhood in the suburbs. His stomach did another flip, and he resolved to drop Brianne's number in the trash as soon as he got home.

He ran next door to the grocery store; he didn't want to waste any more time getting home. He didn't want to waste the flutter in his stomach on a stranger. Not when Nelle would be just getting out of the shower.

5

Evan pulled around the tight corner and into the driveway as fast as he could without losing control of the car. Slowing down too much could be a little hairy. The speed limit along Wrightson Road was thirty-five, but everyone drove fifty, and their driveway was right around a semiblind curve. The BLIND DRIVE AHEAD sign didn't dissuade anyone from opening up on that stretch of road, just like the double yellow line didn't keep anyone headed in the other direction from cutting the corner. People came flying by their driveway without being able to fully see what was ahead. Nelle had almost been rear-ended twice coming home from work. He mused on the hidden flaws of a house that only appeared after you moved in. A dangerous driveway or a dead, widow-maker branch high up in a tall tree in the back yard. He was going to have to hire a guy to get to *that* before it fell and crushed his skull. *Brained while mowing the lawn would be such a weak way to die.*

At the end of the drive, he angled around and backed into his spot beside Nelle's car in front of the garage. After parking on the street for years, they'd been excited to have a garage, even if it was only big enough for one car. And then they filled it with stuff almost immediately, keeping either of them from parking inside. He'd promised to get it cleaned out so Nelle could park the Prius inside during the winter. Still, they had the long driveway, which meant a house set far back from the road and its noise. The peace was worth small inconveniences.

He shut off the engine and grabbed the shopping bags off of the passenger seat, then he pressed the button on the garage door remote and got out of the car.

It was a beautiful day. Later, after breakfast, he would suggest they take a drive up to the trailhead and go for a hike or maybe over to that sculpture park in Lincoln. It felt wrong to be cooped up in the house. He felt great and wanted that sensation to last.

The garage door rose, rattling in its tracks. He ducked under and headed for the door to the dining room. Inside, he expected to find Nelle in her habitat, sitting on the chaise in the nook, reading. She wasn't. He pushed the button that sent the garage door clattering back down and closed the door behind him. "Hey, Nelle! I got you something special," he called out. No reply. He huffed and set the reusable shopping bags on the counter. "Where you at, minha querida?" He slipped a bottle of sparkling wine out of the bag and stuck it in the freezer to chill. It'd be ready to drink by the time he finished cooking.

First, Nelle.

He peeked out the window above the sink into the back yard, thinking she might be sitting outside in an Adirondack chair reading. She wasn't there either. Behind him, Evan heard a muffled thump. He turned, expecting to see her standing in the hallway looking down at whatever she'd fumbled and dropped, but the hall was empty. He walked toward the next place she liked to occupy when she read. Since they'd moved in, she had found a favorite quiet spot in nearly every room of the house. Depending on the time of day and the light (or whether the music he was playing on the stereo matched her mood), she moved from room to room, living in the *entire* house. "We're not going to be those people who never use the 'drawing room.'" she'd said, stabbing air quotes with her fingers around the fancy words.

Poking his head into the front room, he said, "Nelle? You in here?" It was empty as well. Another faint thudding sound came from behind him. He jumped and spun around. What was it his mother used to say when he was little? *It's the sound of the house settling.* That had freaked him out. Creaks and groans were not the sounds of something that was supposed to be solid and safe.

"Stay together, girl." He patted the wall.

The sound seemed to come from the basement. That wasn't good. Since they'd bought the place, the furnace had kicked out twice and the water heater had had a small leak. Maybe Nelle was down there, futzing with whatever had gone wrong. Since she had been taking one of her marathon showers when he left, he placed his bet on the water heater.

He opened the door and peeked down the stairs. From the landing at the top, there was nothing to see. Both appliances were over at the far end, beside the foundation wall. He turned back and grabbed the mini flashlight out of the utility drawer in the kitchen — the lights in the cellar weren't bright enough to see into the tight spaces under appliances and in corners — and went back to get a better look.

"You down here, Nelle? Everything okay?"

Another loud thump. He climbed halfway down to get a better look. Nothing looked out of place. That was the insidious thing about these sorts of problems; they looked fine until you got close and saw the spreading water, dark on the concrete floor, or the alarmingly bright glow inside the furnace.

He heard a squeal and a grunt like an animal.

What the hell was that?

It sounded big and upset and unlike anything he'd ever heard before. He wondered how an animal of any size could even get into the cellar. Through one of those little windows? *Why didn't she text me? Oh yeah, because I left my stupid phone behind.*

Halfway down, he leaned out over the edge of the staircase and peeked around to get a look at it to see if it was something he could take care of himself or if he needed to call Animal Control. He hoped it was a cat. A racoon or a possum would be a totally different situation.

"Jonesy. Here kitty, kitty. Meow." He shined the light into the dim cellar.

He nearly fell off of the end of the stairs when he spotted Nelle sitting in the guest chair under the dim glow of a fluorescent bulb. At first, he couldn't process what he saw. It made no sense that she'd just be sitting there waiting for him. Their cellar was unfinished, and while not the ancient "haunted basement" they'd shared with the neighbors in Cambridge, it still wasn't comfortable or even welcoming. It wasn't anywhere she enjoyed being. There didn't seem to be an animal. Only Nelle. His mind reconciled the various pieces of what he saw, one at a time.

It's not a cat.

She's taped to the chair.

Is that tape over her face?

She's *the one making the sounds.*

Nelle bucked in her seat and grunted louder, her eyes wide with panic. Evan leapt off of the staircase and rushed to help his wife. She was screaming behind the gag and shaking her head wildly. Her damp hair whipped around and stuck to her face. By the time he registered the sound of footsteps behind him and what they meant—what the *whole thing* meant—the blow to the back of his head made everything dark.

6

Nelle watched the man flow from out of the circuit breaker room like smoke. He'd heard the garage door open and Evan come in the house calling out for her, and faded into the shadows of the small room where they stored their holiday decorations. She tried to warn her husband. "EEH UHN OO! EEH UHN OO!" *Behind you.* Three syllables. Two words. One exclamation point. No use. Evan reached for her while she shook her head, but he didn't understand. His head was full of other things that muted her message.

The man whipped around the staircase and raised his arm, something dark in his hand like a piece of shadow pulled from the murky room. Evan's eyes went wide with realization just as the man's arm swung down and the black injection-molded mini bat that Evan usually kept by the front door bashed against the back of her husband's head. He went down, limp and loose like a doll, his chin bouncing off her lap on the way to the floor.

She screamed through her gag.

The man sneered down at Evan and reared back with the bat for another blow. But Evan didn't move, so the man slowly lowered the weapon. He grinned, and it was horrible.

"Thanks for letting me borrow this," he said.

She screamed again. Howling in rage and terror and frustration and more that flowed through her with the speed and force of a river.

He raised the bat and said, "Shut. The. Fuck. Up." But she screamed incoherently at the intruder through her gag.

He said it again louder, and the words formed in her mind slowly. He took a step closer, with the bat over his shoulder.

Nelle stopped screaming, though she couldn't keep herself from making grunts and small peals of desperate sound. Terror deranged her. Behind the cotton in her mouth and the tape over her lips, she formed Evan's name in her throat, needing to say it, needing to wake him, but too out of breath to give volume to her urging. *Oh god he's dead don't let him be dead oh no please no I love him so much!*

The man took a step back, lifting his knee high and stepping over Evan's body. He tossed the bat behind him without looking and grabbed her husband's wrists. He dragged Evan over to the weight bench. He glanced up at Nelle and, for a second, seemed surprised at the look she gave him. Maybe he expected fear, or concern for her husband. He seemed not to have anticipated hate. But she *did* hate him — more than anyone else she'd ever known or even thought of. She hated him more than cancer and domestic violence and depression and drunk drivers who killed whole families and everything else she'd ever seen at work that ruined lives. If she got the chance, she'd kill him. She wanted to do it now. Bash his brains in with the bat he'd clubbed her husband with. But that had clattered away into the shadows. It might as well have been on the moon.

Before she knew what was happening, the man drew the gun out of the back of his pants, stepped over to her, and hit her in the face with it. Lights flashed behind her eyes and the room spun. "You don't get to give me those looks, y'fuckin' bitch," she heard him say from what seemed like far away. "Not if you want him to live through this."

Not, "if *you* want to live through this." Want *him* to live through this. She wanted them both to survive . . . whatever *this* was. *On the news they call it a home invasion,* an unhelpful voice in her head informed her. Other stories filtered through her daze. That one about the doctor and his wife murdered in Connecticut. The other one with those kids who killed the woman up in Mount Vernon. She couldn't recall a news story about a home invasion ever ending with the occupants of the home surviving. It was always, "they were found dead at the scene by investigators," and "the victims of the deadly break-in included . . ." There wasn't any reason to take the man at his word about

Evan's survival, or the slight implication of her own. He'd brought a gun into their home; she figured he intended to use it eventually.

Stunned from the blow, she tried to soften her expression. She'd go along with whatever he wanted until she thought of something better . . . or she died. Nelle tried to think of something better.

The intruder turned away, shoving the pistol back in its holster. He rolled Evan onto his back and grabbed him under the arms. He started to lift him, but stopped when his grip slipped and had to reposition his hold. Evan was slender, but fit, and weighed more than he appeared to. *He's deadweight.* She tried to push the thought away, but it lingered, an intrusive melody. *Deadweightdeadweightdeadweight.* Evan's head lolled as the man ducked down to get a better grip on his body. He lifted him again, pulling him up and onto the slightly reclined weight bench.

The man lost his balance stepping over the dusty dumbbells and almost dropped Evan again. When he finally got her husband up onto the bench, he was panting. Evan's head rocked forward, and he slumped down. The man caught him in a bear hug and shoved him back. He steadied Evan against the backrest and stepped away slowly, hands out waiting to catch him if he went over, like a narrow-bottomed vase. For the moment, Evan stayed where he was. The backrest was inclined, and he sat there reasonably well-balanced.

The man grabbed the duct tape and pulled a strip off the roll. The terrible ripping sound made Nelle's stomach turn. She watched as he taped her husband down like he'd done to her.

At least he won't fall.

He started at Evan's midsection, taping him over his chest and arms to the backrest before moving on to his wrists and ankles. Every minute he spent binding Evan, Nelle's hope faded. She was near to losing it completely when he finished.

The man stepped away, returning to the laundry dryer behind her. He reappeared and stuffed a piece of clothing into her husband's mouth before taping over it as well. Nelle grunted and shook her head, knowing that it wouldn't do any good and might even get her pistol-whipped again, but beyond caring. Her cheek where he'd hit her was mostly numb anyway. A little hot.

"Shut up." The man's voice was hotter. Mean.

Nelle did as she was told.

"Good girl."

Good girl. She'd bristled. *I'm not a dog, motherfucker.* She couldn't say it aloud, but her defiance, even silent, was the only thing she had. *I am* not *a dog.*

The intruder wiped an arm across his forehead and sighed. He turned and went upstairs.

Nelle wondered what unrealized need was keeping him from killing them. What was it he wanted? She listened as he paused overhead in the kitchen. She heard the sound of clinking glass and then the faucet. He was getting himself a drink. *Choke on it, you son of a bitch.*

A movement from the weight bench drew her attention. From the corner of her eye, a shadow seemed to flit away into deeper blackness behind it.

Evan's head tilted slightly. A short bob up and then down again. She saw it. Saw him move. Nelle tried getting his attention, grunting his name, which came out "Ea-uhn." But his head didn't right itself; his eyes didn't open. She worried that even if the intruder didn't shoot him, Evan would still die. Did he have a concussion? Bleeding in his brain? *He's dying right now. He's dying and I can't see it except I can totally see it and I can't call for help or get his attention or even say his fucking name.* There was a feeling she got at work, that the world was an unfair place and embalming the dead gave her a front row seat to its many injustices. She'd gone to mortuary school because she wanted to help people, even if just meant helping them say goodbye in a loving and dignified way. But then she'd have to work on a child who drowned or a college student killed in a drunk driving crash, a young mother with cancer, and there it would be, right in front of her. No matter how many good people populated it, the world wouldn't be any less terrible for them or anyone else, because it was the world. Cruelly absurd and indifferent. Sure, standing over the table was different than being the family member waiting for her work to be done. It was different than being the person *on* the table. At the end of the day, she walked away, went home, and had a glass of wine with the love of her life and watched TV or read a novel until she got drowsy and retired to a warm bed. And then in the morning, she did it all again. She was — *they were* — part of the world's unfairness — willing participants, and now it was their turn on the table.

She shook her head, trying to dispel her dark thoughts. They would only hinder her from finding the will and the way to get free. She looked around the cellar for something she could use to cut the two of them loose. Their meagerly appointed toolbox was upstairs in the garage, and everything else around her was either unwieldy or ill-suited. And none of it was worth a damn if she was stuck in this chair and couldn't raise a hand to reach it.

Nelle tried working at the tape around her wrists, focusing on her right one. Freeing her dominant hand would lead to everything else being undone. If she could get it loose, she could get free. And then she'd grab a weight or a bottle of wine out of the rack to use as a weapon. A wine bottle seemed like a better cudgel than a dumbbell. But the duct tape held — as it was made to do. It always tore so easily from the roll, but wrapped around her wrist in multiple layers, it might as well have been a steel handcuff. Her fingers were beginning to lose feeling. She realized couldn't feel her feet at all, the man had tied her so tightly. She struggled harder, rocking the chair, but it was no use.

She felt like crying again, but that was wearing her out, making her head hurt. Or was it being smacked in the face with the pistol that did that? Worst of all, tears made it hard to see clearly, and while the irrational part of her was fine with that, the rational part knew that seeing was important. She needed to be able to see the intruder when he came back, watch his movements, his face.

More than anything else, she needed to be able to see Evan.

She promised herself she'd close her eyes only when the end came. She'd allow herself that kindness.

She kept her eyes open and worked at the tape.

She wondered how long the man had been watching them.

III

◆

CLOSING

7

FORTY-FIVE DAYS BEFORE CLOSING

It was the fire that made them fall in love. Evan and Nelle had seen plenty of places they liked, a couple they even called their agent about, but the market was competitive and they were beginning to lose hope. There didn't seem to be anything out there worth putting an offer on, let alone having a bidding war over. They'd been to so many open houses and seen so few worth the money the sellers were asking. Even the fixer-uppers were selling for above listed value. One place, for sale "As Is," with brown nicotine-stained walls and sagging, angled floors, had still gone for fifty thousand dollars more than asking. It depressed them that even an *uninhabitable* house that was probably going to be knocked down to build a McMansion was outside the price range they'd set for themselves. They could afford anything they wanted, but they'd agreed to a budget. They had to be disciplined, even while looking for a house they both knew they shouldn't buy right now.

They'd started out cautiously, but after a while, house hunting got to feel like being a shark. They wanted to keep moving, keep searching. If they didn't go to at a least a couple of open houses a weekend, it felt like sinking. Even if there wasn't anything worth seeing. They kept telling themselves it was December and most sensible sellers were waiting for spring to list their homes. There'd be more in March and definitely April.

Despite the snowy roads and cold temperature, this open house was busy. People moved through the place, clutching flyers the listing agent handed out at the door, pointing at features they liked and disliked, trying to imagine their things inside instead of the show furniture. They flowed around the other buyers, trying to get a sense of the space as it would feel with only them inside, instead of a crowd. Everything about the first story open floor plan connecting the living room, kitchen, and dining room felt right. The colors the walls were painted, the fixtures and appliances, the hardwood floors — they wouldn't have to spill a drop of paint or even change a light bulb to make it theirs. And then they saw the fire burning out in the back yard through the kitchen window.

The realtor had shoveled a path through the snow from the back door to the built-in patio fire pit. They walked outside and held their cold hands out to the flames. Nelle looked around at the bright white yard. "It's big," she said.

Evan nodded. "We can get a lawn mower."

"Are you going to buy one of those riding ones?" She smiled and shoved at him with her shoulder. "You want me to send in your subscription to *AARP* magazine when you get it?"

"It's not *that* big. The day I say I want a riding mower, you are allowed to shoot me and put me out of my misery."

"Deal!" she said. "*After* you're done with the mowing."

The agent came walking outside, rubbing at his arms to keep warm as he carefully stepped off the icy deck onto the patio. He sidled up next to them in front of the fire and smiled. "Great, isn't it?" He held out a hand. "I'm John. It's so busy in there I didn't get a chance to ask your names."

"I'm Evan. This is my wife, Nelle." Evan shook the realtor's hand. The salesman let go quickly, though, and leaned over to shake Nelle's hand. The guy's grip was a little too forceful. Still, it was better than that knuckle-up tilt other male agents gave her, like they wanted to give her some chivalric kiss on the back of her hand.

"Evan . . . and Nelle." He said it and paused. Nelle caught sight of a small gold cross at the hollow of his throat and knew what was coming next. "Really? Like . . . ?"

She said, "We didn't plan it that way. It just worked out."

John the real estate agent smiled again, broader this time. His front teeth on the top and bottom were a different color than the rest. Extra white. Nelle tried not to stare, but it was jarring to see dentures in someone she'd assumed was their own age. She guessed either a traffic accident or hockey. Probably hockey around here. He had that look. Stocky and a little cagey, like life moved too slowly for him without skates.

"Do you have any questions about the property or the neighborhood?" he asked. He looked over his shoulder at the house, belying the fact he was there to let them know *he* knew they were there, not to take them seriously as potential buyers. They were young. Outside of today's demographics of home buyers, and their look didn't help. They'd started out dressing conservatively to tour open houses, but after a few, abandoned the effort. People still treated them like they weren't serious, no matter what they wore. In their retro outfits, they looked like half a *Mad Men* inspired punk band. And no one imagined a couple of rockabilly hipsters would have the money for a down payment on a place like this, let alone the income to pay a mortgage. At least it was cold out and he couldn't judge their tattoos through long sleeves and gloves.

Nelle held up the flyer and shook her head. "I think everything we want to know is covered here. Except why anyone would want to sell this place." She let out an awkward laugh, knowing her joke wasn't all that funny, but trying anyway. She didn't ever know what to say to the real estate agents they met. It was a weird situation to be in. After spending only twenty or maybe thirty minutes in a place, she and Evan were trying to make a decision whether to spend three quarters of a million dollars on it. And the real estate agents all wanted to make small talk as if that would help people come to a decision instead of distracting them from actually getting the feel for the house.

John nodded vigorously. "It's definitely beautiful. The owners have done a complete renovation over the last couple of years. He's handy, and she's got a home redecorating/remodel business. They put a lot of effort into making it a showpiece for the business. They vaulted the ceiling in the dining room themselves and converted the sunroom you just came out of from a three-season to an all-year family room. The hardwood floors in the dining room and family room are brand-new too." He pointed toward the end of the yard where a low New England rock wall bordered the property. "You've got a neighbor on the other side of those bushes, but no one else back there or to the north for a couple miles. That's the Cabot Woods State Park. Miles and miles of hiking trails and gorgeous forest. You folks have kids?"

It was the sort of thing well-meaning people all over asked every day without any thought other than that it was a conversational bridge. If the answer was yes or "we're planning on it," Nelle imagined the man would segue into a monologue about how the house and the yard were perfect for a family—though they were already a family, just one without children. But what if the answer was "we've tried, and we can't"? Plenty of their friends were happily "child free"—that way by choice. She and Evan were child*less,* coming around to accepting that unless they chose to adopt, they'd always be a family of two, never three or four.

It wasn't a cruel question, but sometimes it felt that way.

She didn't want to make the man feel uncomfortable, so she merely said, "No."

Evan didn't miss the beat. "The park is part of what has us looking at a place this far out from the city. We love to hike."

Nelle picked up on his redirection. "Are the trails close to the property? Can you get to them from here?"

"The trailhead is up the road about a mile or so at the Scout camp, and the paths stick pretty far away from people's property lines. No one wants to go for a hike just to see patios and swing sets, you know what I mean. From here in the yard, you won't see a soul. Just trees. You have complete privacy. It's perfect."

"Do you mind me asking why they're selling?" Nelle asked. "The listing says they only bought the house three years ago."

The realtor smiled with half his mouth and winked. "Life happens, you know. Point is, this house is ready for *you.* But, as you can see, it's getting a lot of interest." He glanced over his shoulder at the open house full of people looking to buy. The implication that there wouldn't be *another* open house hung in the air between them. He'd walked right up to the line of a hard sell and pointed across without stepping over.

"Sounds great." Evan and Nelle both smiled politely. The guy with his false teeth and hard pitch gave them a bad feeling. But then, they'd only really met one real estate agent who didn't strike them as odd, and that was their own. Nelle could see from the look in Evan's eyes, he wanted to call Dave as soon as they could.

"Can I tell you anything else?"

Evan shook his head. "No. I think we've got everything we need to make a decision." He started for the door to return inside, Nelle falling in beside him. The agent followed them in, through the house, and to the front door. Nelle hesitated there, looking at the glowing green keypad next to the coat closet.

"Is that an alarm system?"

He nodded and pointed to a motion sensor in the corner of the front room and another in the hallway. "Sure is. Totally protected."

"Do you *need* an alarm system in this neighborhood?" Evan asked. John furrowed his brow and shook his head, but didn't say a word. Evan nodded. "Gotcha."

Evan and Nelle walked out the front door to find another couple at the bottom of the steps waiting for them to pass before going in. Once in the yard, Nelle paused and looked to the right. With the large bushes running between the properties, they could hardly tell they'd have a neighbor. In Cambridge, their kitchen window looked right into the neighbor's apartment, and the noise from Mass Ave was loud and constant, all day and night. Standing in the yard, she could barely hear the road. Though the neighborhood continued just on the other side of the highway, from there in front of the house, it felt like they would be completely alone. Secluded. Everything they wanted.

"You okay?" Evan asked.

"Totally fine."

He leaned over and kissed his wife. "Just like you." She smiled at him and shivered a little. It was cold outside away from the fire, and her cute winter coat with the faux leopard collar and cuffs wasn't as warm as it looked. Evan grabbed her hand, and they walked down the long driveway to their car parked on the shoulder of the highway.

Inside the car, he started the engine and cranked the heater. "What do you think?"

Nelle pulled off her gloves and held her hands in front of the vent. "I think we need to call Dave right now."

"Yeah. Me too. I want this place."

Though neither of them wanted to say, "Dream home," they both knew that was exactly what it was. Evan pulled out his cell phone and dialed their real estate agent.

8

The **he man looked through** spotter's glasses at the couple sitting in their car. They were talking on the phone, excited and laughing. Though he couldn't hear them, he knew what they were talking about. He watched them finish their phone call, kiss, and look back at the house they'd just exited one more time before driving away.

He kept his watch, staring at another car pulling into the space those two Halloween rejects just left.

9

CLOSING DAY

The radiator let off a low hiss and a short burst of steam, adding a touch of rusty-smelling humidity to the closeness of the room. Nelle thought about getting up to crack a window and let in a touch of the morning chill. There was no one with them in the Registry of Deeds signing room to stop her, but the building itself seemed to carry the kind of air that said the conditions of life inside were not alterable — not unless one was clothed in the power of the court. So, she sat in the hard wooden chair and glanced at the time on her phone again, trying to ignore the heat and her growing anxiety.

The sellers' attorney was late. Evan and Nelle's lawyer shrugged; he'd worked with this guy before, and he was professional, just not always punctual. No cause for worry. Telling Nelle not to worry, though, was like telling a sparrow not to fly. She was less nervous about the sellers' attorney being professional than she was about the sellers themselves.

During the inspection, they'd uncovered a few issues with the house that hadn't been disclosed prior: a minor carpenter ant problem by the front deck; the antique water heater well past its replacement date; a ceiling fan that needed to be replaced. Nothing catastrophic, but things Evan and Nelle's attorney wanted to negotiate a credit back at closing to pay to repair. It'd taken the threat of pulling out of the deal after that for the sellers to agree, and ever since, it seemed like the sellers were fighting them. Now they were late. Nelle imagined them pulling out at the last minute to make their point in the most aggravating way possible.

Evan put his hand on Nelle's knee under the table to get her to stop bouncing her leg. Their attorney, Peter, had told them, while this sale was weirder than most, it'd all work out. He leaned over conspiratorially and said, "The sellers are a couple of flakes, but trust me, this is going through. My associate recognized their names from the family court docket and looked up their pleadings. Their split isn't what you'd call 'amicable.'" He whispered, "Mister's got a girlfriend, but doesn't want to get divorced, so he contested it. It's all very sordid." Peter grinned, having delivered the gossip. Their attorney had a casual style that Evan and Nelle liked, as though he was telling them a story over beers. He laughed a lot; they liked that too. He was a former assistant attorney general, and when he bit, it was to taste marrow, not blood. A good lawyer to have; a bad one for the other side.

Nelle's face scrunched up.

Evan looked anxious. "Is that a problem for us?"

"No. This home sale is to distribute their assets. It's gotta go through."

Nelle nodded. "But that's why they've been so difficult."

Peter nodded. "Yup. She's already checked out, and he doesn't want to sell, but has to. She's got an order of protection out against him on top of it all. But once everything gets signed here today, their shit doesn't affect you anymore."

"An order of protection? What happens when he doesn't show?" Evan asked.

Peter grinned like a wolf that wants seconds of farm fresh lamb. "*If* he stalls or sinks the sale, then we sue 'em. Get your money back, and you guys buy a house without carpenter ants."

It was hardly comforting. They didn't want to sue anybody, and they didn't want a different house. But Peter liked a fight, even if he'd left the cracking skulls business for a general practice. He was a hammer always looking for a nail.

"It feels weird. Buying it because of a divorce seems like taking advantage of someone else's misfortune," Nelle said.

Peter held up a hand to stop her. "Enough of that. *They* put the house on the market. If it wasn't you guys who bought it, it would have been someone else, that's a certainty. There was another offer, same as yours on the table. *No one* is being taken advantage of. This is the way the world is." He smiled. "Except for good folks like you, naturally."

A man burst into the room in a flurry of apologies too practiced to be only occasionally employed. Peter stood and shook the man's hand. He turned and gestured to the table where he'd already arranged the papers for the closing. "Evan, Nelle. This is Doug Edgerton." He turned to Doug and held up his hands.

Edgerton began unpacking his briefcase and explained, "Neither of the sellers will be coming today." Evan took an involuntary breath in, nearly a gasp, and tried to hide it by coughing into his fist. Edgerton glanced at him and continued. "I have power of attorney to sign everything on both their behalf."

"Well, we're good to go, then!" Peter patted Evan on the shoulder with the back of his hand. It was Nelle's turn to squeeze his leg to try to calm him down.

The two lawyers made chitchat while they signed papers and put in front of Evan and Nelle more to be signed. Peter handed over the cashier's checks and Doug removed a single key from his suit coat pocket. He held it out to Evan. Nelle took it and said, "Shouldn't there be two?"

Edgerton's brow furrowed. "I just have the one. If the other isn't in my office, I'm sure my client left it on the kitchen counter or the mantel."

"It's no big," Evan reassured her. "We're going to have the locks changed anyway, right?" She didn't look satisfied by either man's response, but one key or two, she'd be happy to be done with this meeting.

Edgerton started to scoop papers into his briefcase. "Well, if that's it, I've got to be off. It was nice meeting you two."

"Likewise," Evan said. Evan and Nelle smiled politely and shook Edgerton's hand before he walked out in nearly as much of a hurry as he'd walked in.

Peter came around the table to give them both a hug. "Congratulations," he said. "You're homeowners! I've got to go record these next door to make it all legal and official like. But you two are clear to go to your new home." He gathered the papers off the table and excused himself to the clerk's office.

Evan and Nelle stood in the sweaty, two-century-old room and looked at the house key. Nelle turned it over in her hand. On the back was a small reflective sticker shaped like a flower. "You won't forget to call the locksmith?"

He closed her hand around the key. "I'll call him this afternoon.

Let's get out of here. We've still got to pack up the last of the apartment."

"You want to move a few things over today?"

"You bet! But let's go take a look at *our new place* first."

Evan held the door open for her. She dropped the key in her pocket and walked out.

10

An electronic chirp greeted them as they opened the door. Nelle struggled to pull the key out of the slot while Evan slipped over to the security system keypad to look at the display. It read SERVICE NOT AVAILABLE. The key finally came free, and Nelle shut the door. The system chirped again throughout the house, and she said, "Is it going to do that every single time we open and close a door?"

He shrugged. "At least you'll know when I get home from work so you can bring me my pipe and slippers."

She slapped his shoulder playfully. Evan grimaced and clutched his shoulder, groaning dramatically. "Jeez, bruiser! Watch where you're swinging those." On their first date a decade earlier, they'd gotten very drunk and she'd challenged him to a game of slap hands at midnight in a city park. She'd won overwhelmingly, and the backs of his hands ached for two days after. When she challenged him to a rematch on their second date, he said, "You have fingers like gloves full of rocks," and was taken by the look of delight that had blossomed on her face. Ever since, he played it up like her touches were the whips of a fraternity paddle. It always made her smile.

"Oh stop, you big baby."

"You watch it. I've been working out. You won't be able to push me around for much longer." He kissed one of his biceps, bringing on peals of warm laughter from Nelle.

He looked around the empty front room of their new house. *Our house. Ours.* It seemed unreal, after searching for so long. They'd spent nearly a year trying to find a place they liked well enough to make an offer and then, a month and a half after walking through the door for the first time, it was theirs.

The room seemed different now than when they'd done the final walkthrough, but he couldn't put his finger on why. The seller's furniture had already been moved out by then, so it wasn't the emptiness. He stood there puzzling it out while Nelle walked past him into the kitchen. A moment later, she called out. "Evan! Come see this!"

He rushed into the kitchen. She turned around and gestured with both hands toward a tall bottle sitting out in the middle of the countertop. Relieved it wasn't a problem, he said, "They left us a bottle of champagne. How thoughtful."

"Come *closer.*" She drew a hand across the label, Vanna-style.

He leaned down to get a closer look and read the label aloud. "Martinelli's Sparkling Cider. Contains no alcohol." He looked at Nelle grinning down at him and said, "The bottle is dusty. Think they had it cellared for a special occasion?"

"Who cellars *apple cider?*"

Evan and Nelle loved wine, and their small collection of nice vintages and new twenty-four-bottle fridge was waiting to be unloaded from the back of the RAV4 in the driveway. There was no way they were trusting the movers with *those,* no matter how highly recommended the company had come. He blew on the cider bottle, creating a constellation of dust mites in the beam of light shining through the window above the sink.

"No one does, minha querida. They found it in the back of a cupboard or something and left it for us."

"It's more passive aggression."

He straightened up and pulled Nelle closer. "Hey, now. You don't know that. Maybe . . . they're Mormon and it's sincere. Don't go getting dark on me." As long as they'd been married, Nelle had been prone to somber moods. She wasn't a negative person overall, but little things got to her in a way that pulled her deep into the shadows for a while. Little things like a broken barrette on the sidewalk or a personally inscribed book in the used section of the Harvard Book Store would send her spirits south, and it'd be a day or two before she was fully herself again. She said it was the cost of setting aside her emotions at work, but

Evan had seen how sensitive she was to small cues of disappointment *before* she got the job at the funeral home. Since they'd . . . come into their money, the darkness had grown somewhat less frequent. What did they say? Money can't buy happiness, but it can buy off unhappiness. While her melancholy remained, still, she was resilient. She always pulled herself out of the shadows. And if she needed it, he always had a hand ready for her to hold on to.

She looked in his eyes and said, "No darkness. Only light."

He held up his little finger. "Pinky swear?"

"Pinky swear!" She entwined her finger around his and kissed his knuckle.

He kissed hers and smiled. "Okay, then. You know the deal. You break that swear, I get to break your pinkies." He let go and cast his eyes toward the cupboards. Nelle furrowed her brow as Evan reached for the bottle.

"What are you doing?"

He nodded at the bottle of cider in his hand and winked.

"Oh no. I am *not* drinking that. No way."

He tore the foil away from the neck, finding a bottle cap instead of a cork. He pulled his keys from his pocket and pried the cap off with the bottle opener on his keyring. Instead of a pop, it made a hiss, more like an evil spirit escaping an ancient tomb than a fresh bottle of bubbly. Lacking anything to pour into, he raised it in a toast and said, "To our new home."

"You wouldn't!"

He gulped straight from the neck of the bottle.

She watched with amusement as his expression changed from mischievous to disgusted and waited to see how much he could chug before it came back up.

Evan pulled the bottle away from his lips and turned toward the sink. Nelle shook her head as he spit down the drain. He turned on the faucet and drank straight from the tap. Without a dish towel to dry himself with, he dragged his shirtsleeve across his mouth and made one more contorted face before holding the cider out to his wife. "Want a pull?"

Nelle laughed and covered her mouth with a hand. "It's all yours, sweetie!" He lifted the bottle as if to take another drink. Nelle turned away, pretending to be sick at the thought.

Back from the shadows.

He upended the bottle over the sink, shoving the neck into the drain and letting gravity finish the job. A strong odor of sugar and apples drifted up, and Evan felt for a brief moment like he might actually be sick. Taking a step back, he made a face and belched. That too stank like apples, and Nelle waved her hand in the air.

"Shall we take a look around and see where everything is going to fit?" he asked, grabbing her hand and pulling her through the kitchen into the hallway, away from the aroma that was likely going to haunt him for the rest of the afternoon.

The bedroom upstairs possessed the same undefinable difference as the front room. He looked around, trying to put his finger on what had changed. Why it felt somehow emptier than merely empty. He could tell that Nelle sensed it too. She stood staring out the windows.

"The blinds," she said.

There had been Roman blinds installed in all of the bedrooms and the family room in the back of the house. Evan ducked out of the master suite into the other upstairs bedroom — the one he thought would be nice to set up as an office or Nelle's den. He headed downstairs past the other guest rooms. The blinds had been removed from all of them. He came back to find Nelle inspecting the window frames, running her fingers over the holes where the screws holding the mounts had once been. "They're *all* gone," he told her.

"They can't do that. Can they? I mean, it's not legal, right?"

He shook his head. "I didn't think so. Should we call Peter?"

Nelle's head slumped. He could see the darkness swirling around her like ink in water. Soon, she'd be completely blacked out and no burping bad cider hilarity would bring her back. "What's the point?"

"Point is, they're not allowed to do it. Want me to call our agent and have him make them bring them back?"

"Fuck it," Nelle said. "Let them have 'em. I'd rather find curtains I like better, anyway." She was lying, but he didn't argue. He put a hand on her back. She breathed deeply and leaned against him. Evan suggested they head to IKEA as soon as they unloaded the wine fridge and bottles from the back of the SUV. "Let's look around to see if they took anything else. We can make a shopping list, have meatballs for lunch, and be back before dark."

"Or, we could call the locksmith and just order in some rogan josh, drink a bottle of wine, and get loaded. And stay here tonight."

"You want to sleep on the floor? How about Plan C: we unload and then head back to the apartment so we can grab a measuring tape and our sleeping bags and pillows? We figure out what size curtains we need, and *then,* after the locksmith leaves, we can fall asleep on the floor after a *couple* of bottles with dinner."

"Pass out. The kids these days call it 'passing out.'" She wiggled her fingers in the air on either side of the imaginary words and smiled. The darkness had blown itself away. He didn't know how, but it had.

Nelle turned and squeezed him hard. "Welcome home."

"Welcome home, my love."

She straightened up and looked him in the face. "Well, what are you waiting for? Go unload the car! Hop to!"

He made a little hop and a skip and headed for the front door.

11

ONE DAY AFTER CLOSING

Their hips and backs ached in concert with their heads as Evan's cell phone alarm went off. He'd set it for earlier than usual so they could get back to Cambridge in time to meet the movers and let them into the apartment. As planned, they'd drunk two bottles of wine with dinner, which meant a light hangover for the both of them. Worse, though, was the effect of sleeping on the floor of their new house. While they'd brought their sleeping bags to zipper together, the blow-up mats to put underneath them were packed with the rest of their camping gear, and the hardwood floors were aptly named. They got up slowly, aching, staggered out to their car, and drove back to Cambridge.

At what they now referred to as "the old place"—even though they'd only spent a single night away—they found the next door neighbor had parked on the street in front of their apartment, despite the signs reserving the space in front of their building for the moving van. Evan didn't bother going to the door to ask him to move his car. The asshole never answered when anyone rang the bell, and his wife pretended to be deaf when anyone wanted her to act like a member of the community. Evan dialed the police parking enforcement number he had saved in his phone to get them to come tow the guy's shitbox. As many times as Evan had called to have that car towed from in front of his driveway, he was on a first name basis with half of the Cambridge traffic cops. He wouldn't miss the neighbor mowing his lawn at a quarter to five in the morning or leaving his old toilet in the back yard for months after he had it replaced inside, but he would miss watching him come barreling out of his house, violin case in hand, late for rehearsal at the orchestra, only to stand on the front walk bewildered by the disappearance of his car.

A-1 Towing was pulling away just as the Intelligent Labor van showed up. A trio of skinny guys in black Misfits and Crass tour shirts, pegged jeans, and Chuck Taylors piled out of the cab of the moving truck. Looking at them, Nelle questioned the decision to hire the crew based on the appeal of their company logo and a couple of good online reviews, but after Evan showed the crew boss around, pointing out the section of the shared basement that needed loading as well as how they'd labeled the boxes so the guys would know which room to put them in on the other end, the boss nodded at the other movers, who immediately went to work.

Evan and Nelle watched one, who'd been leaning against the van complaining of having a hangover, lift a bookshelf twice his size onto his back without help and trot out of the apartment like it was weightless. It had taken both Evan and Nelle to get that thing up into the apartment when it was still in pieces in the box, but the weight of it didn't seem to slow this guy's step even a little bit. Nelle rubbed her head and felt a tinge of shame at how her own hangover depleted her. She had a few years on the movers, but not *that* many. She also suspected that when these guys tied one on, they went harder than a single bottle of wine apiece.

She grabbed the Bluetooth speaker off the windowsill in the kitchen and moved it into the rapidly emptying living room. She selected "Cramp Stomp" from *Big Beat from Badsville* on her phone and pushed PLAY. One of the movers looked at her and nodded approvingly. Inspired by the Cramps, Nekromantix, and HorrorPops, they finished loading the truck before lunch.

Crammed together in the cab to set off for Ripton, the crew boss said, "We're going to stop to eat. Be there around two, if that works." Nelle handed him a fifty-dollar bill and told them lunch was on her. The guy took it without argument, smiled and thanked her, and stuffed the bill in his shirt pocket. After they pulled away, she regretted not giving them more. Fifty dollars for four men seemed like too little. Evan said he doubted they were headed to an expensive gastropub, adding if they worked only half as hard unloading the truck as they had loading it, he still planned on tipping them well enough to ensure a week of hangovers.

Evan and Nelle walked back inside the old place looking for anything that had accidentally been left behind. Anything that could say they had once been there. Nelle looked out the dining room window at the brick wall of the gas station next door. She grinned at the thought they'd somehow spent the last ten years with this scene outside and never thought it was anything but the view they had. Evan sidled up behind her, wrapping his arms around her waist, and kissed her neck. "You going to miss it?" he asked.

This was *their* apartment. Each room contained the memories of a decade together. This was where they'd made love for the first time back when it was just *her* apartment. It was where they'd discussed their future together — getting married, starting a family — where he'd held her while she cried and spotted after the miscarriage. The apartment was where he'd worked a telecommute job he hated so she could finish mortuary school. Once she got the job at the Tremblay Funeral Home, they'd decided there, over takeout, he should quit and work for himself. All the good and bad times in their lives together had happened in this city on this street in this apartment. It was the end of an era of their lives. Now they were off to a fresh start far from Mass Ave traffic, blocked driveways, and blasted drunk college students being sick on their front steps at two in the morning.

"Not even a little bit," she lied.

12

But, he's dead."

The words sounded thin coming out of Sharon, a breath dispersing in an airless room. They passed without resonance, failing to elicit even an acknowledgment from the man across from her. She couldn't give him what he wanted. It was all gone, seized with warrants and subpoenas. She thought of her husband's things, laptop computers and external hard drives, micro flash memory chips and whatever else, all taped up in plastic bags and labeled with stickers that read EXHIBIT 1, EXHIBIT 2, EXHIBIT 3 and on and on, stored away in a municipal vault no one could get to. She had no illusions that the police would return a single item. It would all eventually be destroyed, if it hadn't been already. She didn't know how to get this through to the man sitting in her living room.

He considered her with a kind of detachment she associated with someone observing a thing, not a person. His gaze made her shiver, and she had no one to help her fend him off. Her husband was dead and buried in Ridgelawn Cemetery. Her understanding of his crimes was a patchwork of suspicions based on what the police and prosecutors claimed. And, yes, things she'd observed, but placed in that part of her consciousness that nurtured doubt. The part that believed her husband wasn't a bad man; he'd never *hurt* anyone. The specifics of what he'd done were detailed on a sealed grand jury indictment she never got to see, though it was still ruining her life.

Her husband's alleged *indiscretions* had cost her and her son everything. Losing his income was one thing; she worked, and the house was paid for — he'd insisted it be recorded in her name alone, as if he knew it needed to be sealed off from him — but the stories in the papers and on television had stripped any kind of life from them. Colleagues avoided her; the partners moved her into administrative work, isolating her from interactions with clients. Everyone she knew socially, friend and acquaintance alike, had cut her off. They stopped calling, dropping by. "Innocent until proven guilty" was a *legal* standard, something for the courts to determine. But friends and co-workers were free to make their own judgments and impose sentences of isolation and exclusion as they saw fit. She'd defended Bryant at first, but his guilt had been established on the radio during the drive to work, on the way home again, and on the nightly news. Everyone she knew assumed her complicity, if not collaboration, even though she'd neither been arrested nor charged. Defending her husband had only made it worse. What was left was a network of men she didn't *want* as friends, but had to utilize when things needed fixing that Bryant wasn't around to handle. Her relationships with her neighbors bottomed out when one of those men registered her address as a place of employment because the handyman job he was doing on her front steps was going to last a few weeks. The police had come around with flyers and knocked on doors to notify all the neighbors that a Level 3 sex offender was working for her. That was the end of even a sympathetic glance or wave as she drove by. None of them would acknowledge her, let alone engage her in a conversation. Bryant had left and taken everything in the entire world but her son, this house, and his own reputation, which hung over it all like a pall, interring her alive inside.

And now she had this stern-faced man in a black suit, black shirt, and black tie sitting in her living room demanding her husband's secrets. As if she knew them. As if she knew her husband at all.

The man's brow furrowed and then eased back to indifference. "There is a saying where I'm from. Tol'ko samyy nizkiy vor kradyot y svoih. The lowest thief steals from his own village. Alive or dead, he stole from us, and we want back what he took."

"I can't give you what I don't have."

Her visitor shrugged. "Your husband was smart enough to know I would be coming eventually. He knew I would visit this house, where his wife and his son live, and he knew what it would mean for them if I didn't get what I wanted."

Sharon straightened up as best she could under the emotional strain. She said, "I can't give you anything. Do you think I'd still be living here if I had anything to show for what you say he did?" She gestured around her meager living room, letting her hand pause before the crack running up the wall beside the fireplace.

He considered her for an uncomfortably long time before letting out a breath and getting up from the chair he'd pulled over to the coffee table opposite her. He smoothed the front of his trousers and buttoned his suit jacket the way she'd seen so many lawyers in the firm do, as though they'd gotten everything they wanted, the deposition was over, and it was time to go. "I had hoped we would've had a more productive conversation," he said. The man turned and walked to the front door. He opened the door, and all the air in Sharon's body rushed out of her at once, leaving her breathless and desperate. She was unable to move. This was drowning on dry land.

The man waiting outside was half a head taller than his companion. He seemed more weathered, as though the time he'd spent standing in the sun in situations like this, waiting to be invited in, had leathered his skin. The first man could've easily passed for one of the attorneys at the firm, with his well-coiffed hair and manicure, if it weren't for the tattoos on his hands. But this one, despite his expensive suit, didn't look like anything but a killer. The similar tattoos on his hands and neck, along with the gun that appeared in his hand as he stepped into her house, dispelled any notion that these men would leave her alive.

Her thoughts turned to her son, still at school, but for how much longer? The bus would drop him off somewhere around four o'clock, and though she usually met him at the stop, when she didn't today, he'd find his way right home anyway. He was good like that. And then what would he discover when he arrived?

"No," she eked out, wanting to bargain, though unable to find the words. "Please, no!"

"If it makes any difference," the first man said. "I believe you. Stas, on the other hand, will take convincing. He is . . . uh, how you say, a skeptic."

The man closed the door.

13

The movers emptied the truck in half the time it had taken them to fill it. Evan tipped the guys, and they left with smiles on their faces. He watched them drive off, glad to see the boss was a pro who left intact the trees along the driveway with their spreading branches. If he could drive that thing through the narrow side streets of Cambridge and Somerville, he could take it anywhere. Evan turned away and stared at their new house. Their *home.*

From the outside, it didn't look like much. They'd seen so many places with outward promise that turned out to be "fixer-uppers," or even full-on dumps on the inside. At first blush, this house was a bland, light yellow, slightly updated, two-story Colonial with nothing to distinguish it from any other place, apart from the shed built off to the side in the front yard, instead of out back. Though it was odd, the look somehow worked. It had a kind of prosaic New England charm. But the façade was truly just a mask; inside it was something extraordinary masquerading as average. And they could always have the siding replaced. They could do anything they wanted—it was theirs, and they had the money. More of it, in fact, than they could spend in a lifetime.

Now they were moving into their dream home. A place with an open floor plan where they were always in sight of each other unless one of them sought privacy in the expansive bedroom upstairs or the lavender-painted front room. (They even thought about breaking through to create a cutout wall to open up into that space too, but were still undecided since a nice breakfast ledge in the kitchen also meant even less wall space for art.) Evan's office was no longer also the dining room slash library slash workout room slash whatever-else-it-needed-to-be. Not to mention the reduction in noise. No longer neighboring a gas station, only the low drone of distant traffic and, more presently, the rustle of the light breeze in the trees penetrated his office. A crow cawed, and then the whole place was quiet.

Evan had started to walk up the front steps when a loud car engine starting up halted his step. He turned with interest to see what kind of whip was making such a roar. Their old street in Cambridge was a neighborhood of college students and older homeowners who all owned sensible cars, performance luxury rides like an Audi or a BMW, or junkers that could get dinged up in urban driving. People in that part of the city didn't often buy trucks or muscle cars. Here, though, there seemed to be a lot of teenage boys with big giant trucks that had big giant American flags waving in the wind on tall poles in the back, and as many throaty muscle cars driven by white-haired guys who looked too old to still be having midlife crises. While not Boston or Cambridge, Ripton was still in Massachusetts, though a different one than they were used to.

A blood-red Dodge Challenger pulled away from the shoulder and took off, kicking up a small cloud of dirt and grit. Evan wondered what the driver had been doing there. On that side of their driveway, there wasn't a neighbor for maybe a mile or more. Just thick trees and conservation land. Evan walked to the end of his driveway and looked up the street for the car, but it had already disappeared around the next bend. Whatever the guy had been up to, he was long gone now.

Evan checked the mailbox. Inside were a couple of coupon flyers and an oversized postcard ad for a local dentist. They were addressed to CURRENT RESIDENT. That was them now. Soon they'd start getting their own mail, addressed by name and everything. Probably tomorrow, he figured. Then they could go update their driver's licenses, reregister to vote, and do anything else that required proof of residence. But there was no rush.

He thought again about the car that peeled out. It hadn't been *idling;* he'd heard the engine start. It must have been there for a while because he hadn't heard it pull up. He'd have noticed the growl on a beast like that. He shrugged and told himself to stop being paranoid. He'd only taken note of it because it was a Challenger SRT Demon. If it had been a Prius or a hybrid RAV4 like their own cars, he might not have even looked back at the sound of the engine turning over. Not that he was into modern muscle cars; he wanted a classic two-lane blacktop hotrod—a '41 Ford Club Coupe or a '32 Deuce—something that'd go with their rockabilly style better than a fucking crossover SUV. He wanted to go to the Grand National Roadster Show or the Hootenanny with Nelle next to him, leaning against the fender of something almost as beautiful as her. But *that* muscle car. What had it been doing *there?*

Stop. There'd been a moving truck in the driveway. People got curious about new neighbors. It was a thing that happened and didn't have any other sinister connotation. He rolled up the junk mail in his hand, intending to drop it in the recycling bin, and walked back up the driveway toward the house.

14

THREE WEEKS AFTER CLOSING

The **driver behind her** laid on the horn as Nelle slowed to make the sharp turn into her driveway. Despite turning on her blinker long before approaching it, the guy still had to stomp on his brakes and swerve to avoid rear-ending her. After the day she'd had, the sounds of screeching tires and a horn set her heart racing. It was long past time for a drink. Fortunately, as she angled the car around in front of the garage, she saw lights on in the dining room.

It had only been a couple of weeks, but there wasn't a thing about her commute that was going well. In terms of time, it hadn't increased by much — only about ten or twenty minutes, depending on traffic — but the difference between driving and riding the subway was significant. Instead of staring at a book and unwinding from the day lost in another world, she stared through the windshield at brake lights and only got to read political bumper stickers. NPR wasn't doing it for her either. She resolved to try audiobooks and see if that helped.

She hadn't quit her job or found a new one closer to Ripton yet. She'd worked hard to learn how to do what she did, so it seemed like a waste not to keep at it for a little while longer; plus, she really liked her boss. She wasn't sure what she'd do if she stayed home all day, anyway. *I'll read and snack too much and forget to work out. That's what I'll do.*

Saying it in her head, it didn't actually sound that bad. Gaining a few pounds wouldn't be the end of the world. It'd likely suit Evan just fine if she got a little more hourglassy.

It took a couple of tries with the clicker to get the doors to lock after she climbed out of the car. The battery in the fob probably needed to be replaced—yet another thing piled on top of a difficult day. Enough of them and she'd buckle. *Not tonight. Go get a drink and chill out, bebê. Leave tomorrow for tomorrow.*

The front door was unlocked; she let herself in and threw the deadbolt out of habit. The alarm chirped its illusion of security as she opened and closed the door. They'd made the decision not to resubscribe to the service, but the system still had power and it kept making the sound every time someone came or went. The chirp was mildly annoying, but what she really hated was the glowing keypad mounted on the wall by the door. It looked trashy. If they weren't going to have an actual alarm, she didn't want the keypad or any of the plastic motion sensors high up in the corners. She didn't want a gaping hole in the wall or a clumsy patch where the keypad had been either. Neither she nor Evan were handy enough to make it look like the alarm had never been there—hell, she didn't even know if they could remove it without electrocuting themselves—so, eyesore that it was, it was staying until they could hire someone to deal with it.

Evan's shoes were lying on the floor where he'd kicked them off. She pulled off her boots and picked both pairs up, lining them up on the shoe rack beside the door. She set down her bag and shrugged out of her coat. She hung it in the closet instead of on the coat tree and padded into the kitchen, where her husband was making dinner. He had the music turned up.

"Honey, I'm home," she shouted.

He started and his face turned red. "You scared the shit out of me."

"You didn't hear the alarm?" He shook his head and nodded toward the Bluetooth speaker on the dinner table. It was blaring the Reverend Horton Heat. He shouted, "Alexa, turn it down." The music quieted enough for them to speak normally.

His brow furrowed. He wiped his hands on a dish towel and stepped away from the stove. "Rough day? You want me to fix you something? Bar's open." Despite her attempts to hide her mood, he could sense it. He could always tell when she didn't feel good. Still, she tried not to burden him with her problems at work. She wanted nights with her husband to be untainted by grief and stress.

"Fix me a sidecar, bartender. And don't skimp on the brandy." She didn't have enough Don Draper in her tonight to do more than put on her best smile.

"Coming right up!" He turned the flame on the gas range down to WARM and went to the kitchen island they'd repurposed as a bar.

She picked his glass of wine up off the black granite countertop and sniffed at it. A cabernet. He'd be in trouble for opening a pinot noir without her, but a cab was fine. She took a sip and put it back on the counter. "You want to talk about it?" he asked.

Nelle didn't often discuss her work, and she definitely didn't when the work was hard. She was well-suited for her job because she was good at the physical mechanics of it and the direct sights and smells of dead bodies didn't faze her much. She could look at a corpse and know it had been someone's grandmother or father or spouse, but the person they had been before had fled, leaving behind the natural consequence of being mortal. Their remains. Nothing more.

Beyond suffering.

She wasn't religious or spiritual and didn't think anyone she saw had gone someplace better—or worse—they were just gone. Most of the time they were older folks, passing after prolonged illnesses. Their families remained, however, and needed the comfort of what the funeral home provided: an opportunity to say goodbye and have a meaningful experience moving through this massive transition. A person's death was a milestone that deserved recognition like any other. It was good for people to acknowledge it, be present with it, and make peace, so they could continue to live. And she took comfort in knowing she helped ease them through—a gentle guide for the living and the dead. She thought of herself as "death positive."

It was hard to be positive about anything when it was a kid on the table. There was something about staring down at the body of a person who should be just beginning their life that couldn't be put into words. Any person with a heart understood the injustice of an untimely death. Still, as much as she could intellectualize such a thing, it was hard to put it in an emotional box labeled *The Way Life Is.*

Especially this one. "Some drunk asshole blew through a light and crashed into the back of the family car. She was . . ." Nelle trailed off.

She couldn't think of the right word. *Killed?* That word wasn't enough. *Ruined?* The sight of this poor girl's battered body had nearly broken her. Nelle thought she looked like the girl of her own she'd wanted to have. She'd swallowed her anguish and done her work the best she could for the sake of the child and her family, reminding herself the entire time, it wasn't *her* on the table.

Someday it would be.

That was the constant that kept her going. She didn't feel death breathing down her neck, no matter how many times she encountered its work. Because, though it was inevitable, it wasn't her. Not today.

The last shreds of her pretense fell away. "I worked on a little kid today."

Evan abandoned the shaker and came to take her in his arms.

"I'm so sorry," he said. Her eyes welled up with the tears she'd been holding in since she had picked up the child's body at the hospital. Evan held her close and smoothed her hair down and whispered, "Shh," while she let it out onto his shoulder.

After a while, she pulled back and smiled weakly. She wiped at the big tearstain on his shirt, unable to make it go away. The cry helped; now she just felt raw and tired.

"I'm sorry. I'm going to go take a hot bath, if dinner'll keep. I just feel nasty."

"It'll be fine. I haven't put the pasta in yet. Everything can simmer. Take your time." He slipped back over to the bar and poured her drink into a coupe glass. "Take this too."

She took a sip and said, "It's delicious; just what I need. This, and a little time to decompress. Thank you."

He leaned closer and kissed her again. "No darkness."

"Only light," she replied. She didn't feel it yet, but after a drink and a bath, she hoped she would. She turned to go start filling the tub, but paused by the mail sitting on the kitchen counter. She picked through the bills, ad cards, and flyers. "Is this all that came today?"

"Yuppers."

"I'm expecting something from Mom."

"They said it'd take a little while to reroute whatever goes to the old address. It'll get here."

Nelle said, "She told me she mailed it to this address. It doesn't need to be rerouted."

He shrugged. "It'll probably show up tomorrow. If not, we can try to see where it is, if she kept the tracking number."

Her mood was dark and darkening further.

Evan pointed to a plate of chocolate chip cookies covered in Saran Wrap sitting on the counter next to the pile. On top, a small note read *Welcome Home.* "That's the only other thing that was waiting for us today," he said. "It's from the Darnielles, next door."

She pulled back the plastic and slipped a cookie out from the plate. Evan reached for the treat in her hand. "Whoa whoa whoa! I haven't checked to see if those have nuts yet."

Nelle gave him a knowing look and took a bite. She chewed for a second and declared through a dry mouthful of cookie, "They're fine." She chased the bite with a sip of her sidecar. "I'm getting in the bath now." She stuffed the rest of the treat in her mouth, grabbed a second, and disappeared into the bathroom.

He called after her, "Your extra EpiPens are still packed with the rest of the medicines in the box by the sink!" There was more than a tinge of fear and actual anger in his voice. When they were first married, she'd accidentally eaten half a cashew. Her eyes swelled shut and her throat closed while he was rushing her to the emergency room. After a shot of epinephrine and an eighty-dollar Benadryl, the ER doctor made them wait until after one in the morning before she would release them to go home. And all that time, he kept beating himself up for not having brought her autoinjectors to the party with them and not asking about the food. Ever since, he'd been hypervigilant about anything edible not prepared by him.

Nelle had a twin pack of EpiPens in her purse in addition to the ones that were packed away. Though the pair she carried around were likely expired. In any case, she hadn't thought to check the cookies for nuts because *how could the day get any worse than it's already been?*

She started the water, stripped, and finished the second cookie before taking another drink of her cocktail. It was perfect. Yeah, she could quit work and comfortably gain a couple of pounds. Wider hips would make the cute little Marilyn flare dress she liked hang better. *Slightly* wider.

She set the coupe glass on the floor beside the tub, lit a candle, closed the Venetian blinds, and turned off the light before getting into the water. It felt good to just lie in the warm dark for a while and try to forget. She listened to her husband in the next room clanking around the kitchen to the muted sound of the Reverend Heat's "Psychobilly Freakout," and the stress of the day started to seep out of her body into the water. What was it her mother had always said to her when she was little? "We're safe as houses." She'd never understood what that meant. But lying there in the warmth, in the dark, it sounded right.

Safe as houses.

15

He tore open the flap of the small Flat Rate box and shook out the slip of paper and taped up Bubble Wrap inside. The paper was a small piece of salmon-colored stationery like old ladies used. It smelled like lavender. His wife bought lavender-scented bags to pick up the dog's shits when they took it for walks, so the smell always made him think of dog shit, and that always made him upset. He hated that he had to pick up the mess with his hands. People were such assholes about it. Especially that one bitch who'd put up the little cast iron sign shaped like a squatting dog with NO! engraved on it at the edge of her lawn. He tried to get Maxim to piss on the damn thing every time they passed by. After a while, the white paint on the word NO! started to turn a dull yellow. He loved that.

Unfolding the stationery, he read the short note written in careful, tight cursive. Old lady writing.

Dear Eleonora,

I found this in the attic. I forgot I had it, and I thought you might like to keep it. It was your great-grandmother Ella's before she gave it to my mother. Gran gave it to me and I put it in a chest and, I hate to say, forgot about it. It was one of the few possessions your namesake took with her when they left Poland. I think she'd be happy to know that you have it now, even if it's not the sort of thing that's in style to wear. It's come a long way to be with you. I'm sorry I didn't give it to you sooner. It's hard to let go of things, but this belongs with you. Maybe one day . . .

The pictures inside are of your Great-Gran Ella's parents Josef and Esther. They died in Treblinka.
I love you,
Mom

He set the note beside him on the sofa and unwound the packaging from around a locket at the end of a length of chain. He snapped it open with his thumbnail. Inside, the pictures were faded with age, but still recognizable. Recognizable to someone who might have known them, anyway. To him, they just looked like another couple of old Jews.

He sniffed his fingers. They smelled like lavender, and that made him angry. He wished he still had his dog so he could get it to piss on the pictures, the letter, and the envelope. He tossed the necklace on the table, got up, and walked to the bathroom to wash his hands. After a hard scrub, he sniffed at his hands again.

The fuckin' smell won't come off.

"Treblinka," he said. He liked the sound of the word. "Treblinka. Treb-lin-ka." He thought that if he ever got a new dog, he might name it that. He could call it 'Linka for short and no one would ever know. But he wasn't going to get a new dog. There wasn't time enough left.

He went to the fridge for a beer. Behind him on the table in the eat-in kitchen next to the blue polo shirt he'd special-ordered online sat the shopping bag that had been in the trunk of his car. He popped open the beer, took a long pull, and set it on the table. He pulled the oilcloth bundle out of the bag and unwrapped it carefully, as though it held one of his own grandmother's porcelain figurines—the kind that were always praying, the ones that, every once in a while, he'd "accidentally" break, even though his grampa would tan his ass for it. The Heckler & Koch HK45 pistol was much heavier than one of those. The firearm was expensive, but that's what money is for: spending.

Like the necklace, you can't take it with you.

IV

◆

NIGHTMARES

16

TWELVE WEEKS AFTER CLOSING

Evan was lost in a black void. His body was heavy, and when he tried to move, it felt like gravity doubled, making his arms and legs leaden and immobile. His head ached and he was disoriented and woozy, like he was drunk and blacked out, but not completely *passed* out. He remembered staging breakfast and having to run to the store. And when he'd come home, Nelle was gone. He went looking for her. Finding her was the last thing he could remember. He remembered tape over her mouth. More holding her to the chair. It was wrong and scary, and he'd taken a step toward her without thinking because she needed his help, and then her eyes and panic and . . . the void.

He was still floating in it. No, not floating. He could feel his body, and it was seated on something hard. He was sitting up. Not lying on a floor or in bed. Though he couldn't understand why, if he was sitting upright, he couldn't move. Something cut into his wrists and ankles. Rope? *Tape,* like over Nelle's mouth and arms. It felt tight and pinched, and he realized that while he could feel the seat against his body, he couldn't feel his hands. No. He *could* feel them. They hurt. But the pain in his head made it hard to focus on the rest of his body, as if his mind was sunk in a pool too deep to see the surface.

He tried to lift his head and open his eyes, but the surge of pain in his skull brought forward a wave of nausea. He wanted to retch, but following that thought was the awareness there was something in his mouth. Something thick and dry that made it hard to breathe. Panic swelling, he tried to take a deep breath in through his nose. The effort made everything feel a little less real. The void resurgent. Nothing made sense. Nothing but the throb of pain that pulsed in his skull.

My skull.

His thoughts about his body were fragmented, as if he was only a collection of parts that hadn't been put together properly and weren't fitting. Hands. Back. Skull. Consciousness, misplaced deep down, not where it should be, in brain and skull. Why was he all apart? Why was he so deep down in this abyss? Another surge of pain and nausea crested and waned like a wave crashing over rocks and then gently flowing away, its particularity reoccupied by an oppressive whole.

Far off, he heard voices, caught phrases that made no sense in a lost context.

". . . good girl . . ."

". . . if you scream . . ."

". . . water . . ."

"I've been good."

There were two speakers. He worked to focus on them, but it was hard. One was Nelle. She didn't sound right, but after a decade together, he *knew* her voice in all its variations—normal, hoarse, whispered, and shouted. Nelle was with him. They hadn't been separated. It was the other one he couldn't place. It didn't belong to anyone they knew. A man. Not familiar. Not a friend.

More pain.

He tried to open his eyes again. While he felt closer to the surface, he couldn't break through. He was stuck in the void. In the distance, though, he thought it was becoming lighter.

He heard heavy footsteps moving away. Up the stairs.

Closer to the surface. Almost there. Almost awake and back in his body. Just a little further.

And then, "Please wake up, Evan."

His heart sank, and he wanted to be back in the abyss. He wanted to be drunk and passed out because if he was lit and laid out at a party, then this wasn't happening.

"If you can hear me . . ."

Oh god, I can *hear you. I'm in here and I can hear you and I don't want to hear any of this!*

17

Nelle thought she saw Evan move again. His head turning just a little to the side, maybe. A little toward her. It could have just been gravity, but then his eyelids fluttered a little.

Did the man see it too? He stared at her husband, but his face gave up little. She thought she caught a hint of disappointment before his expression reset. Was he upset that Evan was still unconscious? The man took a step toward Evan. Nelle watched as he reached out for her husband's face. He grabbed Evan by the jaw and tilted his head up. Evan's eyes didn't even flutter. He looked dead. Except she could see his chest moving ever so slightly. He was breathing. That didn't mean he wasn't dying, though. He could have a brain hemorrhage or swelling. She'd seen the end results of head trauma, most often motorcyclists who tried to get around the helmet law by buying a little "brain bucket" that wasn't DOT compliant. Once, she'd worked on a woman who'd drunkenly fallen off the platform at Wellington Station, landing headfirst on the steel rail. She knew what closed head wounds like those did. She knew all about worst-case scenarios. She was living one right now. The man had clubbed her husband with a bat.

He let go of Evan, letting his head slump down again.

She exhaled through her nose, and the man glanced at her with narrowed eyes, annoyed that she was making noise. She couldn't help it. She couldn't breathe through her mouth because of the gag, and the tape around her midsection was tight. She felt light-headed and couldn't tell if it was because she wasn't getting enough oxygen or if it was from the beating he'd given her upstairs. Either way, she wasn't feeling well and was certain that the sensation was only going to get worse as the hours dragged on. Her stomach growled. It seemed an inappropriate response in the face of larger problems, but she hadn't had breakfast. She already felt weak, and it was hard to think clearly. In a few hours, it'd be hard to run or to fight. Even now, thinking of her stomach was a distraction from her most pressing problem: the man standing in her cellar.

Focus.

She grunted at the intruder. He looked at her again, with less patience than before. She grunted again and made a movement with her head like she was trying to shake off the gag. *Take it off, please,* she was trying to say. He furrowed his brow and seemed to be trying to make sense of her muted request. As obvious as she thought it was, he didn't seem to be taking the hint. She did it again, tilting her head in a come-here motion that took all of her will to perform, not because her head hurt — though it did, badly — but because the last thing in the world she wanted was for this man to come any closer.

The man stepped away from Evan. She nodded and pled with her eyes. He smiled that terrifying smile and said, "You wanna say something?"

She nodded.

"If I take this gag off, you going to be a good girl?"

She didn't know what he meant by that. She'd already figured out that screaming would be no help. With only one marginally close neighbor who was out of town for the long weekend, she could scream her head off and no one would come to help. Maybe he meant something else. Spitting or biting. She was smart enough not to antagonize a man when she couldn't even lift her arms to protect herself. No, she wouldn't spit or scream. She nodded.

"Okay, then."

With his left hand, the man picked a corner of the duct tape on her face loose, and yanked. It came halfway off, catching at her lips. She yelped and jerked in the chair, her arms wanting to come up so she could paw at her face to see if she'd lost skin, if she was bleeding, but the tape around her wrists held. The man paused and then ripped it the rest of the way off. Her face stung brightly and her lips felt numb, like she'd been punched in the mouth.

He took a step back, his brow furrowed, holding the tape out like he might slap it right back on. Nelle could see he didn't realize that he'd hurt her. He didn't see her pain. She pushed the cloth out of her mouth with her dry tongue, gently letting it fall in her lap. She spit it out demurely, not to avoid offending her captor, but because she didn't want it to fall on the dirty cement floor. If he was going to end up shoving it back in her mouth, she didn't want it to be covered in grit and whatever else was underfoot.

Inhaled deeply through her mouth, the cool, musty air of the basement was the most satisfying breath she could remember ever taking. She breathed deeply again and said, "I'll be good." It came out as a hoarse whisper. Her tongue was dry, and her throat hurt. She tried to swallow so she could repeat her promise a little louder, except there was nothing in her mouth to swallow. She tried again anyway, forcing a bit more volume. "I'll be good."

"Right. Because if you try anything, I'll make you regret it." He held up the piece of tape in one hand and made a fist with the other. His hands weren't delicate. They looked like they were used to being thrust against things. Like he was the sort of man who got angry and punched walls, punched other men — Nelle knew for a fact he punched women; she was living proof. He continued, sticking a thumb out from the fist and jabbing it over his shoulder at Evan. "I'll make *you* regret it, and I'll make *him* pay for it."

Nelle looked at Evan. His lids weren't fluttering anymore. His head hadn't moved again. Maybe she'd imagined it. It was possible that it was a trick of the dim cellar lights and one of her dizzy spells. She wanted him to wake up, but she wanted to be the first one to speak to him when he did.

"Can I have . . . some water?" she said. Her voice was still a croak, but it was audible. "I'm thirsty."

"A drink?" the man said, as if she'd asked for something unreasonable.

She nodded. When he stood there, saying nothing, she added, "I've been good."

He smiled. "Hard to be bad when you're tied down and have a pair of panties stuffed in your mouth."

She looked at the ball of cotton in her lap and saw it was indeed a pair of her underwear. A pair she'd bought recently that were cute and relatively inexpensive. She'd yelled at Evan for being too rough taking them off of her during foreplay when she first got them. She didn't want him to tear them. Women's underwear like that didn't come in packs of eight like his boxer briefs. She felt a tinge of embarrassment and anger. She tried to conceal the signs of either feeling but couldn't hide her hot ears filling with blood.

"I'm being good," she said. "Please, may I have a drink of water?"

The man looked around. His eyes alighted on a stack of plastic red Solo cups they'd bought for the housewarming party a few weeks ago. He grabbed one off the stack and scanned the basement. She wondered what he was looking for, until she realized he was searching for a faucet. There was a spigot at the bottom of the water heater that'd release filthy, scalding hot water, and there was the pipe that led to the washer hookup, neither of which would pour a drinkable glass of water. She said please again. "You have to go upstairs."

He shouted, "You want a Perrier? Want me to squeeze a fucking lemon into it?"

She flinched. "No. I . . . just . . . There's no tap down here."

His back straightened, and he gave her an exasperated look. He stood; his breathing quickened as if merely talking to her was making him angrier. She got the sense her *existence* made him angry.

"I know that!"

He stomped up the stairs. She listened to him in the kitchen. When she was certain he was out of earshot, she whispered to her husband, "Evan, can you hear me?" While his eyelids fluttered again, he didn't move; he didn't wake up. The water upstairs began to run. "Please wake up, Evan. Please, *please* wake up." She willed him to snap his eyes open and lift his head to her.

The clank in the pipes above her head as the water shut off made her flinch.

"If you can hear me, bebê, maybe just keep pretending to be out, okay? If you can hear me, work at the tape, but *don't* let him know you're awake."

The man came stomping back to the landing at the top of the stairs. Nelle watched him coming down but tried to look at Evan out of the corner of her eye, wanting a sign that he'd heard her. If he gave her one, the man might see, so she hoped he'd stay still almost as much as she yearned for him to blink, just once, to let her know he'd understood.

"Here." The man held out the Solo cup, sloshing water onto his thick fingers. She hadn't noticed the reddish-brown stains under his fingernails and in the cracks of his knuckles before. The horror on his hands made her want to shrink away, but she couldn't. Not after she'd asked for the drink. She craned her neck forward to remind him that she needed help. He stepped closer and tipped the cup toward her lips. She took a big gulp of the water pouring out. It splashed against her face and a little went up her nose and she sputtered but kept swallowing as it spilled down her chin and onto the front of her shirt. The man stepped back and set the cup on the steps. "Only a little. Too much and you'll have to piss."

Her face grew hot with embarrassment at being spoken to like a child. Of course, she'd have to pee eventually. She'd gone to the bathroom before getting in the shower, but she'd also had a cup of coffee right before that. Chances seemed fifty-fifty that he'd let her wet herself right there in the chair rather than free her so she could use the bathroom upstairs or even squat over a bucket here in the cellar. While she wanted to be free, pissing in her pants seemed like a better option than being cut loose and having him follow her to the bathroom. Better than undressing, even partially, in front of him.

Then again, the only way to fight was to be cut loose.

"Thank you," she said.

"That's nice."

The wetness of her shirt chilled her a little. She felt gooseflesh raise on her arms. The man seemed unaffected by her discomfort; he just stared. She felt exposed with the wet fabric clinging to her while he stared.

"What do you want from us?"

"I want you to shut the fuck up. Keep talking, and I'll seal you up again."

"If I knew what you—"

The man got up faster than Nelle could process what was happening and slapped her across the mouth. The crack of his open hand on her face echoed through the cellar.

She tasted blood, and her neck hurt from being whipped around by his blow. She wanted to apologize, say *I'm sorry.* She was afraid he'd hit her again if she did, so she just sat there.

"Did that hurt?" he said. "You learn something from it? Now, imagine how much worse this feels." He tented his fingers next to the knife he'd set next to her phone on the book box. "You got me?"

Nelle nodded.

"Good girl. That's what I thought. You have plans this weekend?" She raised her eyebrows in reply. He gave her permission to answer the question.

"No." They hadn't made plans for the weekend. Patriots' Day coincided with the Boston Marathon *and* the start of spring break for Massachusetts schools, meaning the roads would be snarled in all directions. The Mass Pike was the world's longest parking lot on a normal Friday night, let alone at the head of a long weekend and a major annual sporting event. So, rather than dinner with friends or a drive to the Cape for a long weekend, they'd settled for grilling in the back yard and opening a lot of wine and maybe a hike or two in the woods behind the house if it was warm enough and didn't rain. A "staycation" to avoid the stress of having to compete with other people in order to get away from other people. And also to keep that low profile they promised they would and always seemed to fall a little short of doing.

"No, what?"

Nelle felt a tinge of contempt gnawing around the edges of her fear. Did he want her to call him "sir"? As if it wasn't enough that he'd beaten her and taped her to a chair. She was helpless and frightened, and he could do anything he wanted to her. And still he wanted more. He wanted her to concede his supremacy. The urge was there. *Go fuck yourself.* Just three words. And then, his reply. Delivered with fist or knife or gun. Her chances of getting out of this got weaker every time he hurt her. There would come a time when he wasn't satisfied with slapping her, or punching her, and his hands might wrap around her throat. And then it was all done. All for want of a single syllable. *Sir.* The utterance was compliance; it was submission. But, she told herself, she could *pretend* subservience for a while.

She said, "No, sir."

He frowned and undid his belt buckle. "Maybe next time, you won't have to think so hard about it."

18

Evan tried to listen, tried to figure out who their captor was, why he was doing this to them, but if he knew the man, he couldn't place him — not through his semiconscious haze and the throbbing in his head. Evan picked up pieces of what was being said, but couldn't track the whole. Things were becoming clearer, but nothing was entirely clear.

He heard the man shout at Nelle and felt a swell of anger that made his head hurt more. He wasn't one of those spouses who got bent out of shape anytime someone spoke to his wife sharply. Nelle could be headstrong, and sometimes she was too direct for some people's liking. But he didn't jump in to fight her battles like a white knight; she could take care of herself. Except this wasn't just some asshole stranger on the street who didn't like how she drove. Evan wanted to stop the guy from yelling at her again . . . or worse. Worse seemed like an inevitability. No. Didn't *seem* like. Worse was definitely coming.

He'd heard Nelle tell him to "work at the tape." He tried to focus, to find a way to make sense of what his body was telling him. But he felt dizzy and unstable, while at the same time, heavy and rooted to the spot. Not rooted. Tied down. *Taped* down.

A groan escaped his mouth. He couldn't help it. No. Not his mouth. He couldn't open his mouth. It was taped, like his hands and feet. The groan rose up from his throat and escaped through his nose. He couldn't hold it back. What was the other thing Nelle had said? "Don't let him know you're awake." *Easy. I'm* not *awake.* But he was waking. And once the groan was out, he wanted so badly to take it back that he thought he might've moved again, as if he could reach out and grasp the sound in his teeth before anyone caught hint of it drifting away from him.

She'd said other things to him, but by the time he'd risen up enough from the darkness to listen, he'd missed much of it. She implored him to work at the tape, and not let the man know he was awake. Nothing else. It felt wrong, pretending to be unconscious. But then, he wasn't pretending, not entirely. He was only half awake. Still, feigning a blackout made him feel cowardly. It made him feel afraid too; it was the old nightmare all over again.

When he was six or seven years old, he'd watched a Godzilla movie with his dad one night and then gone to bed and dreamed that a gargantuan monster was coming for him. In his dream, he hid behind the sofa, in the closet, under the bed, but the monster always peered through his windows with a giant, jaundiced eye and beheld his vulnerability. Once seen, he would run to another hiding spot, and then another, until the monster ripped the roof off of his house and little Evan had to run across a wide open plain to escape. There were no wide open plains where he'd grown up in New Haven, Connecticut, but in the dreaming world, his house was all that existed for miles, maybe eternity. Him, his house, the monster, and no one else to save him as he ran. The giant thing came lumbering after him, the earth shaking from its weight and speed, and just as he felt its hot breath on his neck, the threat of being devoured in a single agonizing bite realized, Evan would awake in a pool of sweat — sometimes piss — his eyes wide with fear and heart racing. The thing in the night had almost eaten him alive again.

But it was just a dream.

The memory of it coalesced around his mind, drawing clouds that obscured the reality beyond his eyelids. He was alone in the expanse, and there was no escape, because how could you hide out in the open from something that was so much bigger, faster, hungrier than you could ever imagine? How could you escape the monster that was the perfect embodiment of your helplessness?

Evan tried to banish the nightmare and find the clarity he needed to run out of the dream house, out into the open, and get away. But what he needed was to get out of the endless void and back into his mind. He needed to run into the house, not away. Nelle needed him.

Wake up wake up wakeup!

19

Oh, look who's comin' around." The man looked at Evan. He finished slipping his belt out of the loops and folded it over in his hands, snapping the two half lengths of leather together. The sound echoed in the cellar, bouncing off the concrete foundation walls, somewhere between a whipcrack and a gunshot. Despite knowing the sound was harmless, Nelle flinched. The man's gesture was a promise of harm. With what he'd done already, nothing he threatened was empty.

"Leave him alone," she snapped, trying to draw the man's attention away from her husband. She hadn't wanted his attention a second ago, but she couldn't bear watching him fix on Evan.

He took another step, so she called out, "Leave him alone!"

He paused and looked over his shoulder at her. His eyebrows raised in surprise at how clearly she had communicated. The expression on his face under that surprise made her mouth shut so forcefully that her teeth clacked together. Nelle shook her head in frustration. She wanted to scream at him, but . . . Gun, knife, belt. *You have to be* smarter *than him,* she reminded herself. *You can't outfight him or outrun him. You have to* outsmart *him. And that means staying calm.*

"Did you say something?"

She answered him with less volume, but similar urgency. "Leave him alone, please."

He smiled. "No."

The man lashed Evan. The long strip of leather slapped against her husband's thighs, making another loud snap, though not as loud as the first. It was the long groan of muffled pain that came from Evan's throat that echoed in her ears loudest. Her stomach did a flip, and she thought *this* time she was definitely going to vomit. The man lashed Evan's chest, and Evan's head whipped upright instead of lolling, his eyes tightly shut against the pain.

And then he opened his eyes. Wide and panicked. Nelle felt a small part of her give up at the look of fear in them. If *he* was afraid, what hope was there for her? He was the rock she clung to when things were too hard to bear alone.

The intruder glanced at Nelle, a broad smile on his face. A lifetime of resentment and bitter anger swelled up in her. Hate so strong, she thought she might not ever feel anything again. She repeated herself. "Leave him alone, you fucker!"

The man's smile faded. "What did you call me?"

Nelle wanted to tell him that she knew he heard exactly what she'd said. *You fucker.* Instead, she furrowed her brow and stared, letting her gaze communicate for her.

He got the message. In two long strides, he was at her, swinging the belt. It slapped at her shoulder, and pain flashed like fireworks. He hit her again. Neck. Shoulder. Breasts. She shut her eyes, buttressing herself against the pain, waiting for the next blow and the next. What had she done? Her mind scattered as she lost sense of what part of her body he was striking. And then she heard the jangle of the buckle; it muted and she felt the belt loop around her neck. Her eyes snapped open as it tightened. The man held the long end of the belt out and up like a hangman holding a noose, and he pulled. Her vision narrowed as he cut off the air to her lungs, the blood to her brain. The buckle pinched at the skin of her neck, a clear point of sharp pain in the dullness of strangling.

She struggled in the chair and against the tape, unable to reach up for the strop of leather choking her. Panic made her wild.

After a moment, the belt loosened and she felt blood surge into her head. She took a deep breath. To her left, Evan was screaming through his gag. She hadn't been able to hear him before, but now that the belt was loose, she could. The intruder ignored him and leaned down close to her face. If she could've spit in it, she would've, but she couldn't get a breath to force what little moisture was in her mouth past her lips. Her tongue protruded.

"You going to be a good girl? Or do I need to tighten the leash again, bitch?" He jerked the belt. The buckle shifted and this time pressed right up against her windpipe. Fresh tears sprung to her eyes.

She shook her head.

"No? You're *not* going to be a good girl?"

Nelle nodded. She wanted to tell him she'd be good. That she'd do whatever he wanted. Just not to pull the belt tight again. She couldn't get the words out. So she nodded. *Good girl. Good girl.*

"That's more like it," he said. "You know, you got a dirty mouth. Guys would like you better if you acted like a lady." From the small of his back, he pulled the gun out of its holster. Evan began to buck against the weight bench. The man turned and pointed it at him. "Settle down, or I'll settle you down." Evan reluctantly complied. The man returned his attention to Nelle.

He traced the line of her cheekbone down to her jaw with the muzzle of the gun and then tilted her head up so she'd look at him. The front sight dug into the flesh under her chin and made her wince. It still hurt less than being choked. "Good girl," he whispered. "Now, you have to make up for offending me."

"What do you want?" she choked.

"I want you to be nice."

She tried to blink away her confusion, but nothing resolved into any greater clarity. The man stared at her, brow furrowed as if she'd done *him* wrong and not the other way around. No part of this made sense to her. She nodded at him.

"Say it."

"I'll . . . be nice."

He let the belt around her neck loosen. "I know you will. Because if you don't, I'll kill him and make you watch."

You're going to do that anyway.

She swallowed the thought, hiding it deep down in her belly so he couldn't read the words on her face. "I'll be nice," she whispered. "Just tell me what you want from us. We have money. Is that what you're here for? The money?"

"The money," he said. His voice was flat.

She perked up. If that was why he was there, he was still likely going to kill them both after they gave him the bank account numbers. But the thought he might not was a single thread of hope. A very narrow, short thread that she intended to hang on to as tightly as she could. "We'll give the money back. I mean, we spent some of it, but the rest is still—"

He yanked the leash, reducing her voice to a strangled whimper. His face purpled, it had filled with so much blood. She imagined it reflected her own, except he wasn't being strangled.

"You people think you can buy anything you want. You think you can buy your way out of trouble? You think you can buy me off?"

She shook her head, not wanting to argue, but feeling unable to let the accusation go unanswered. "I don't—" she choked.

He stomped heavily on the concrete floor next to her foot to shut her up. His tan work boot thudded dully, but still made her shudder. She couldn't move out of the way of his next stomp if he chose to bring it down on her toes or her instep.

His face was redder than ever and his red-veined eyes bulged. He stared as if expecting an answer, some kind of rationalization or continued bargaining, but she couldn't find the right words. "You're going to start with an apology. And if I don't like it, he dies."

"I don't . . . understand."

"APOLOGIZE!"

"I'm . . . s-sorry. I am sorry for upsetting you," she said in a measured tone she hoped wouldn't antagonize him further. "I swear."

Holding on to the belt, he shoved his gun back in its holster and started undoing his pants. "You're going to make me feel better. And then we'll talk about what else you can do for me."

Nelle turned her head away. The man yanked her face back toward him, hurting her neck. His grip on her chin pinched painfully. He squeezed tighter and glared, as if wanting to see the look in her eyes that told him she felt him. She tried to give him the look he wanted. He let go and pulled his zipper down.

Evan began thrashing against the weight bench again.

The man whipped around. "SIT STILL AND SHUT UP!"

With a look, Nelle tried to implore her husband to be calm. To quietly and covertly work at the tape like she'd asked him. His brows knitted, and she nodded slightly. Tears filled her eyes, but the weight bench stopped rattling with his struggles.

The man refocused on her. "You're going to give me the apology I want."

"I'm sorry, I swear. I swear."

He leaned in. "If I don't like it, I'm gonna take my knife to him and really give you something to swallow."

"Don't do this. Please don't."

He let go of the belt and grabbed a handful of her hair and said, "Be a good girl now."

20

Evan struggled to remain still. He'd thrashed and fought, and all he accomplished was reclining the back of the weight bench even more. His line of sight from this new angle was worse. And the man kept looking back at him, making sure he saw. As if his reaction was part of it. As if it got him off to be seen like that. For Evan to see *her* like that. He wanted to take that away, to frustrate the man's pleasure, his satisfaction in knowing he was seen. So, he closed his eyes and turned his head.

Hot shame burned in his chest at looking away. Stopping the man was a thing beyond his ability. The son of a bitch had blindsided him. Clubbed him unconscious and tied him up. *That* wasn't his fault. When Nelle looked in his eyes, though, and he looked away, that was the failure of his heart. The beginning of the end of everything. Shame filled him so full he felt like bursting. Shame at his weakness, shame at his inaction.

He felt shame at turning away from his wife. At not wanting to see.

21

Nelle felt like she was floating a foot behind her head, as if her consciousness couldn't quite stay seated in her skull. Her thoughts were unmoored from the present, finding shelter in the past instead. Evan's voice slipped through the fog, whispering words of encouragement like he always did when things were difficult. *You got this,* he'd say, like she was standing toe-to-toe with her problems, capable of fighting. But today she didn't feel like a warrior on the battlefield; she felt like Giles Corey being pressed to death under stones. Corey wanted to defy his accusers and die faster, but she didn't *want* a heavier burden. *She* wanted to live, and she wanted not to be in the cellar, in this chair, with this man standing in front of her. She wanted to follow her conscious mind and float right up out of the house and away. But she was rooted to the spot.

She tried to focus, force herself back into her body and brace herself for what was about to happen — the intruder's hand gripping her hair, pulling her head forward as everything in her wanted to lean away. She waited for the sight and smell of his cock and the feel of it against her lips. She forced herself to let her jaw relax and stop clenching her teeth together as tight as a sprung bear trap . . . because she wanted to be an open one instead. She resolved in that instant that she'd suck him off for a few seconds — not much longer, just enough to let him think she wouldn't fight — and then she'd bite down as hard as she'd ever bitten into anything in her life. She wanted to spit it at him and watch him fall down and bleed and scream all day long while she and Evan freed themselves. Of course, as soon as he felt her teeth, he'd probably pull that gun out of the back of his pants and shoot her. She was a dead woman anyway if she didn't do anything at all. He'd broken into their house, tied them up, beaten them, and was about to rape her. Murder was, without any doubt, a part of the plan. The end of the whole affair. No one in their right mind would do all those things and then think they could just walk away, leaving her and Evan alive. It was beyond naïve to hope for that end. Nelle gave herself permission to keep fighting, even if it meant dying, because it meant dying on her own terms. The alternative, going along, ended the same way, but with more suffering.

Bite.

The man shoved her face into his groin mashing her nose and lips against skin and hair. The rough fabric and open zipper of his jeans dragged against her lips and cheek. His cock was limp. She didn't care if he couldn't get it up. Her teeth would go through his dick better if he was flaccid.

Her phone on the plastic box behind him buzzed and chirped. The man glanced over his shoulder at it, still holding her hair firmly in a fist. He turned his wrist, and her neck bent back, pulling her face away from his body. The cell chirped a second time, and he let go and took a step away from her. Nelle felt a fresh wave of despair come crashing down.

She whined a little when he stepped away. The intruder looked at her with surprise and a little confusion on his face. His expression said he didn't know how to process the idea that she might've wanted this. She didn't. And she did. Letting him in her mouth was at once the very last thing she wanted in the world, but she had the nerve to fight *right now.* Later, she might not have the guts. *This* was the moment. Right goddamn now.

He turned toward Evan and smiled. It was a cruel look that overtook his face. "Did you know that about your wife, Evan? Is it a thing with you two? Are you a cuck?"

Evan looked at him with undisguised hatred. Nelle feared that look turning toward her. She didn't *want* that man in her mouth; she wanted a chance to hurt him. Take the risk. Do the terrible thing to try to buy any chance at all. Though the man had removed her gag, she couldn't find a way to talk to her husband. The words wouldn't come to her lips, though they raced through her mind at light speed. *I'm sorry, Evan.*

I'm sorry, but it's what I have to do to save us. I can't do anything else, but I can do this.

"You wanna lose that look, cuck. I mean it, or I'll come cut it off your fucking face."

Evan didn't change a thing. He stared at the man with a thousand miles of hate behind his eyes.

"Leave him . . . alone," she eked out. The man's eyes flashed at her with contemplated violence. His knuckles turned white as he gripped her phone in his hand. His face reset, and he took a deep breath, getting himself under control. Everything he did was deliberate. He was in control. But Nelle could see he was close to losing it. A push too hard and he'd snap. Considering what he was willing to do with a clear head, she didn't want to think about the things he was capable of if he lost control. Then again, the end might come quicker if he let loose. That might be another weapon in her arsenal. Or at least a quick way to end it — suicide by psychopath.

"So, you *want* to suck my dick?"

Her voice was low and meek, but she tried to sound convincing. "Yes."

"Yeah, I'll bet you do." He stuffed himself back into his pants. He looked at her phone and stabbed at it with a stiff finger. His face reddened and clouded as he read whatever it was that had been sent to her. He looked at her and said, "You're going to make a call. You're going to do what I say, say what I tell you to, or else I'm going to fuckin' kill him and make you watch me do it. You get me?"

She nodded. She didn't understand who he could want her to call, but then she didn't understand anything he was doing. If he was there for their money, why were they tied up in the cellar? Why wasn't he asking them about it? Why was he so preoccupied with her cell phone?

She said, "The signal down here is — "

"SHUT UP! I DIDN'T SAY YOU COULD FUCKIN' TALK!"

Nelle clenched her jaw. She opened her eyes wide, trying to convey that she wanted to help. He took a deep breath and blew it out long and slow. "Tell me."

"The Wi-Fi makes it seem like it should be good, but our phones always drop calls in the cellar," she said, testing. When he didn't snap back or threaten her, she continued. "E-mails and texts go through, but you have to go upstairs if you want to make a call." *Go upstairs. Go and make all the calls you want. Call your bestie and talk until I run out of minutes. Please.*

"Where's the best signal?"

"In the Prince Room."

"The what?"

"The . . . f-front room. The one with the l-lavender walls."

The man didn't smile at their cute nickname for the front room. He stared at her blankly for a second. He bent over and picked his belt up off the floor, Nelle flinched, waiting for him to lash her with it again. The buckle jangled as he threaded it through his belt loops. "Good girl," he said, taking a step back as he refastened his pants.

He clacked his teeth at her.

Blood flushed in her cheeks and ears. He knew. She wouldn't get the chance again. Not like that. Nelle let her head drop and stared at her lap. Though she felt a small measure of relief at not having to do what she had been prepared to, she still felt ill and not quite there, as if she still had to pay the emotional toll of going through with it without any of the payoff. She felt far away and dull, like time had slowed and parted to flow around her instead of carrying her along into the future. There was no future, she realized. Only the present, and this room, this man, and her and Evan, unable to reenter the flow of time before it ended for the both of them. There was only right now. Not a minute ago, not five minutes ago, not an hour a day or a week. All that was past was prologue. There was only now and no future. Wondering how she'd gotten to this place was worthless.

A shadow in the corner seemed to resolve into the shape of the little mortally wounded girl peering at her from behind the water heater. Her half caved-in face and hair matted with blood and stuck to her cheek, obscuring the eye she couldn't open. She tried to smile with half her mouth. Her eyelid fluttered, and Nelle *felt* her saying something. The girl's voice was inside of her.

This is dying. Why fight it?

Nelle pictured her body on the cellar floor. Evan's next to it. The two of them, gone.

She went behind her eyes, and the image of herself on the embalming table at the Tremblay Funeral Home came rushing back. A collection of tools arranged on the surface beside it ready for use. She stared at her body, discreetly covered by a white shroud while her boss leaned over her getting ready to work. It wasn't the first time she'd imagined herself lying on the table — not even the first time that day — but it was the first time she couldn't banish the image from her mind by turning on NPR or sending an affectionate text to her husband as a distraction.

No darkness. Only light.

Except the dark vision intruded and she welcomed it and watched as Tony pulled the zipper on a PVC bag down slowly, revealing her white face and purple throat and the paper hospital gown she'd undoubtedly be in. He'd cut that away, revealing her shoulders and the tattoo of sparrows under her collarbones holding a banner in their little claws that arced across her sternum above her breasts. *True Until Death.* The ring in her navel and her earrings and wedding ring and the necklace her mother had promised to send her would all already be in a personal effects bag.

No. Not the necklace. She didn't know where that was. The mail had never come.

Since she wanted to be cremated, he'd return those things to whoever was there to collect them. Likely her mom. Everything except for the necklace.

In the mortuary register, Tony would fill out her name, the date she died, her age, where she'd been transferred from, and who brought her to him. He'd write the same things on the whiteboard for his assistant to see — though she was now dead and wouldn't see.

Like she'd done with the girl, he'd treat her with care and respect. He'd wash her with disinfectant and massage and bend her limbs to break out rigor mortis, in order to get her into her clothes. He'd put in eye caps to keep her eyelids from looking sunken and close her eyes before gluing them shut. Then he'd sew her mouth closed — through the gums so it wouldn't show. He'd remove whatever blood was still in her body after her autopsy. She knew she'd have an autopsy because she was a murder victim, and they'd *have* to perform one. He'd fill her veins with formaldehyde, glutaraldehyde, methanol, ethanol, phenol, water, and a little dye to give her skin a lifelike color for the viewing.

She concentrated on a good death.

No light. Only darkness. Forever.

The little girl stepped back into the shadows behind the water heater and disappeared like she wasn't really there, because of course, she wasn't. But Nelle was beginning to lose her hold on what was and what wasn't, and the girl was her guide into that world of disassociation. She would lead Nelle away from the really real world, so she could let go and die more easily.

The man slapped her, forcing her to return to the cellar, and said, "I'm gonna cut you loose. And we're going to play Simon Says. You do anything I don't say, and you'll regret it. You and me, we're going upstairs to make that call." He stopped and narrowed his eyes. "Do you get it?"

Nelle nodded. He hadn't needed to ask; she understood his threat the first time. He thought he was clever. Letting him know she didn't agree was dangerous. She tried to look suitably frightened of his threats. It wasn't difficult.

She wished the girl would come back. But she was only a coping mechanism of a mind that couldn't process everything it needed to.

"Got it," she said.

He knelt down beside her and sliced at the tape around her left ankle with his knife, then repeated the gesture on the right. He cut her wrists free and moved up to the strip around her midsection. She was free. Free to stand and run or fight. Though she couldn't do any of those things, since her hands and feet were numb. And he hadn't said. She sat in the chair, waiting.

The man stood up, folded the knife, and stuck it in his pocket. He stared at her while he did, satisfaction growing on his face. "Good girl," he said. She wanted to stab him once for every time he said that. "Stand up."

She stood. He lurched toward her, a fist drawn back, and she fell into the chair, almost toppling over backward. She raised her hands to protect her face, waiting for the blow to land in her stomach instead and for her bladder to let go. He didn't hit her. Instead, he said, "I didn't say 'Simon says.'"

"Y-you're S-Simon. I assumed any-anything you said was s-something I sh-should do."

He smiled. "Get up." She did. He didn't threaten to punch her again. Instead, he drew the gun from behind his back and held it down beside his leg. "You going to behave, or do I need to tape your wrists together?"

She thought about the tingling in her fingers as blood returned to her hands, and didn't want him taping her at all again, even if it was just her wrists. She nodded, keeping her arms stiffly at her sides.

He smiled with one side of his mouth and nodded at the staircase. "You first."

Nelle stood carefully and took a hesitant step forward. Her legs were shaky, and her feet were tingling pins and needles along with her hands. That was good. That was feeling. She could run on feet with feeling. She took another step and then another.

At the staircase, she hazarded a look back at her husband. He looked away from her, letting his eyes drift downward. *It's okay,* she wanted to say. *Everything's going to be okay.* That she didn't believe it didn't mean she didn't need to say it. But then, "Simon" hadn't said she could talk to her husband. In her mind, she said goodbye. If she got the chance, she was going to take it.

I love you, Evan.

Then she climbed the stairs, leaving him alone with the dead girl in the shadows.

22

Evan watched them go upstairs, Nelle leading the way with the piece of shit following behind her, holding a gun to her back. The image of them wavered and blurred for a second and then all he saw was the man's legs, and then the empty staircase. He listened for their footsteps above, but the pounding in his head made it hard to concentrate. It was difficult to hear through the rush of blood churning in his ears. Hard to do anything at all but ache and feel useless.

There was a heavy thump above and then another and then silence. Evan wanted to tear out of his bindings and rush the man who'd broken into their home, but he was taped too tightly, and could barely move his wrists, let alone his whole body. He couldn't do anything but sit there and look at the floor. He had to keep working at the tape around his wrists—pull and twist and hope to stretch or weaken it, since he couldn't actually reach any of it with his fingers. He had to focus on that and trust that Nelle could manage by herself. In any other circumstance, he'd feel assured she could. She was more than capable of holding her own. But the man in their home wasn't some pimple-faced goon who goosed her ass at Dan Brereton's signing table at Comic-Con or some idiot Internet tough guy making threats from his mother's basement. He was a real threat. He was present death.

Strong as she was by herself, they were better together. So he kept pulling at the tape, and trying to hear what was happening upstairs.

23

At the top of the stairs, Nelle hesitated. She thought for a second about bracing herself against the wall of the narrow hallway and trying to kick him down into the cellar. He might shoot, but what were the chances he'd hit her? Fifty-fifty? The man was so close, shoving the gun into her back, it was more like eighty-twenty. Still, she was moving, and he'd be caught off guard — maybe he'd miss. The odds were . . . well, better than her chances of winning the lottery. She decided to gamble.

Nelle lurched forward, nearly falling into the wall ahead of her so she could use its stability for extra force. She raised a leg to kick and banged her knee into the molding beside the bathroom door. It hurt, but she ignored the feeling, ready to drive her heel backward. Before she could piston the kick, the intruder slammed his forearm into her back, across her shoulder blades, and pushed her up against the wall hard. Her neck popped, and her face, already stinging, mashed into the wall. A small shadowbox painting she'd bought at a friend's gallery exhibition years ago fell off of its nail and clattered away down the hallway.

"The fuck do you think you're doing?"

"I — I tripped. I swear. I tripped."

The man shoved her harder against the wall, and she felt the barrel of that fucking gun jam into her back, just below her floating rib. A bullet there would rip through her kidney, and maybe her liver. Or maybe it'd tear apart her intestine, if it deflected down off her rib, or go up into her lung. Every potential path was her ruin.

He shoved again with his forearm. Her upper spine popped several more times, and her neck ached as it was wrenched around by the pressure against her back. Her arms were as useless as when she'd been taped to the chair. She couldn't push off the wall, or swing at the man, or even claw at him. She just let them drop to her sides, submitting. Showing him she wasn't doing a thing.

"Tripped," he said.

"I swear. I'm s-sorry. My legs ... are wobbly from sitting in that chair."

One final shove that pressed the air out of her lungs, and he was gone. No longer up against her body but somewhere else. He moved in her house like a ghost who could slide through walls and disappear into shadows. *Like the girl.* Except he was real.

It wasn't fair. Nothing about this was fair. He had all the advantages and she had none.

His voice floated out of the shadow behind her, and she turned to face him. He stood in the hallway between her and the kitchen, his gun still pointed at her. They stood at the confluence of the front room, the kitchen, and the bathroom. Each space offering its own avenue of revolt or escape, and all of those options stunted by the man standing in front of her. Not four feet into the kitchen, a butcher block stood on the counter, bearing an assortment of large knives. Evan kept them all very sharp, but she knew which one in particular she'd run for. The year before, for his birthday, she'd bought him a cimeter carving knife. It was ten inches long and curved upward at the tip, resembling something out of a Friday the 13th movie more than a kitchen tool. But when she saw Evan carve a rack of ribs with it for the first time, she understood why he'd asked for one. It cut through meat and cartilage like butter. Yes. That's what she'd run for. The cimeter. Except the intruder knew better than to let her into the kitchen. He stood in the archway, blocking it.

The bathroom beside her offered nothing. A closed window she'd never get open in time to even try shimmying through. No. The bathroom was as worthless as the kitchen was blocked.

All that remained was the front room, where he was herding her anyway. If the front door was still unlocked, she could sprint for it, hope he didn't just repeat the move he had at the top of the stairs, slamming her with a forearm into the beveled window in the upper half of the door. He was so fast. She imagined being shoved face-first through the pane, sharp edges of glass shards slicing through her skin like Evan's finely honed knives. She imagined leaning through the window, bleeding out onto the front steps, and dying in the shade of the overhang where she liked to stand and look at the flowers she'd hung from a hook next to the downspout and listen to the breeze wake the Japanese wind chime beside that, delicately complementing the patter of her blood sprinkling on the composite plastic boards below.

"Stop it," he said, his look telling her he sensed what she was doing.

"What do you want?"

He jerked his head toward the front room. "I want you to sit your fat fucking ass on that couch and shut the fuck up." The man ushered her into the room and gestured toward the sofa. He grunted at her to "siddown," moving closer, the heat of his hostility pushing against her. She sat. Defeated.

Compared to the chair downstairs, it was like landing on a cloud. Her aching neck and back still hurt, but she didn't care. Any relief at all was worth it. She placed her hands flat on the fabric at her sides and tried to calm down. Straight ahead, there was a purple orchid standing on the bay window ledge. It was blooming and in the daylight looked perfect, like a picture from a gardening catalogue. Beside it was stacked a pile of books she had yet to find a home for. One of her many to-read piles, this one acquired the weekend before at the Ripton Public Library book sale. "Where are you going to put those?" Evan had asked. "Right here," she told him, knowing that he was right about her being out of space for new books, but unable to help herself. *Give Me Your Hand* sat beneath *The Open Curtain,* which was beneath another called *In the Valley of the Devil,* and topping them all, *Your House Is on Fire, Your Children All Gone.* Beyond them, through the window, the bright daylight shone on their front yard, shadows from the trees wavering in the unmowed grass. She looked at the driveway and remembered seeing it lined with cars at their housewarming a month ago, and how much fun it had been to have a house full of friends, laughter echoing off the walls along with Evan's music, and the smells of spring and lamb grilling on the back patio drifting in through the open windows while she sipped wine and told stories. All the people they'd left behind when they moved to Ripton.

How did we get here?

V

◆

MEMORY

24

THIRTEEN MONTHS BEFORE CLOSING

The thumb drive sat on her desk. It was a little more than a half inch wide and maybe an inch and a half long in a black, rubberized plastic shell. The question how anyone could swallow such a thing flitted through Nelle's mind. She knew chances were the man on her embalming table hadn't *swallowed* it at all.

The memory stick had gone undiscovered during the subject's autopsy at the medical examiner's office. Cause of death had been clear: he'd shot himself in the head. Nelle knew that the ME did a thorough exam, removing all the organs and inspecting them before placing them back in the man's body cavity, but she was also aware that if the cause of death was clearly a self-inflicted bullet to the brain, an ME running behind might skip procedures that weren't necessary for their report. Procedures like a rectal exam, for instance.

She'd only found it because Tony insisted that Nelle place an "A/V closure" in bodies she embalmed. It was like a trocar button for closing up incisions, except for natural orifices. In other words, a plug. It was to keep them from seeping or leaking. Not everyone used them — some morticians used epoxy or cotton — but the screw closure was Tony's practice. Most people outside of the business didn't know about them at all. And when they found out, they were either appalled or amused, depending on how dark their gallows humor. And that was how she found it. She'd begun to insert the A/V closure into the body and felt something strange, like a little tap on something solid. For a moment she thought about just shoving a little harder, placing the plug and getting on with the job so she could leave at a decent hour and have an unhurried dinner with Evan. But then curiosity got the better of her.

Every once in a while, someone died with a baggie of something illicit inside of them. "Butt drugs," a friend in mortuary school had called them. The young woman said she dreamed of one day finding butt drugs, a special prize hidden inside a cadaver, like a golden ticket under the wrapper of a chocolate bar.

"Would you actually *do* butt drugs?" she'd asked her classmate.

The woman shrugged. "I don't know. But wouldn't it be cool to *find* some?"

Nelle wasn't sure then if it'd be "cool" or not, but at the moment she felt her heart flutter a little at the idea of discovering something hidden. Something secret. With a long hemostat clamp, she'd removed the object, wrapped in cling film. And that was how she found herself staring at a black and red memory stick, wondering whether she should call the ME's office or the police, or insert it into her laptop to see what the stick contained.

Curiosity got the better of her, and she pulled the cap off and stuck it into the USB port on her work laptop, figuring she could call the ME afterward. She wanted to know what a person who was about to kill himself wanted to hide so badly. The saying *you can't take it with you* flitted through her mind, barely noticed.

The system recognized the device, and she ran a quick scan to make sure it wasn't going to infect her computer. When the scan turned up nothing, she opened a window to show what it contained. On it was a single file named kinaccts.xlsx.aes. Nelle had no idea what any of that meant. Her finger hovered over the touchpad while she debated clicking the file. She drew her hand away and picked up her cell phone instead.

"Hey, minha querida, what's up?" Evan answered.

"You busy, bebê?"

"No. Just, you know, smokin' some endo, sipping my gin and juice. Same old."

"Very funny, Medium Pimpin'. Really, though," she said, "I've got a question for you. Are you busy?"

"No. I'm just waiting for a diagnostic to finish running. I've got time. Shoot."

"What's an AES file?"

"It's a kind of encryption. Usually what comes right before that extension is the file type. What's before AES?"

"XLSX."

She heard him let out a short breath through his nose. "Oh, that's easy. That's an Excel spreadsheet. It's one that's been saved with an encryption program so nobody can open it without the password."

"It's password protected?"

"Wouldn't be much of a cipher if it just opened itself. Why do you ask?"

"No reason."

"Are you trying to break into Tony's books? Not very nice, Nelle."

"What? Never! Look, I'll tell you later." Nelle pulled the phone away from her ear, intending to end the call — they liked to just hang up on each other like characters in the movies; it made them both laugh. But she hesitated and looked behind her at the dead man on the table. *He didn't want this to be found. He'd . . . hidden it before he killed himself, so whatever was in that spreadsheet had to be important. Curiosity killed the cat.*

"But satisfaction brought it back."

"Say what?" Evan said.

"Oh, nothing. Hey, do you think you could crack a password on a file like that?"

Evan was quiet for a second, and then he said, "Maybe. Most people's passwords are something stupid like 'one two three password.' Depending on the person who encrypted it, it could be done. AES isn't like the most impenetrable program out there. Whoever locked up that file isn't a black hat hacker or anything."

"Okay. Thanks."

"You be —"

Nelle ended the call, thinking about what Evan had said. *Depending on who encrypted it.* Who this man was, was the kind of guy who shoved a jump drive up his ass before eating a bullet. She had her doubts he was thinking several moves ahead. Not if he ended the game by blowing his brains out. She, on the other hand, was thinking about what could be stored in a file he wanted to hide so badly that he couldn't bear the thought of it being out of his possession even after he was dead.

You can't take it with you.

She ejected the drive, put the cap back on the device, and stuffed it in her pocket. She'd finish getting Mr. Shearman ready for his funeral and *then* worry about his secrets.

25

Evan screwed up his face, leaned back in his chair, and looked at the device he'd tossed onto the table like it had burned him. Nelle smirked at her husband's fussiness about touching the memory stick. He'd had a lot of jobs, oil change mechanic, line cook, web designer, and now computer security consultant. He kept getting cleaner as he went. Nelle had only ever had two: nanny and mortician. Both were dirty. At least as a mortician she got to wear gloves. "Calm down, Howard Hughes."

"Not wanting to touch something that has been up a dead man's *butt* does not make me *eccentric,* Nelle. It makes me like the normalest person ever." He leaned forward and picked it up between two fingers.

"You going to sniff it?" she asked, a smile growing on her face.

"Guh. No!"

"You were. You were totally going to smell it. You are so gross!"

"What is wrong with you? How'd you even find this? I thought dead people, you know . . . pooped when they died."

"Pooped? Are you three?" He looked at her with growing impatience. She relented. "Fine. Yes and no. Not always. Your muscles always relax, but if you've got nothing to evacuate, there's no 'pooping.' And this wasn't coming out without something behind it pushing." She didn't bother explaining how she'd become curious that something was up there in the first place. She'd told him about the A/V closures once, and he declared that he never wanted to hear about them or anything else she did at work again. "It was wrapped in plastic *and* I cleaned it, okay? Do you think I want what was inside him on *my* fingers? If I touched it, you can totally touch it."

Evan made a pouty moue with his lips. She thought he looked like Martin Freeman when he did that. A cute, vulgar hobbit with a big—but not too big—nose, ears that stuck out a little, and a perpetually sad expression. "Do you want me to crack this or not?"

Nelle dropped her head with faux shame and nodded. He gingerly pulled the cap off the drive, set it on the table, and plugged the device into the side of his computer. He opened the window and clicked the file. A dialog box opened, asking for a password. Nelle watched as he opened another program she'd never seen before and started working with it.

"You're not going to guess?"

"I don't know who this guy is. The password could be his cat's name."

"I thought you said most people used something like 'A B C password.'"

He nodded. "That's right. But most people aren't *all* people. This is better. Especially if he has a self-destruct failsafe on failed attempts. If I enter the wrong code too many times, it could fry the file."

She didn't know what "this" was, and she didn't ask. She understood what he did as well as she knew how to overhaul a transmission. Which was not at all. She kissed him on the cheek and said, "How long is it going to take?"

He shrugged. "I'll let you know," he said.

"I'm going to go read, then," she said, and left him to work on the file.

Close to an hour later, just as she was really getting into the new book she'd started, he called out from the office, "Got it!" She glanced at the page number and set the book on the end table next to the sofa.

Evan was hunched over his laptop looking at the file when she walked up behind him. "So, what is it?"

"It's a spreadsheet, like I thought. But it's . . ."

Nelle leaned over to take a look. "It's what?"

"It's confusing." He pointed to the screen. "This column here is dates, for sure. And this one looks like it could be money maybe, but it's, like, crazy big amounts if it is. These last two columns I don't get at all. They're just a long string of numbers, and I don't know what the headers are supposed to be. If they're encoded, it's some other kind of encryption the guy had written down or had in his head or something. It's nothing I can unscramble without a key."

Her stomach did a little flip, and she felt slightly queasy. She pointed at a cell in the grid. "That's an IBAN," she said.

"A what?"

"An international bank account number." She looked at her husband. "These are offshore bank deposits."

"How do you know that?"

How indeed.

Nelle sighed. "My dad," she said, swallowing hard at the thought of him. "He used to work in finance."

"Wait. David? I thought he was a teacher."

"No. Not him. My bio-dad, Harold."

"I thought he ran off when you were a kid."

Nelle felt a tinge of defensiveness well up in her. She'd told Evan she was raised by her mother after her parents split, but never explained why he'd left them. She didn't want to tell him now either, but it seemed inescapable. She'd kept it to herself for so long, it felt like a growth. Something rock hard she felt whenever she pressed her hands against her belly. "Uh, sort of. My dad . . . he uh, went to jail for securities fraud."

There. It was out.

Evan looked at her, mouth hanging open with astonishment. Then his expression melted into that one she loved so much, that he wore so easily and readily when she needed it: caring. He said, "You never told me. I'm so sorry, Nelle."

She raised a hand to hold him back as the memories of her childhood flooded her mind. She hadn't ever told anyone the story. If she didn't get it out now, she never would. "He left us with nothing. Mom scraped to get by. She couldn't afford the mortgage on the house, but she insisted we stay there as long as we could. She wanted me to keep going to school in Newton.

"She pretended nothing was going on, even though all the neighbors watched the news and they knew. The government wanted to take the house — it was in his name — but Mom found my dad's bank account information and tried to negotiate with them. He'd stashed money in foreign banks all over the world. Money that the government wanted more than they wanted to sell a house at auction. He had it all written down in a ledger he'd hidden in his office. All the deposits were there. He'd recorded everything. Everything except for the account numbers. She tried to bargain with them, get them to leave us some of the money if she could get him to tell her where those were. But you know, that money wasn't ours any more than it was his; he'd stolen it from other people. The US attorney promised that they'd 'take care of us if she cooperated with the investigation.' We couldn't have any of the money Dad stole, naturally, but they said they'd treat us like informants and give Mom, like, a stipend or something. I don't know. I was, like, nine, and it didn't make a lot of sense to me. I just remember them telling us we'd be okay.

"They sent her to talk to my dad on visitation days at the jail, but he wouldn't tell her anything. So, after a while, they had me try. They gave me a script. 'Mom found your account book. We're going to lose everything. We need money. What's the password?'" Nelle recited the lines she'd memorized more than two decades earlier to her husband, the feeling of betrayal at their utterance as fresh and stinging as a new wound. Her eyes started to well with tears, and she blinked rapidly to hide them. Evan reached out and held her hand. She hadn't concealed a thing.

"That's fucking horrible. How could they make you do that? How could your mother go along with that? You were just a kid."

She shrugged, as if to say, *What's there to do about it now?* She let go of his hand, wiped her eyes, and continued. "At first, he didn't tell me anything, but I wore him down, and he told me to tell his attorney to give Mom the accounts in '*CH*' and '*LU*.' He made me memorize it. *CH* and *LU*—Switzerland and Luxembourg. I did like he said, and the lawyer gave us the numbers. The feds cleaned out the accounts, and me and Mom were left with nothing because the prosecutor lied to us. The money was gone, and Dad never spoke to me again. We went to visit him in jail a couple of times, but he knew what I did. Even if he would've listened, there wasn't anything I could say to convince him I didn't betray him. He'd sent us the information through his attorney. He was smart enough to figure it out when his lawyer told him the money was gone. And the only way the feds could've gotten to it is if we were cooperating with them. If *I* was. He knew who got him cleaned out. He never spoke to me again. After he was paroled, he disappeared."

Evan's eyes were wide. "Holy shit, Nelle. I had no idea." He stood to embrace her. She shrugged and took a step back and wiped at her eyes in a way that looked like she was banishing her tears more than drying them. She tried to put on a brave face and act like it didn't matter, though it did. It mattered a lot and had colored the way she looked at men and relationships her entire life. It affected what she shared with her boyfriends and eventually her husband, and how she thought about the secrets other people kept from each other. And what "unconditional love" meant. She'd always thought her father's love was unconditional, but it wasn't. It had conditions. And when she failed to live up to them, he left her and her mother alone and destitute.

She knew he probably found someone new to love and to marry eventually. Maybe he even had another daughter. And he loved her. Did all the things that dads did with their little girls, except maybe trust her. Nelle thought she could've lived with his distrust because she didn't know any better back then when the prosecutor tricked her, and a part of her never stopped loving her father, because he was her dad and she was his child and they were supposed to be like that forever. That was how families worked, right?

In concert with her imaginings about her father, her mother eventually remarried, but by the time she found the right guy, Nelle was eighteen, and he wasn't a father to her. She wouldn't let him be. He was "Mom's boyfriend" and then "Mom's husband," and when they spoke, he was always David and never Dad. It was too late for that, and the title belonged to someone else, whether or not he deserved it.

"Yeah, well. It's ancient history, I suppose," she said.

Evan nodded and told her he understood. But he didn't really, and that was why she'd kept that recollection to herself. He didn't understand that she'd been willing to lie to her father and get the account numbers so they could take the money he'd hidden, because deep down she wanted to hurt him for leaving them. It had been important to her then to make him hurt the way she did every time she had to visit him in jail. The way that he'd injured her mother so she blissed out every night on wine and Xanax. The way Nelle felt having to grow up all at once because she was the only one who ever thought to make her lunch for school the next day or knew when her laundry needed to be done.

She'd wanted to hurt him, and since money was the only thing he really loved, that was the way to do it. And then when he left, it hurt worse than anything, and deep down she knew it was her fault.

"Anyway," she said, pointing at the screen and trying to get Evan to turn his attention away from her, "I've seen these before. When the lawyer gave me those account numbers on a piece of paper, they looked like this."

"Wow. So, these are Swiss bank account numbers?"

She took a deep breath and leaned in. "No. See the one that starts with SG?" She pointed at the screen. He sat back in his chair and looked. "I'm pretty sure that's Singapore. HK is definitely Hong Kong." She pointed at the bottom of the screen. "Scroll down." He did. Her stomach knotted. "That's the balance."

"That's the *balance?*" he shouted.

She shushed him, even though there was no one around to hear. She nodded.

"Who is this guy?"

"I don't know. Just some dude who killed himself." She pulled a dining chair from the dinner table up beside Evan and sat. "Go to the web and look up . . ." She had to stop and think for a moment. "Byron Sherman, I think. No. *Bryant Shearman.*" She spelled it. *S-H-E-A-R-M-A-N.* Evan did as he was told. Nelle pointed to the first hit. "That one," she said, "Click it." The lede made her feel like she might throw up.

The article left them both feeling breathless.

> Bryant Shearman, 52, Natick, was found dead today as authorities attempted to serve an arrest warrant at his home. Police executed the warrant after another criminal defendant, Arie Jacobi, 60, Cambridge, implicated him as part of a federal trial as an accessory in the operation of an international child pornography ring trading in images and films of torture and sexually explicit material involving children on the "dark web." Shearman had been previously indicted in state court on charges of rape, three counts of rape of a child by force, and six counts of indecent assault and battery on a child under the age of 14, and was free on $500,000 bail awaiting trial. Jacobi testified that Shearman was "the accountant" responsible for managing the income received by the website, known to its users as The Kinder Garden [sic] and allegedly had access to millions of dollars of cash collected from members of the site globally. State

prosecutors filed a motion to revoke Shearman's bond last week, which was granted by Judge Marisa Dunfries. Though Shearman's lawyer promised that his client would turn himself in, Shearman was not present in court at the time of the hearing, and failed to appear at the designated time for his surrender early this morning.

Police discovered Shearman's body when they entered his home to serve the warrant for his rearrest. A police spokesperson later said Shearman appeared to have died from a self-inflicted gunshot wound to the head, though an official cause of death has yet to be released by the Office of the Chief Medical Examiner.

Evidence of Shearman's financial involvement in any crimes has not been confirmed by police or the district attorney at this time. Federal prosecutors declined to comment on how Shearman's death affects their prosecution of Jacobi.

Shearman is survived by his wife and minor son, neither of whom were home at the time of his death. Sharon Shearman did not respond to a request for comment for this article.

"You're embalming *this* guy?" Evan said.

Nelle's face was white; she was shivering and holding her arms like she'd been caught out in the cold without a coat. "Yeah. His family wants an open-casket viewing."

"How's that even possible? It says he shot himself in the head."

Nelle straightened up in her chair and rubbed her palms on her pants as if she was trying to wipe them clean, then pointed her index and middle fingers up just under her nose like a gun barrel. "He shot through the roof of his mouth. The bullet came out clean through the top of his skull. His face is totally intact, so Tony only had to reconstruct the top and back of his head. Once I glued his lips shut, you couldn't tell he didn't die peacefully in his sleep."

"I can't believe Tony accepted this guy's body." Evan took a deep breath. "Are there going to be protesters again?"

Nelle's mood darkened even more. The Tremblay Funeral Home had embalmed the remains of the Evacuation Day Killer, Gary Pinsky. He murdered nine people and wounded twenty-two more in his rampage at Quincy Market before the police finally killed him. A half dozen funeral homes turned his body down before Tony agreed to take it. Nelle had just started working there, and things seemed to be going very well. Then, overnight, there were angry protesters outside the funeral home and people were screaming at her when she went to work. A protester had stalked her back to the apartment one night. He followed her onto the subway, glaring at her from the next car until she got off at Davis Square. Though she thought she'd left him on the train, when she looked over her shoulder on the path headed home, he was there, behind her. She sprinted the last three blocks and fumbled her way inside the front door, waiting for the hand to fall on her shoulder . . . or worse. Evan started to tell a joke about her taking up jogging, but was quick to see that she was terrified and jumped up to comfort her. When she explained what happened, he was livid. He ran outside to find her stalker, but no one was there. Next to the door, he found one of the protest flyers stuck in their mailbox. He came back inside clutching the piece of paper in a clenched fist, and they had an argument about her quitting. She couldn't. Not after only five weeks—she'd never get hired again in the industry, and they had her school loans to pay. He relented, she stuck it out, and things eventually calmed down after Pinsky was smoke and ash. But the memory of it still made Evan angry. She sympathized; she knew he'd felt as helpless as she did. Together they were safe, but apart, he had to trust she *could* take care of herself. And she could, against all manner of problems. But not if someone pulled a gun or blitzed her from behind. That's what they were both afraid of.

"No, hon. It's all very hush-hush. The family turned down the webpage memorial. Nobody knows we have him right now except the guy's wife and the clerk at the city morgue who signed his body out to us."

He sighed and let his shoulders relax a little. "Can you finish embalming him with something that makes him rot faster? I don't even want his fuckin' corpse in the world."

"Right? I wish. Oh god, I can't even believe I had my hands on him. Even wearing gloves, I feel nasty—like he's on my skin." She looked closer at the news article and pointed at the screen. Evan leaned closer and read the words above her finger. *The Kinder Garden.*

"Yeah? It's fuckin' gross. And?"

"Switch to the memory stick window." Evan did as she said, and the jump drive window expanded to fill the screen. She pointed at the file name, kinaccts.xlsx.aes. "Kin accts? Do you think this could be the money the police are looking for?"

Evan didn't reply, but Nelle knew exactly what he was thinking.

It had to be. Eventually, he said, "Why would he put this on a drive and . . ."

"Shove it up his ass? I don't know. Why would he do anything they say he did? Maybe he thought we'd find it when we embalmed him and return it to his family. Kind of an end run around the search of the house he knew the police would do."

"I don't . . . It seems . . ." Evan rubbed his hand down his face and leaned back. "Are you going to hand it over to the DA?"

She stared at the screen for a long moment and shook her head. "Fuck him."

"Minha querida?"

She held her breath for a moment and then sighed quietly. She felt that old familiar sensation creeping up in her. She wanted to hurt this guy, except he was already dead. She had an idea how to hurt a lot of people like him, though. She raised her eyebrows as she trailed off: "What if we . . ."

Evan got what she was suggesting right away, though she was a little disappointed he hadn't had the same idea on his own. She waved a hand to dismiss what she hadn't said. "No. It's a bad idea. You're right."

He didn't disagree with her. He didn't say anything at all.

26

Evan stared at the computer screen. While it didn't look like anything had really happened, he could see everything had worked. The display was staid and understated, like everything else about the bank website. It appeared the designers assumed a higher level of sophistication from its users than online banking sites in the States.

"Did it go through?"

He pointed to the figure at the side of the screen under the word BALANCE.

"We're millionaires." Nelle whispered.

"We are," he agreed. They spoke quietly, as if saying anything too loudly might wake them both from the dream. "Oh my god. We are." His stomach turned. They'd researched how to do a transfer and looked at whether any of it was traceable back to them. In the end, he decided it was safe enough to try a personal computer over a Wi-Fi network, but paid cash for a brand-new laptop he intended to return as soon as they were done. They found a quiet study room at a library and logged on through a VPN he assured Nelle was as safe as they were going to get anywhere. Chances were good that no one was trawling the signal at the Waltham Public Library for people checking their bank balances. Evan still found it stressful. He expected to watch the account balance drop to zero in front of his eyes as someone in another carrel outside their private study room funneled it right into a different untraceable account. Instead, the number remained constant and unimaginably large.

"What now?"

"Now I guess we pretend we're not rich for a while. We can start parceling out a little bit at a time, but not so fast that it looks like we just . . ." He wanted to say *stole almost a hundred million dollars from an international kiddie porn network.* He chose instead to say, "Like we just won the Nigerian lottery."

They'd been dreaming for days of all the things they could do with the money. Fantasizing like they did on the rare occasion they bought a lottery ticket — when the prize was big enough and it was "worth it." They imagined buying quality things instead of settling for less because it fit their budget, and paying off their student loans, and having a well-stocked wine cellar, and going on wonderful vacations to distant places that made good memories.

He wanted to buy Nelle a book he'd seen once. The special edition of her favorite novel, with the Smyth-sewn bindings, embossed endpapers, and gilded edges. It came in a tray case that folded out with the book in a box on one side and an art print on the other that looked like a piece of the ancient manuscript the characters in the story used to defeat the ancient evil that was after them. There were only twenty-six copies of that edition of the book in the world. Hand-signed and lettered, A through Z. The one he'd seen in person — *that* one was even the letter N in the series, making it almost like the author had personalized it just for Nelle. It was long sold out, but he imagined there were copies on eBay or at Powell's Books maybe. But they resolved to play it safe. No muscle cars or $2,500 books. Let the money trickle out so they were comfortable, but not so obviously it was clear they'd come into unearned wealth. They wouldn't buy anything right away that they couldn't afford to make the payment on with their own income. And eventually, when Evan had done sufficient "creative accounting" for his home business, they could branch out and buy a little more. Buy something a little nicer. Move up one step at a time. And if it ever felt like there was too much attention on them for what they did, they'd stop and wait on that step for a while. Careful and slow.

Someday he'd surprise her with the book. But not today.

They'd both asked themselves, what good was money they couldn't spend? The answer they each came to on their own was that it was better than money they couldn't spend because they were in prison. With this plan, they were set. Loan payments and rent could come from their own income. Everything else they needed would "grow in the garden." They also decided on eventually making a large anonymous donation to a children's charity or two. Evan found a couple that looked like they did real work protecting kids. One was called the Legislative Drafting Institute for Child Protection that wrote model legislation to toughen laws for people who hurt kids. Twenty percent was the fee for living the rest of their lives afloat on a sea of blood money. They figured that would buy off guilt.

They could live with that.

Evan closed the laptop, smiled, and brushed Nelle with his shoulder. She stared into the distance. If they were in a British romantic comedy, she'd snap out of it and say, "Sorry. I was miles away." But they were in on a heist, and it felt like the moment right before everything went wrong. That breath before the opening credits where Mr. Blue or Green, or whichever, gets shot by the cops as they try to get away with the jewels.

This wasn't a heist movie either. It wasn't a movie at all. It was real life.

And they'd just gotten away with it.

Everyone who doesn't get away thinks they're going to get away.

Evan took a sip of coffee from his travel mug and nudged Nelle again. She snapped back and said, "Sorry. I was miles away." He laughed a little too loudly. The sound echoed in the private study room, and he imagined a librarian around the corner shooting him a nasty look. "What?" she asked. "Whaaat?"

"Nothing. Everything is fine."

27

ELEVEN WEEKS AFTER CLOSING

T**ony thought the man** standing in the foyer of his funeral home didn't belong. Something about him suggested he wasn't there out of bereavement or even business. Tony knew everyone processed loss differently and he shouldn't make snap judgments about a potential client, but no one had ever walked into the Tremblay Funeral Home and made him feel so unsettled. Stepping into the foyer, Tony swallowed, then held out his hand to shake. "Good afternoon. What can I do for you?"

The man looked at him. His eyes were more gray than blue, and *he's blind* flashed in Tony's head, until he realized that the man had walked through the door unassisted by a guide dog or even a white cane, and picked up a business card and a brochure from the table in the entryway. Now he stared at Tony with a gaze more penetrating than amaurotic. He reached out and shook Tony's offered hand. His fingers were cold. Firm grip, but not painfully so. He was assured, had nothing to prove. At least not in the shake.

"I hope you *can* help me, please. Are you the proprietor of this establishment?"

"I am. I'm Anthony Tremblay. How can I help you?" Anyone else, Tony would've immediately brought them into the reception room and invited them to take a seat either at the big table or on the sofa. Instead, he stood his ground, hoping he could tell the man that he couldn't provide whatever was needed and show him the door.

"Very good. I understand a dear friend of mine was . . . I don't know how to say it. Processed here." An unpleasant sensation grew in Tony's stomach at the vulgarity of the word. The man continued. "After his funeral, his family was so bereaved, I believe they may have neglected to retrieve all of his personal belongings. I am here to see if there is anything left behind."

"And you are?"

The man's eyes narrowed briefly before he smiled. "I am Lev Yevseyenko. I was friends with the deceased, Bryant Shearman."

Tony was ready to say, *I'm sorry, we didn't perform services for anyone by that name,* when he recalled Shearman. They'd cremated him over a year earlier. Tony felt his anxiety spike at the mention of Shearman's name; he always remembered the controversial ones. While Tony made it a practice never to turn away someone truly grieving, he didn't want to deal with anyone who'd claim to be that dead man's friend. And seeing this visitor—his name had already fled Tony's memory—something *shenko*—he especially didn't want to.

"I'm sorry, Mr. . . . sir. But I'm not able to release any personal belongings, or even information, for that matter, to anyone but family or perhaps a family attorney. And even then, we wouldn't have kept anything this long. If I recall, Mr. Shearman's memorial was over a year ago. Any personal possessions that might've been left behind would've been returned to his next of kin long ago. I'm afraid I can't help you."

The man's smile disappeared. He clearly wasn't accustomed to being told no. Tony didn't know what else to say. They wouldn't have anything belonging to Shearman, even if it *had* been forgotten. They didn't store personal effects.

"Are you absolutely certain? Because his family is very distraught over the loss of a personal item they cannot find. They think it may have been on his person, perhaps in a pocket."

"I'm sorry, but anything personal we might've found while preparing Mr. Shearman we handed over to his wife. I don't know what to tell you."

The man's tone changed from lightly appeasing to harder edged. "Did *you* process Mr. Shearman's body?"

"We don't *process* anyone, sir. We're not a meatpacking plant." As soon as the words came out of Tony's mouth, he regretted them, but it was too late to take anything back. He was getting upset and wanted this man gone. "Whatever you're after, even if we had it, we couldn't release to you. But like I said, we have nothing belonging to Mr. Shearman or his family; we don't store belongings here. So, I'll ask you to leave."

"Did you?"

Tony felt another surge of panic. What if he *had* worked on Shearman? What then? How was who prepared the body in any way related to whether or not they'd held on to a personal item after his funeral? After a second's reflection, he recalled it had been Nelle who'd worked on the body once he'd finished the reconstruction of the man's skull. They'd been busy with multiple services that week, and she'd taken on almost every aspect of dealing with Shearman except for the one he was better at — there weren't many tasks in that category.

"It's none of your business who worked on whom."

The man took a step forward. While Tony wanted to stand his ground, he was unable to help stepping back. He bumped into the welcome table. The plastic stand holding the Tremblay Funeral Home brochures toppled over, spilling flyers onto the floor. The flowers rocked, but didn't fall. The man looked deeper into Tony's eyes, staring hard. Tony forced himself not to look away, not to be cowed by this thug.

The man seemed to look through Tony's eyes into his mind, deeper, down into his consciousness, probing those secrets Tony hadn't ever told and intended to die keeping. *But telepathy isn't real,* Tony reminded himself. At best, this visitor could read body language and expressions, but he wasn't learning anything that wasn't freely given to him. He wasn't a supernatural creature, just a man. Tony could stand up to a difficult man.

"I understand. My apologies if I upset you. If you say it is not here, then I'll take your word for it." The man let his face relax and took a step back. He said, "I appreciate your time," and turned to leave.

Tony held his breath, waiting for a last word or a final flash of intimidation. Neither came. The visitor opened the door and hesitated in the threshold. Tony expected him to say something that'd bring all of the wordless threatening back into clear focus. Instead, he raised a hand in a farewell gesture and stepped outside.

The door fell shut behind him, and Tony felt a heavy weight in his bladder and an ache in his lungs. He let go of the breath he'd been holding and quickly closed the distance to the door. He threw the deadbolt before hurrying to the bathroom to piss before he ruined his pants. He was glad Nelle was off work. After what she went through with the Evacuation Day Killer, she didn't need the stress.

Lev climbed into the car. "Starik govorit, chto u nego yego net." The old man says he doesn't have it.

Stas hadn't had much confidence in the information that led them to the funeral home. They didn't know if the Shearman woman knew about the computer her husband had stashed away in the attic that the police had missed. If she did, she had unimaginable will. She still wouldn't have lived if she'd given it up to them, but she wouldn't have lived as long—and as badly. Her husband had hidden the thing well enough that the police hadn't found it, but Lev had an insight into the nature of hidden things. Where other people saw wasted space or poor construction, he saw places he knew existed solely for concealment. And when he'd found the small crawlspace opening that only a child could fit through in the attic of Shearman's house, he knew there would be treasure on the other side. Her son had been happy to oblige them if Lev would make Stas leave his mother alone. It worked. With the computer and everything else, they didn't need either one of them anymore. The boy fit so well in that space, they'd only needed to cut up one body.

The computer hadn't yielded any information about the missing money, though. Not at first. Eventually, Lev found the information the Trojan program was sending. They'd both been in police custody when that program had first started sending updates. Bryant Shearman had been good at stealing, but not at all good at hiding. That was how he got caught, and how the rest of them got swept up as well. Whoever had stolen from *him* was the opposite. The tracks they'd left taking the money were easy enough to find. But not who'd made them.

The first report they'd found led them to an apartment in Cambridge. Worthless. The people there knew nothing. But then they went back farther, and that led them here. "Should I go in and ask again?" Stas asked.

"Nyet." Lev handed Stas the business card he'd taken from the table in the foyer. "*She's* the one."

ELEONORA A. PEREIRA
Advanced Planning Consultant / Licensed Funeral Director
TREMBLAY FUNERAL HOME
& CREMATION SERVICES
617-555-8974 eapereira@TremblayFuneral.com

"Where is she?"

Lev shrugged. "She won't be hard to find. She will come to work tomorrow or the next day. And then we'll follow her home, where we can have a long talk."

VI

◆

SECURITY

28

ELEVEN WEEKS AFTER CLOSING

Nelle sat on the sofa in the Prince Room. It was her first day off in a week and she felt restless, as if sitting down and doing nothing but reading all day was somehow irresponsible. Naturally, there were things to do — laundry, dishes, the lawn, grocery shopping, the car needed to be washed. All of it could wait, though. She was almost done with her book and wanted to start a new one. She envied people who could tear through a novel in a week or a day. But then, she liked to think of herself more as a thoughtful reader than a slow one. Either way, it didn't stop her from buying more books. Her library made moving tedious and expensive, but in her heart, she knew a *home* was filled with books.

She turned a page and reached for the cup of tea on the table next to the sofa. Her drink had grown cold, but that was okay; it was getting hot outside, and a tepid cup of tea was just fine. She took a sip and tried to set the cup down without taking her eyes off the words that were speeding toward a calamitous end. The cup rocked half off the coaster, and she jerked to catch it. A bit of her drink sloshed out onto the table. "Shit." A few drops would clean up in a minute just as easily as they would at that moment. And the words didn't want to wait. She was almost through with the chapter.

The doorbell startled her, making her jerk a little on the sofa, doing a little dance to keep from dropping her book. Through the faceted glass window in the door, she could see a man in a bright blue shirt. The kind of color only people who were selling something wore. She sighed, took note of the page number in her head, and set the book down on the cushion beside her.

In the short time they'd lived there, salesmen had come to the door trying to give them free quotes on a new roof, lawn care, and cable television. They were never sales*women,* not unless it was Jesus they were selling. Commercial door-to-door salespeople were always men. Always pushy. *The joys of homeownership,* she thought as she got up. She decided, whoever this guy was, she'd politely tell him no, and then immediately get online to order a NO SOLICITING sign to stick on the siding outside next to the doorbell. And if a book happened to fall in her virtual shopping basket when she did that, well . . . things like that happened from time to time.

She opened the door. The man standing on the porch didn't look like the salesmen who'd come knocking before. They were almost always young. In their twenties or early thirties. This man was approaching forty, if he wasn't already. She'd have thought he was there for some other reason if his shirt hadn't had a company logo over the breast, the words VIGILANCE SECURITY SYSTEMS embroidered beneath it. Beneath that it read AUTHORIZED DEALER. The man held up a laminate card hanging from a lanyard around his neck and introduced himself.

"Good afternoon, Mrs. Pereira." He pronounced it with a long *I* sound that sounded almost like "pariah." "I was hoping to talk to you about switching from American Total Security to Vigilance Security Systems. VSS offers the most comprehensive home security system in New England, and—"

"I'm sorry. Did my husband call about a consultation?"

The man smiled. His teeth were a dusky yellow. "No, ma'am. I'm here today in the neighborhood doing some work for one of your neighbors, and I thought I'd drop by to see—"

"How do you know my name?" Nelle clutched the door tightly, ready to slam it if he gave off a bad vibe—a *worse* vibe than he already did.

"I'm sorry." He laughed a little. It was an ugly sound that didn't relax her, if that was his intent. He smiled broader and said, "The company pays attention to new filings at the Registry of Deeds. My supervisor gave me a list with your and your husband's names on it." While he held a clipboard, he didn't turn it to show her the list. "Evan and Eleonora Pereira, right?"

Nelle's stomach did a little flip at the sound of her full name. At least he didn't have her middle name. Or her maiden name. Did he? She considered him another moment. He was solid-looking. Again, like a guy who worked harder for a living than ringing doorbells. She supposed he could be a gym rat. She let her grip on the door ease up a little as she convinced herself there was no reason to go lunging for the molded plastic bat Evan kept leaning against the wall behind the door. She was being silly. It was the end of the book she was reading that had her hackles up. Jack Ketchum did that to her.

"Your name is?" she said.

He held up his laminate. "My name's Paul Michaels." She leaned forward to get a look at his credential. He continued. "Anyway, Mrs. Pereira—"

"Puh-rare-uh. It rhymes with barbera," she corrected him. A nascent panic grew in her chest the minute she uttered the words. She hated when people mispronounced their last name, but men, in her experience, hated being corrected even more. She waited for his tone to turn hostile. Instead, he kept smiling and apologized again. But there was a twitch in his cheek that let her know his smile took work to maintain.

"My apologies," he said. His back straightened as he said it.

She waved her free hand. "No. I'm sorry. Go on." She hadn't wanted to hear his spiel, but felt obliged, as if correcting him had somehow indebted her to listen to the pitch.

"Thank you. As I was saying, I was hoping to discuss the possibility of switching you from ATS to Vigilance. We offer a comprehensive program that can be controlled and monitored from your computer or smartphone. We have very competitive rates and a twenty-four-hour customer service line staffed by real people right here in Massachusetts." His eyes kept shifting over her shoulder. She didn't dare look back. Looking away from him seemed like a bad idea.

"How did you know we have a security system?"

He pointed at the small triangular sign sticking up from the garden plot next to the front porch.

"Oh, that." She'd thought about pulling the sign up and throwing it away, but for no good reason other than inertia, hadn't gotten around to it. There was no harm in letting people think they had a working system, was there? And that was it. Though her previous encounters at the door had been unremarkable, this one was sending up red flags. She couldn't pinpoint exactly why. She wanted this man to walk away thinking she could summon the police at the push of a button. Of course, if he had bad intentions, he'd be well into whatever it was he had in mind long before they could send help. Still, she closed the door a little and said, "I'm sorry. I'm sure your company is great, but we're happy with the service we have. If we want to make a change, we'll look you up on Angie's List, okay?"

"Can I leave some literature with you, at least?" He pleaded with eyes that reminded her of a shark's. They were flat. When he smiled, the expression didn't reach his eyes.

"Sure," she said. He pulled a brochure off of his clipboard and held it out to her. For a moment she considered telling him no after all. *No point in agitating him. Take it and shut the door. Shut it and lock it.* She chastised herself for being irrational again. If this guy wanted in her house, he would already be inside. *You're just wigged out by the book. Stop being a fraidy-cat.* She took the pamphlet and said, "Thank you."

The man — she'd already forgotten his name — he had no last name, just first ones — touched a finger to his forehead in a little salute and stepped off the porch. He stopped and turned. "Do you mind if I come back by when your husband is here, so I can talk to you both? When would be best?"

She felt herself shaking her head. "I, uh . . . We'll give you a call if we want to talk."

"Okay. Thanks. I look forward to hearing from you."

Don't fucking count on it. She shut the door. The alarm system chirped like it always did, though it wasn't monitoring a thing. Nelle twisted the deadbolt lock slowly, so he wouldn't hear it click into place, and then ran into the dining room to watch him leave through the blinds. He walked halfway down the driveway and looked back over his shoulder. Though she was hiding behind the curtains, she jumped back from his gaze. He couldn't have seen her. He was just looking at a missed commission.

The look on his face, though.

It wasn't disappointed or, as she'd feared when she corrected him, annoyed. It was hostile. She might have even described it as malevolent, though she'd only glimpsed it for a second before the force of it thrust her back and she lost sight of him in the dark. She crept to the window again and stood to the side. She didn't want him to see her silhouette through the curtains. She peeked through the gap between the wall and the fabric, hoping that he wasn't still standing in her driveway staring daggers at the house — at her.

He knows I'm here alone. I practically admitted it! Stupid stupid!

She couldn't see him in the driveway. He'd gone. She let out a breath and tried to relax, but ease was slow in coming. She grabbed the short bat from the closet by the door. It felt good in her hands. She gave it a short little wiggle, not quite a swing. She felt better holding it.

A throaty engine revved at the end of the driveway. She clutched the bat a little tighter and returned to the window. She spied the front end of a muscle car parked next to the mailbox. And then, with a squeal of tires, it pulled away. If that was the guy, he wasn't being honest about "just being in the neighborhood." Not driving *that* kind of car. *If he was working at a neighbor's house, wouldn't he be driving something that could carry tools or equipment?* She tried not to overthink it. He was gone and everything would be just fine. Wouldn't it? Her mind kept returning to ideas she didn't want to think about. People she didn't want thinking about her, as if holding them in her mind was a beacon to their consciousness. Why *didn't* they resubscribe to the alarm service? Because wasn't that the point of moving to this place? To be somewhere they could sit outside and have a drink and not have to breathe bus exhaust and hear the drone of helicopters looking for the suspect who fled on foot? Somewhere quiet and safe. But was anywhere really safe?

She chided herself for being irrational. This was just some random grifter — yes, someone looking to con a naïve pair of first-time homeowners into a "consultation." That would turn into a sizable down payment reserving "today's prices," and then they'd never see him or his company again. It was a garden-variety scam — low-rent fraud — not their chickens coming home to roost.

She returned to the sofa and set the bat on the cushion next to her. She picked up *The Secret Life of Souls* and tried to read, but couldn't get past the first sentence on the page. The mood was spoiled. She set it back down and decided to go fix herself a cocktail instead. Evan wouldn't be happy she'd started drinking without him, but that was what he got for leaving her in the house alone on her day off.

29

He **tossed the clipboard** on the passenger seat. The census addressed to Evan and Eleonora Pereira from the Town of Ripton fluttered in the breeze blowing through his open window. Ringing the bell had been a risk, but he wanted to see inside. He hadn't gotten a peek any farther than the front room, but still, he'd seen what he wanted. The security pad behind Eleonora had chirped, but the message display on the screen had read SERVICE NOT AVAILABLE. They hadn't changed carriers or even renewed the system subscription.

He grabbed his cell phone off the dash and looked at his text message inbox. Nothing new. He started the car and goosed the gas. He didn't want to bring attention to himself, but it was so hard not to give the Demon a kick. She begged for it. He pulled out and drove back to the apartment, almost ready to get started.

30

Nelle slipped between the low rock wall running along the road and the end of the burning bushes that divided her yard from the Darnielles' property near the end of the driveway. The branches tugged at her hair and shirt, but it was safer than walking all the way down and stepping out onto the highway.

Around the other side, she turned up the driveway and walked toward the neighbors' house. With each step closer, she felt a little less sure of her reasons for going over. Running through the encounter with the man at her door a half hour earlier propelled her forward, though. They hadn't talked much to the Darnielles other than a couple of short conversations in passing and the one time she went over to return the plate on which Juanita had delivered the Welcome Wagon cookies. Whether the visit would confirm or deny her suspicions, she also wanted to be a good neighbor and get to know the people who lived nearby, make friends.

She rang the doorbell and waited. At the end of the driveway — not quite as long as theirs, she thought — a truck wailed by. Otherwise it was quiet. They'd wanted to live somewhere quiet. The reality of that choice was beginning to settle in.

As Nelle reached to ring a second time, she saw her neighbor's silhouette through the glass in the door. The blurry shape through the faceted window resolved into Juanita, and Nelle let her hand fall away from the button.

Juanita opened the door and called out, "Nellie! So nice to see you."

"Nellie was the mean girl on *Little House on the Prairie.* I'm just Nelle." She said it with a big smile to try to mitigate her gentle correction. Juanita flushed a little and apologized. A much different reaction than the one from the man who'd stood on her doorstep earlier. She seemed honestly embarrassed by her error.

"I'm so sorry, *Nelle.*"

"That's okay. It's been a thing, like, forever. No big." She dipped her head, ashamed to have begun the conversation this way instead of how she intended.

"Would you like to come in? I don't have any coffee made, but there's a bottle of wine on the counter from last night you could help me finish off.

Nelle smiled. "That's so nice of you to offer. I'd love to have a glass . . . or six. But I don't want to impose. I'm just dropping by to ask you something."

"It's no imposition." Juanita smiled and stepped back to make room for her to come inside. Nelle felt the pull of not only alcohol, but friendly companionship. She hesitated at the threshold. She'd only intended to be gone for a few minutes, and then never really out of sight of her house, but now she was going inside and she felt like returning home to check the front door, assure herself she'd remembered to turn the bolt. The tug at her back was almost as strong as the one pulling her forward. *I locked it. I know I did.*

Juanita closed the door behind them. She led Nelle into the kitchen and pulled a pair of stemmed glasses out of the cupboard. Where the mudroom just inside the door was dim and confined, the eat-in kitchen was open and bright. Light shone through the skylights above, making the little reflective flecks in the snow quartz countertops sparkle. Everything was perfectly in its place; no clutter or awkward appliances that looked like there was just nowhere else for them to live, so that's where they ended up. It was model-home clean, like a movie set. In the corner, a small Bluetooth speaker played an '80s pop mix. Men Without Hats faded into the Fixx. Juanita and Colin were older than Evan and Nelle. Gen Xers. Nelle felt a little of the tension drain out of her at the thought of Juanita with big poufy hair, wearing an orange and lime colored dress at a middle school dance.

"I hope white's okay," Juanita said. "I opened a riesling with dinner last night and didn't finish. Colin's a beer drinker and never has any."

Nelle nodded. "Anything's fine, thank you." Juanita poured her a glass and handed it over. She took a little sip. White wine almost always gave her a hangover, but this was crisp and fruity and felt nice in her mouth. She drank again, a bigger swallow this time.

"You needed that?"

"I guess so." Nelle chuckled. "It's been a weird morning. Speaking of weird, that's kind of the reason I came over. Did you have a guy around today to do some work on your alarm system?"

Juanita smiled broadly. She had perfectly bleached white teeth that seemed to shine even though she had her back to the kitchen window. She led Nelle over to the kitchen table and offered her a seat. "Oh, sweetie. We don't have an alarm system. Shit, we don't lock our doors unless we're headed out of town for more than a night."

"Not even with the trails back there?" Nelle asked.

"We've lived here fifteen years, and all we've ever seen back there are Boy Scouts and dog walkers. Anyone who's willing to fight their way through the poison ivy and ticks on the way to our yard isn't going to be stopped by a lock on that door." Juanita nodded at the sliding glass door leading out to the back patio. Juanita's expression soured. "Is everything okay? You seem spooked."

Nelle nodded again. She was beginning to feel foolish. "It's nothing, really. I just spooked myself, I guess. Some guy came to the door trying to sell us a new alarm system. He said he was doing some work in the neighborhood and decided to hit up a few of the neighbors. I just thought . . ." She took a breath and waved a hand dismissively. "It's stupid."

"Oh, we used to get that too. When we first moved in, it was kind of frequent. Mostly those assholes at Comcast, or whatever they call themselves. X-somethingorother stupid. A few summers ago, we had a resurgence of salesmen from a solar company. They were pushy. It's so frustrating, but it tapers off after a while."

Nelle smiled. Juanita's calm was catching. Nothing seemed to bother her. Of course, Nelle barely knew her at all. She was sure to have ups and downs like everyone else. But something about being around her was soothing. Or maybe it was the wine. "Did the guy from the alarm company come over here too?"

Juanita shook her head. "You're the only one who's rung my bell today, hon. I wouldn't worry about it. But I wouldn't buy anything anyone's selling door-to-door either." Her face settled into a serious mien, and she added, "And I certainly wouldn't let anyone in."

"Oh, definitely not." Nelle finished her glass, set it on a coaster on the table, and stood up. "Thanks for the drink. I suppose I should let you get on with your day."

Juanita stood. "Any other day, I'd insist you stay, but I need to finish getting things ready for our trip."

"Where are you headed?"

"Colin and I are going to Hyannis for a few days. We're taking the whole week off, leaving early and not coming back until after the long weekend. I always tell him that we don't need to leave *days* before the traffic rush, but he likes to be ahead of everyone else. He's practically obsessed with the news stories of people getting caught in Cape traffic. He keeps reminding me, 'It took 'em six hours to go ninety miles, Johnnie.'" She mimicked her husband's deep voice. She rolled her eyes and leaned in as if she were telling secrets in the halls in between classes. "He gets so . . . *fussy* about things like that, so we just make it a whole vacation."

Nelle hadn't met Colin yet, but if he was married to Juanita, she figured he had to be all right. She liked that he called her Johnnie. She wondered if she'd get to know her well enough to be allowed to call her that.

"Evan isn't much of a planner. He waits to pack until the night before we're leaving to go someplace. Like, *late* the night before. Maybe the two of them can be a moderating influence on each other."

Juanita let out a small laugh and stood. "Oh, I've been trying for years to get Colin to unclench. I doubt there's anything Evan can do. But you never know." She led Nelle to the door and opened it. "When we get back, we'll have you both over for dinner. Let the boys meet and officially welcome you to the neighborhood, such as it is. We loved the Nilssons when they lived in your house, but the people who bought it from them weren't very sociable. It'd be nice to have neighbors over more often. I hear they have a chili cookoff a few blocks down. I'd love to try something like that."

"Only two couples isn't much of a cookoff."

Juanita laughed. "I guess it isn't. We'll have to come up with another idea."

"Anything would be lovely. I can't wait." Nelle slipped her shoes on in the mudroom and said thank you again. "Have a nice time on the Cape."

"We'll see you when we get back. Don't go letting any strange salesmen into your house, now." Juanita winked, but there was a tone of seriousness underscoring her play that made a heavy stone settle in Nelle's guts. She smiled at the joke and stepped outside.

The air outside had a tincture of the approaching spring—damp earth from rain and maybe a hint of pollen, like the trees were about to bud. It was early for that. Grass, perhaps. People's lawns were starting to green up. She smelled smoke on the breeze. It seemed early to light a fireplace. It'd had always felt to her like an after-dark, get-cozy kind of thing. But then she didn't really like the smell of smoke or even the look of a fire. It reminded her of work.

She turned and waved at her neighbor as she walked back toward the gap near the road and shimmied through to her own driveway. Juanita smiled and waved from the doorway before disappearing inside.

Nelle looked as she passed around the end of the burning bushes for the sportscar the security salesman had been driving. It was nowhere she could see.

Inside, she poured herself a glass of water and looked out the kitchen window at the deep woods bordering her back yard. Maybe a hike would help clear her mind. It couldn't hurt to get out of the house for a bit—out with other people enjoying the day, like her husband was doing. She didn't play racquetball or squash or whatever it was he was up to, but she should've gone with him into the city. She could've visited the MFA or the Isabella Stewart Gardner Museum or something. But he was long gone, and it'd be an hour drive to get into the city. Cabot Woods was closer, and she thought it'd be better to enjoy the outdoors while the weather was still warm.

She couldn't remember if the real estate agent said they could reach the hiking paths from the back yard, but it looked like it'd be a snarl to get through the tight brush—and there were probably ticks, like Juanita had said. She stared out the window at the line of trees beyond the back yard, the frontier where her stable, controlled world met the wild dark beyond. Though it wasn't entirely wild. Civilization and all of the dangers she knew well enough encircled the forest on all sides. The afternoon was getting late, and the sun was behind the tall trees. From where she stood, it looked black as moonless night back there. If someone *was* back there, she'd never see them. Watching.

Stop it. Stop it! You're letting that guy get way too far under your skin, Eleonora. *Everything's fine.* He didn't really know her name—not the one she went by, anyway. Just what he'd read off a deed at the probate courthouse. His job was making people feel insecure so they spent money on security systems they didn't need. *We're fine without it.*

Everything was just fine.

She stepped away from the window, grabbed a stemmed glass, and went to soothe her nerves at the wine rack while she waited for Evan to come home.

She'd go hiking another day.

VII

◆

DIE OF FRIGHT

31

TWELVE WEEKS AFTER CLOSING

Nelle felt defeat creeping in at the edges of her will, telling her that she should give in, give up, lie down, and accept the inevitable. Her stomach rumbled, and she crossed her arms over her belly to try to hush it. Yet it ached. A combination of hunger and lingering pain from being punched that morning. The man didn't react. If he heard, he didn't appear to care.

The front room was bright; its light purple walls appeared almost a faint gray in the glow shining through the bay window. The light wasn't direct, but it was still strong. Not shaded. The way the sun tracked, that meant it was still before noon, but it couldn't be much before. She tried to suss out how much of the day had passed. She'd gotten out of bed a little after nine, kissed her husband, who was getting ready to fix breakfast, and sat down to check her phone. After finishing her coffee, she jumped in the shower and stayed in maybe ten or fifteen minutes. She spent perhaps five minutes looking for Evan after she shut off the water. Ten at the most. That made it around nine forty-five or ten o'clock when … But then, she had no idea how long anything that morning had actually lasted. Time worked differently since this person had come into her life. It distorted, alternately slowing and hastening, depending on the moment. When the man had tied her down — when he'd taped Evan to the weight bench too — time elongated. Every tear from the roll stretched out, and the process felt like it'd never end. Another tear. Another eternity. And then, when he'd gone to fetch her the glass of water, it had seemed like she barely had the chance to say her husband's name before she heard the man returning to the cellar staircase. Nothing in her perception seemed reliable, time least of all. Still, how long *did* it take to buy groceries early on a Saturday morning? What else had he been doing?

Stop it! It takes as long as it takes. Evan didn't nip off for some tryst while I was in the shower. He wasn't gone that *long. Long enough to drive up and get eggs and prosecco.* The way he texted her and posted pictures online, she had a pretty steady accounting for nearly every hour of his day. If he was keeping secrets — or was somehow having a *relationship* with someone else — he had a talent for deception that would've made Patricia Highsmith gasp. No. She trusted Evan as powerfully as she loved him, so she pushed down her resentment for his absence that morning. Ruminating on what might have been was as useless a meditation as imagining herself flying away on a magic carpet. No matter how many conceivable realities there might be, *this* was the one she inhabited. *This* was the world in which the consequences of their choices were playing out. And it was the one in which she had to try to survive, because there wasn't another waiting behind a veil of obscurity. She did it because she loved him, and because the only way the two of them were getting out of this house was *together.*

Nelle stared at the floor while the man typed into her phone. She didn't want to look at him, but the view out the window only reminded her how helpless she was. The curtains were wide open, and he made no effort to close them because no one could see them. So she stared at the floor. The memories of eating takeout, getting drunk, and making love there on their first night in the house were better.

Out of the corner of her eye, she saw it. A glimmer of hope. Her purse.

It rested on the floor next to the sofa, under the end table. Inside, she didn't have a can of pepper spray or one of those collapsible baton thingies. She didn't even have keys in there she could slip between her fingers — *those* were hanging on the hook by the front door. But sticking up out of the inside pocket she saw the orange flip top of the cylinder that held her EpiPen.

Lifesaving medication.

She slid a little to the side on the sofa. Not much. An inch or two.

"You want to live through this?" the man said.

She froze. It was a stupid question. Insulting. Of course she did, and he knew it. He was counting on it. Nelle nodded anyway.

The feeling that she knew him nagged at her again. Something recognizable in the tone of this word, or the familiarity of that look. If she didn't *know* him, at least she'd seen him before. Talked to him. Through the fog of disorientation and fear, she couldn't think where that might've been. Everything about him was upsetting, but something in particular, something she couldn't put her finger on, stuck a little farther out.

A hint of a subtle movement behind him caught her eye. A fleeting shadow, a small wrongly bent ankle that disappeared into the darkness of the coat closet by the front door. She thought she heard the echo of a child's voice. *I'm going crazy.* Her eyes traveled to the alarm system control panel on the wall behind him. The panic button on the keypad glowed a faint green. It wouldn't summon anyone, no matter how urgently she pressed it. SERVICE NOT AVAILABLE. Though she needed to keep her eyes on the man, the keypad drew her attention as if it held some insight into her predicament. *The fucking seller's agent told us we didn't need an alarm out here, and we believed him.*

That fucking keypad.

She felt the blood rush out of her face. She knew him. He'd been clean-shaven then and wearing glasses. It was a Clark Kent kind of disguise, but it had fooled her. A face looked different with a pair of glasses on it, without a beard, in bright sunlight instead of lit by a shitty fluorescent spotlight bulb in a dark basement. Now, standing in the front room, he looked both different and the same. She remembered, and that seemed worse. So much worse. He'd been to their house before. He'd come to her door . . . to sell her a security system.

She started to say, "What do you wa—" and then the loud pop made her swallow her words and flinch. She cried out. She couldn't help it. The sound just came out of her like someone else in her body was vocalizing for her. A primitive bark of fear and anticipated pain.

The man's arm shot out straight, the bore of the gun settling on her face. She flinched again and shut her eyes, waiting for the punch through her skull. The feeling of a bullet slamming into her forehead and then, nothing.

But there was no shot. No oblivion. Just her and the man.

"The fuck was that?" he shouted. He stomped away from her.

Your chance! This is it!

She opened her eyes and lunged to the side, toward her purse.

32

The bang in the kitchen startled him; he jumped and raised the gun, thinking that somehow the woman had gotten ahold of something. But no, the sound had come from the other side of the wall behind her.

He lurched toward the archway, wondering how her husband had gotten free. How he'd been able to sneak into the kitchen without being seen. He could shoot the fucker now if he wanted. The guy wasn't necessary for the plan. He was only keeping the husband alive because he figured as soon as he killed him, the bitch would come unhinged and be useless. Women were like that, he thought. Admittedly, killing her husband would be a *big* thing, but still, it would shut her down, and he'd be left with a sobbing, hysterical mess unable to wipe the snot off of her own lip let alone make a single fucking phone call. If he killed one, he might as well do them both at the same time.

Leading with the gun, he ducked around the corner, trying to keep an eye on the front room and the kitchen. He paused in the archway. He couldn't leave the woman alone — she'd try something; she had already shown him she was always going to do that. *Bitch was going to bite me. She tried to kick me down the stairs.* But he couldn't ignore the sound either. When he didn't see anything, he slipped back into the front room. The woman was sprawled out flat on the couch.

"Get the fuck up! The fuck are you doing?"

She said some gibberish, and he grabbed a handful of her hair and yanked her off the sofa, twisting her around. He shoved her ahead of him into the kitchen, his gun aimed over her shoulder. "Motherfucker! Come get some." There was no reply. Not one he could hear over her whimpering, anyway. "Shut the fuck up, bitch," he insisted. She didn't shut up. Just kept on sobbing and saying some shit he didn't want to hear. The buzzing in his head was too loud, like flies, and he told her to shut up again.

"The freezer," she said a third time, her words finally penetrating his haze. He glanced at the fridge, not wanting to take her bait. *Bitch. Witch. Bitch. Witch,* cycled through his head. The two of them with their fucking goth occult shit. She was bewitching him.

That's why he hadn't gotten hard downstairs. Fucking witchery. He'd show her. *She can't bite with her asshole.*

A clear fluid leaked out of the freezer drawer at the bottom of the appliance. He blinked at it a couple of times. She wasn't lying. Something was wrong with the fridge. It'd popped the line that led to the water dispenser on the front or something. Except it wasn't water, and there was a smell. A sweet smell like . . .

Grapes.

"It's prosecco," she said.

"What?"

"Like champagne."

"I know what fucking prosecco is," he said through clenched teeth. There wasn't a thing about these people or this house that didn't make him want to set fire to it with both of them inside. The couch in the "Prince Room" was "architectural" and hard cushioned like it wasn't ever meant to be used. *It* made him angry. The painting on the wall above it, with its broad brushstrokes, looked like something a first grader might do after he came in from recess, except he knew that it had to have cost a fortune from some pretentious faggot gallery. *That* made him angry. There were shelves and shelves of books, and he wondered who had the time to read so goddamn much? He hated every last one of them. *Real* people worked for a living, all day, and then they came home and had more shit to do. Repairing things that needed fixing and then the lawn on the weekends, and maybe if he was lucky, he got to watch some of the game. But these two weren't sports fans. He could tell from their fancy fucking paintings and the furniture that looked like torture equipment and the racks of wine. And that made him even angrier. *Racks.* One in the kitchen and another in the cellar. And more on the counter and in the fridge. He wanted to break a bottle over the bitch's head and watch the red—wine *and* her blood—pour down and listen to her cry about the upholstery. And then he wanted to fuck her in the face to shut her up about it. His stomach clenched at the memory of his first attempt to do just that. Some instinct had saved his ass, he reckoned. Not his ass. She was a biter, and his *dick* knew it. That was it. Nothing wrong with him. He knew something about her deep down, and it'd saved him from getting bit. Still, it was upsetting. He tried to push it out of his head, but it sat there. Limp now as then.

He wanted to *shoot* her in the fucking face.

But not before she did what he wanted. As much as he hated to accept it, he needed her. For the moment, anyway. Once he was sure he was set to get what he really wanted, he'd waste her and her pussy husband, and really get down to what he wanted to do. It sure as shit wasn't these two. He had to admit there was something thrilling about watching them think it *was* about them. They were so self-absorbed, they thought *everything* was about them, when no one in the world gave a shit about Evan and Eleonora Pereira, rhymes with barbera. *Fuck you!* He'd had to look up "barbera," and when he found out it was a kind of wine, he'd almost thrown his phone across the room. It was bad enough she corrected him, but that she had to show how much smarter and more cultured she was when she did it pissed him off even more.

He glared down at her and thought about pulling the trigger. If only he didn't need her. *Do I really?*

He pulled on her hair, jerking her back so he could see better. She yelped and stumbled, falling to her knees. He staggered a step to the side, not letting go of her hair. "My husband put a bottle in the freezer." She was crying.

It made sense. The faggot put a bottle of champagne in the freezer, too stupid to know if he forgot about it and it froze, it might explode. He hadn't snuck past. The idiot was still tied up in the cellar. *Trying like hell to get out of that tape, I bet.* He had to work faster. He couldn't leave the guy downstairs unattended for too long or else he'd be dealing with the very situation he thought he had on his hands a second ago.

"Get up." He yanked her hair to get her to stand. She blurted out in pain and stayed on her knees. He pulled again, harder, and she stood.

He led her back into the front room and shoved her onto the sofa again. She flopped on it and gave him one of those looks. The kind that made him want to hurt her more. The same kind his wife gave him. Those looks were going to be the end of both those bitches. He'd make sure of it.

33

Nelle landed on the sofa on top of the EpiPen case she'd dropped when he grabbed her hair. She turned and sat, careful to keep the autoinjector behind her. She tried to put her hands on it without looking like she was grasping at something, but felt certain she looked as guilty as she felt. Guilty. It was an odd feeling to have, but that was it. She was trying to get away with something and didn't want to be caught. She knew the feeling well. It was far from unfamiliar, but this was the most intensely she'd ever felt it. Because the ramifications of being caught now were instant and irreversible. She wasn't sure how she'd get the injector out of the case and use it without him seeing what she was doing, but she would find a way.

The man stared at her. The small muscles at the back of his jaw flexed as he clenched and unclenched his teeth. He held his pistol at his side, his hand wrapped around the frame, not the grip. The barrel pointed at her. His hand was turning white around the gun. He was hitting the side of his thigh with it, as if he was trying to make up his mind what to do.

He took a deep breath and let it out. "Time to make a call."

"I don't . . . understand. Please just let us go. We don't know who you are. You can have anything you want, and I . . . *we* can't tell anyone. We don't know who you are."

He gripped the gun tighter. He put his finger inside the trigger guard. A small part of her wished he'd just get it over with. What could either of them give him that he couldn't just take? The money, that was all. And then they were dead. That was the cost of stealing it. Even though he was going to kill them as soon as he had it, she wanted to offer it again and again until he listened to her and agreed to let them go.

"Look, we have money. You can have it all. Please, just don't hurt us." Of course, he was going to hurt them. He was going to *kill* them both. But she couldn't keep from uttering the words. They were as automatic as not wanting to die. "You can have it all," she said. "We'll transfer it. I'll get you the account numbers. Just let us go."

"I DON'T WANT YOUR FUCKING MONEY!" The man's face stretched into a red rictus. He raised the gun and aimed it at her. Nelle's breath caught. She tried to inhale but was unable to take in any air. She could feel her heart pounding in her chest, in her pulse in the sides of her neck. The man's knuckles turned white as he squeezed the pistol grip. "I want what's mine," he said through clenched teeth.

The sight of him stole the air from her lungs, and she had to work to push the words out without being able to put a breath behind them. "I don't know . . . what . . . what you . . . want from us."

"I want you to talk to my wife." He held her cell phone in front of her face.

Her lips moved for a moment, soundlessly searching for what to say. "Wh-what?"

"You're going to tell her that something doesn't work and you need her to come over to help you figure out how to fix it."

"Tell who?"

"My wife. Fuckin' bitch."

She couldn't tell whether he meant her, his wife, or both of them. Nelle suspected he applied the sobriquet to all women. "I don't . . . understand. I don't know your wife. I don't know who you —"

"Shut up. You know."

She tried to keep her voice calm when she spoke to him, though she couldn't control the quaver that crept through. "I don't. I swear."

"DON'T TELL ME YOU DON'T KNOW WHO I AM! YOU'RE SITTING IN MY FUCKING HOUSE!"

Nelle tried to blink away her confusion, but nothing resolved into any greater clarity. The man stared at her, brow furrowed as if she'd done *him* wrong and not the other way around. No part of this made sense to her. He stared as if expecting an answer, some kind of rationalization or continued bargaining, but she couldn't find the right words.

"This is our house. We bought it from . . ."

You.

He smiled at what had to be the fluid shift in her face from confusion to realization to fear. He saw what she knew, and it amused him to see it terrify her in a completely new way. Her terror seemed to please him.

While he and his wife hadn't been at the open house, the walk-through, or the closing, he'd come to her door to sell her the security system. He wasn't a *stranger* who'd been stalking them for their money. While she'd known him by name only, the revealed link between them was somehow more frightening. Everything shifted—his motives, her strategies for survival. She was starting over with new information. It wasn't the money. It was . . . *personal.* Whatever it was he was after, she feared it was something she couldn't give him even if she wanted to. She had to think of something to say, but couldn't.

She recalled her attorney telling her about the divorce. *She's leaving him, but he's contesting it.* He wanted her to talk to a woman who'd left him, who wouldn't talk to him herself, likely for reasons related to exactly what Nelle was going through at that moment. His anger, unreasonable demands, irrationality. What could she say to a woman who knew him like an ex-wife did? She wanted to say that she wasn't about to lure someone to the house for him to tie up and murder along with her and Evan. Instead, what came out was, "What if she . . . she tells me h-how to . . . fix it over the phone? Why would she c-come over to help?"

"Play stupid. All you cunts do that. Make her believe you're too stupid to figure it out and you need her to *show* you."

"And then wh-what?"

"I want her to listen to me. And if she's here, in *our* house, she'll listen. I need to show her something. And then . . . I'll let you go."

Nelle knew something else about him: his lies were effortless. She wondered if he was going to shoot her after she made the call, or wait to do it after his wife rang the bell. The question was pure speculation, because Nelle knew his ex would *never* come over, no matter how convincing she was on the phone. There was only a slim chance the wife was going to answer a call from an unfamiliar number to start, and even less possibility, if she did, that she'd rush right over on a sunny holiday weekend to show a stranger how to work something that wasn't her problem anymore. Nelle knew it wouldn't work, because if *she'd* already escaped this man, there was no chance she'd ever get anywhere near anything associated with him ever again.

Her eyes shifted to the gun in his hand. She scooted back on the sofa, feeling the EpiPen against her backside. She had to make it work. *Had to.* As much as he promised otherwise, his only intention was to murder them. He could be crazy as a shithouse rat and still realize that taking her and Evan hostage was going to land him in prison if they told anyone. His only way out was to kill them both. And his wife. That was what he wanted her here for. He meant to kill all *three* of them. And then what? *He'll kill himself too.* At the end of it all, his exit plan was to save a bullet for himself. How many times had she heard men say, "If I go, I'm taking as many people with me as I can!" as if it was somehow more tolerable to die a mass murderer than by oneself? She'd heard it enough not to believe it when this man promised to release her.

The fog that clouded her mind was drifting away.

The intruder's wife had walled off her ex-husband, and he couldn't find a way to break back through to her. If he'd come to Nelle for help getting in touch with her, he'd run aground with every other option. That meant her distance was the only thing keeping her and Evan alive. If she was successful in getting his ex to come to the house, they were all dead. The thing was, if she didn't help lure her to the house, they were still dead. He wanted to use Nelle as bait to lure his ex into a trap. Murdering his ex-wife was the man's endgame. And if he killed her, there was no getting away. If he got what he wanted, *he* was dead too.

There was no point in trying to find common ground. For one of them to win, the other had to lose.

She wanted to cry. Not the little sobs she hadn't been able to control when he pulled her hair or hit her. A long, soul-racking cry. The need was there, like a pressure building in her chest. Eventually, she wouldn't be able to hold it back, and she'd sob. And then *he* would know something about *her.* That she had no more fight left in her.

Not yet. Don't cry. Don't be a fucking weakling. Don't cry.

She took a shuddering breath and said, "You could have asked me to c-call her b-before. I w-would have helped you if you'd just asked. You didn't have to do . . . all this."

He let out a snorting laugh through his nose. "No, you wouldn't've.

Females aren't like that. You can't just ask; you have to convince them." He hit the butt of the gun against his thigh. Nelle prayed to all the gods she'd ever heard of that he'd accidentally pull the trigger and shoot himself. He didn't have to blow his head off. In the leg was good enough. He'd focus on the wound in his thigh and she could swing around with the needle and stick him in the neck. A dose of epinephrine in a muscle wouldn't hurt him, but a shot of it right in a vein would stop his heart. At least she *hoped* the neck would do it.

But he didn't shoot himself. He remained focused intently on her.

"What . . . what do you want me to say?"

"What I told you, stupid. Tell her you don't know how to reset the heater in the sunroom and you need her to come over to show you. Be convincing. Play dumb. Shouldn't be hard." He looked down at her phone and tried to unlock it again, but seemed to have trouble remembering the code. She started to repeat it to him, but he barked at her. "I know. Shut up." It took him two tries. His hands were shaking.

While he was focused on her phone, she reached behind herself with one hand and opened the cap on her EpiPen cylinder. She tilted the container, letting the device slide out. The scrape of plastic on plastic seemed so loud to her, her heart beat faster and it felt like she couldn't get a breath. The room swam a little, and a thought appeared in her mind like it had been spoken by someone else: *You're going to die of fright; that's what this is.* She wanted to silence that voice, but it lingered in her head, like the scraping of the autoinjector sliding out of its case. A ringing in her mind couldn't be silenced.

Die of fright. Die of fright.

But he didn't hear. She jammed the empty tube into the gap between the seat cushion and the back of the sofa and held on to the device, waiting.

The man's face relaxed as he opened her phone app. He looked up at her. Her palms were sweating. *Not doing anything here. No sir. Just waiting for you to figure out how to dial a fucking phone. That's all I'm up to.* Tears stung her eyes. She wasn't crying yet, but close. Stress was eating at her resolve like decay. Soon, she'd have none, and the corpse of her will would presage her own cadaver.

He held the phone out in front of her. "Can I hold it?" she asked. He was just out of reach. *Come a little closer. Take your medicine.*

"Fuck no, you can't hold it. You keep your arms right there at your sides. I'm going to put it on speaker, so I can hear too."

"It'll sound weird to her on speaker. I just want to be able to hold the phone so it sounds right."

"And I don't want you to have it. What's so fuckin' hard to understand?"

"What can I do with a cell phone?"

"What can you do? You can throw it at me, try to hit me in the face with it." He pointed to the long scrapes under his eye that she'd given him earlier in that very room. His face grew redder, and he took a step back. "You think you're smarter than me, but you aren't. With your fucking snooty wines and your big city bullshit. You get tired of living in the city, so you sell your fancy-ass condo and buy a quiet place in the suburbs, and you think all the bumpkins out here are going to kiss your ass and bring you cookies because you're classing up the neighborhood."

"That's not it at all. I'm not trying to trick you. I *want* to help."

"Oh, really?" he said through clenched teeth. "Well, Miss Pereira" — he said, drawing it out, daring her to correct him — "I'll just do whatever you say, then." Nelle shrank down, waiting for him to hit her. His back straightened as she cowered. In a low voice full of venom, he said, "I hate all you entitled, rich cunts. You get everything handed to you along with a participation trophy, and you think you just won the game." He stepped closer and stuck the gun up under her chin. "*You* want to help *me.*"

The muscles in her shoulder tightened, ready to swing. If she hit him now, all he had to do was pull the trigger. She froze again. Her resolve from earlier had dissipated.

"I'm sorry. I'll make . . . the c-call however you want me to!" Nelle tried to calm her voice. "Let me t-talk to your wife. You can hold the phone. I'll say anything you want. Just put the g-gun away and let me d-do it." She tried to give him a sense of retreat and surrender with her body. She hunched her shoulders and tilted her head back to seem smaller, more vulnerable. Not a threat.

The man's face went slack. He pulled the gun away from her chin, dialed the number, and then activated the speakerphone. He held the device in front of Nelle's face — it shone brightly into her eyes, the phone app keeping the glassy surface of the smartphone from being reflective. She was happy not to be able to see herself. It would only remind her how frightened she was—how slim her chances of living were. Getting slimmer.

While the signal upstairs was much better than in the cellar, it still wasn't great. The phone had two bars. The sound of ringing on the other end was faint and distorted. Her impulse to lean closer to be heard better warred with her repulsion at the thought of being nearer to the man. She felt like a drunk sitting there, wavering like she couldn't stay upright without effort.

After a few rings, a woman's voice declared, "You've reached Samantha's Studio."

Samantha! That's her name!

"It's her voicemail," Nelle whispered. "What do I do?"

The frustration on his face lingered a second before he returned to his inscrutable baseline. This was a guy who, when people told him to smile for a picture, believed he was smiling and would defend his flat mien despite everyone else around him looking different. She didn't want to get to know this man, even as little as how to read him.

"Leave her a message," he mouthed. She looked a question at him; he bugged his eyes out in response. She could see that he wanted to say something mean, but didn't want to get picked up by the device—even though it hadn't started recording yet. He widened his eyes at her again. She was suddenly glad to be on speaker if it kept him from threatening her.

She felt a new panic rising. *What the hell was her name? She* just *said it. Why can't I remember? Sa Sa Sarah . . . no!* Samantha. *Like the TV witch. Samantha* Roarke. *And he's . . . he's . . .* Malcolm!

The voice on the phone said, "At the tone you know what to do." A second passed, and a sharp beep crackled from the speaker. Nelle tried to keep her voice steady as she spoke. "Uh, hi, Samantha. This is Nelle . . . Eleonora Pereira. My husband and I . . . uh, bought your house . . ." She glanced up at the man—Malcolm. One of his widened eyes twitched at the words *your house.* She continued. "If you could give me a call when you get this message, we're having trouble with the uh, heater in the family room, and we *really need your help.* Trying to get it ready for fall, you know, and it won't . . . work. Anyway, we really *need* your help because we're in, uh, kind of a tough situation, and a little *help* would be great. You probably, uh, have it in your caller ID, but my cell number is 617-555-4671. Thanks." She nodded at him. The man—she didn't want to think of him as Malcolm. He probably didn't go by that name, anyway. It was too soft for a man like him, she guessed. He'd fight it. Use his last name for everything. It'd sound stronger, like something military. The man, Roarke, stabbed the button to end the call. She thought she heard something in her phone pop. His fingers gripping the device were turning white.

"The fuck was that?"

"I was . . . trying to make it sound . . . urgent. Like you said."

"You were sending her a code. *Need. Help.*"

"I swear, I wasn't. I just wanted it to sound like it wasn't just a little thing, you know? Urgent. I didn't know what else to say."

His hand whipped out and she felt her phone against her face before she realized what was coming. She cried out, and he hit her again, harder. "All you had to do was say what I fucking *told you!* You were trying to signal, you cunt—"

Nelle screamed, "No! I swear!" She let go of the EpiPen and held her hands up to ward off another blow.

"Shut up," he shouted. He put the barrel of the gun to her head.

She couldn't get a breath.

Die of fright!

"Stop! I'm only doing what you said. I'm trying to get her here, I swear. Please! Don't!"

"Liar! You took my house, and now you're trying to warn Sam. I'll show you how to ruin a marriage. I'll fucking end yours." He threw her phone on the sofa and grabbed her by the elbow. She grasped at the EpiPen behind her with her free hand and barely caught it before he dragged her to her feet and away toward the cellar.

He marched her down, gun jammed into her back. She stuffed the autoinjector into the front of her sweats as discreetly as she could on the way down, hoping the stretchy waistband would hold it in place until she got a chance to use it.

At the bottom of the stairs, he spun her around and hit her hard in the stomach with a closed fist. Her legs dropped out from under her and she crumpled to the floor, gasping for air and retching. He snatched a bottle of wine off the rack and reared back with it like a club, ready to swing at her head.

Though it was muffled through the cloth and tape, Evan unmistakably grunted, "Leave her alone," from the other end of the room. Roarke's head whipped around, his face finally finding a new steady expression: enraged. He threw the bottle. It tumbled end over end as it flew, and smashed into the concrete foundation behind the weight bench. The room filled with the aroma of pinot noir, and the sound of tinkling glass echoed through the air as shards scattered across the floor. He'd missed. Roarke roared his frustration and stomped toward Evan, glass crunching under his boots. He jammed the muzzle of his gun hard into Evan's chest and shouted, "Is this what you want?" He turned to look at Nelle, still in a ball on the floor. "I can take *everything* away from you. EVERYTHING!"

Nelle choked on her saliva as she tried to get a breath. Coughing and sputtering, she couldn't plead aloud, so she shook her head, holding up a hand to beg for mercy. A gossamer line of saliva slipped out of her mouth and dangled briefly from her lip before it fell and wetted a spot on her thigh. It ran down her leg, over her knee, leaving a shiny trail. Though she was far beyond feeling shame for drooling on herself, it was a humiliation that broke her a little more. Another small thing adding up to the weight that would soon crush her spirit entirely. She swallowed and focused on finding her breath. Her voice.

"Stop. Please." She lost control of the hitch in her voice and openly sobbed, not caring anymore whether Roarke took any pleasure in her tears. "Just stop. I'll do . . . anything . . . you want."

He stuffed the gun in his waistband holster and pulled the folding knife out of his pocket. He grabbed hold of Evan's jaw and pressed the knife to his cheek and pulled it back, bearing down. Evan's muffled scream filled the basement despite the gag; snot burst out of his nose, coating the duct tape over his mouth. Nelle answered with her own rising howl, wild and irrational.

Roarke let go and turned to face her, red knife in hand. Blood ran from Evan's cheek, dripping off of his chin onto the front of his shirt. Roarke stomped back over to Nelle. He snatched the pair of underwear off the floor where they'd fallen and stuffed them back into her mouth. She tasted her husband's blood on the man's fingers and gagged as he shoved the cloth deep into her mouth. She wanted to bite, but his hands were so far in, like he was trying to pack her throat, and she couldn't get the leverage to resist. All she could do was gag and try not to vomit. If she threw up, she'd choke to death. She realized that was how it would've worked before. She'd never have been able to bite hard enough.

He jabbed forward once with his fingers and let go. He tossed the knife on the plastic box where he'd set it earlier and she heard the loud rip of silver tape coming off the roll. Then, he pressed the strip to her face, covering her mouth. He was clumsy with rage, and it stuck high up, partially over her nose. She snorted hard, shooting out blood and snot that reflected back up onto her cheeks. He jerked his hands back, as if getting *these* fluids on his hands was a line he was not willing to cross, and glared at her. His jaw flexed as he gritted his teeth. Nelle shook her head, crying and struggling to breathe. He slapped her again.

Dieoffrightdieoffrightdieoffright!

He yanked her up off the floor and set her hard in the dining chair, pulling strips of tape off the roll. He started with her wrists and moved on to her ankles. When he taped her around the midsection, he covered the lower half of her breasts, pinching them painfully.

No more, she thought. *I'll do anything.* She tried pleading with him through the gag, but her appeals were muted and went unheard. It didn't matter. What little faith she'd had in his willingness to listen was gone. There wasn't a way she could imagine getting Evan and herself out of bondage and out of the house that involved either his compassion or mercy. He was on a mission to kill as many people as he could, and nothing would sway or even slow him when he finally decided to get started. She hoped that he'd use the gun and be quick so they didn't suffer. And she hoped he killed her first so she didn't have to watch her husband die. It was selfish, but among all the pains of the world she thought she could handle, that one was too much.

She cried. The sounds she made were ugly and desperate, but she was beyond caring, so she let herself make honest sounds.

34

Upstairs, **an airy digital melody** trilled in the front room of the house, unable to rise above the sounds of crying and shouting filtering through the floorboards from downstairs. After a few rings, the call redirected, and after a moment's silence, the phone chirped a final short burst of notes, letting the empty room know that Nelle had a voicemail.

And then it was silent.

VIII

◆

PHANTOMS

35

The man patted his pockets searching for something. Nelle wondered what he could want. He looked at the book box and his face darkened. It was her phone he was missing. He rubbed his temples. "Fuckin' upstairs," he mumbled.

She could see the beginnings of his unraveling, where he'd appeared in control only an hour or two earlier. Things weren't going the way he wanted, and that was throwing him. There was no denying he was good at sneaking up on people, good at hurting them, but it was becoming clear he didn't know a thing *about* people and what made them work. This was a guy who heard cracking and still applied pressure.

She looked at her husband's still-bleeding face. The cut was long and deep. It was red and angry as anything she'd ever seen. A flooded red river overflowing its banks.

Roarke would kill them when he saw no other end.

Whatever he did *after* that didn't matter. It was the time leading up to his eventual realization that things weren't going his way that counted. And that time was shortening with every new frustration.

The EpiPen in the front of her pants pressed against her belly, still secure in the waistband of her shorts. She had gotten lucky and he'd hit high when he punched her in the stomach. He was taller than she was and hit just under her ribs. And then she was lucky a second time when she went down and it didn't fall out of her pants. Now her hands were taped to the chair again, and the spring-loaded needle was as useless as everything else in this basement. Still, she felt it, right there in her waistband. She had it. And maybe she'd get the chance to use it. Maybe. If she was . . .

Lucky.

Evan groaned.

Roarke put his hands up to his head and pressed against his temples. "Shut up, the both of you! I can't think," he said, as if the slight sounds she and Evan made weren't the direct result of him doing awful things to them. He tromped up the stairs.

Nelle listened to him rummage in the bathroom. His head hurt. *I hope you're having a fucking stroke.*

While it was a pleasing mental image, she banished the fantasy of a blood vessel in his brain bursting open like a crimson grenade and instead tried to focus on how to get out of this situation. She could cooperate all he wanted, and at the end, the game was rigged for only one winner. If she wanted to come out ahead, she had to get out of this chair.

36

Malcolm Roarke — Mack to everyone who knew him — fumbled through the cabinet in the hall outside of the bathroom looking for anything to beat back at the headache that'd been with him all day but in the last couple of hours had become nearly unbearable. Dealing with the bitch downstairs made him feel like his skull was going to pop from the pressure. She looked at him just like his wife did. The way they all did, with that silent judgment that said she thought she was better than him. Well, fuck her. Fuck all of them. The pain throbbed, and he squinted and looked closer, imagining that he had to be overlooking what he wanted. The closet outside the guest room was just full of towels and skin lotion and hand sanitizer. "Where the fuck are the pills?"

He stomped into the bathroom and yanked out a drawer. A bunch of bottles rattled against each other. All he could see were the tops of plain white caps; everything looked alike. During the renovation, Sam had him hang a big black-framed mirror above the sink instead of a medicine cabinet, so they had to find somewhere else to keep their prescription meds and personal things. It was frustrating. Normal people stored things where they could see the damn labels. But then she got her big mirror, flat against the wall instead of a blocky medicine cabinet, because it fit her "design sense" better. To hell with convenience.

He started pulling bottles out of the drawer and tossing them in the sink until he finally found a bottle of generic ibuprofen. He twisted off the childproof cap with some effort and shook several pills into his hand. He counted out four, and then two more before tilting the rest back into the bottle. He replaced the cap and dropped the bottle into the sink with everything else. He had an urge to replace everything as it had been, but it passed. It didn't matter what he tore apart in the house. It wasn't his anymore, and it wouldn't ever be again. He knew that. He wasn't crazy. The news would end up saying a lot of things about him, but he knew it'd eventually end up spinning what he did into "our unaddressed mental health problem in America." He was white, after all. *But I'm not crazy. There aren't any talking dogs telling me what to do. I'm settling scores is all.* Scorched earth might be desperate, it might be irrational, but it wasn't crazy. "I'm not crazy," he said to his reflection. It mouthed the words along with him. *See?* he thought. *Nothing wrong there.* Still, everything *was* going wrong. It had been for the last year, but today, everything awry reached a kind of terminal velocity. Sam wasn't returning the texts or taking calls — he'd only ever put the chances of her responding to his deceptions at fifty-fifty anyway — still, he wanted what he wanted. And that was to hurt her worse than she'd hurt him. The hang-up in the plan was that he couldn't find her. She hadn't been at her new apartment or her parents' place. Her boyfriend's condo in Worcester was empty too. And that was the only reason he'd kept the people living in his house alive. Without any other way to track her, they were the only way he could think of to reach Sam before the end of the weekend. That had been his timetable. When people returned from the long weekend and tried to get back to their lives, they'd see what he'd done. Then it would be all over. Best case scenario, he figured he had until Monday evening at the latest to do everything he wanted. Now, though, it was going to be over much sooner. If his wife wouldn't answer her phone, that meant there was no reason to wait to kill the couple downstairs and move on to the endgame. He regretted not having the chance to show Sam what he had waiting for her in the trunk of his car, but she'd still find out. Maybe the cops would show her pictures. He hoped they did. And when she saw them, she'd know. If he couldn't have his wife and his house and his life, then nobody could.

He looked at the blood and snot on his fingers. He'd had enough blood on his hands — that wasn't a big deal to him — but something about her snot repulsed him. He ran the tap and washed them.

The phone in his pocket buzzed and pinged half a dozen times. He jumped like it was a scorpion stinging him. Sure, now that he was upstairs, it had a signal. It was downloading everything that hadn't come through before. He had no idea if his phone had ever got a signal in the basement. He rarely went down there when it had been his house. Sam had turned the downstairs into a workshop for her antiques hustle, and he didn't have room to do a thing down there except throw the circuit breaker when the lights went out. He'd wanted to finish the basement and turn it into a TV and game room. But she was always down there sanding and painting old pieces of shit she pulled off the side of the road or bought at yard sales. That was *her* space. She told him she couldn't refinish antiques in a "man cave." He did his work in the garage, where it was too cold half the year to do a damn thing. And he had to share his work space with the snow blower and the goddamn bicycle she never rode. He—

The chirp of the door alarm broke him out of his reverie and snapped him back into the present. It sounded again. Behind it, he heard the soft click of the front door latch catching. Someone had let themself into the house. He thought for a moment that it could be Sam, but then the bitch downstairs had only just left her voicemail message. She couldn't have come already. Not unless she was already in the neighborhood. Her parents lived on the other side of town. But he'd already been by that place, and Sam hadn't been there. And if she'd dropped by to visit her folks today, she wouldn't be here now.

And she wouldn't just walk in.

But the police would.

Mack peeked out of the bathroom into the hallway, trying to stay out of sight. He saw a pair of dark figures standing in the front room—men silhouetted against the light coming through the faceted glass in the front door. The word *police* flashed in his mind again like a red alarm beacon. He wasn't ready for the cops yet. Behind the pair, through the window, he saw a black Range Rover parked in the driveway. Not a cop car. *They could be detectives,* he reasoned.

How didn't I hear them pull up?

He knew how. Evan and Nelle had been screaming loud enough to muffle the sounds of an airplane landing in the driveway. He'd been washing his hands. He had a headache that was dulling everything. But then, if it weren't for the door chirping, he wouldn't have heard them enter the house either.

For a second, they stayed still, as if they were only the memory of figures who'd once been in the house. Then one of the phantoms moved. It detached from the light behind it and moved toward him with such suddenness all Mack could do was backpedal away into the bathroom wall. The man closed the distance before Mack was able to reach under his shirt for his gun. A closed fist redirected his attention from the small of his back to his nose with sudden efficiency. Mack had been hit before, he could take a punch, but this one felt like the end of the world. He saw an eruption of lights behind his eyelids, and his stomach turned with instant nausea. His head hit the bathroom window, and he thought he heard it crack. Felt something wet under his hair. Unaware of anything but his own disorientation, the phantom caught ahold of him and yanked him forward, throwing him into the front room.

Mack lurched forward, his own weight propelling him toward the second phantom. The other man hit him hard in the midsection, again with a punch that felt superhuman. Mack retched and fell to his knees. He had no air and struggled to take a breath. The phantom kicked him in the gut, and he fell over. The gun in the small of his back jammed into his spine. Again, before he could reach for it, the other man was on top of him holding him down, a knee on one biceps and a foot pressing down on the other forearm.

The first phantom stepped up and stuck a gun in Mack's eye. "Stop." He spoke the word calmly, without anger or even a sense that he'd been exerted. Mack's head throbbed, and he felt nauseous. The pain in his head surged, and his skull suddenly felt as if it might explode from the pressure inside. The other man got up off of him, but the first kept the gun barrel stuck in his eye socket, pressing down. Holding him in place like an insect on a pin.

Then their hands were on him, lifting. The pair of phantoms lifted him effortlessly up onto the sofa. He sat heavily, having to exert significant effort not to fall over onto his side.

A phantom spoke. "If you do not do what I say, I will shoot you. Do you understand?" Not detectives. His voice was accented like the livery company owner Mack used to drive for when he was in his twenties.

Vlad something. No. Vadim something. He was Russian. He'd been indicted for racketeering and money laundering through that same livery company and went to federal prison.

"Do you understand?" the man who sounded like Vadim Something repeated.

Mack said yes, though a thickness in his throat made it hard to speak.

The phantom with the gun was pointing it at him, muzzle staring at him like a pupil. The stare of cyclopean death. At the sight of it, he involuntarily pushed into the sofa cushion behind him; his own gun still in its holster pressed against the small of his back. He fought the urge to reach for it, and kept his hands at his sides. He knew better than to move for his piece; they'd shoot him. It's what he would've done.

His head hurt so much, it was nearly blinding. He had trouble taking air in through his crushed nose and breathed instead through his mouth. One of the two shades broke away and left the room, moving like a man coming out of a corner after a bell rang: determined, fierce, and direct. Mack heard him move through the house with speed and intention. He covered the first floor and then went upstairs. His footsteps overhead weren't soft; he didn't bother trying to conceal his movement. He wasn't looking to sneak up on anyone anymore.

Mack sat there staring at the shadow with the gun. The phantom slowly resolved into a man as his eyes adjusted, though he was still blurry. The guy was wearing a suit. Or, something like it. Dark clothes. Everything black. His suit coat looked like it might be leather. White guy. Thinning, graying hair. He was angular, like his face had been knapped out of a piece of stone, the way you'd make a primitive ax.

Mack blinked and tried to clear his eyes. Things eventually took clearer shape, but occasionally the room seemed to yaw like a plane in bad winds. He took another deep breath and tried to settle himself.

The man pointed the gun at him, unmoving. Black tattoos on three of his knuckles resolved into clarity. *KOT.* Mack had no idea what it stood for, but figured it didn't mean "mercy."

A few moments later, the other man returned and rejoined his partner in the front room. They spoke to each other for a bit in what Mack guessed was Russian. He didn't understand a word of it. Just the rhythm and tone of the language.

The man who'd gone looking removed his suit coat. Mack saw a glint of metal on his hand. Knucks. *Those are illegal in Massachusetts.* As if it mattered to these men, or him.

The man refitted the brass on his fingers and tightened his fist. "Where is your wife?"

IX

◆

SAMANTHA

37

THREE YEARS BEFORE DEPARTURE

Samantha and Mack walked through the house, trying to imagine their own things in each room instead of the sellers' hideous furniture. The real estate agent said that the place had been built in the fifties, but was updated in 1977. It looked it. The breezeway between the house and garage had been converted into a dining room, but the wood paneling and low drop ceiling made it feel more like a cave, or a singles bar with the word *grotto* in the name.

"How long have you two been married?"

"Six months."

"Newlyweds," the agent practically shouted as he led them through a door into a room with windows on three sides. It was bright, and there was a stationary bike and a stair step machine in front of a big CRT television and an antique-looking VCR. "They used this as an exercise room, as you can see, but it wouldn't take much to turn it into family room or a game room. You could put a pool table right there."

Mack smiled and said, "It's perfect."

Sam's brow furrowed and her lips tightened into a thin, straight line. "Could you excuse me and my husband for a minute?" she said. The man smiled and told them he'd be in the kitchen if they had any questions. As he walked out, he reminded them that there were cookies. She turned to her husband and said, "Are you crazy?"

"What? It's perfect."

"Did you see that room in there? Or the living room? Frosted mirrors, Mack. All it's missing is a disco ball and a fishbowl for the key party."

"It's a cosmetic fixer-upper. The foundation looks good, and the construction's decent. They built these places sturdy back in the day. Yeah, it's out of date, but this is the showcase for our home decorating business."

"I told you I don't *want* to have a home decorating business. I don't want to live in a mess. I want to restore antiques and open a shop."

"Selling old junk? Don't you wanna do more? I mean, you can keep on with the bits and pieces, but the real money is in making places like this look good again. Lots of rich people in old houses want to update. I can do the structural work, and you'll make it look like those places in the design magazines." He held up his hands, splaying his fingers out as if he was showing her a marquee. "Roarke Remodeling and Restoration. We spend a couple of years —"

"A couple of *years?*"

He spoke through gritted teeth. "We spend a couple of years on the weekends making this look like one of those fuckin' dream homes offa HGTV while you do your antique thing on the side, and then when we get a few jobs based on our show house. I'll quit work, and we go into business full-time. It's perfect."

"Weekends are when I do 'my antique thing.' How am I supposed to restore furniture and teach during the week?"

"Nights," he said, as if the single word was a solution to a problem so easy it barely needed to be answered.

"I grade papers at night. I prepare for classes the next day at . . ."

Mack's face started to turn red, and he got that twitch in his mouth, like he was trying to smile or scowl and couldn't decide which. Sam knew better than to contradict him when he got like this. He wanted what he wanted, and he got upset — her dad said "mean" — when anyone disagreed or told him no. But she wanted to tell him no. She didn't want to fix up a house and go into business as a remodeler. She wanted to live in a nice modern home *now* and paint some furniture so she could quit teaching other people's bratty kids and open a cute shop downtown. Open for business when *she* wanted with no toxic co-workers undermining her with the school administration. Her dad had told her that the old bookstore next to the bistro and wine bar she liked was struggling to pay the rent and would probably be out of business within a year, or maybe eighteen months, tops. If she worked hard, she'd have enough floor stock to fill it by then, and he said he'd help her with the buildout and setup. She knew what she wanted to call the shop: Samantha's Studio. *That* was what she wanted. Not this.

The real estate agent poked his head back into the exercise room and said, "You two want to see the back yard? Big enough for dogs, and it looks right out onto Cabot State Park. You have neighbors on one side, but a hedge runs the whole length of the property. You'd never know anyone was there. Total privacy."

Mack turned to him and said, "We love it!"

"As soon as you walked in the door, I said, this is the kind of place for a couple like you. Take down the paneling, paint a little—"

"I want to blow that out," Mack said, gesturing at the drop ceiling in the dining room. "Put in a vaulted cathedral ceiling and a chandelier." He turned and nudged his wife with an elbow.

She flinched as he hit the bruise already on her biceps. She forced a smile. "I guess I can see that."

The agent said, "That sounds like the makings of a dream home!"

"Broker'll call you with our offer," Mack said.

Sam's stomach dropped. The agent laughed and beckoned them to come have a cookie. "I'll give you guys some privacy if you want to call your agent right now." He leaned a little closer to Mack like he was about to share some really great betting tip on the big game. "I'm not supposed to tell you this, but the sellers are motivated. Their parents, who lived in the house, died this year, and they want to make sure the place goes to a good family who'll love it like their folks did. You two have kids?"

"Not yet," Mack said. "But we're working on it." He tried to nudge Sam again, but she ducked out of the way, saving her bruise from getting worse.

"No kids," she said.

"It's a perfect place for 'em. Schools here are great."

"I know. I teach at Mayr High."

The agent blinked at Sam as if her telling him she knew more than he did about the subject didn't register. He continued. "They're pumping a ton of money into the local schools, and we're outperforming Boston *and* Cambridge on the MCAS. It's a great place to raise a family."

Mack had his phone out and was dialing. He looked over his shoulder at Sam and said, "We can make great things happen here. We can make this a house we'll want to spend the rest of our lives in." He turned away when their broker answered. "Hey, Dave. We found one we want to make an offer on. We really like it."

She tried to imagine herself in the house in ten years. Five.

She just couldn't picture it.

38

THREE DAYS BEFORE DEPARTURE

Samantha sat on the sofa scrolling through her Facebook feed on a smartphone with a waning battery. She kept going back to look at the number of likes on the last post she made on her Samantha's Studio page. Despite having over five hundred followers, after a little more than two hours, it was holding steady at only twelve tiny thumbs-ups. One of them was her own. She closed Facebook and went back to Pinterest, looking for ideas for the secretary that she'd picked up off the side of the road. She wasn't sure what to do with it and wasn't all that invested in it; the thing was more trouble than it was worth. Probably why the owners had dumped it on the sidewalk in the first place.

She set the phone aside when Mack pulled up in the driveway knowing Samantha was done for the night. "Sam" was on the clock now. She hated that he called her that. She'd been Sammy until fifth grade, but the minute she started middle school, she became Samantha and never answered to anything else. Until she met her husband. No one called her Sam but Mack. At least no one used to. It was catching on the more he used it around their friends.

The rumble of the garage door vibrated faintly through the walls, and she heard him let himself in through the dining room. There was a pause while he took off his boots and dropped them, *thump, thump,* on the dining room floor. It had taken getting the hardwood floors redone, but he eventually came around to not wearing his Timberlands in the house. She listened as he walked to the refrigerator, opened the door, and popped open a beer. He gulped down three big, loud swallows before he shut the fridge door and called out to her. She replied, "In here." A moment later, he tromped into the front room, freshly painted a lovely light purple.

The house was coming together more quickly than she'd anticipated. While she hadn't entirely hated the process of updating it (her choices about liking it were limited if she didn't want to live in the Disco Den), she still didn't want to renovate homes. She didn't want people giving her orders and telling her that they didn't like her choices. Still, it was a nice room.

He strode over to where she sat on the couch—an English roll arm she'd bought at an estate sale—and leaned down to give her a kiss. His breath smelled like beer and the onions he must've had in his lunch. Under that, there was something else, subtle, but impossible to ignore. He wore a faint hint of perfume and a fainter aroma of excited pussy on his skin. She kissed him because that was what she did when he wanted it. If she refused or turned away, he'd get pissed off and storm around the house like a giant toddler. So, she kissed him and asked how his day was, when she knew how at least *part* of it had gone. He smiled and told her it wasn't bad.

Not bad. I bet.

He straightened up and took another drink of beer. "This is the last one," he said, the implication hanging heavy in the air. She hadn't been to the store.

"I'll grab some tomorrow when I go to my hair appointment."

"That doesn't help me tonight, Sam." He stared at her as if she wasn't picking up on his heavy unspoken suggestion that she get up off her fat ass this minute and run to the package store. She read him clearly; she just didn't feel like going. Not when he could have bought some after he finished fucking his whore. *And stop calling me Sam.*

"It's going to take me a minute to get dinner going, if you want to run up to Sippy's Liquors. You have time."

He frowned. He could have a drink or dinner when he liked, but not both; not unless he took care of one of them himself. "I just got home," he said, as if that somehow trumped the fact that she was equally inconvenienced by his lack of forethought.

"I'll get started on dinner while you enjoy that one." She stood and turned to head for the kitchen. He grabbed her arm tightly and stopped her. She braced herself, waiting for him to scream at her, his breath strong in her face. While his grip hurt, his expression was flat. She looked to see if his jaw was flexing the way it did when he was holding something back, like when he got angry in public. It wasn't. His face was pale, without a bit of the flush she was used to seeing rise in his cheeks when he was upset. She couldn't read him. That was always the worst. Her stomach cramped a little at the memory of the last time he looked like that. Sometimes her back tooth still ached. She steeled her resolve. *So close. You're so close, just stick it out a little while longer.*

He said, "You wanna go out to eat?"

She blinked a couple of times while she processed what he said. "Sure," she agreed carefully. "We can do that."

The white impressions of his fingers in her flesh darkened to red after he let go. Tomorrow there'd be bruises where he grabbed her, and she'd have to wear a long-sleeve shirt to work, despite the late season humidity. Her other hand wanted to float up and rub at the aching spot, but she held her arms down at her sides. She imagined him noticing her massaging her arm and asking, *What? You think that was hard?* Instead, she stayed still, and he said, "Let me get changed and we'll go. I've been sweating in these clothes all day." He walked off to the bedroom. He never changed after work. Sometimes, he'd wear the same thing two days in a row, only taking his clothes off to get into bed and then stepping right back into a pair of pants that could almost stand up by themselves. She figured he must've smelled his mistress on himself. It didn't matter. He could spruce up all he wanted. He'd confirmed what she knew already. *What* she knew, but not who.

He emerged a minute later, dressed almost identically to what he'd been wearing before, except clean. A Patriots T-shirt, a pair of tan dungarees, and white socks. His face clouded over for a second. He stepped out of sight and returned a minute later with his boots. "You ready?" he asked.

She followed him to the car. Once upon a time, he'd been gentlemanly and had held doors for her — pulled out her chair like a high school boy following his mother's instructions how to treat a girl, though they were both in their thirties. Those chivalrous gestures faded as they dated, having mostly disappeared by the time they were engaged. Once they celebrated their first anniversary, the bloom was off the rose, as her grandmother used to say. He'd kept up the pretense for as long as he needed to. By the end of the first year, they'd bought the house and were established in it. And he was done with courtship gestures. The best she knew she could expect was when he used the fob to unlock his door, he might think to click twice to release hers too before climbing in.

He was backing up out of the driveway before she had her lap belt fastened. He didn't ask where she wanted to go. It didn't take but a minute to realize he was driving straight to the Hadley Maison.

Despite the exotic name, it was a townie burger bar that looked like the only way it could pass inspection was with an envelope full of cash. It was his favorite haunt. He seemed to always have a friend or two sitting at the bar.

Sam wondered if he brought the whore there for lunch.

The waitress smiled when she saw Mack and told him his table was free and said she'd be right by. *He has a table? How often does he come here without me?* They sat by the window, him in his usual seat with the better view of the restaurant and the big screen television over her shoulder. The Red Sox were playing. The batter hit, and the people at the bar cheered and whistled like they were in the stands at Fenway. The waitress came over and asked if they'd like something to drink. He ordered a Narragansett, stepping on Sam's attempt to get out, "I'd like a glass of chardonnay, please." The waitress smiled and winked at her, leaving to go fetch their order.

She stared out the window at the water. Across the pond, the lights of other people's houses reflected in the ripples made by the evening breeze. The restaurant was right in the middle of a lakeside residential community. She wondered how many of those people came around to eat at the Hadley. Probably not as many as wished the owners would give it up so the property could be razed and developed for another expensive house on the water instead of this dive.

One of Mack's friends from the bar said something, and he laughed. She didn't hear what it was, but had a feeling they were laughing at her. The noise in the place deadened her ears, and she felt a little disoriented, kind of like being drunk, except she hadn't had anything to drink. Not yet. She wished that the waitress would hurry up.

After a few minutes, the server returned with their drinks and took their order. When she came back later with their food, she had a second beer for Mack in hand even though Samantha couldn't remember him ordering another. The server didn't ask if she'd like a fresh glass of chardonnay.

They ate without saying much. He stared at the TV above the bar, and she did her best not to distract him from the television. She figured his enthusiasm to eat out that night was motivated by the game and not an interest in relieving her of the burden of fixing dinner. There was no TV in the dining room at home, and they were in the habit of eating together at the table. She wasn't sure why he insisted on that when most nights he rushed through his meal to get to the sofa and the flat screen. Still, the Buffalo chicken wrap she'd ordered was tasty — it had bacon bits in it — and she had no dishes to do.

A third beer arrived, and she started to worry about the drive home. Mack didn't let anyone drive the Demon. Not even her. He had a high tolerance for alcohol, but three beers was three beers after all. *No. Four. He'd had one at home before they left.* Tolerance or not, Narragansett was going to be his copilot, not her or Jesus. Nor was he becoming more patient and loving as he got deeper in the glass. He wasn't a happy drunk, though he was an amorous one. He was a vigorous — if selfish — lover, but the last thing she wanted to do that night was pretend his half-erect alcohol cock was anything capable of pleasing her. Four beers was four beers, and there'd probably be a fifth before they headed for the exit.

She pulled her cell phone out of her pocket and checked Facebook again. Still only twelve little blue thumbs. She browsed away to a friend's page and looked at her pictures of the new puppy they'd gotten. Sir Arthur Corgi Doyle, they'd named it. She clicked the heart emoji and then realized that she'd forgotten to take their own dog, Maxim, out for his afternoon walk. It was a near certainty that they would return to a pile near the front door or in the middle of the dining room, and she'd be the one to clean it up. It *was* her fault he didn't get a chance to do his business before they went out. After work, she'd gone right to her computer instead of walking the dog.

Another play and the bar erupted in more cheers and clapping. She jumped a little and realized how badly she had to pee. She stood and set her napkin on the table.

"Where're you goin'?" Mack asked.

"I have to use the restroom." She waited a second and then added, "And then we should probably go. The dog needs to be let out."

He waved a hand at her and returned his attention to the game. If another cheer startled her, she was going to wet her pants.

On her way to the restroom, she stopped by the waitress station. Her server looked up and smiled. Something about the way she looked at Sam was off. Her husband definitely brought his mistress here. *What if* she's *his mistress?* Sam looked the woman up and down quickly, assessing if she was her husband's type. Though she was a little skinny, it was possible. Sam had met one of his exes, and that woman was nothing like her or this waitress. If he had a type, it might be as simple as has-a-vagina. But the woman's perfume wasn't right. The scent she'd caught on Mack was less assaultive. Less intended to cover the odors of kitchen grease and spilled beer. She smiled and said, "Could we get the check, please?" The woman said, "Sure," and turned to print out their ticket. Sam went to the bathroom.

When she returned to the table, Mack was looking at her with a furrowed brow. "The dog needs to be walked," she reminded him.

"There's no beer at home."

"We can stop on the way."

"I'll miss the end of the game." She sighed and sat down, resigned to cleaning up dog shit. "You gonna pout about it?" he said.

"If I'd known we were staying for the whole thing, I'd've brought my phone charger."

He rolled his eyes. He knew she didn't like baseball, had known since they were first dating, though early on, she'd tried to learn to like it. It didn't work. She thought the game was boring, but you weren't allowed to say that in Massachusetts, let alone in a townie bar crowded full of people wearing red and white jerseys. "Fine. If you're going to be a fuckin' baby, we'll go. Jesus."

She didn't argue. There was no point to it. Mack turned and announced that his mom said it was time to get his jammies on. One of his friends at the bar said, "Maybe she wants to breast feed you."

Mack laughed, picked up his beer glass, and said, "I'm strictly bottle fed. I'd starve otherwise." The friend looked at Samantha's chest and laughed. She crossed her arms over her breasts and tried to kill him with her glare. He winked at her and took a drink.

He knows. Everyone here knows my husband is sleeping with someone else.

Her face flushed with rage and embarrassment, and she turned to leave. She was halfway down the stairs before she heard Mack following along.

The ride home was a little harrowing, but could have been worse. Her husband had the route between their house and the Hadley committed to muscle memory. *He could probably make the drive dead asleep.* Half drunk wasn't asleep, though. He kept drifting into the oncoming lane of the narrow, twisting New England road. She clenched her jaw and held on to the side of her seat. Along the way, he stopped at a package store and went in to get more 'Gansett and a pint of Maker's Mark. Once started, he was determined to finish. That suited her just fine. Drink made him horny, but *drunk* might make him pass out.

At home, he parked in the driveway at a crooked angle and climbed out, forgetting his house keys in the cup holder. She pulled them out so she could unlock the front door before he started swearing and kicking at it. When she climbed up the steps to let him in, he tried to pinch her ass but almost dropped his bottle of Maker's and figured he couldn't risk it. She was quietly thankful for small blessings.

Inside, she was relieved to find that Maxim hadn't made a mess on the floor, but he was looking at her with an expectancy that said if she didn't turn around and take him out for a walk that very instant, he wasn't going to be able to hold it any longer. So, she hooked the leash to his collar and told Mack she'd be back soon. He grunted and headed to the living room with his six-pack and whiskey. She was barely out the door before she heard him hollering at the game.

She and the dog hustled into the neighborhood across the highway. It was a longer walk than they needed to take — Maxim had done his business not twenty feet from the front step. But she wasn't ready to go back in. Not yet. Though it was a pain getting across the highway, and the neighborhood was a little far, the dog needed the exercise, and she needed the time away. She hated being so far from everything, and craved having other people around her, even if they were mostly behind closed doors. Looking out and being able to see a house across the street or someone else walking their dog felt less like being an exile. On nice evenings, she'd sometimes run into people walking off dinner over there, getting their steps in on fitness trackers. They'd wave and say, "How ya doin'?" But not tonight.

It was dark. She'd forgotten a flashlight, and her phone battery was too low to waste. It was fine. Like Mack knew the way home from the Hadley, she'd stored the walk through the neighborhood in her muscles and bones. She took Maxim around their regular circuit, peeking in people's windows as they passed, mostly seeing big televisions tuned to the game. She walked the dog up a different street than usual just to stay out a little longer and window peep. Eventually, though, she had to go home. Tonight, anyway.

They circled around and headed home, having not spoken to a soul.

Inside, as soon as she let the shiba inu off his leash, Maxim raced off to find Mack.

She peeked into the living room at her husband. He looked like he might be asleep. Maxim shifted on the sofa, and Mack put a lazy hand on his back. Not asleep. Not yet. But close.

When I go, I'm taking that dog with me, you asshole.

She went into the bedroom to change into her flannel pajamas. Even though it was warm inside, she liked how cozy they were — and how unflattering. Her husband's dirty clothes lay in a pile at the foot of the bed. She kicked them aside and *that* smell wafted up to her. The scent of perfume and something else. There was no way she was going to sleep in a room with that smell. She grabbed his shirt and tossed it into the laundry hamper. Picking up his pants, she dug into his pockets to pull out the inevitable scraps of paper, receipts, and business cards that always ended up clotted and ruined in the wash. Her fingers brushed against something soft and silky. She withdrew a pair of women's underwear from his front pocket.

Her fingers sprung open, and the underwear fluttered to the floor. Her heart started to pound, and she felt breathless. Whether his mistress gave them to him as a gift or he just took them, there was the memento of his faithlessness right there on the floor in front of her. A pair of stinking panties with a faint yellow streak in them.

She picked them up between thumb and forefinger and contemplated going back into the living room and throwing them in his face and screaming at him to get the fuck out of her house. She knew how that would play out, but it didn't matter. If he finally followed through on his threats and hit her somewhere it would show, she could call the police and have him arrested. She didn't want him arrested, though. He'd just bail out and come home. And then she was right back where she started. No. *She* had to be the one to leave. But restoring furniture wasn't enough to live on without her teaching salary. Not yet. Having a second income and the craft shows on the side meant she could save up for the first and last on the shop lease and the buildout, but if she had to rely on teaching to pay the rent, she'd never have the time or energy to even think about opening the shop. What choice did she have? Dreams deferred again. Another year treading water teaching French with her head down, and then she could try. She could get her down payment on the house back and use that. But first she had to divorce Mack and force the sale of the house. A lawyer would cost more of her money. And before everything, she had to leave him. That was another thing entirely.

She stepped lightly over to the closet and got down on her knees. She pushed aside the stack of shoe boxes piled on the floor inside and reached for the pair of Mary Janes she'd bought on clearance a year earlier. They hurt her feet and gave her blisters, so they stayed in the closet. The stubby screwdriver was right where she'd left it, inside the toe of the left shoe. She took it out and prised up the single floorboard she'd loosened during their restoration while he was at work. When it was in place, you couldn't tell it wasn't a fully lacquered and secured part of the hardwood floor. She wasn't just good at restoring *furniture.* Her dad had shown her a thing or two. His little girl, the carpenter.

The underwear went in the compartment next to the shoebox she filled with the cash she skimmed off her sales at craft fairs and garden shows. Mack always bitched about her doing those because she never made any money. As far as he knew, she barely made enough to buy new junk to fancy up. And she kept it in a box instead of a bank account because she thought he might be smart enough to install a keylogger on her computer, but he wouldn't think in a lifetime to pry up floorboards under her shoes. This cash was as good as locked away in a fortress.

She looked at the second box — the one under the floorboards with his gun and bullets. He never shot it, and she was sure he thought it was still up on the shelf up above in the closet. Hiding it from him was another insurance policy. While she could live with a beating, if he got drunk and angry enough to go looking and got his hands on the thing . . .

She thought about how good it felt in her hands. As much as she wanted to take it out and hold it, feel its reassuring weight and the deadly potential in it, she resisted. Not tonight. Not ever, if she could help it. Though she might not be able to help it.

Could I kill him? No, she realized. Because she knew she'd pay if she did. She'd go to jail. And *he* was not going to make her pay any more than she already had.

Samantha stuffed her husband's stinky silk trophy in the hole and fitted the board back into place. She replaced the screwdriver in her shoe, got up, washed her hands in the bathroom sink to get the smell of that damn perfume off. In the morning, she resolved to swallow her pride and call her dad to ask for help. She could take all the I-told-you-so's he could utter if it got her out of this house.

She went back into the front room to look at her phone and see if anyone else had liked her post. In a while, she'd go to bed and hope that Mack stayed on the sofa and didn't wake up until it was time to get ready for work.

Thirteen likes. The night was looking up.

39

DEPARTURE DAY

Sam watched Mack rifle through the laundry, digging down to the bottom of the hamper, pulling out clothes, and looking behind it while his agitation grew. "Whatcha looking for?" she asked. His head whipped around, and he made a small, startled high-pitched yip. She almost laughed, but didn't. She waited for his answer, eyebrows raised. "Maybe I can help you find it," she added.

He blushed deep red and turned away. His ears looked like if she poked one with a needle, it'd spray a firehose gout of blood like in one of those Tarantino movies she thought were so disgusting. He stuffed the clothes he'd pulled out of the hamper back in and half shoved, half kicked it into the corner with his foot. "I was looking for the pants I wore the other night.

"Oh, I washed those. You said they were dirty. Was there something in the pocket you needed?"

He straightened his back and took a deep breath. When he turned around, his face looked like she imagined it did as a boy when he got caught doing something dishonest. Wasn't that exactly what was happening now? She'd known long ago he was cheating, but it was only a few days ago that she finally had found real proof. The proverbial nipped candy bar in his pocket. And he couldn't claim it was an innocent mistake.

Finally, he said, "It's nothing." He tried to leave the bedroom, but she wouldn't step aside. He stopped in front of her and nodded for her to make way. She smiled.

"No, really. What was it? I bet I found it in the wash. If it was money, I already spent it when I went out with the girls the other night."

His expression soured. "You *know* it wasn't money."

"Then what?" She was playing a risky game, but she wanted this moment. He wasn't smart enough to talk his way out of it. He could shout and argue and even hit her if he wanted to, but he couldn't say or do anything that would cast into doubt what she knew to be true. No amount of denial or gaslighting would make the evidence disappear from under the floorboard. *The smell-tail heart.* She almost laughed at the thought. At him. She wanted this because it was the last chance she'd get to see him wrestle with her having more power than him. No matter what he did to her at this point, she was going to come out on top. With what she'd saved up combined with what her dad had promised when she called him to say she wanted to leave, she had enough for first, last, and a deposit on her own place. It had been hard to admit her dad had been right about Mack, and she almost hadn't been able to work up the nerve to make the call, but she did. And her dad hadn't said "I told you so" even once, but rather that he'd help any way he could, starting with getting her out of that house. She could stay with him and her stepmother until she could get her own place. He already knew a lawyer, and said he'd gladly pay for that. But it was time to go. The antiques store could wait, but not her departure. Not any longer.

All she had to do was be frugal for a few weeks. Save up enough so she didn't slip underwater and she could get away for good. Stand on her own and leave her mistakes behind. Eventually, everything would be all right. She was moving on, and this moment was what she wanted to leave in her wake.

In a calm voice that defied her desire to laugh in Mack's face and spite him for being pitiful and stupid, she said, "Tell me what you are looking for, and I'll tell you if I found it."

He didn't say anything. He nodded for her to get out of the way again. She stepped aside and let him leave. Though she didn't get to hear him confess, he'd all but admitted it with his sullen silence. His inability to construct even an attempt at a lie communicated clearly he was aware of what she knew. He'd gotten pass-out drunk and had forgotten about his trophy. By then, it was far too late to do anything about it. He was caught out.

Mack stomped through the kitchen into the dining room. She

heard a chair groan across the floorboards and his weight settle into it solidly as he sat to put on his work boots. She followed along, stopping by the stove to watch him.

Without looking up from his boots, he said, "You think you're so smart." It came out "smaht." She almost laughed again.

Smaht enough, Mahky Mahk.

"I'm smarter than you," she said.

Another sharp inhalation. He let this one out slowly through his nose. "Yeah, maybe you are. But I still know something you don't."

"Yeah? What's that?"

He looked up from tying his boots and said, "I know which one of your friends you shouldn't tell secrets to."

A sudden tightness grew in Sam's chest. One of *her* friends? *It can't be any of* my *friends, you stupid son of a bitch.* All the same, her mind started racing with worries about what she'd said to whom. Whether she'd told any of them that she had her stash in the hidden space she'd built in the bedroom, that she was leaving him. Was that why he was so calm? Because he knew and already had a plan to undermine her escape? No. He couldn't know because she hadn't told anyone yet. Not any of her girlfriends, anyway.

"You think I'm messing with you. Maybe I am a little," he said. "But you're smart; you'll figure things out." His accent wasn't funny to her anymore. He stood up and grabbed the small, hard-sided cooler he used as a lunch box off the dinner table. He opened the door to the garage and stepped out. He lingered a moment in the doorway, waiting. When she didn't reply, he said, "Take out steaks for dinner. I won't be late." He closed the door behind him.

Sam's mind raced. She couldn't know whose underwear he'd brought home, but she'd found hairs on his clothes too. Blond. Not all of her friends were blond. Lisa was a redhead, and Randi had dark hair like hers. Siobhan was blond and so were Sarah and Rebecca. She tried to think if any of them wore perfume like she'd smelled on him. A couple of them did, but she'd never smelled *that* scent before. At least she didn't think she had. Was it because it was mixed up with that other smell? *No. You bought it for her, didn't you, you pig? You bought her the perfume, and she wears it special for you.*

Samantha wanted to run to the closet and dig out that pair of underwear and burn them, but she stood her ground by the oven. He was goading her. He was waiting in the garage, trying to trick her into running to her secret stash and showing him where she'd hidden his trophy. She wasn't going to fall for it. A second later, she heard the garage door roll up and his car door open and slam. The Demon's engine growled to life, roaring through the house like a monster that lived in the cellar. He sat there for a moment, revving it like a teenager before he tore out of the driveway.

Sam stood where she was, listening until she heard his car roar down the road and away. Once he was gone, she sprinted for the bedroom, falling to her knees in the closet and clawing things out of the way to get to the board. She yanked it open, half expecting to see everything that she'd saved up over the last few months gone, replaced with a note that read *You think you're so smaht?*

Everything was right there where she'd left it.

She pulled out the shoebox and opened the lid. Her craft show money was still inside, bundled neatly in like denominations and bound with rubber bands. She set the box aside and reached for the second one. It was heavy and felt good in her hands. She set the box on the floor between her knees, opened the lid, and peered inside. The yellow oilcloth was still there. She unwrapped the revolver and pulled it out of the box, feeling the weight of it in her hand. She popped out the cylinder and carefully loaded five bullets in. She'd read it was safer to leave the chamber under the hammer empty. But she felt better with all five filled. It was more dangerous, yes, but it was psychologically satisfying. She wanted all the chambers to count.

She stuffed the gun in her hoodie pocket and got up to retrieve her suitcase from the basement. She was going to miss having a basement. It was unlikely that she'd find an apartment with space to continue to restore and store antiques at home. But that was temporary. She'd find a way to make it work. It'd be small pieces, things she could manage out of her car and a smaller place. And then maybe in the spring *next* year she could quit teaching. Nothing was going to stop her. She patted the gun in her pocket. Nothing.

Upstairs, she packed her favorite clothes and a few other things she'd stored away. The day had come. She was doing this. She turned to grab the last of her stuff when she heard a car door slam. She fumbled the pistol shoe box and dropped it. A box of bullets fell out and broke open, scattering rounds — the gun nuts online called them that, *rounds*—around the closet. She froze, waiting to hear the sounds of Mack walking in the front door. That was impossible. She hadn't heard his engine come back up the road or pull into the driveway. The dog wasn't barking to greet him. Still, she sat quietly, hand stuffed in her pocket, listening, wondering if she'd have to shoot him. Wondering if she could. After a minute, she let out a breath. It was probably Juanita's car next door. Samantha scrambled to collect the bullets she'd spilled. She dropped them loose into the shoe box and set it next to her suitcase. She stood. There was so much left. Her nice clothes, the rest of her shoes, the furniture in the basement, pictures and personal things. But for now, she just wanted to pack the most important belongings and get out.

She took one more look inside her secret space, to be sure. Everything was in her suitcase. Everything except the stranger's underwear. She picked them up and rubbed part of the waistband elastic between her fingers. She tried to get a good sense of the perfume scent for some other time. It was faint, but there. She'd know it when she smelled it again. A night out with the girls and hugs hello.

He's just getting into my head. None of my friends would fuck him.

But it wasn't bullshit. He'd lied to her about things before to manipulate her. Get her to change her mind, forget something shitty he'd done. Every time he'd done that, there was a tiny little itch in the back of her mind that said, *It's a lie.* Not this time. The way he'd said it, like it was meant to be a kick in the soul, had convinced her. One of her friends couldn't be trusted.

She thought about saving his souvenir to give to her lawyer. But then she set the underwear back in the hole and replaced the board. Fuck him. Let him be near what he wanted but never able to actually have it. He deserved far worse, but she only wanted out. *Remember what Dad said. When you've won, you can quit fighting.* She hadn't won yet. But this was part of it. She could get the divorce without that thing, and she didn't need to keep it with her. A trophy of her pain, her bad choice in husband, and the failure of her marriage.

First marriage. Lots of people have first *marriages.*

Samantha stood and grabbed her bag and walked through her house toward the front door. Mack left through the garage, but god damn it, she was going out through the front.

In the front room, she lingered for a moment, looking back at the house she'd lovingly redecorated. At her home. The room still smelled faintly of paint. She'd thought it would be hard to abandon it after putting so much labor and time into it. But no. After finally breaking free from him, that part was easy.

"Maxim! Maxey Max!" The dog came trotting into the room, mouth open, tongue hanging loose. His little vulpine face looked like a crazy smile, and his curled tail wagged hard. "You want to go for a ride?" The dog barked excitedly and ran up to her, waiting patiently for her to attach his leash. He was a good dog. She couldn't hold it against him that he loved Mack. She had once too.

She walked out with her dog and closed the door behind them. In the car, she dialed her father. "We're out," she told him.

"I've got the truck. Me and the boys will be over in twenty minutes." He'd shut down the build site for the day, enlisted two of his biggest laborers with promises of time and a half, and rented both a Ryder truck and a storage unit to fill with her things. She imagined what might happen if Mack came home early. She didn't want that. The idea of a pair of mountainous men with rough hands holding Mack while her father "tuned him up," as Dad said he wanted to, appealed. But more than that, she wanted him to come home to a house with big empty spaces. Without the smell of dinner cooking, the sound of their—*her*—dog greeting him, and the taste of a cold beer. "You sure everything you want us to get is on the list? Because we have room in the truck."

She looked at the dog in the passenger seat and thought about the gun in her suitcase. "Everything I couldn't carry on my own is on there. If you treat yourselves to all the beer in the fridge, that'd be fine, but I don't need anything of his."

"Okay, Sam I Am. Love you." He was the only person in the world who'd ever be allowed to call her Sam from now on, and only with *I Am* at the end like he'd always done.

"I love you, Hop on Pop."

She hung up and dialed in to work, telling them she needed to take a couple of days off, and then backed out of the driveway.

X

◆

MACK

40

NINE MONTHS BEFORE DAY ZERO

Mack **looked up** from his desk, expecting the man approaching him to be a co-worker. Gerry, perhaps, with a new location assignment. But it wasn't him, or anyone else he recognized. The others in the office watched in mute astonishment as the man marched right up to his desk, having stridden past the low swinging gate that separated the lobby from the office space without asking if he could enter. The office was an "open plan" meant to foster a collaborative work space. What it really did was force them to pretend that the person at the next desk wasn't talking too loudly about last night's game or making a personal call during working hours. Except no one pretended not to notice the stout man standing in front of Mack. No one had stopped him to ask where he thought he was going. They all stared, not making any effort to spare Mack the indignity of what was about to happen.

"Malcolm P. Roarke?" the man said. His voice was gravelly and possessed a jaded, bored tone. Mack nodded at the name plate on his desk. It read MACK ROARKE. The man didn't look amused. "I can see you're sitting at his desk. Are you he?"

"Yeah, I'm him."

The man reached into his jacket, and Mack had an awful moment where he imagined staring into the barrel of a gun before it blossomed fire. The man withdrew an envelope from his pocket instead and held it out. Mack didn't reach for it, so the man dropped it on his blotter. "You've been served, Mr. Roarke."

"With what? What do I do with this?"

"I can't advise you, sir. Have a good day." Mack thought he caught a hint of amusement in that last sentence. The process server turned and walked away. Everyone in the office waited until the man was out of the office before they approached Mack's desk to find out what had just happened.

Mack picked up the envelope and read the return address. It was from the Civil Service Division of the Sheriff's Office. Beth asked what it was. He shrugged. Gerry, his supervisor, shook his head but didn't say anything. Rob offered his condolences for the mere fact of being served process for whatever bullshit it was.

Mack tore open the envelope and withdrew the papers inside. At the top of the first sheet, it read

```
Commonwealth of Massachusetts
The Trial Court
Probate and Family Court Department
COMPLAINT FOR DIVORCE
```

Under that was the line Mack knew was coming, but still made him want to smash his fist down on his desk and break something.

```
Samantha Zamyatin-Roarke, Plaintiff, v.
Malcolm Peter Roarke, Defendant
```

Since when is she Zamyatin-*Roarke?*

"Tough break, man," Rob said. "I'll give you the number of the guy who did my brother's, if you want it. He's good. Saved him from getting taken to the—"

"Robert," Beth scolded. "Leave him alone."

Mack looked up from the paper and said, "Thanks, Rob, but I'm not getting a divorce."

Rob smirked and said, "Looks like you are, pal." Mack's stare made him back away from the desk, holding up his hands. "Whatever you say."

Beth leaned in closer. "I am so sorry. That girl never appreciated you, Mack. You deserve better than her." She turned and walked away, dragging Rob along with her before Mack could retort.

He read the paper again, scanning over each line where Samantha's assertions had been typed. He paused in the middle of the page at a paragraph marked *Item 5*.

> On several occasions during the parties' marriage, the defendant at Ripton, Massachusetts, engaged in acts of adultery as part of an ongoing sexual relationship with Siobhan McKinley, a friend of the plaintiff. The defendant has also been cruel and abusive to the plaintiff on numerous other dates and occasions.

Yes, he'd slept with Siobhan, but she'd seduced *him,* not the other way around. He'd fucked her because she was begging for it and was sticking her tits and ass out every time she saw him, and he was a man, god damn it. What did Sam expect? She'd gained weight after they got married, so if his eye wandered a little, it wasn't like she was without blame. When she wasn't in a classroom, Sam was either in the car looking for yard sales or sitting in the basement all weekend painting the junk furniture she bought and snacking. She barely stood up, let alone did any exercise. She spent her days either on her ass or her knees. Siobhan, on the other hand, was a ServiceFit instructor. She was fit as hell and always wore those yoga pants. She called them leggings, but they were tights. The way she wore them, they were a single step away from nothing at all. And she came to him wanting some attention. She talked to him. Laughed at his jokes and understood his frustrations. Siobhan *got* him.

He was only human.

So, he'd fucked her. He'd counted on her friendship with Sam being important enough to keep their secret. But she was a crazy bitch, and she must have ratted him out to his wife, burning both of them.

From across the office, Mack heard Rob whisper to Gerry, "I can't believe she had him served at work."

Mack leapt out of his chair and threw the first thing he could reach at Rob. The stapler bounced off the wall next to Rob's head, and he barked in surprise. Mack screamed, "I am not getting a divorce!" He tried to shove his desk out of the way. It screeched a half foot across the tile floor and stopped. He banged his thighs into it, bounced off, and shouted, "FUCK! YOU!" at the object. He pushed around the table and stormed toward the door. Gerry broke away from the wall with his arms held out.

"Mack. Calm down. It'll be okay. Take the rest of the day, and—"

"Keep your fucking hands off of me," he shouted as he shoved Gerry out of the way.

The supervisor staggered and fell over a rolling chair, landing on his back. Rob and Beth ran to help him. Gerry sat up, brushing away his co-workers' hands, his face bright red. "Take the day off, Roarke. Go home and use the time to write your fucking resignation letter."

"Fire me, you chickenshit." Mack stormed out of the office, slamming the low gate behind him. Rob and Beth watched him go, mouths agape.

The crumpled divorce complaint and summons remained on his desk where he'd thrown them.

41

FOUR MONTHS BEFORE DAY ZERO

The clerk stamped the form with a red seal below the judge's signature. She took the papers over to a photocopier and made duplicates. When she returned to the bar separating her work area from the public, she slid the photocopies under the gap in the bulletproof plastic shield between them. Mack had to strain to hear what she said to him as he took the papers from the tray.

"These are your copies of the abuse prevention order and the notice regarding the same. Read the notice carefully. It will explain what you need to know. This is a *final* order, by the way, and is in force for a year, as the judge already told you. During that time, you are not to have any contact with the plaintiff whatsoever. You may not contact her in any way personally or through someone else, unless authorized by the court. You must remain away from the plaintiff's residence and her workplace, even if she's not there. While this is a civil order, failure to conform to these conditions is a criminal offense and will result in your arrest and prosecution." Her brow furrowed as she glanced at her paperwork. She looked up at him and said, "I remind you that if you have any firearms, you need to surrender them to the police along with your FID card, immediately."

"I already told you people, my gun was . . . stolen."

The woman stared at him, her face screwed up with displeasure but not surprise, as if she'd heard that same line many times before. Perhaps she had. It didn't change the fact that he was telling the truth. His entire experience at the court had been one of swimming upstream against the tide of the presumption against him. The judge barely looked up from the bench when he tried to defend himself in the hearing. When she did, it was to announce that unless Ms. Zamyatin — the divorce wasn't even final and she was calling Sam by her maiden name — had anything to say, she was going to extend the restraining order for an entire year. Mack wanted to shout that it wasn't right, but he knew better than to raise his voice in court. Especially in front of a lady judge. He looked around the courtroom and saw the female clerk, stenographer, and even a lady sheriff's deputy. *These bitches are all looking out for each other. This whole thing is a setup from soup to nuts.*

The clerk behind the glass partition brought him back to the present. "You need to discuss the status of your firearms with the police. If you haven't surrendered them, you're in violation of the order."

He rolled his eyes. "Fine." He hadn't spoken to the police and had no intention to, now or later. He wasn't supposed to have a gun, and he didn't. So what was the point of talking? He could tell the truth, that his soon-to-be-ex-wife took it, and cops would still be cops. All of them, from the judge to the court clerk and the bailiffs, were automatically on her side. He had to work to prove himself innocent every step of the way. If he told them she had it and didn't have a license for it, they'd probably just think he was lying to retaliate and get her in trouble and then he'd end up in an even worse situation. No. He couldn't see an upside to saying anything at all. Let her get busted with his piece and no license. Knowing her, she probably threw it away or gave it to her father or something. He thought about dropping by the old man's place to ask about it, but the guy had never liked him. Last thing he needed was to get popped for trespassing. Or worse, a violation of this order if she happened to be visiting him. Which brought up another thing.

He pointed to the no contact provision of the order. "How am I supposed to talk to her about selling the house when —"

"Sir, you have the forms. If you have any questions about them, you need to consult with your attorney. *I* can't advise you."

"But you just went through . . ."

The woman turned away from the glass, leaving Mack standing at the window, staring at her. She seemed unaffected by his gaze as she took her seat at a desk in the middle of the office.

He looked at the heavy bolts holding the thick shield in place. To the right of the window was a solid door with a sturdy-looking metal keypad above the knob. He'd seen a couple of people enter through it while he was waiting for the clerk to process his paperwork. They were careful to both block the code from view when they entered it and to linger in the threshold, pulling the door shut behind them before moving on. They were cautious. But they couldn't stay behind a barrier all the time. They all drove to work, and there wasn't a fuckin' bulletproof shield in the parking lot.

He took another good look at the woman. She was talking on the phone and smiling. The bitch didn't care that she'd just delivered the written form of his railroad job.

All in on it together.

Out in the hallway, he paused to read the papers in his hands. They weren't any different than ones he'd received when this whole thing got started, except for the dates, and that this one was marked *Final* instead of *Temporary*. Everything else was the same bullshit lies and exaggerations concocted by Sam and her new boyfriend to punish him.

Boyfriend. That didn't take long.

He suspected that she'd been seeing him before they split. That would fit. While Mack slept with her friend, that didn't *mean* anything. He always came home to his wife. He didn't love Siobhan. Sam was the one who was unfaithful. She'd lost faith. And filing for cause was another way of hurting him when she could have gone with a no-fault divorce and not dragged his name through shit.

He considered balling up the papers and throwing them away, but there wasn't a trash can he could see in the courthouse hallway. It was as if they were afraid that people angry about being abused and picked apart by bitch judges might start a fire or hide a bomb in one. An image of a trash can exploding and forcing the employees to come streaming out from behind their locked doors and protective glass walls flashed in his mind. He watched their gossamer shades run through the hallways in a panic while he calmly walked behind them, the weight in his hand kicking as he—

A woman stepped into the hall with her lawyer and gasped, snapping him out of his fantasy. He looked around to see what had startled her. There was no one in the hall but the three of them and another couple of empty suits way over by the staircase. And she wasn't reacting to them.

Can't be me. I was just thinking.

It dawned on him that he'd begun scowling, his lips pulling away from his teeth while he was lost in his fantasy. He tried to find a suitably neutral expression for a setting as austere as the Middlesex County Probate and Family Court. His face didn't feel like it was cooperating, though. He tried smiling; the muscles around his mouth and eyes twitched. Her look went from concern to fear, which made him feel just fine. The woman's attorney grabbed her by the elbow and led her away. She tottered ahead of him on high heels that clacked on the marble floors. Another slut. Mack watched them go, wondering where the sucker they'd just screwed over was. Somewhere in the building was a guy just like him, standing with a restraining order in one hand and his dick in the other.

This whole place was making him feel less stable; he was sinking in quicksand. He needed a beer. It'd help settle both his stomach and his nerves. He remembered seeing a bar around the corner; it had some stupid generic name the hipster faggots liked, like Pub or Drinks. He'd passed it on his walk from the parking lot to the courthouse. He tried to gather his composure a little more and walked out the door to find a place to sit for a while and have a couple before he headed home to a house full of half-empty boxes he needed to finish packing. Sam's fucking lawyer had gotten the judge to order that he agree to sell the house if he couldn't buy her out. Of course he couldn't afford to do that. She'd made the down payment from her trust fund, and he didn't have some rich grandfather who'd left him a bundle like she did. They hadn't owned it long enough to have any equity to split — not with all the money they'd borrowed to finance the remodel. She wouldn't agree to a payment plan either, so they had to make . . . What had the lawyer called it? "A quick and equitable distribution of property." There was nothing "equitable" about it, he thought. She was getting paid money she didn't earn, and he was getting screwed out of a house he'd invested years of sweat and labor in.

He walked around the block, stomping through the dingy rain puddles pooling in the uneven sidewalks and found the place right where he remembered seeing it. The sign swinging in the breeze outside of the pub read THE BAR. Beside the name of the place was painted a white wig sitting on a table next to a mug of beer. He got it now. The Bar. He thought of Daffy Duck. *Ha ha. It is to laugh.*

He stepped inside and immediately regretted it. Everyone inside except him and the staff was wearing a suit. It was a liquor oasis for lawyers working the courthouse. It was early, and the place wasn't busy, but still it was clear who was welcome and who wasn't. He wanted a drink, though, and he wasn't going to go pay to get his car out of the garage to find another watering hole. Not when there was a perfectly good row of bar stools and taps right there.

He took a seat at the bar. The bartender approached him and asked if he wanted a lunch menu. "No. Just a drink."

"What can I get you?" she asked.

He shook off his coat and draped it over the stool next to him. "'Gansett."

"Which one? We have the Temple Sticke Altbier and the lager."

"What the hell is a sticky alt beer?"

"Gotcha," she said, and walked off to pour his drink. A couple of women in suits in the corner were looking at him and appeared to be holding back laughter. He tried to ignore them and checked his phone for e-mails. He'd had to silence it when he went into the hearing and had forgotten about it until he was sitting there with nothing else to do. His inbox was empty. Sam was constantly on her cell, checking in with her social media garbage. He had a smartphone so he could look things up on Google and get e-mails from work while he was out on the job. And since he'd been fired, he didn't have work e-mails anymore. When he got home, it went on the table by the sofa, and he didn't look at it again until morning unless someone called. No one ever called. The kind of time she wasted on her phone was staggering. She'd sit through an entire ball game, never once looking up at the television, playing some game or typing with someone on Fakebook. Instead of talking to him or even just reading a damn magazine, she had long conversations with people she'd never actually stood in a room with and wouldn't ever meet, living a fantasy life while their marriage withered. Whether or not she realized it, she'd forced him to go looking for someone who would pay attention to him. Someone who really *got* him. And her "good friend" Siobhan had been there.

He downloaded the Facebook app onto his phone. While it installed, the bartender came back with his beer. She set it down and left without asking if he wanted anything else, which suited him just fine. After another minute, the app opened and he was prompted to log in.

He clicked CREATE NEW ACCOUNT. It asked him for a name and a password. He entered his grandfather's name, Jack DeLuca, and created a profile with a fake birthdate and hometown. He declined searching his contacts list for "friends," and eventually was released from the setup and could go looking around. He touched the search bar at the top of the screen and entered *Sam Roarke.* No result. There were plenty of other Roarkes listed—his sister in New Hampshire and his asshole cousin in Boston at the top of the list—but no Sam. He tried again with the hyphenated last name she'd put on the original divorce complaint. *Samantha Zamyatin* came up in the results instead.

Shoulda known.

He clicked the link and started scrolling down his wife's page. Pictures of the antique shit she restored were mixed with videos of his fucking dog, Maxim, and other cloyingly cute images with inspirational garbage typed on top of them.

TO BE BETTER THAN YOU'VE EVER BEEN
YOU HAVE TO DO SOMETHING YOU'VE NEVER DONE

He held down his gorge and scrolled to the pictures she'd posted of their home restoration and the fire pit that he'd risked heat stroke to build last summer so she could use it when the weather got chilly. She made exactly two fires in the goddamned thing before it was "too cold to sit out." He'd said, "I thought that was the point of a fire pit." She didn't argue. She just typed something into her phone and ignored him. He hated the way she did that and felt angry sitting there in the Bar just thinking about it. She always dismissed what he said like he was a stupid child.

The women in the corner laughed again, and he looked up from his phone at them. He caught them looking and they turned away quickly, one of them holding a hand up to her face like a blinder, as if blocking her view of him meant he couldn't see her. They chittered again like loud insects rubbing their legs together, looking for a male to decapitate and consume.

He went back to the top of Sam's page and clicked on the link for her pictures. There was one of her and the skinny guy she'd run off with. The guy's name was under the picture. *James. Not Jim or Jimmy.* He touched it and the screen changed to the man's feed. And right there at the top was a selfie of him and Sam at Walden Pond. *Fucking*

Walden Pond. Like she ever read a book, let alone that one. Mack hadn't read it either, but he figured her cuck boyfriend, *James,* probably had. He had his arm around her, and her head rested on his shoulder in the picture. They were smiling like they were on their honeymoon. *Faggot,* he thought. He clicked the word ABOUT on the page and looked at the guy's profile. He lived in Worcester. He taught at a fancy private school. An *Academy.*

He wouldn't be hard to track down.

The bartender came back and asked if he wanted another beer. She looked impatient. Mack hadn't realized that his glass was empty. He'd drunk it on autopilot. He looked at his watch. Almost an hour had passed without him noticing, and the bar was starting to get busier with the lunch crowd. He smiled and said he'd like to settle up. She left a slip on the bar and walked off without another word. *Eight bucks for a 'Gansett. Fucking rip-off.* He pulled out his wallet and dug out a ten. The bartender took it and came back a minute later with two singles. She dropped his change on the bar, expecting him to get up and leave it there. He pocketed it. She was pretty, but stuck up. No smile for him meant no tip for her. *Another bitch.*

Mack stood and walked out of the bar. As he left, he noted that he couldn't see a clear emergency exit out the back of the place. There had to be one, but it wasn't easy to spot. The front door was the only obvious way in or out. If there was a fire here, a whole bunch of sluts in suits might burn to death. The thought made him genuinely smile as he pushed out into the afternoon sun.

42

FORTY-FIVE DAYS BEFORE DAY ZERO

He sat in his car across the highway watching people file in and out of his house through the spotter's binoculars he'd bought at Red's Armory up in Nashua. Almost all couples. All greedily looking at the work *he'd* done, deciding whether to put down money for *his* labor — and he was going to get none of it.

A couple came walking down the driveway toward their car dressed up like fucking Halloween. She had a hairdo like some chick from the fifties, short bangs in front and a red bandana wrapped around the back. He looked like a low-rent greaser Elvis. No way they'd have the borrowing power to buy. But then they got in their brand-new hybrid car and pulled out a smartphone the size of a brick. He watched them make a call sitting in the road like they had no idea they'd parked behind a blind curve. They smiled and laughed, and he wished a big dump truck full of road salt would tear around the bend and rear-end their shitty little Prius.

They ended the call and kissed. He set his binocs down next to his new gun and watched them drive away. He thought about following them, but decided to stay put. If they ended up buying the house, he'd have plenty of time to figure out who they were. *And* it wasn't like he wouldn't know where they lived.

43

DAY ZERO

Mack turned the house key over in his fingers, looking at the edges barely starting to wear after only three years of use. And then, what? He had to fucking give it away? The broker had messaged him looking for the key. It went to Eleonora and Evan Pereira's house now. The Halloween couple. How the hell did a pair of ghouls like that get the money to buy a house? Probably a trust fund like Sam's, but even bigger. More unearned money. Privileged shits, when he had to work and still lost everything. He thought about them living in the house he'd restored. Eating in the dining room where he'd vaulted the ceiling and built out the breezeway to widen it. Showing their friends his work and being congratulated on it as if they'd done a thing to the place. Sleeping in his bedroom. Fucking in it.

He set the key down on the table next to the notice he'd gotten in the mail today that the "nisi period" was over and the divorce was final. It was *all* over. *What's that stupid saying? Tomorrow is the first day of the rest of your life. That makes today what?*

Day Zero.

Sam was gone. She wouldn't talk to him. She'd blocked his number and his e-mail address. He hadn't been careful enough, and she'd even found his fake profile on Facebook and blocked that too. Got a fucking restraining order out on him. Claiming he was stalking her, and she felt in danger. He didn't even know where she was living. She'd taken the dog just to fuck with him. And now, as of today, it was all gone. The house, his dog, his job, and his wife. All he owned was his tools, his wedding ring, and the Challenger Demon. His unemployment was running out, and without a job, he'd have to stop making insurance payments for the car soon enough. If he got caught driving without insurance, they'd take that too and he'd have nothing left but a restraining order, a worthless gold band, and this house key. It didn't go to *his* house anymore. That part stung. Fuck them and everybody like them.

Last time he'd been there, to pick up some mail to get to know them a little better, they still hadn't changed the locks. His key worked in the front door. He could let himself in anytime. He hadn't wanted to test the alarm system to see if they'd reset that yet, but figured they probably were as lazy and stupid about that as they were about the locks.

He figured he'd pay them a visit soon. He had to go up to New Hampshire first, sell the tools, use the money to pick up some different ones to make his visit more productive. More interesting.

They'd help him get everything back. With the right incentive.

XI

◆

ASCENDING

44

TWELVE WEEKS AFTER CLOSING

The **man in front** repeated himself. "Where is your wife?"

Mack blinked hard trying to make sense of what the man was saying. *My wife? My wife. She's not here. She's . . . I don't know where. That's why* I'm *here.* He tried to speak and almost vomited instead. He took another deep breath through his mouth and tried again. "My . . . wife. My—"

"Where is Eleonora?" The man's accent and Mack's throbbing head made it hard to parse what he said. *My wife's name is Sam . . . Sam-antha. Not Ell-ee-nora. Who the hell is . . .* As it dawned on him what they wanted, Mack almost laughed. His face hurt when a small smile crept up his mouth, and he winced instead. "I'm . . . not . . . I'm not—"

The man moved with frightening speed, and the brass knuckles impacted solidly against Mack's sternum. It felt like he was having a heart attack. The pain spread out from the center of him and the lights went out for a moment. When he opened his eyes again, the man said, "You are as original as you are convincing, Mr. Pereira. Don't think we haven't heard that before. It took some time to track you and your wife down. But a little virus told us where you were, eventually. A little virus that was in one computer, and then in another, and that led to . . . Well, the whole thing is rather boring. Let's just say, you are not as good at hiding as the man who *originally* stole from us. We didn't know what was missing for a long time. But once we did . . . That you stole from *him* is no insult, of course. He was a blyad' kusok der'ma."

The Russian with the gun broke in. "Mortvyy kusok der'ma seychas."

His partner agreed. "Yes. A *dead* piece of shit now." The man continued. "But he did cause our concern quite a significant loss of money and business, and we're here to recoup on that loss, Mr. Pereira."

"Not. Me. I'm not him," he choked out.

"This is *your* house, and you are *in* it. We are not here to fuck around. You cannot protect her. So tell us, where is your fucking wife?"

"I'm not—"

The man backhanded Mack. He fell over, like he'd been trying not to do. Something moved, skipping across his tongue and back into his throat. He choked, and a molar fell out of his mouth, landing on the cushion. Mack looked at the bloody tooth, this piece of him, no longer a part of the whole, and realized they were going to kill him. He knew it before—the gun communicated it clearly enough—but this little piece of him spoke loudest. *They're gonna take you apart until there's nothing big enough left to call Mack Roarke. Just pieces.*

That had been his intention all along. Get his wife over to the house and show her what he had to show—say his piece—and then call the cops. And when they arrived . . .

Plans changed.

A heavy thud from the cellar drifted up to them in the lull. The Russian men didn't seem to notice. "I'm. Not. Lying."

"Who are you if you aren't the man who lives in this house?"

Mack pushed himself up on the couch. The tooth rolled off the edge and bounced away on the hardwood floors into a shadow. Gone. "Mack." It sounded like a cough. He cleared his throat and tried again. "I'm Malcolm Roarke. We . . . I used to own this place. The Pereiras . . . bought it."

The Russian reared back to hit him again, Mack held up his hands and pleaded the best he could. "I can show you. My wallet." Slowly, Mack reached back to pull out his billfold, expecting the Russian to stop him. But he didn't. Why would he? Evan was just some guy. A citizen. Well, maybe a thief according to them—he tried to reconcile what they said about Evan and Nelle stealing from them with what he thought he knew about the couple—but not a gangster out doing gangster shit, by any means. Why would he have anything hidden behind him? And of course, the other one still had his gun aimed right in Mack's face. If he came back with anything but his wallet, he'd never even get a shot off.

It hurt to turn even the little bit to reach his wallet. He grunted when he twisted. His heart pounded, and he wanted to take a deep breath, but he just couldn't get in enough air, no matter how hard he tried. He got his fingers on his wallet and pulled it out. He flipped it open and tried removing his driver's license. The Russian snatched the entire thing away from him. He looked at the license and back at Mack and then back again before throwing the license and the wallet in the cold fireplace.

"If you aren't Evan Pereira, what the fuck are you doing here?"

He tried to smile again, but couldn't. He grimaced a kind of rictus and felt a little saliva or blood — probably both — slip out of his mouth. "I'm here for the . . . same reason you . . . are. They . . . stole from me." He took a breath and said, "They're in the basement. They're tied up in the basement."

"Tied up. Downstairs."

Mack nodded. He brushed at the drool hanging off his chin and wiped the pink smear on the back of his hand onto the sofa.

The man's face clouded. He looked at his partner and spoke in Russian again. The man with the gun shook his head and said one of the few words Mack understood. "Nyet." He wasn't much of a talker, it seemed. The other one said something else, and his partner nodded. "Da."

Another sound drifted up from below. This time the Russians heard it. The one who spoke English returned his attention to Mack. "These people, they stole from you?"

Mack's jaw was hurting, and he could feel his face swelling where he'd been hit with the knucks. He didn't want to speak if he didn't have to. He nodded.

"I understand. I am sorry for the confusion."

Mack sighed. He raised his hands in a what-can-you-do gesture.

"But our debt comes first." He turned to his partner. "Ubey yego."

The black pupil erupted with a bright yellow flash. Mack never saw it.

45

N**elle clenched her teeth** and made tight fists as the thunderous clamor of Mack's stomping above their heads sounded like he might be returning to the cellar door. She looked up anxiously, waiting to see him come careening down the stairs, ready to deliver what he'd promised a moment ago, but he didn't appear. He'd stopped. She couldn't tell if he was lingering in the bathroom or the front room — not that it mattered. She wondered if he was trying to text his ex again with her phone. *I can take everything away from you,* he'd said. Except, there *was* something he wanted from them that he couldn't just take. Something they had to give willingly: cooperation. When another round of texting didn't work and he came back downstairs, unable to convince Samantha to come over, that was it.

The best case she could imagine was a prolonged standoff with the police before he murdered everyone in the house and then himself. Wasn't that how men like this worked? They started by going to their parents' or a girlfriend's house to get warmed up — to work up the taste for it and close off their options behind them — and then they went to the office or a school or a concert. This wasn't Roarke getting his momentum. What was happening now was just a stall in the plan — a pause while he put the last pieces in place, because his wife wouldn't take his calls. And like most people these days, she wouldn't accept a call from an unknown number. When she listened to that voicemail, she sure as hell wasn't *coming over.* Samantha's silence wasn't the end of the storm, though. It was a lull in the weather. The eye would eventually pass, and the storm would rage harder than ever, until everything was laid waste. Roarke would kill them as soon as he decided that they didn't have a role in his plan any longer. Whether or not Samantha returned Nelle's call, the black clouds were in motion. Nelle couldn't wait for Samantha's silence to doom them. If they didn't get out right then, they never would.

She looked around the cellar for something, anything, she could try to reach to help get free of the tape. An exposed nail head or even just a sharp corner. There wasn't anything that looked helpful. Nothing stuck out. Everything on the shelves in their bulk store larder was useless. There were boxes of Ziploc baggies, dryer sheets, and a value-size bottle of laundry detergent — canned food, boxes of mac and cheese, Smack Ramen, and condiments. And among all of it there wasn't a single thing with a sharp edge. In the rest of the cellar were boxes and boxes of books and garbage bags of ill-fitting, out-of-style clothes they couldn't bear to give up. And the wine rack — minus the bottle that had been smashed against the foundation wall. He'd plucked out an expensive one they'd been saving for a special occasion, and she'd mindlessly thought, *No please, not the Stag's Leap,* before it occurred to her that it didn't matter at all which one he smashed over her head. This was the point at which all there was left to do was hold hands and wait for the end.

That was it.

She jerked in her chair, trying to move it. The legs skidded slightly on the concrete floor. Not far, but far enough to encourage her to do it a second and a third time. The tape around her ankles kept her from moving quickly, but it didn't keep her from moving. She was able to shift the chair an inch or so forward, turning a little left, and then another couple of inches to the right. Making her way bit by bit. The distance between them felt uncrossable. It was only ten or twelve feet, but moving an inch at a time, it seemed like it would take days. That was time she didn't have. So she worked harder. The chair flexed as she moved. *If only the damn thing would break.* It held together, but loosened and flexed more with her effort, giving her a little more mobility. Two inches instead of one. She moved double the distance now. A small victory was still a victory.

Nelle scooted across the floor, thankful for the felt pads she'd stuck on the bottom to keep the inexpensive chair from scratching up the hardwood upstairs. They dragged a little on the rough concrete, making it harder to slide than if the ends of the chair legs were plastic or bare wood. Still, she was moving more or less quietly, instead of scraping. That was good enough. The tape at her midsection kept her from leaning forward and getting up on the balls of her feet, but it didn't matter; as long as she could twist side to side, she could make it another little bit. And another, until she was halfway there.

Evan watched her come closer, his eyes darting from her to the stairs and back again. Nelle wanted to look back, to see if he was trying to warn her. *He's right behind me, isn't he?* was a joke they made often. She froze, waiting for the feeling of a heavy hand on her shoulder — the blow to the back of her head. She let out a breath. Evan nodded for her to come closer, flexing his fingers. He'd figured out what she wanted before she had to try to explain it to him. He was her best friend and soul mate, finished her sentences, and always knew what to get her for her birthday. Without her having to tell him, *Pull at the tape around my wrists,* he knew. She loved him so.

She scuttered her chair closer and closer still, until she was right next to him, then twisted around so she was facing away and backed up. She stopped when her hand jammed in between the weight bench and the chair. It hurt like hell, but the gag deadened her sob, so she let it out instead of trying to stifle it. It wasn't any louder than the chair legs on the floor. No louder than Roarke upstairs, doing whatever it was he was up to.

She felt Evan's fingers close around hers and squeeze, and for a moment she feared that he hadn't actually divined her intentions and instead was going to merely hold her hand. It was just a moment's reassurance, though. He let go, and she felt him starting to pick at the tape. His breathing hastened, and she felt his pulling little by little, loosening the tape the same way she'd crossed the room: by increments. A little bit would eventually become enough, given time.

The security system chirped. Was Mack leaving? Had he had a change of heart and decided to abandon his plan? No, Nelle told herself. If he was going anywhere, it was only to come back with something worse in mind and hand.

They heard footsteps overhead. Heavy bodies that made the floorboards above them groan. Evan stopped pulling, and they both looked at the ceiling with wide, frightened eyes. Nelle imagined policemen, standing resolute in crisp blue uniforms and shining badges. But policemen having responded to . . . what? She could've walked out into the front yard and screamed, and the neighbors across the highway wouldn't notice. No. It was not the police. She hadn't heard the doorbell ring. Had they knocked and she didn't hear? Why would he open the door for anyone? If it was a couple of Jehovah's Witnesses or one of those fucking Comcast assholes, they'd never know Mack wasn't supposed to be the one to answer the door. He could politely say he wasn't interested—even take a flyer or a copy of the *Watchtower*—wish them a nice holiday weekend, and shut the door softly, locking it after them, and that would be the end of it. But that would take a minute, wouldn't it? He had to go open it and say no and shut the door. And it sounded like they were inside. Whoever it was, it gave her and Evan at least a minute more than they had without the interruption. Whoever it was, she hoped they were persistent—kept Roarke's attention while she and Evan got free. Whether they were religious or secular salespeople, she was thankful they were working on the Saturday of a long weekend. *Thank all the gods for capitalism!*

But . . . they were *inside*. They probably weren't salesmen. She avoided the most frightening implication and tried to focus.

She nodded impatiently at Evan to start picking again, and he did. Though now he seemed distracted. His brow was creased in worry, and he glanced toward the stairs frequently.

Heavy rushed footsteps overhead.

Nelle tried to gasp at the sound of it, but the tape over her face kept her from doing anything but taking a shuddering, wet snuffle though her nose, followed immediately by another short blast of snot.

Evan's fingers worked harder and faster, and his breathing was becoming frantic.

He didn't stop when they heard the loud thump above and the sound of whoever it was collapsing on the floor. They knew it wasn't Mack going down. There was no way. More heavy footsteps thundered above them, and Evan picked harder. Nelle couldn't feel any difference in the tape binding her. She tried wringing her wrist, hoping that would loosen things and make Evan's job easier. It didn't seem to have any effect except to pull painfully at her skin and hair. She tried again and her wrist moved a little more. And then it caught again.

It wasn't working.

She was breathing so fast she was beginning to feel dizzy. She tried to control her breath, afraid she might hyperventilate, but couldn't do it. They were running out of time. Something bad was going on upstairs and, whatever happened, she knew time was not theirs.

She heard a voice. Not Roarke's. Oh, how well she'd come to know his voice in such a short time. Not deep or high, but midtoned with a hint of gravel, like someone who didn't smoke but liked his whiskey. A good voice for radio or maybe audiobooks if it weren't for the tones of condescension and threat or the implacable Massachusetts accent. No, this was not his voice. It was much scarier.

Nelle dropped her head in frustration. She was ready to give up, grab Evan's hand, and ride their descent to the end. The smell of pinot noir was stronger over by her husband. The bottle had smashed behind him and spilled wine pooled under the weight bench. Dark shards of glass winked up at her, glistening with wet red beads she'd never taste again. She wished it hadn't gone to waste; she'd have liked one more glass before dying. One more bottle with friends. The special one that was now puddled at their feet.

Evan picked and picked. His quickened breath told her he was growing frustrated and more worried. He might have sobbed behind his gag.

And then another idea occurred to her.

She tried to stop his fingers from grabbing at the tape, but she couldn't reach his hand while he worked. She shook her head and grunted a soft but insistent "no" at him. He paused. She shuffled away from him. He pleaded with her to stay put. Let him keep at it. She ignored him and lined herself up as best she could with the biggest, thickest piece of glass she could see. A part of the bottle base, with a long, vicious-looking shard pointing straight up.

She looked to her left at Evan. His cheek above the cut was swollen, and the blood coating the side of his face was turning maroon in the dark basement. She couldn't smile through the duct tape to reassure him, so she winked. He blinked in response. Then she rocked toward him and then away. Left and right and harder and again and once more until she fell over.

The chair didn't make a sound hitting the floor because her shoulder and arm took all of the impact. There was still a loud pop she feared was her shoulder dislocating, and her elbow blossomed pain. A small piece of glass jammed into her biceps. She didn't want to scream, but it was so hard not to. It hurt so much, tears sprung from her eyes and she saw stars. Before today, she'd never realized that was not just a turn of phrase — "saw stars." Bright points of light erupted behind her eyelids. She wondered if she'd hit her head going down. The cellar came back into focus, and she tried feeling for the shard she'd aimed at. Evan grunted excitedly. She thought she might have heard him attempting to say, "Up, up," and so she pushed herself a little in a direction that felt like up.

Her hand brushed against something wet. It made a tinkling sound as it skittered away from her clumsy fingers. She scooted again and grabbed at the shard a second time. The sharp edge bit into her fingers, but she didn't let go. She held on and felt around the piece, trying to find the point without hurting herself any worse than she already had. She found the tip and started digging at the tape at her wrist.

Something heavy thudded upstairs — a body — and she stopped for a second before renewing her effort at a quicker pace. She listened while she tried to jab at where the tape felt like it was around her numb wrist. She pushed and tested and felt the glass pierce the tape. She did it again and wrenched her wrist as much as she could, trying to start the tear she could finish without the glass. She had no idea whether she was cutting it, or merely making random punctures in the binding that would do no good at all.

Then it worked.

She pulled, and the sound of the tape ripping was like cloth tearing. She inhaled sharply; it seemed so loud in the basement. But Roarke didn't come running to see what it was. She pulled again and her arm twisted around free. She wriggled out of that, losing most of the fine hairs on her wrist and maybe a little skin. She slid her arm out from under her, experiencing another long moment of disorienting pain. It passed, and she set to work sawing at the tape around her midsection. And then her other wrist. When both hands and her body were loose, she tore at the tape holding her legs.

Free from the chair, she pushed up onto her hands and knees. Her left shoulder hurt bad — *real* bad, the kind of pain that could make a person crack teeth trying to grit through it — and it wouldn't support her. She almost fell, but she caught herself and got up on shaky legs.

She hobbled over to her husband and cut him free. The glass kept nipping her fingers with small cuts, but she didn't care. The slices were short and shallow; as long as she didn't go too deep or cut a tendon, she could take it. The next unbidden thought to enter her mind was, *Fuck your tendons. Fuck your fingers. Having a hook for a hand is better than dying.*

Freed, Evan reached up pulled his gag off. She winced at the movement of the gash in his cheek as the tape came away from his face, but he didn't seem to notice. Or perhaps he was beyond caring. The tape left a square of irritated red skin on his cheek where the blood from his wound had flowed and dried over the tape. It was a terribly odd look, and it gave her pause while she tried to reconcile the image of it with what she expected her husband to look like.

He removed her gag gently, though as quickly as he could. She spit out the underwear and tried to kiss him. He winced and pulled away from her. Then leaned down and gave her a light kiss before whispering urgently. His voice was a croak, and it sounded like his lips were numb. But she understood. "We gotta go." They looked at the ceiling. An unsettling silence had descended, and everything was quiet upstairs. A lump grew in her throat that felt like she'd swallowed her gag.

Evan nodded to the wooden door behind them. "That way." It was barred with a two-by-four and a latch lock. Beyond that, up a short flight of concrete steps were the steel storm doors that led out into the back yard. "We'll go to the Darnielles' next door and call for help." He didn't say what they both knew: neither of them was in any condition to fight. They had to run or they would die.

"Juanita and Colin won't be home until Monday. There's no one to let us in." Her throat was so dry. It hurt to speak.

"I don't care. We'll break a window. We've got to get help. You call, and I'll look for a weapon. Maybe Colin has a gun in the house."

The thought of having a shootout with Roarke ... or whoever else ... seemed suicidal. Maybe not as much as going upstairs and trying to have a fistfight with him, but still. Maybe Colin Darnielle *would* have a gun and they could hide and wait with it for the cops to come. And if someone followed, and they saw him first before he spotted them ...

She hoped Juanita and Colin had a whole collection of guns. An arsenal.

Such are desperate dreams made of.

They started toward the bulkhead door. Nelle had to hold Evan steady. Despite being awake, he was still dizzy and unsure on his feet. As much as she wanted to get out the door and put distance in between them and Mack, her husband definitely wasn't up for a long run. He seemed barely fit for the sprint across the yard. They had no other choice. The only two ways out of the basement were through the bulkhead doors or up the stairs.

Nelle wasn't ready to face what was upstairs. Not yet. Not ever.

Evan stopped. Nelle said, "What is it?"

"My glasses. He knocked off my glasses. Do you see them?" Evan wasn't blind without his specs, but he wasn't entirely sighted either. She cast a quick look around, trying to see if they were anywhere out in the open. She didn't want to look any harder for them. He could see well enough to make out a door and her. He could squint and find *9* and *1* on the telephone.

"Forget about 'em. You need new ones anyway." She shrugged closer under Evan's arm and tried to hurry. Pain arced up the back of her calf, and she almost fell. She yelped. Her guts cramped at how loud the unbidden utterance had been. She might as well have screamed, *Come and stop us! We're escaping!*

"What is it?" Evan whispered.

She looked at her foot and hissed, "Shit." A long shard of green glass stuck out of her heel on the same side as her hurt ankle. She reached down and tried to pull it out. It was slick with her blood, and her trembling fingers made it hard to get ahold of. It took two tries, but she slid it out of her heel. The length of the shard that had pierced her made her stomach do flips as it seemed to keep coming and coming like a magician's rainbow handkerchief. The wound was deep. Maybe an inch. She'd never thought that seemed like much, not until she held a piece of red-stained glass that had been that far inside her flesh. Gritting her teeth, she stood for a second, trying to deal with the flare of pain that was growing. The raw hole rent in her heel screamed. It bled. She tried to take a step. It hurt so much to put any pressure on it she almost fell. Still, she could walk on the ball of her foot. She had to — this couldn't be the thing that stopped them. Not now that they were free and so close to getting away. She couldn't be the reason they died. They hobbled a few more steps, and she stopped and looked back. Blood stained the floor like a trail out of a fairy tale. "Fuuuck."

Evan let go of her and staggered back to grab the duct tape and the underwear that had been in her mouth. "I'm sorry," he said, holding them close to his face to see what they were. "I'll buy you a new pair." He meant it. He was sorry for ruining them. She couldn't have cared less, and it made her want to laugh, but then he pressed the cotton up against her wound and began to wrap it tight with tape, and the faint feeling of mirth she'd felt abandoned her. When he finished, he pulled her back up to her feet and together they hobbled the last few feet to the cellar door.

Now neither of them were steady on their legs. They held each other close; their escape like a three-legged race. She almost laughed again at the thought, then worried that she was coming undone.

A loud sound, unmistakably a gunshot, erupted in the house, and Nelle felt the bottom fall out of the ecstasy of their near escape. That was the sound of something ending; definitely not the beginning of their salvation. Roarke had killed whoever it was in their house, and now he'd be coming down to finish what he started.

Evan let go of her and lifted the two-by-four blocking the door out of its brackets. The thing was wedged in there, and it took some effort, but the board came free. "We should keep that," Nelle whispered. She imagined bashing Roarke in the head with it. Killing him was better than running, wasn't it? Much better. But all they had was a piece of wood that either one of them would probably fall over trying to swing, and he had a gun. Evan held on to it.

"When I get this door open, you run."

"*We* run," she insisted.

"That's what I said."

Nelle didn't argue. She stepped into the dark stairwell, tripping on the bottom step and catching herself against the wall. Pain shot up her leg, and she jammed a finger. All the little hurts felt like huge humiliations. *Riiight. Run. Keep it together.* Her shoulder and elbow and arm and foot all hurt, but she had clear eyes and no concussion. She had to keep it together for the both of them.

Evan twisted the latch bar that unlocked the storm doors and slid it back. He pushed against the steel door, and sunlight streamed in. He looked like death in the daylight, blood covering half his face. Nelle lost a little more of her optimism at the sight of him. He looked better in the dark. The shadows had hidden how bad things really were. He needed stitches. Evan's cheek was bruised and swollen, and his eye was closing. Even if they got to the hospital right away, she worried he'd lose his eye. If it weren't for the coagulated blood gummed up in the slash, she imagined Evan's cheekbone would be visible. White and wrong in the sunlight.

Cut to the bone or not, he's still standing. Keep going.

He pushed the door open wider. The hinges creaked loudly. It had never occurred to them to oil them — who cared if the bulkhead squeaked?

Footsteps overhead came crashing across the floor and toward the cellar stairs. Evan threw the door open the rest of the way, the latch catching it and keeping the thing from slamming back down on top of them. "Go."

The steps behind them thundered under Roarke's weight. Evan snatched the two-by-four that had been bracing the door out of Nelle's hands and shouted, "Go!"

The bullet that hit the wall next to them sent fragments of concrete pelting into Evan's face, and he flinched.

"STOY!"

Evan stepped in front of Nelle to block Roarke's next shot. She froze as the unfamiliar voice shouted again. "Stoy! Ostanovis' pryamo tam!" She knew she should run. Hurry out through the door and across the lawn. She looked over her shoulder into the daylight and winced at the painful brightness of it.

She thought she saw a girl standing in the yard. Her broken little body teetering on bent legs and an arm that reached out, beckoning, *this way.* She wanted to go, follow the child, escape. But the sunlight hurt her eyes, and the child frightened her because seeing her meant she'd lost touch with reality. What was real?

The sound of the gunshot made her breath catch and her muscles seize, as if the gun had fired an interruption in time instead of bullets. It was thunderous in the cellar and seemed to come from everywhere at once. Stabbing little bees stung her neck and face. That was real. Had to be. She blinked, and the girl in the yard enticing her away was gone. Just stark sunlight on green grass and the fairy-tale darkness of the woods beyond. Of course, she was never there. Nelle turned her back on escape.

Another man stepped out from behind the one holding the gun.

Calmly he said, "Mrs. Pereira. Close that door and come back inside. Let's talk."

Nelle wished he'd shouted. Shouting would've been so much less terrifying. She twisted the lock bar that propped the bulkhead open and eased the metal door down, restoring darkness, until her sun-dimmed eyes were blind.

46

Evan spun around, trying to see in the dark cellar. The blue afterimage left by the sun hovering in his vision blurred everything more than it had already been. He saw shapes he recognized by their position as the staircase and the weight bench, but couldn't make out details. In between them was the shape that shouldn't be there—the one that moved.

A second man stepped out from behind the first and spoke in English. His tone was firm and held them like the concrete steps had melted around their feet. He didn't speak to Evan, but rather to Nelle. Called her "Mrs. Pereira." Yet another stranger who knew their names. And that was the spell that held them. The name. It said, *I know you. Run and I'll still find you, because you aren't capable of hiding. Not without your name. Not* from *your name.*

This wasn't the person who'd been torturing them. Who the hell *were* these men?

Evan's thoughts were muddy. Whatever the guy had hit him with that morning, it felt like the asshole had cracked his skull wide open. The left side of his face was hot and stiff. He could see enough, and he could think *just* enough to know that he and Nelle had only one way out and it was the opposite direction of the man who'd just spoken. But Nelle had closed the door, and even if it were open, they couldn't outrun bullets.

The man in front shouted again, something more guttural to Evan's ears than lingual. Evan gripped the board tighter and tensed, ready to fight and give Nelle the time she needed to get a head start, even if it was only a few feet. It was something he could do. An advantage she didn't have otherwise. *Any chance at all is better than no chance.*

The accented man spoke again. "Put down the weapon."

Evan wanted to stand firm and say no to this man who intended to do them violence, just like the other. But unlike the other, this man's presence communicated rational disaster. Intentional atrocity. The other one. The man they'd left upstairs. His threat was unknowable. Scattered and subject to the whims of his madness. These men weren't insane. They were deliberate. And when they commanded him to drop the board, it grew heavier in his hands. Evan opened his fingers and let the board clatter to the floor.

"Good. Come have a seat, please."

Nelle's fingers wrapped around Evan's upper arm. He put his hand over hers. This was not a reprieve. This was their end. More certain death, but hopefully at the hands of men who took no particular pleasure in killing—at least no more than a butcher delights in his trade—and would afford them the mercy of efficient, painless ends. Together, they walked back into the cellar and toward the chairs that the man had repositioned for them, side by side.

The man with the gun tracked them as they moved. Evan and Nelle both took their steps haltingly. Evan was dizzy and nauseous, and he felt more than a little drunk. He knew that was very bad, but doubted it would be the concussion that would kill him. Nelle hobbled beside him, favoring her wounded foot. They paused at the chairs. The man who'd asked them to sit stepped back. He showed no concern that being near them was in any way risky to him. He merely gave them room to move. Nelle helped Evan sit.

She knows. It's obvious I'm not right.

She took the seat next to her husband and reached down to hold his hand. Evan tried to focus on the feeling of her fingers entwined with his. A strong root in this world. He wanted to send her strength, but at that moment, the flow was running the opposite direction. She squeezed, and he could feel her trying to reassure him. She was giving him her energy, her hope, because his had fled.

"Your name is Evan Pereira, yes?" Despite his ears still ringing from the gunshot, the man's voice carried. It was as clear as any detail in this nightmare.

Evan nodded. "What do you want?"

"Don't be in such a hurry, Mr. Pereira." The man looked at Nelle. "You are Eleonora Pereira, mortician at Tremblay Funeral Home. Nelle to your friends. This is correct?"

"Yes," she said. Evan heard a tone in her voice he knew well. Resignation. He squeezed her hand, wanting to silently tell her, *No darkness; only light.* But there was only darkness here. They'd closed the door on the light.

"Good. Now that we know we're talking to the right people, we can talk about what we want. To begin, we can discuss the matter of money."

All of Evan's fears coalesced around the word. *Money.* The money they'd taken, that they'd used to buy the house and bottles of spilled wine and all the little things here and there that they thought were beyond notice. But it wasn't a pinot noir or a nice shoulder bag that had doomed them. It was this house. Haunted as it was, not by ghosts or devils, but by money taken from terrible men who'd done, and were willing to always do, unimaginably terrible things. Hundreds—no, *thousands*—of children who'd paid for this home with their bodies, their pain and innocence, alive though they most likely were all across the globe, *they* haunted the house. Evan and Nelle had invited the profit of their pain to come live with them. And it was their ghosts who'd led these men here. None of them were innocent, and they deserved what was about to happen.

Nelle said, "You can have it all. Just please let us go."

The man smiled with half his mouth. It was not an unattractive smile. But it was made ugly by the cruel denial behind it. He didn't have to lie or make threats. The smile was threat enough.

"If you're just going to kill us anyway," Evan said. "Why would we give you anything?"

"There is a Russian saying. 'Life is hard but, fortunately, also short.' Your life can be hard and short, or it can be slightly longer, and . . ." The man shrugged and held out his hands as if he were a bureaucrat apologizing for the unreasonableness of an arbitrary policy instead of a mobster threatening to torture them. "We are offering you mercy—a thing you do not deserve, incidentally. There is no bargaining. You accept what we give you or not. We will leave here soon with the money or . . . *later,* also with the money. He looked at his partner and then back at

Evan. "It's not at all surprising how people change their minds after Stas convinces them."

The man with the gun, Stas, made a movement with his mouth, not a smile, not a sneer, but some kind of contortion that looked like acknowledgment, somehow. While he'd yelled at them in another language, he seemed to understand English well enough to follow his partner's cues.

Stas took a step toward Nelle. Her hand tightened around Evan's painfully.

"Stop," Evan pleaded. He said it to the man with the gun, but his wife recoiled as if he'd barked at her. He squeezed her hand, trying to keep her with him, though he had no idea where he was leading them.

Stas took another step, undeterred by Evan's command, and reached out with his free hand, grasping a handful of Nelle's hair in his fist. He wrenched her head around so she was looking up into his face. She grimaced and let out a cry of pain.

"You can have it all! We'll give you anything you want," Evan cried. "Just . . . don't. Please!"

Stas turned his attention to Evan. His face reformed into a very recognizable expression: disappointment. Evan's prior impression that these two weren't madmen who loved hurting people proved wrong. Whatever the other man's interests might've been, Stas had been looking forward to convincing them.

But then, their predecessor had already softened Evan and Nelle up. These monsters' work was almost completely done for them before they ever arrived.

"Where is the money?" the unarmed man asked.

"It's in a Swiss account. We have to go upstairs. Use the computer in the office. I can transfer it to you. Easy." That last word was a plea for mercy as much as it was a description of how tough Evan thought giving them what they wanted would be.

The man looked at his watch as if *he* was surprised they'd broken so soon. He said something to Stas that Evan couldn't even begin to comprehend. He spoke fast in a language that, maybe, in another setting, he thought Nelle might've found lyrical or beautiful, flowing like something that hummed with the same resonance as one of the world's great novels. But to Evan, it sounded like death, a looming resonance.

Stas let go of Nelle. "Da."

The man who spoke English pulled a pistol out of the back of his pants and held it pointed toward the floor, as if he didn't have to aim it at Evan to get him to comply. He was right. "Let's go," he said. He didn't ask where anything was. Evan understood what he was expected to do, and there was no amount of feigned or sincere ignorance that would extend his time or buy them reprieve.

Evan squeezed Nelle's hand one more time and opened his fingers. She reluctantly let go.

"I love you," she said. No sass. No snark. Just three words, spoken with sad resignation.

"I love you too."

A heaviness settled in his stomach, and he felt like gravity wouldn't allow him to stand if he tried. But he forced himself to rise from the chair because the weight of staying still would crush him. The men in front of him parted. The unnamed one gestured toward the stairs. Evan walked between them and stepped onto the first riser. He paused and looked back at his wife. In myth, he'd turn to salt or watch her fall into the netherworld for daring this glance, but he couldn't help it. She sat in the chair where he'd left her, watching him go with eyes that had only ever beheld him with love or humor, never sadness, like now. In that moment, he understood Orphic despair, as the life he'd thought of as mostly comedy, sometimes farce, and often romance, became undeniable tragedy. The presence of the man at his back urged him forward, and he moved, feeling more certain with each step that the last time in his life he'd ever see his wife had passed. Evan ascended, leaving Nelle below.

47

At the top of the stairs, Evan turned quickly to the left toward the guest room he and Nelle had reappointed as an office. In the action of trying to get free, get away, it was hard to pinpoint the sound from below the floorboards, but he was pretty sure things had gone south in the front room. Though he couldn't see well without his glasses, he didn't want to see the aftermath of what happened in there. He didn't *want* to see a dead body, whether or not it belonged to a man who'd slashed his face and tried to sexually assault his wife. So he made a sharp turn and started down the hall away from horror.

The man following kept in step, close behind. Evan imagined if he stopped abruptly, the man might run into him. Not that it would do him any good. He could use the momentary physical disorientation to try to wrestle for the gun. Or maybe he'd just be shot by a man who wasn't stupid enough to fall for a self-defense maneuver based on a slapstick prank. He walked on.

"This is it," he said, as if taking the man on the nickel tour of their house. *And over here are the downstairs bedrooms. Ours is on the second floor, so this one is for guests, and the other we turned into my office.* He pushed open the door and flipped on the light. It wasn't much, yet. A modular desk stood in the middle of the room with a shabby bookcase behind it and half-size metal filing cabinet with the inkjet printer on top; they'd thought someday they'd get nicer things and turn the room into a proper den or something you could call a study. In the middle of his desk sat the laptop, cover closed. He moved around behind the desk, opened the computer, and pushed the power button.

"Keep your hands where I can see them." The man continued to hold the gun down beside his thigh. While he was more than threatening enough without it aimed directly at Evan, the second it would take to raise it felt like time that was on Evan's side if he got the chance to fight back.

There was a long uncomfortable silence as the computer started up. Eventually, the log-in screen appeared, and Evan entered the code to finish the process. The screen was blurry. He was pretty sure he had a spare set of glasses in one of the drawers in his desk. He hadn't bothered to pack the contents of those when they'd moved, instead, merely taking them out of the desk and wrapping them in moving plastic. The prescription in those wasn't strong enough, but it was better than looking at the screen with his uncorrected astigmatism. He also knew that if he went digging through his drawers looking, he was going to get shot. Evan resigned himself to squinting and leaning close to the screen.

He said, "Do you have a SWIFT number you want the money transferred to?" when the Windows desktop finally appeared.

The man shook his head. "I'm not a banker. You will confirm that the money is in the account, and then you will give me the relevant information. I'll take it back to my people to effect the transfer."

You want your money, but you're not even prepared to take it?

"Okay." Evan sighed and took a step out from behind the desk. The man's gun hand lashed out with a speed that didn't register in Evan's mind until the barrel of the gun was already slamming into his already cut cheek. The room went white, and he fell sideways into the wall. The bookshelf behind him rattled and swayed forward, threatening to topple over. A couple of small fragile tchotchkes Nelle had stacked on the upper shelves rained down on him and broke on the floor, but the bookcase remained upright. When Evan's vision cleared, the man was standing over him, pistol back at his side.

He didn't move or even flinch. He stood as solidly as a statue, and said, "What are you doing? I told you to bring up the account information."

Evan touched his cheek with a trembling hand. His fingers came away freshly wet with blood. His face was hot and swelling, though, mercifully, mostly numb. He swallowed and tasted blood. His tongue probed at his upper molars. A couple felt loose. Speaking hurt. "The . . . uh . . . account information . . . is in a safe in the closet over there."

The unnamed man leaned over and pressed the barrel of his gun to Evan's kneecap. "What you need is in the safe. Along with your pistol, yes?"

Evan shook his head. "I don't own a gun." A sharp jolt of pain moved through his skull. He winced. A chill shuddered through his body. He couldn't beat this man. Not on his best day, with his glasses, without having been tortured. He was outmatched, and he would die.

"You did not think to mention this before?"

"I'm not . . . thinking clearly. It's been —" What was there to say that wasn't a profound understatement? *It's been a stressful day. I'm feeling distracted.* "I'm doing my best. Considering the circumstances."

"Consider the circumstances." The man shoved the end of the gun against Evan's kneecap, emphasizing his point. It hurt, but not as bad as anything he'd already gone through. Still, the promised agony was very present in the gesture. "If you are thinking of doing something stupid, you will pay a price for it."

I'm sure I will either way.

48

Nelle tried not to appear like she was cowering from the man standing in front of her, though her body badly wanted to quail. Held in place only by fear, she imagined getting up from the chair and running. She wanted to fight back, swing the chair, batter the thug, and find her husband before these men could accomplish what they'd come to do, and she and Evan were no more use except as a lesson to anyone else who'd dare transgress against them. The man had a kind of terrible presence that kept her ass rooted to the chair, wordlessly compelling her obedience.

She tried to keep her hands still, but they crept up to her waistband, feeling for the needle she'd secreted away to use on Roarke. Though there were two EpiPens in her purse, she'd only taken the one. And she wasn't even sure *that* would do the job.

The thought of talking her way out of this flitted through her mind, teasing with the fiction that he might be swayed if he understood her humanity. If she could talk to him . . . But she knew better. Though she had plenty of her own tattoos, the marks on his skin told her that he could not be swayed, could not be reasoned into seeing her as anything other than . . . a thing.

His knuckles sported tattoos of black rings with crowns at the tops and the numbers 1 9 8 9 below. *If that's the year he was born, he's younger than me.* The tattoo of the dagger piercing behind and reemerging on the other side of his Adam's apple frightened her most. Ink on hands and necks were what tattoo artists called job killers. These just made him look like a killer. Those and the gun he pointed at her.

She listened as the footsteps upstairs receded and then stopped altogether. They were in the office. And once Evan transferred the money, what then? The man in front of her would pull the trigger with one of those tattooed fingers, and that would be the end of it. She hoped that would be the end of it. A quick death. From what she knew about men, especially men who felt like something they were entitled to had been denied them, it wouldn't be as easy as that. Nothing ever was.

Nelle slipped the autoinjector out of her waistband, hiding it in her hands. She tried to pry the safety-release cap off the end without being obvious. It was soft plastic and slid off without a sound. Once removed, she had nowhere to put it. If she let go of the cap, it'd make a small clatter on the concrete floor for sure. She let it drop between her thighs, and slowly parted her knees so it might fall the rest of the way to the seat. She felt it slip along the skin inside her thighs and then disappear. She closed her knees again, hoping he hadn't seen the bright blue cap fall. The other end, hidden under her hand, was bright orange. The devices were designed to be obvious so people could find and use them quickly. She worried he'd see. He didn't seem to, though.

Upstairs, Evan cried out and there a heavy thud followed by a kind of rumble. Nelle flinched at the sounds. The man in front of her calmly turned his head to look toward the staircase. She could see a vein in his thick neck. Right where she wanted to jam the device. But he was so far away, and the gun was still pointed at her.

Her heart felt like it might explode, and she was dizzy. She tried to keep herself from panting.

The man — Stas — turned his face toward her again, and his look stole Nelle's breath. There was the barest hint of a smile at the corner of his mouth. It was the scariest thing she'd ever seen.

49

Evan sat on the floor waiting for the man to move so he could stand and walk to get the password book out of the small fireproof safe they'd stuffed in the back of the closet. He refused to crawl. It was one thing to be murdered after getting knocked on his ass, but he would not die on his knees if he could help it. The man took a step back when Evan gestured toward the safe. "You unlock the safe, I will pull what you want out of it."

Evan nodded. Despite having a combination wheel and a pop-out tubular lock on the front, he only ever used the key to secure it. The thing was hard to open by design, and neither he nor his wife could ever remember the combination or how to enter it (was it one full rotation around after the first number or two?). That was written down on a sheet of paper stuffed in a folder marked *Home Loan* in the file cabinet in the corner. Evan realized that the key to pop out the button lock on the safe was hidden in a ring box in his sock drawer upstairs. Security masterminds they weren't, but the only things in the safe were their passports, birth certificates, and the password book with their Netflix account information and the means to access millions of dollars in stolen blood money.

He opened his mouth to say that they needed to go upstairs to retrieve the key, but couldn't find the words when he saw movement behind the man. The dark part of his mind reckoned that the man he'd called Stas had quietly killed Nelle and was coming to rejoin his partner. Despondency shuddered through him like a winter chill, freezing his resolve to do anything but stay on the floor and give up.

The gunshot in the hallway was deafeningly loud and resounded in the small office with the force of a thunderclap. Evan's ears deadened, and his eyes shut involuntarily at the sound. Somewhere, far away, he heard a shout, and the grunts and pounding of hurried violence, as if a struggle was happening outside in the yard. But it wasn't outside. His ears were dead, and it was happening here. He forced himself to open his eyes and saw the man who'd brought him up from below disappear into the darkness of the hallway, a blur of black suit and red blood. The framed pictures on the wall in the office juddered, and one fell, its glass smashing on the floor.

Who the fuck is he fighting with? Nelle?

Evan got to his feet and lurched out into the hall to help his wife. How she'd gotten the better of Stas, he didn't know, but two against one meant they might live through this after all. He pitched through the door to help his wife.

It wasn't Nelle. The man was fighting with someone else. Another man. It was hard to see in the dim hallway, but it wasn't Stas. There was only one other person it could be.

Evan turned and ran. He heard another gunshot and the heavy sound of a body collapsing on the floor. He didn't look back. It didn't matter who'd won. Unless he somehow got the upper hand, both he and Nelle would lose.

Another report blasted in the hall, and a bullet sent bits of a closet door frame splintering as he turned the corner. He sprinted for the cellar door, hoping he wouldn't hear gunshots coming from downstairs. It was a certainty that Stas was waiting at the bottom of the stairs, alert and ready, hearing the sound of the chaos above him, but Evan didn't care. He hoped that he'd have a second. Just a second to try to save his wife. To give her a chance to get away.

He flung open the door and plunged down into the basement. The footsteps of the man behind him sounded like they were close enough to be his own.

50

Stas's head whipped around at the sound of the first shot. Heavy footsteps scuffled over their heads, and Nelle heard the sounds of bodies banging into walls, stomping the floor. The echoes of the fight drifted down, and she understood Evan had taken his chance. This was hers. Stas still aimed his gun at her, but his focus was on the stairs, not her. He took a step away, as if he might get a better glimpse at what was happening on the floor above if he found the right angle to peer through gaps in the floorboards.

Nelle gripped the EpiPen tight in her hand and sprung off of the chair. She lurched at Stas, rearing back with the injector. Stas looked at her, his face red with rage that made her want to stop and shrink away. But she flew forward. Above them, the door at the top of the stairs banged open, and he again turned to look. The gun in his hand went off, but wherever the bullet went, Nelle didn't know. It didn't hit her. Not that she knew, anyway.

She collided with the man and jammed her fist down as hard as she could, aiming the end of the injector for the hollow above his collarbone — the supraclavicular fossa. There was an "artery island" there — the external jugular, transverse cervical vessels, supraclavicular vessels, and subclavian veins and arteries — all waiting to take her medicine.

The device clicked, and the man roared. If she'd been administering the shot to herself in her thigh, she'd want to hold it there for ten seconds to ensure all of the epinephrine inside was delivered. That was an eternity — a chasm of time she couldn't cross, though she tried. She held on, shoving hard down, bearing her weight down on the autoinjector behind the man's collarbone with one hand while trying to hold the pistol away from her body with the other. Stas shoved at her, but she held on. She counted in her head, *two, three, four* . . . before she was flung away. She let go of the EpiPen, hoping it would remain jammed into the man's body, sticking up like a plastic collarbone erupting out of his body. The spring-loaded safety tip did its job, though, and as soon as she let go, it snapped into place, pulling the needle from his body, rendering the device safe and inert. It clattered to the floor at his feet.

Another man hurtled down the stairs, moving with abandon and nearly falling, but catching himself on the rail and staying upright. Nelle didn't have another weapon. If it was the other Russian, she was dead.

It was Evan.

Stas raised the gun to shoot her husband, but Evan hit him hard, driving him into the wall. The firearm flew out of the man's hand, clattering away into the shadows. Nelle felt her body jerk toward it, wanting to put her hands on the weapon, turn it against its master. But she lost sight of it in the dark recesses of the cellar behind the weight bench and water heater. Barefoot, and already wounded, she didn't dare run over there among the rest of the broken glass to go looking. Instead, she turned and ran for the two-by-four they used to bar the bulkhead door.

Evan swung into Stas's midsection and the big man fell, his face an even deeper red, and his lips spread open in a clench-toothed rictus. He clutched at his left arm. Nelle had hit him where she wanted; his heart couldn't take the direct shot of epinephrine. He was going into cardiac arrest.

"Evan!" she screamed.

He looked over his shoulder at her. Another man came lurching down the stairs. "Run!" Evan shouted. "Get out of here!" He turned to face the dark figure on the stairs.

51

A **hot bloom of pain** erupted in his shoulder at the same time he heard the report of the gun. Still, he reeled forward, letting his momentum carry him into the shadow staggering down the stairs. He couldn't see who it was clearly, but it didn't matter. Another man with a gun. He had to fight. He ducked at the last instant, trying to shoot for the man's midsection, hoping for a takedown like he'd learned in jiujitsu classes long ago but hadn't practiced in years. The man moved, and he didn't take the guy down. They collided, and the man shoved him back, hard. Up close, he could see who the figure was. Not a third Russian as he'd first thought, but their original captor returned as a nightmare version of himself, face bloodied and almost unrecognizably twisted with rage. Together, they slammed into the edge of the doorway leading into the smaller room where he and Nelle stored their holiday decorations. Where this man had hidden to ambush him hours earlier.

The man barked something as Evan shoved him into the sharp corner of the foundation wall. He felt the butt of the gun slam down on his wounded shoulder twice. Evan cried out and shoved forward again, ducking out of the corner, trying to get out from under the man's blows. He drove a hard hit into the man's ribs, under his elbow. He felt a hard exhalation in his face and heard a faint clatter that he thought might be the weapon falling out of his opponent's hand. Following the sound, Evan took a step back and looked for the gun. He spotted a dark shape nearby he thought might be it. Everything was dark and blurry.

Maybe it was the gun. Maybe it was something else. If he bent over to grab it, chances were even that he'd fall down trying. He tried to kick it toward Nelle, and it went skidding away, clattering into the far end of the cellar.

Evan felt something hit him in the gut. The air rushed out of his lungs, and it hurt to try to take a breath. Still, he gasped and swung back with a tight uppercut he hoped would find its mark. His knuckles popped and ached as he landed against something hard, yet yielding. A head rocking back. He heard the hard clack of the man's teeth jamming together and a dull knock as his head hit the wall behind him. The man fell forward into Evan, and they both tumbled to the floor in a heap of intertwined limbs.

Evan felt his own head bounce off the concrete floor and saw a brief, bright flash of light. He wanted to shout at Nelle to get the gun and shoot, but the darkness took him, and he was deep again. His last thought before he went back under was of her.

At least she's got the gun!

52

Mack's head was spinning. He had thought the husband looked like a hipster pussy, but the guy hit hard. That he felt badly muddled from being shot added force to the guy's punch. Still, he was conscious, and however off course he felt, it wasn't enough to stop him.

He looked up to see the bitch standing over him with something long and heavy-looking in her hands. The pussy husband didn't put out his lights, but that broad might. He tried to roll away as she swung it. The thing still hit him, but in the shoulder instead of in the head, where she was aiming. It hurt, but not like being shot in the face. He took it and lashed back at her, missing, but feeling like he'd caught a touch of her in the swing. A brush.

She shrieked with surprise and stepped back. Mack felt a trace of satisfaction. She was afraid of hitting him — or missing and hitting her man. Either way, it made her pause long enough for him to lunge for her. He got ahold of her leg and yanked. Her knee folded and she went down like a rag doll. The board fell out of her hand and clattered away. Thanks to the gunshots, he couldn't hear much, but still he heard the thump of her body hitting the floor, and that sounded *fucking great*. He got up onto his hands and knees, ready to show her what it cost to fuck with him. He fumbled at his pocket for his knife, wishing he'd brought the bigger one with him.

The fist that caught him in the jaw seemed to come out of nowhere. She rocked his head harder than her old man had done, and for a second he imagined she'd broken his neck. It didn't snap, though it popped a half dozen times, and the hard twist made his mind feel extra fuzzy. She swung at him again, missing his face this time and catching him in the collarbone. She hit hard, and pain arced up his neck into his jaw. He shouted again, more out of anger than pain, though he felt plenty of both. He reached for her, but she was gone. Instead, his hand fell on the board. He pulled it toward him and rocked back on his knees, swinging it blindly, just to keep her at a distance while he got his shit together. He shook his head and got up onto one foot. The room pitched and yawed like a boat in a white squall, and he fell over on one hand before righting himself again.

Mack's eyes cleared, and he spotted her in the far corner trying to reach under the gap beneath a shelf. He shouted, "You're dead . . . bitch! Fugging dead!" His words were mush, and it hurt to speak. He was missing more than a few teeth on the left side of his mouth where the Russki's bullet had deflected and torn out of his face. It was still mostly numb, but he could tell it was bad. Bad or not, he was alive, and they weren't.

She turned at the sound of his voice. The look on her face when she saw him—*really* saw him—*that* look excited him every time he saw it. She was piss-her-pants terrified of him, and the exhilaration of it ran through him like a bump of cocaine. His head began to feel tight. His already deadened hearing turned from a whine into a buzz. He pushed up with the board and got to his feet and took an unsteady step closer to her. She pulled her empty hand out from under the shelf and backed away.

"Dead. Bitch," he panted. He could feel the blood and saliva running down his jaw and neck on the ruined side and thought it had to be a particularly frightening image. It almost made him feel all right about being shot in the face. The room rolled again, and he shook his head to clear it. When his vision came back into focus, she wasn't by the shelf any longer. She'd made it to the doorway leading outside. "Stop," he yelled. She disobeyed him. The metal bulkhead door shrieked as she shoved it open. He threw the two-by-four at her like a javelin. It clattered impotently across the room. She bounded up the steps and out into the daylight.

"I'LLFUGGINGKILLYOUYOUFUGGINGBISHYOU'REA DEADCUNT!"

His utterance was as worthless as the board, and it only made his head and face hurt worse.

He staggered over to the shelf he'd seen her fumbling under. He hadn't seen what happened to his pistol, and probably never would've thought to look for it there if it weren't for her. He got down low and tried to reach under, but couldn't get his thick arm into the space past his elbow. He staggered over to the board, grabbed it, and went back. He jabbed with it under the shelf trying to find the damn thing, but it was dark and he couldn't feel the gun at the end of the stick. He'd guessed this was the shelf and not some other only because this was where he'd seen her kneeling, trying to reach under, and assumed that she'd actually seen where it had gone. After another few seconds, he pulled the board out and, sitting up on his knees, hurled it across the room again. It clattered into the corner behind the furnace. His head ached worse than ever. Another bitch who'd taken a gun from him.

He looked right at the other Russki. He sat slumped against the wall, blank eyed and slick with sweat. He wasn't breathing. Somehow, one of them had killed the monster. Good for them. Good for him. He looked for that man's pistol, but it was gone too. He could go upstairs and get the one from the other dead Russki in the hall. He knew where that one was. But that would take time. Time he didn't have. She was getting away.

He stumbled over to her husband, still out cold on the floor. Mack couldn't tell whether the pussy was alive or dead. It didn't matter. He stomped on the man's face twice. A red bubble grew on Evan's lips and popped. Still breathing. But like the man upstairs, not going anywhere.

Mack looked at the door to the back yard. It was bright outside. It wouldn't be hard to see her running. He could catch her, and when he did, he was going to make her look in his face until he got as much of that look on hers as he could stand. *And then I'll fucking kill her too.*

He headed toward the light.

53

She shoved the bulkhead door open, bracing herself against the blast of sunlight that tried to blind and stop her, scrambled out of the cellar, and tried slamming the door shut to buy some time. But the safety arm caught and held it open. She shoved again, and a small cry of frustration escaped her throat. To free it, she'd have to bend back down into the stairwell and lift the release bar. Fighting with it or stepping inside to release it both took time she didn't have. Roarke was coming.

The board had hit him in the shoulder, not his head. It might've hurt, but it was *miles* from deadly or even incapacitating. Standing there waiting to swing at him, she'd felt like a Van Helsing hovering over a coffin. And then she missed. Fucking no good at all. He'd looked at her with that tattered undead face—a neat little hole under the cheekbone below his left eye and a huge, gaping tear by his ear that seemed almost yonic and vulgar in its bright red exposure—and she had wondered if he could be killed. If it would really matter if she hit him in the head or at all.

In her head, she heard an echo of Evan saying, *Get away!*

Leaving him in the cellar was the hardest thing she'd ever done. But if she didn't get away now, she couldn't get help. Neither one of them would make it.

Nelle turned and lurched toward the hedgerow of burning bush trees separating her yard from the neighbors'. The bushes were grown together too thickly for her to push through on her feet unless she ran to the end of the row down by the road. No time. Nelle got down on her stomach and started to shimmy under, waiting for the feeling of a tight hand closing around her ankle or a hard stomp in the small of her back. Neither feeling came, and she emerged in the Darnielles' back yard, filthy and choking on dirt. She tried to stifle her coughing, but the soil she'd kicked up scrambling beneath the tight branches was in her throat, and she couldn't inhale without gagging. She swallowed as well as she could and ran for the sliding door at the end of the patio.

She grasped the door handle and tugged. It didn't move. Juanita's voice called out from her memory. *Oh, sweetie. We don't have an alarm system. Shit. We don't lock our doors unless we're headed out of town for more than a night.* They were gone for a whole week and had locked the house up tight. Peering inside, she couldn't see a telephone — she didn't know if they even had a landline, or if they were like her and Evan and only used cell phones. She hadn't ever thought to look for a telephone the times she'd visited. Who did when everyone had one in their pocket or purse?

She spun and looked for something to smash the glass with. Behind her were a pair of molded plastic chairs that wouldn't help her break a sweat if she swung them all day, never mind a pane of glass. There was a picnic-style table with fixed benches at the other end of the patio that was the opposite of the chairs — heavy and unmovable. She searched for something in the Goldilocks zone — not too light, not too heavy, but just right. She ran toward the low wall bordering the edge of the patio and wrenched a brick from it. Her injured shoulder resisted the effort, but she bit down against the pain and forced herself to pull the block free. Huffing it back to the doors, she tried to throw it as hard as she could. The brick hit the glass and bounced off. Nelle had to skip out of the way as it returned to her. While a round spiderweb pattern of cracks appeared in the door, it remained as solidly impassable as before. She picked up the brick and threw it again. The shatter pattern grew larger, but the door held. She wasn't getting inside. Not this way.

She tried to remember what the Darnielles' front door looked like. Was it half glass like her own? She picked up her brick and took a step toward the path leading around the side of the house. Even up on the balls of her feet, moving made her heel feel like hell. The adage that you didn't have to run faster than the tiger, only faster than everyone else running from it came to mind. Except there was no one else running with her. That meant she *had* to be faster than Roarke.

Nelle stumbled, and the heavy brick slipped out of her hands and landed with a dead thump in the lawn in front of her. She tripped on it, hurting the toes on her good foot and sprawled out facedown in the grass. The silence that followed was somehow more horrible. No shouting or sounds of a struggle. If Evan was alive, he'd keep fighting. And if he'd won, he'd be standing in the yard now calling out for her, telling her it was okay. It was all over. But he wasn't there. Mack had somehow gotten the gun that she couldn't reach with her slender arms, and he'd . . .

She shoved the thought down. She hadn't heard any shots. She didn't know for certain Evan was dead. She didn't know he wasn't, and the silence didn't offer any evidence to the contrary. Instead, her darkest fears settled into her mind and whispered the worst things. They had lost. There was no more fighting to do.

Without Evan, what remained but dying?

He'd want me to live. He'd want me to run.

Run where? I don't even know if Juanita has a landline. What if I waste time and make a bunch of noise trying to break another window and there isn't a phone? What then? She knew what would happen, phone or no phone: she'd die in the Darnielles' house waiting for the police to come while her killer leisurely made his way over to find her. Or she could head for the next house down the highway and hope they were home instead of also at the Cape or in the Berkshires. That way wasn't escape either. To get to the road, she had to run all the way around the house and down the driveway. If Roarke caught up to her, there was nowhere to hide and nothing she could try to use as a weapon. Sure, maybe if she made it to the highway someone would be passing by in a car at just the right time and would stop to help. But with the blind bend in the road, they'd be as likely to run her down as stop. And if they did stop, Roarke might kill the Good Samaritan too before finishing her off.

Why had they moved so far away? Why had they picked a house on the outskirts of town? If they were *in* the city, she could stand in the road and scream for help, and a hundred people passing by would all hear her. If she screamed, "Fire," they might even come to her aid. Their first few nights in the house, they'd slept poorly because there were no sirens in the distance like there were in the city. Now, in Juanita's back yard, she realized that those sirens were the sound of people rushing to someone's rescue. Fire engines responding to put out a blaze. Ambulances speeding to get someone to the hospital and lifesaving care.

The police coming to stop a man with a gun.

A light breeze rustled the trees behind her. She looked at the reservation land and couldn't help feeling like a character in a fairy tale. Not a modern bowdlerized one — an ancient version, where the red-hooded girl dies in the woods as a cautionary fable to teach children to listen to their parents, not to stray from the path. She was Red Hood in this tale. And the wolf was coming. But what else was there to do? Where else to run?

The Scout lodge at the trailhead. It'll have a landline. With all those kids there in the summer, they have to have a reliable way to call for help if one of them gets hurt. The path leads there. Disappearing in the trees seemed better also than trying to hide in a house she couldn't lock behind her once she broke in. It'd be better to disappear fast. The trees, though still bare, offered cover. She could hide. She could find a branch or a stone to swing. She could creep and eventually sneak until she found another back yard and someone at home to beg for help. Or the welcome center.

Nelle rose up and abandoned the house for the woods.

At the back of the Darnielles' yard was a low New England rock wall separating their property from the Cabot Woods behind it. She climbed over and headed for the less passable bramble of bushes and deadfall branches beyond, piled there to discourage wanderers on the path from straying into private yards. As she scrambled over, the pile shifted and fell out from under her. She tumbled down. Noise surrounded her, and she let out a racking sob of frustration. Everything she tried was a failure. She wanted to quit. Let the clown-faced piece of shit find her. A numbness settled over her. Every time she thought she'd experienced the worst, there was something even more terrible waiting right behind it. There was pain she hadn't yet even begun to fathom, the little nagging voice in the back of her mind insisted.

Run, a different voice told her.

She pushed on over the rough barrier into the woods beyond. The low brush resisted her passage, catching and pulling at her hair and clothes. She kept going. Every movement seemed to make noise; leaves and twigs underfoot rustled and snapped like Lunar New Year crackers in her ears. She heard a truck pass by on the highway and regretted the decision to run for the trees instead of the road. But *what if* and *if only* were as distant as Jupiter and Saturn. This was the way she'd chosen. The only direction to go was forward. She pushed ahead harder, ignoring the noises she made and trying to put distance between herself and the man in her house.

A few yards farther, she caught sight of movement and stopped, ducking behind a thick tree trunk to hide. Roarke emerged from the bulkhead opening. He climbed the steps deliberately, carefully, like a man unconcerned that he needed to defend himself.

Nelle's knees felt weak, so she dug her fingers into the bark of the tree to hold on. From the distance, she could see his red face, bloodied and torn, and felt a small swell of satisfaction at someone having hurt him, even if it wasn't her. He wasn't an immortal from a slasher movie that couldn't be stopped. He was a man.

She could kill a *man.*

She *wanted* to kill a man.

She wanted to kill *him.*

Nelle stayed still and shrank further behind the tree as he scanned the far end of the yard. Her breath stilled as he seemed to look right at her. Then his gaze tracked on past. She didn't let the breath out, but held it, afraid that the sound of her exhalation would draw his attention again. She knew, as had been true all along, he held all the power she lacked.

Who am I fooling? I'm not killing anybody.

Roarke looked to his left at the Darnielles' house. He moved so suddenly Nelle's heart skipped. He staggered around the side of the house toward the neighbors'. He had to have heard her trying to break the window. He was following her there, not into the woods. She watched him move quickly toward the end of the hedgerow. If he wasn't going to get on his belly and crawl under like she had, he had to turn his back on her and go the long way around. All of a sudden, she had time. He was going the other way.

The breath held in her lungs hurt, and she wanted to let it out—sigh with relief. As soon as she did, though, she'd take a great, noisy gasp in, and that would be the same as calling out to him.

She mentally urged him on. *Go. Go! Chase me that way. GO!* He stopped and looked over his shoulder at the forest edge again, and Nelle pressed against the tree and tried to stay still. She trembled, and it felt like being naked. The tree trunk could only hide so much. But he didn't come closer. He resumed his walk toward the driveway.

Nelle held her breath and slipped away. This was her head start—the only one she'd get. She took it.

54

Mack felt dizzy and half blind, having emerged from the cellar into the daylight. His head felt tight, and the pressure seemed to grow once confronted by the sun, disconcerting him even more. He tried to focus, clear his mind, and center his thoughts, but it took effort. The pain and whatever else was happening in his head addled his brain. He reached up and felt at his cheek where his wounds began. The small hole under the eye that wasn't focusing. His fingers were cold, and a light touch felt good. But when he pressed down a little harder, his head swam and the world turned gray, an instant fog falling over him. He moved his hand around to his cheek, or what remained of it. An image of someone standing next to a blackened, burnt tree with a scorched hat and a gormless smile on his face popped into his head. *I was struck by lightning and lived to tell the tale. A tornado threw me a mile away, and I'm here to talk about it. It exploded, and I was the sole survivor.* He took a deep breath and felt the air rush over the aching broken stubs of what used to be his molars and out through his ruined cheek. *I got shot in the fucking face. But I survived.* It didn't feel like a victory. What hadn't killed him hadn't exactly made him stronger.

He hadn't counted on anyone else showing up with their own score to settle. He remembered wondering where a couple like this got the money to put down the deposit they had, but he'd figured they had to be spoiled shits like Sam. Rich brats with a trust fund from Mommy and Daddy that meant they could look like rejects from *The Addams*

Family and not have to worry how they were going to be able to make a living. But now he knew. They weren't like her. They'd stolen the money from bad men who'd come howling. Those men tried to kill him, even though he hadn't done a thing to them. Still, they were dead now, and *he* was the one still breathing. And that was something. Those Russian thugs couldn't stop him, and neither could Sam or the Pereiras or fucking anybody. Nothing would stop him.

A throb of pain made his stomach lurch, and the fog descended again. Why was he standing out in the sun when he had things to finish inside? *The bitch. What was her name again? Evelyn or something. No. Eleonora. She got out.* She was out and on the run. Where?

He remembered hearing the sound of the window cracking next door. She was at the neighbors'. He hadn't planned on her getting loose. But it didn't matter. Those two gutless shits next door wouldn't have a thing she could use to hurt him. He talked to Colin once, and the guy was a snowflake. Had one of those HATE HAS NO HOME HERE signs in his yard like he wanted to prove to the neighborhood how special and tolerant he was. What'd they call it? Virtue signing or something. She might as well come at him armed with dessert forks or some pine cones in a decorative bowl; there wasn't anything she could find out in plain sight that could hurt him. Kitchen knives or fireplace tools at best. Like that would touch him; he'd been shot in the fucking face and was still on his feet. He'd take her out. He'd take down as many of the bitches as he could on his way out. Sam, the one from the courthouse, Siobhan. *She* thought he was stupid too, but she learned different. Women were like that. Faithless. That was the word Sam used. Like she was any better. Like she hadn't had her new guy lined up ready to go. They both thought he was stupid, but *Siobhan* found out how smart he was. It was a kick to see when it dawned on her face that she'd had him figured all wrong. By then it was too late to make amends. He made her pay for fucking up what was his and telling his wife what she'd done.

They'd *all* pay.

He walked around the hedgerow toward the neighbors' house. His heart beat hard, and he wanted to rush in after Eleonora, knock her down, and bash her face in with his boot heel like he had her cuck husband. But not so bad she couldn't open her eyes and see him before he snuffed her. He wasn't sure he wouldn't let his enthusiasm get the better of him, but the pain in his head made him move quietly, carefully.

He controlled himself and listened, trying to hear if she was still in the yard or had made it inside. Nothing. He'd show everyone what he thought of them. And even though he couldn't finish things the way he wanted, when Sam turned on the news tonight, she'd see what he'd done. She'd know, deep down, it was her fault. She'd set this all in motion. She was responsible for all of it.

He'd show them all.

First, this one.

XII

◆

THE WOODS

55

Each painful step reminded Nelle of the gash in her heel. Her wound was poorly dressed, and the improvised bandage was coming looser with each stride. She couldn't think about it, though. She had to move. Trying to take it easy on her right foot, she lurched unevenly along the path. Her left shoulder ached badly also, so she cradled her elbow in her other hand, trying to take some of the stress off of it as well. The contorted stagger that accommodated her wounds made her hip and back sore, but she loped along as best she could, fighting against the growing assembly of pains within her.

The forest debris underfoot was mostly smooth, but being barefoot made the going slower. The last thing she needed was to step badly on a jagged rock or a broken branch. She couldn't afford to twist her ankle slipping off of a slick stone or to break something splaying out on the path like she had in the yard. She took each step as quickly as she dared, careful not to fall. After a few yards, she seemed to find, if not a stride, then an uneven gait that was fast enough. And like that, she ran.

Other times she'd hiked the path, she'd looked for houses visible through the trees. But theirs was the last house a mile or more in this direction until the parking lot and trailhead for the reservation and the big welcome center building. Summer camp season hadn't started, and the buildings had been closed up. Everything would be locked. But it was all rustic construction, no tempered or even diamond-wired glass. She remembered all the windows in the main building being clear panes. She hadn't inspected anything closely on her casual hikes, but figured a big rock would get her in almost any building she wanted.

Across the highway and maybe a half mile farther up the road from the reservation parking lot was the Ripton Animal Hospital. It was a local clinic, nothing as big as Angell Memorial in Boston, but small as it was, it was still a place where people worked. *They* have *to be open — sick pets don't take Saturdays off. Someone there can help.* Even farther beyond that was town and open-all-year civilization like shops and package stores and restaurants. If she had to make that run, maybe someone driving by would see a bleeding, half-dressed woman in her pajamas running along the side of the road and would stop. *I'd be the sort of thing that would make a person pull over and at least ask if everything was all right, wouldn't I?* First, before she made a mad dash along the highway toward town, she decided to try the welcome center. If that wasn't fruitful, then the vet hospital.

She pushed away the thoughts of what would happen when she called for help and they found a pair of dead mobsters in her house. That didn't matter. She'd take all the heat that came with calling the police as long as it meant getting Evan help. Getting him to a hospital. She'd happily go to prison to save his life.

The woodland path that had once seemed so pretty and peaceful on a quiet day took on a new quality now — darker, colder, more confining, growing ever more haunted with each step, like a fairy-tale wood after the children have run out of bread crumbs, or those places where people are drawn to kill themselves like in Japan or Brattle, Washington. It had never seemed like that before. She'd loved this place. She loved running here so much more than in the city, with its bus exhaust and catcalls. But now she was hungry and dehydrated, disoriented, exhausted, and despairing.

Her pace slowed. Her breath was becoming harder to catch, and a fresh stitch in her side grew. Her step faltered. She stumbled. *I can rest for a minute. Just a minute, and then back up again.* She thought about Evan lying on the cellar floor. Badly wounded — but only wounded — waiting for help to come. He was waiting for her to save him, and every second delayed was more blood lost, a breath closer to his last. *If he's still breathing,* that negative voice nagged. It taunted her, telling her that she was a widow at thirty-four — a tragedy in motion, running toward dinners alone in an empty house with a single glass of wine and a phone that wouldn't ring because no one would know how to talk to her anymore.

She slowed more until she was walking. Her first steps in the world truly alone were these.

And she wept.

56

Mack walked through the front door he'd jimmied open the night before like he had a key. The house was quiet as he stalked through looking for a sign where the bitch was hiding. Nothing gave her up. Not a bloody footprint or a single thing out of place. It made him feel nervous. He'd heard her smash the window; she *had* to be there. He wandered into the dining room, waiting for her to leap out at him with a butcher knife. But she didn't. All the knives in the kitchen were where they'd been the night before when he made himself dinner.

One of the glass doors in the dining room was badly cracked, but not shattered. It stood like a mosaic of clear tiles. He stepped over to the door. The latch was locked and the dowel blocking the door from sliding in the floor track was still in place. Outside, the brick she'd thrown against the door lay abandoned the grass. He smiled at the realization that she couldn't break a glass door with a square foot of patio masonry. *Weak bitch.*

If she wasn't in the house, where had she gone? He hadn't seen any trace of her out front. He looked around the patio at the mess of stains she'd left behind, blood browning in the sun. Her tracks led to the patio ledge and the gap from where she'd plucked the brick out. They led back to the doors and then away again, into the grass, where they disappeared. Because he hadn't seen her footprints in the driveway heading toward the road, he'd assumed she'd gotten in, called the cops, and shortened the time he had left. Except she hadn't gotten in. She'd run away. Toward the forest, it looked like.

He smiled again. She was trying to escape through the woods barefoot and bleeding. Even sticking to the hiking trails, it was going to be slow going, and she wasn't running toward anywhere someone could come find her before he could catch up. *Stupid cow.*

He was a hunter; she was as good as dead.

Mack walked back into the Darnielles' bedroom, pulled out the duffel bag he'd stuffed under their bed, and dropped it on the mattress. He unzipped it and laid out the AR-15 and the extended magazines he'd bought up in New Hampshire. He set aside the improvised explosives he'd intended to plant on the sides of the Pereiras' driveway. Those were a special thing for the cops. He reached in and removed the KA-BAR knife he'd split Siobhan open with and had intended to use on Sam. It felt good in his hand. With this weapon, he could make this bitch look at him with terror. No disgust. No disappointment. Just pure terror. That was what made him feel best of all. Alive. Powerful. *Real.*

With trembling hands, he clipped the knife sheath onto his belt at his side and walked out of the bedroom. On the way, he stopped in the bathroom and took a look in the mirror. His face was a ruin. He looked like a monster. Something out of a zombie movie. The scratches Eleonora had given him under his eye were barely noticeable compared to what the bullet had done to his cheek, but they were there. He could see them. He tried to calm his breath, let his heartbeat slow, but it seemed like every second that passed, he just got a little more excited. His needle was in the red. He was angry and anxious and even a little giddy at the thought of feeling the KA-BAR sliding inside another woman.

He was thirsty. He poured himself a glass of water and tried to drink. The pain of cold water hitting his raw broken teeth and ripped cheek was enough to send him out of the world. He barely heard the clatter of the plastic cup in the sink as he staggered back and hit the bathroom door. He slid down to the floor and disappeared into the dark for a moment. He had no idea for how long. He wasn't clear about much of anything except his pain. That and the need to get after the girl before she got away.

He stood and waited for his head to clear. The room spun once and he thought he might fall again. Then it settled and he kept his feet under him. He left the bathroom, walked through the kitchen, unlocked the back door and threw the dowel away. The door slid open easy, like a dream.

They were hard to see, but once he found the first of her bloody footprints in the grass, it wasn't too hard to find the next. And the next. Her blood was drying and turning brown, and that meant he'd lose her trail eventually in the dirt along the trail, but as long as he got off in the right direction, Mack felt confident he could catch up with her. Sure, she had a head start. Time was hers, but he had *all* the other advantages. He felt at his side for the KA-BAR knife. It was where it belonged. He pressed on.

Once over the deadfall, he paused on the trail and looked left. Nothing. To his right he spied a wet smear of dulled red on a rock and a footprint beyond that.

Too easy.

The huntsman drew his knife and followed Nelle's trail of blood crumbs into the woods.

57

Nelle felt rooted to the ground. Her knees begged to bend and relieve themselves of the burden of standing. It would feel so nice to sit down — no — *lie* down and close her eyes for a while. To just lie down and drift away seemed best. It would be good to feel the soft dirt underneath her body and for the moss to cover her over like a green blanket and to sleep forever. Let the forest floor be her new home and dirt her only clothes. The world blurred a little, and she thought whether she lay down on her own or not, she'd fall eventually. She was bleeding, maybe not to death — not that fast — but badly enough that she felt increasingly light-headed. She looked down and saw that the dressing Evan had used to cover her wound — her underwear — had come free from the tape and was gone. Lost on the trail somewhere behind her.

For him *to find.*

She tore the last dangling strip of duct tape away from her ankle and threw it into the trees. The too-familiar pain of it peeling away from her skin woke her a little, and the feeling of putting down roots lessened. Pain reminded her that she could move — that she *needed* to move. She had to find help and couldn't quit the world until she stopped Malcolm Roarke . . . or at least set someone in his way to do that. And when she had pointed men capable of answering violence with greater violence at him, *then* she would lie down and let go.

She took a step. One became two. Two turned to four and then eight. And before she knew it, she was running again. Her heart thudded heavily, and her lungs took in deep, gasping breaths of air, and it felt good. Her ankle and heel still hurt, along with her hip and shoulder and head, but that all felt like being alive. So she ran despite the pain. To spite it.

The trail sloped downward, and she recognized the bend ahead that led to the road entrance to the reservation and the parking lot on the other side. She ran the last hundred yards without thinking of anything but moving ahead. That, and who she left behind — another foot, a yard, an unreachable distance away with each step she took. Around the bend, she caught sight of the totem pole rising out of the flower garden that stood sentry behind the sign that read CABOT STATE PARK SCOUT RESERVATION. Emerging from the dense trees into the sunlight felt like being exposed for everyone to see. An easy target. But there was no one around. No one to see and either take aim or run to her aid. She was still alone.

Up the lane to the left, not far after, stood the welcome center, where she knew there'd be a phone. She ran as fast as she could along the driveway toward the parking lot and the welcome center lodge. Casting a glance back to look behind her, she felt alarmed to see that although her blood had mixed into the muddy path almost invisibly, it stood out like a beacon in the light-colored gravel. Turning back, she felt her stomach drop and almost fell trying to stop. Rocks jabbed into her wound as she dug in with her heels to reverse direction. There was a car parked in the lot ahead of her. Off to the side, in the shadows, backed into place.

His car.

She remembered him. But she remembered *it* better.

It had been parked at the end of her driveway when he came in the security company disguise. She remembered thinking what an odd car it was for a door-to-door salesman to drive. A cherry red Dodge Challenger, it looked like the sort of thing a middle-aged lawyer would drive on the weekends — a status symbol. A "muscle car" to fight back at the indignities of an expanding waist and thinning hair. The sort of thing a man like that thought he was entitled to own.

At the sight of it, she let out a small squeak and clapped her hands to her mouth. Nothing moved. Not in the parking lot or the woods or up at the lodge beyond the chain stretched between two posts at the far end of the lot. Her heart beat furiously with panic as she waited for the door to open and Mack to step out like a nightmare, gun in hand. He didn't. The only movement came from the shadows of branches overhead swaying in the gentle breeze.

She took a cautious step forward and craned her neck to see, ready to run at even a hint of movement from inside the car. *He parked here so we wouldn't see it. It's easy for a guy to hide, but not a bright red sports car. Not one like that.* She wondered how long it had been parked there. How long had he been hiding in their house? The answer didn't matter. Whether it was an hour, a day, or a week was irrelevant. She'd escaped, and if he behaved in any rational way at all, he'd be coming back to get away in his car before the police showed up.

That he wasn't rational sat in her head like a stone, weighing her down.

Nelle hobbled forward, trusting that she was still ahead of Roarke. The fear that she hadn't eluded her captor but run right back to him made her heart pound harder. He hadn't gotten ahead of her, she reasoned. But he *was* coming. She could creep by, head to the back of the lodge and break the window. He'd never know she was there. But her growing anger at seeing his car right there—*that fucking car!*—made her pause. It made her want to pick up a big rock and smash it down on the hood, on the windshield, against the doors. She wanted to destroy it because it was his and he cared for it. Even if it was only a car, it was a thing he loved, and for that, it deserved to be hurt and defiled.

She grabbed a stone from the border of the lot, one that felt nice in her hand, about the size of her fist, round and smooth but heavy. Gripping it tightly, she crossed the lot and swung once at the driver's side window. The impact made a dull *thunk,* and a small point of white appeared where the stone met the glass. She swung again, harder. This time the window smashed with a loud crack and a soft tinkle of safety glass spilling into the black leather seats. It felt good. She unlocked the door and yanked it open, not sure what she wanted from inside, but needing to see anyway. She sat in the driver's seat, pebbles of safety glass prickling under her ass, and pulled down the sun visor. Of course, no keys fell conveniently into her lap. She flipped it back up and popped open the glove box, hoping to find a pistol, maybe. His registration and insurance were there under a deck of vodka-branded playing cards and a tire gauge, but she found nothing she could use to fight or flee. She closed the glove box and searched the rest of the car, foot wells, back seat, looking for anything, and came up empty. She turned to get out, and her eyes alighted on a small button to the left of the steering column with an icon on it of a car with an open trunk lid. She pushed the button. A soft click sounded behind her. She looked through the back window. The trunk swung up and blocked her view. She jumped out of the driver's seat, quietly shutting the door behind her and hobbled around to the rear of the car. There had to be one of those things in there that loosened the lug nuts on the wheels when someone needed to change a flat—and didn't guys who drove cars like this pride themselves on changing their own tires, spark plugs, oil? There was a weapon to be had here. She just needed to reach in and grab it.

Her scream was uncontrollable and loud.

At first, the woman in the trunk seemed to be dressed in a red leotard, but as Nelle's mind resolved into clarity, she realized that what she'd mistaken for skin tight fabric was blood. Blood that had escaped from wounds, the number of which she couldn't count at a glance and didn't want to inventory. She tried to catch her breath, but it had left her, carried away on the breeze by her scream. She gasped and her eyes blurred with panicked tears and she thought she might've felt a small trickle of urine running down the inside of her leg.

She'd seen so many dead bodies in her life, some savaged, yes, but they were all in their right context: on a metal table, clean, ready to be embalmed and dressed and cared for by her. The dead came to her for her care, and she gave it so they could possess one last hour of dignity in front of their loved ones before she helped take them to the fire or the grave. That was the context of the dead she could accept. This body, though. *This* body was shocking and wrong. Under the dried maroon blood, she was mottled peach and purple and blue—Nelle thought, *she's in hypostasis, past rigor mortis.* Her face was puffy and her tongue stuck out slightly from between her lips. The woman's eyes stared blindly straight ahead, discolored black with tache noir. And the smell that assaulted her . . . It was familiar, but so much more intense than she'd ever smelled before. Of course. This body had been in a hot car trunk for how long? It didn't matter. Any duration, no matter how brief, was longer than anyone should have to lie in this state.

The sight and smell of the woman stunned her, leaving her reeling for a moment like nothing ever had. She took a breath through her mouth and tried to collect herself. *You don't have time to be shocked!*

She needed a weapon.

She tried repeating to herself, *I can do this. I've touched women like this before.* But she hadn't, really. She'd worked on women who'd been hit by cars and city buses. She'd embalmed more than a couple suicides and only ever one murder victim who had been strangled to death. But she had never been near someone like this. Someone who . . .

She retched, but had nothing in her stomach to throw up. *If I don't get it together, this could be me.* Will *be me.* The image of her on the embalming table came rushing back to mind. She fought to banish it, but it persisted, haunting her as relentlessly as a beating heart.

With trembling hands, she reached in under the woman, searching for the tire iron. She pushed against the woman's belly to try to move her. It yielded in a terribly intimate way. Someone else's belly was something that only lovers touched. It was a place of insecurity and self-judgment. If you were allowed to caress a soft tummy, you were trusted. Nelle was not trusted; she was a stranger to this woman. This woman's stomach was violated with terrible gashes and cuts. And when Nelle pushed against it, a horrible reek emerged that made her stomach heave again.

Is this Samantha? It couldn't be. Roarke had been adamant that she call his ex-wife and convince her to come over.

So, who is this?

It didn't matter. Whether a stranger or a lover, the woman couldn't help her.

Her body was cool and soft and her skin tacky with blood that was getting on Nelle's hands and forearms. Nelle tried to hold her breath as she felt under the dead woman's sticky skin with bare hands, searching for something, anything she could use. Nelle's fingers closed on something long and rigid. It was slick and tacky at once. She tugged, but it wouldn't come free. She shoved at the woman, growing angry that she was keeping Nelle from what she wanted.

Help me out here, damn it! We're on the same side.

She shoved hard and pulled with her other hand until she had what she wanted. A tire iron. It was shorter than she'd hoped. Lighter too. But it was a solid piece of steel, with a hard angle and a bulb at one end for tightening and loosening lug nuts. At the other end, it was flat like the end of a screwdriver. She could stab with it, she imagined, but it felt better as a club. *This* would break a window. Or a skull.

She looked one last time at the dead woman in the trunk, unknown to her. "I am so sorry," Nelle whispered. She closed the trunk lid and started away toward the welcome center lodge.

In the distance, she thought she might've heard footsteps.

58

The scream thrilled him. It was distant, but close enough to hear, and it meant that though he'd lost time in the bathroom, lost her trail in the mud, he was headed in the right direction and wasn't far behind his quarry. Mack wondered what had caused her to cry out. Whatever it was, he smiled at the idea of her being so surprised by something that she betrayed herself. He quietly thanked the woodland creature or whatever it was that had startled her and doubled his pace on the path, careful not to make too much noise, but too anxious to creep.

He stopped at the edge of the woods before it gave way to the main entrance road and looked for a sign of her passage. The trail she'd left behind had become clearer for a time after she lost her makeshift bandage — and how he thrilled at the form that "bandage" took, stuffing it in his front pocket — and then waned again as, he assumed, earth caked in her wound and helped staunch the bleeding. Still, he found hints along the way that rewarded the choices he'd made at trail junctions. He'd assumed she was headed for the entrance to the reservation. He knew what she was after; it would be the same thing Sam would make a run for if he had been chasing her instead — someone *else* to solve her problems. *All alike.* But it wouldn't do her any good. Even if she did get inside of the camp office and call the police, she'd be dead long before they showed up.

He felt the comforting heft of his knife in his hand. Its weight and balance. He reminisced about plunging it deep into Siobhan. Pulling it out and opening her anew in another way. He was excited to do it again. Though, he'd have to be cautious about getting caught up in the moment. Taking too much time. *Knock her out. Take her home first. That's what I'll do. I have all the time I want at home.*

Seeing no one out in the open, he emerged from the trees and hustled across the grass in the direction he thought her scream had come from, hoping to pick up her trail again. Halfway across the lawn, he glanced at his car parked in the far corner of the overnight lot. His step faltered as something felt not right about it. It was where he'd left it, but something was odd. He changed course.

Up close, he could see that his window wasn't down as it had appeared from a distance, but smashed. A tight ball of anger swelled in his throbbing head. His mouth went tight, and he tasted fresh blood and a jolt of agony from his shattered teeth. He ignored the pain and looked inside the car. Glass covered the driver's seat. He leaned in further and saw mud and blood staining the foot well upholstery. And a rock.

The bitch was in my car.

He imagined her trying to think of a way to steal it and drive away. If he hadn't been so furious about the window, he might've laughed at the idea of her trying to start his car without the RFID chip in his key fob. He gripped the knife tighter in his hand. *I'm going to skin her,* he promised himself. *I'm going to fucking peel her like an orange.*

59

Nelle wondered if Roarke would've just gotten in his car and driven away if she hadn't broken his window. She'd kicked herself for being so stupid, but seeing him drawn to the car just a moment ago revealed to her how close on her tail he was. It was a mixed blessing. Yes, he was here and he knew she was too. But, because of his focus on the car, she'd seen him and he hadn't seen her. That small advantage was hers, and she took it.

She slipped out of sight around the welcome center building and crept for the back door. She looked at the tool in her hands, knowing Roarke was too close for her to smash a window and not be heard. She wondered whether it would work as a pry bar. She figured she could jam it in between the door and frame with some effort, but even if she did, she wasn't sure she had the strength to bust the deadbolt. It was worth a try. No other ideas were coming to her.

She wedged the end of the tool into the jamb between the knob and the deadbolt above it and began to try to force the door open. Her tool wasn't a crowbar and once stuck in the gap, the bend in the metal pointed straight down, not out, and it was hard to get her fingers around the bar to try to pull. Her fingers were slippery with blood, Evan's, her own, and the woman's, all mixed in a darkening intimacy, and it was difficult to keep hold. She did her best, struggling to be quiet, but the sounds of cracking wood were as loud in her still-ringing ears as the gunshots that'd deadened her hearing to begin with. Nelle worked at the door, wanting desperately to get to the telephone inside.

It wouldn't budge. She pulled the tool out from the frame and jammed the flat edge behind the round plate at the base of the knob. It bent and deformed easily enough, but had no effect at all on how the knob turned — or didn't. Of course, it wouldn't. Locks were designed to hold, and if she could just pop off a cover and get one open, there might as well not even be a lock on the door. And there was still the deadbolt to contend with. She accepted that she wasn't getting in by breaking the door frame or the locks. The only way was to smash a window. And unlike the soft cracks of the wood, however deafening they'd seemed in the quiet of the abandoned woods, glass would be much louder.

It would bring him.

It was too big a risk. If she broke in that way, she'd end up dead while the police dispatcher listened to the last seconds of her life at the other end of the line, if she even got as far as a phone.

Her hands were sweating, and the tire iron slipped in her grasp. She couldn't help gasping in fear as she tried to catch it before it clattered to the flat slab of concrete under her feet. She caught the tool and clutched it tight to her chest, holding her breath. In the distance, she thought she heard Roarke shout. She had to move.

Nelle crept to the far side of the building and peered around the corner at the parking lot. He was standing beside his car. Though his torn face allowed him only a single expression, she could see he was enraged. It was in his body — the way his shoulders hunched and his neck jutted forward. You didn't have to know a man at all to know when he was standing at the frontier of frenzied violence. She'd defiled something that was his, and he felt the violation. More importantly, she could see that she couldn't get out of the parking lot to the road without being spotted.

If she could sneak past, the animal hospital was just a bit farther up the highway. She could make that run along the highway, and then she'd be safe. Wouldn't she? The far-too-common image of a stoic news reporter standing outside the scene of the latest mass shooting or rental truck attack intruded upon her fantasy of sprinting for safety. The throbbing pain in her foot told her that there was no way she'd make it a hundred feet down the blacktop with him chasing her. And there was no possibility of sneaking past him out in the open. She had to lose him in the woods and try to circle around.

The main trailhead was another fifty yards away, past the pit toilet outhouses and a shed. She bent down, and started to creep away from the lodge. Behind the outhouses, she paused and breathed a deep sigh of relief. Her heart was thundering, and the bar in her hands was slick with dripping sweat. She wiped her hands, one at a time, on her shorts and tried to listen for the sound of footsteps following her. When she heard nothing, she made for the shed. Behind that, she didn't dare pause again. She kept going, lumbering toward the trailhead as quietly as she could. A few yards away, she came to the trail marker.

MAHICAN TRAIL ➡
DELL POND TRAIL — CABOT MEETING HOUSE ➡
⬅ TRISTAN LEE PORTER COUNCIL RING
⬅ SPECTRE PATH

The few times she had been hiking on the forest reservation, she hadn't paid close attention to what features were on each trail, except for the Spectre Path. That led to a memorial for a mass grave the town had dug to bury their dead during a smallpox outbreak in the seventeen hundreds. The fenced-in ring of memorial cairns at the end of that route offered nowhere to hide. She picked the Tristan Lee Porter fork and limped off, wanting to step off the path, but knowing that once she did, she would become both much louder and much slower in the underbrush. She stuck to the trail and forged on.

The ambient sounds of the woods made her cringe. She looked over her shoulder as often as she dared, though it led to her stumbling more than once. Each time she turned back, she expected to see Roarke looming behind her, gun raised, ready to fire. But he wasn't there. Not yet. She was ahead of him, and he only had a one-in-four chance of following the same path she'd chosen. And he couldn't be thinking clearly. Not after being shot in the face. Though it wouldn't take much concentration to find her if she didn't do a better job concealing her escape. *One-in-four. One-in-four. Only a quarter chance.* And if she could hide long enough, she could try to circle down through the trees to the animal hospital.

She stumbled around a bend and spied a small cabin up ahead. It was supported by struts in front keeping the building level on the sloping hillside. Nelle could crawl underneath, though raised as it was on this side, it wouldn't offer any more concealment than hiding behind one of the picnic tables out front. If she wanted to disappear here, she had to get inside. She hurried around to the steps leading up to the small front deck. Above her, a sign hung from the front eaves.

POND VIEW CABIN

A brand-new, shiny brass deadbolt lock with a number-pad key box underneath had been installed in the door. She could bust a window and unlock it easy enough, except someone had nailed a two-by-four across the door frame as added security. She wasn't getting that off by hand. The windows on either side were big enough to crawl through, but again, she knew better than to try to smash them to get in. She wanted to hold on to whatever chance she imagined she had in being silent, and didn't have it in her to walk through any more glass. She peered through the window on the left. The late afternoon sun was low, and golden light filtered in through the back of the cabin, illuminating the inside in a warm golden glow. Through the front room, there looked to be a small kitchenette and a back door. She stumbled off of the deck and around the building.

The back was locked with a deadbolt like the front door, but instead of a board, a padlock hung from a loop over a hasp as a second measure. She breathed a sigh of relief. Still difficult, but not impossible. She jammed the end of the tire iron into the shank loop and braced against the body of the padlock. The thing didn't give when she pulled, and she bit her cheek to try to stifle the cry of frustration rising up from deep inside of her. She tried again, leaning away with all her weight, but with the loose lock twisting in the hasp loop, she couldn't put enough pressure on to break it. She pulled the bar out of the lock, stepped back, and took another look.

The hasp. Try against the hasp.

She stuck the bar behind the swinging hasp arm behind the lock and pulled down hard. The padlock stuck out toward her like it had come to attention, and then the thing gave. Not the lock, or the hasp plate, but the screws in the wood holding the whole assemblage in place. They weren't coming out of the new solid door, but the framework around it that was as old as the cabin and weatherworn. Another hard tug, and the hasp came away with a small metal ringing and the faint clatter of screws falling out of the mount onto the flat stone beneath her. She tried twisting the knob just in case. It was locked. A small cry of exasperation escaped her throat. Her impulse was to abandon this cabin and run to the next, but she was tired, and the next place would be at least as well secured as this one, or better. It was this or nothing at all.

In desperation, she swung the end of the bar at the pane of glass nearest the doorknob. The loud clack and crash of glass made her flinch, but the pane broke into pieces on the first hit, falling inside the cabin. She was getting better at breaking and entering. Nelle carefully removed a big shard that remained stuck in the frame and tossed it in the weeds beside the building. She reached through, undid the lock and pulled the door open, slipping inside. She took a long step over the shards on the floor and closed the door behind her, resetting the lock, even though anyone could reach through and undo it again. Whether or not it was a worthless action, the extra second of time it would take to jiggle the knob, then reach through to undo it again seemed like an advantage, however slight. She slipped her arm out the broken window and pushed the padlock hasp up against the door frame again so it looked intact. It wouldn't fool anyone up close, but she hoped everything would look right enough from a distance. Satisfied, she turned to find a place to hide.

Her shadow stretched out ahead of her on the floor of the kitchenette. She stepped to the side out of the light, and it disappeared. Not seeing her shadow felt a little better. Still, it wasn't enough; she needed to find a *real* place to hide. Somewhere for *all* of her to vanish. The kitchenette was wide open, with a bare, round table and a couple of chairs. Against the wall was a sink basin and a narrow counter, but underneath, that was also open to view. No drape hid the space below. This room offered no shelter.

In the next room stood a brick fireplace and rows of bunk beds along the walls, stripped for the season. While a child might hide well enough beneath a low bunk, a full-grown woman would stick out, both figuratively and literally. She turned around, looking for anywhere else to hide. Behind her she saw the trail of muddy, slightly bloody footprints she'd left leading back the way she'd come, from the bunkbeds to the kitchenette and the back door. On the bright pine floors inside the cabin, nothing she tracked in was hidden like it had been outside. Her footprints marked her path through the house like one of those *Family Circus* comics her grandmother used to stick to the fridge when she was little. Her trail was a perversion of the sweet-hearted joke. The dotted line on the floor traced not the distracted path of a child to the mailbox and back inside, but instead the aimless, panicked flight to the place of her death.

She set down the tire iron and yanked at her camisole, trying to rip it. It stretched, but wouldn't tear. She pulled it up to her teeth and bit at the cloth. It still wouldn't tear. Frantic, she picked up the steel rod and shoved through with the tip near the hem at the bottom, finally hearing the sound she wanted as it punctured the thin fabric. She tore a long strip off the bottom. It pulled along unevenly, leaving her with more skin exposed on the right than the left. It would've been easier to wrap the entire shirt around her bleeding foot—it wasn't that big—but bit by bit she'd lost control of everything, except for this one last thing: covering herself. She couldn't say no to the man with the gun or stay with her husband when he needed her. She couldn't even remain in her home and had to run away. But she could stay dressed, god damn it.

She pulled the rest of the strip of cloth off and paused, looking back at her tracks across the floor. She stood and walked to the back door, doing her best to deliberately leave a trail of blood that looked like she'd come and, finding nowhere to hide, had gone. At least that was what she hoped it looked like. Her fresh tracks in place, she sat in a dining chair, wiped off her uninjured foot, and bound up her wound in the other with the tattered piece of her shirt.

The deception was only as good as her ability to disappear. The tracks wouldn't fool anyone if she was caught out standing in the open. And apart from being inside, instead of outdoors, she was still exposed. The entire interior of the cabin was visible through the windows. The place wasn't built for privacy—just shelter. It was a weekend bedroom for boys to stay up late telling scary stories and singing campfire songs.

Then she saw it. A solid plywood door in the next room.

She hobbled over, careful not to set her bad heel down as she went—the camisole bandage held, though it'd be only seconds before she bled through that too. It was a closet. Inside she found a pair of brooms, a dustpan, and plenty of space to hide. She'd be blind, but also out of sight. It wasn't an ostrich hideaway like the main room; it was actual concealment.

In the next room, light shone through a window. She glanced out and her breath hitched when she saw the figure standing in the trees. Her broken girl. She stood staring at Nelle with worry twisting her face. She told herself that the girl was only the psychological manifestation of her worst fears. Of being like her.

But the ghost girl told her something she needed to know. If she could see the child outside, she could be seen *from* outside.

Nelle opened the door carefully, trying not to leave dark fingerprints on the light wood, and stepped into the closet. She pulled the door shut.

To her relief, light filtered in through the gaps at the top and bottom of the door frame. If she leaned close, she could see very faintly through to the room on the other side of the door. It was hard to see well, but she could make out the difference between the folding chairs leaning against the far wall and the bunk beds. Good enough. She tried to settle in for a long wait, wondering how long it would be before she could assume Roarke had given up looking for her or it was clear he'd taken another path. She had no idea. She relied on her gut to tell her when it was time to move; it had steered her right so far. The other voice in her head — that girl's voice — was saying it was not time to stop and hide. It told her to keep running.

The sound of heavy footsteps in the brush outside made gut instinct irrelevant.

There was nowhere left to go.

60

He **stomped up** onto the front deck and paused. From her hiding place inside the closet, Nelle couldn't see him but pictured him leaning close like she had only minutes before, a hand cupped to the dirty window beside the front door, peering inside. Seeing her footprints. The door rattled, and her heart started to race. Outside she heard Roarke say, "I see you!" His words were slurred and his voice deranged. But she understood him clearly enough.

Nelle lost her breath. She clutched the tire iron close to her chest. While she didn't have room to swing it, confined as she was, holding it felt like hanging on to the safety rail that would keep her from falling into oblivion. She couldn't stay there, hiding in the closet like a child, or else this cabin would become that place where she'd disappear forever. Her safety bar wasn't attached to anything; she could take it anywhere.

He stomped away from the front door. The sound of him jiggling the back doorknob made her take a sharp hissing breath in. He laughed and called out, "So. Fugging. Stupid."

She pushed the closet door open quietly and slipped out. She backed into the small sitting room and looked for an escape. The front door was locked and barred, the windows beside it in plain sight. He was at the only other door. If he went straight into the bunkroom, she thought she might be able to slip through the swinging door and out while his back was turned. But the cabin wasn't that big, and the rustic wood floors creaked and groaned underfoot as she moved.

The sunlight shining through the window cast her shadow across the floor to her left. She spun around. That was her only way out. She twisted the locks at the top and lifted the sash, gritting her teeth at the dry sound it made sliding in the frame. The window stuck halfway open. Wide enough for her to try to shimmy out with some effort. She climbed through headfirst.

The sound of Mack unlocking the back door echoed in the tiny cabin. She let out a small squeal. Hanging halfway out, she felt caught. The waistband of her shorts was hung up on something. She pushed up and then shoved hard at the window frame. The wood scraped at her belly and her thighs as she fell out like a limp animal birthed from a standing mother and landed on the ground in a heap. The pain in her wounded shoulder flared, and she saw bright stars again. The tire iron bounced out of her hands and landed with a thud in the tangled weeds a few feet away. She scrambled for it, ignoring the searing sensation in her thighs and shins from dragging across the rough sill. She snatched at it, and the weeds held on, resisting her like some malignance — the animate forest come alive to aid her killer. She tore at them, and the tendrils holding her tool snapped and let go with a ripping sound she was sure echoed through the entire forest. Free of the weeds, she scuttled backward and put her back to the cabin wall below the window, paralyzed, waiting for the man's lunatic leering face to appear in the opening. She couldn't reach to pull the window down. There was no time to try. He'd see which way she'd gotten out, and there was nothing she could do about it.

She was unsure which way to go. Every direction seemed pointless. In her state, running wouldn't accomplish anything except leaving her breathless and tired when Roarke finally murdered her. *Now* was the time she had. All her potential futures had narrowed down to this one moment at the intersection of living and dying.

Through the open window, she heard him shout, "Come out, and I'll shoot you in the head and put your fuckin' lights out quick. Like Evan." She flinched at the sound of her husband's name on his lips. Roarke's footsteps stopped. Then she heard a sound like the closet door banging against the wall, loud as a gunshot. Her legs spasmed, and she pressed harder against the cabin wall.

"GIVE UP OR I'M GOING TO FUCK YOU AND GUT YOU!"

In a moment he'd know she'd slipped out of the cabin and would be coming to follow. She forced herself to creep away from the window and around the back of the building. With shaking hands, she raised the tire iron over her shoulder and waited beside the door. The steel bar felt so heavy, so unmanageable. It was no longer a safety rail. It was an anchor pulling her down. All she could do was hold on tight and try not to scream.

She didn't scream. She waited.

Mack stomped through the cabin to the window. She heard him curse at the sight of it half open and shout through it. "Bitch!" If he followed her through the window, it was over. She was too far from the corner of the cabin to swing at him if he came from that direction. And she couldn't outrun him. No. This was it. Her place to stand. He had to come through the door. *Had* to.

She heard his footfalls pounding on cabin floor as he ran back the way he'd come. Past the closet, through the bedroom, into the kitchenette. Her guts knotted. His boots crunched in broken glass and the door whipped open and she swung by instinct before she saw him.

The feeling in her hands was unlike anything she'd ever experienced. A reverberation of force traveled up her wrists and her forearms; pain flashed in her elbow forcing her fingers to spring open. The bar bounced back and slipped away like a weightless thing floating off into space.

I missed! I hit the fucking door jamb!

She'd failed, yet again, to do a single, simple thing—hit the man, not the wall or the door. She never heard the steel bar hit the ground. It was lost in the weeds. As gone as a final breath. She had nothing left to fight with, and Roarke would emerge in a second to end her. This was her last moment. The white pinpoint of a nearly closed aperture.

When her eyes cleared, she saw Roarke lying on his back inside the cabin, bright red hands up, covering his face. She'd hit him. Actually hit him right where she'd hoped, and he was down. She spun, looking for a stone big enough to bash his head the rest of the way in. Her eyes alighted on one lying in the weeds a few feet away. She lunged toward it. Her foot caught in a tight vine growing along the ground in the same kind of ivy underbrush that had fought her for the tire iron and she fell. But her hand found the rock. Stone in hand, like some savage woman from fifteen thousand years ago, she walked into the cabin to finish what she'd started.

He lay on his back in the kitchenette. She stepped through the door and lifted the rock. He held out a glistening red hand. A fresh gash ran along his forehead, spilling blood over one of his eyes. It ran down, covering his nose and mouth. His lips were pulled back in a crimson snarl, and his open eye rolled, unable to stay focused on her. She felt a touch of satisfaction at how badly hurt he was.

"Wait," he said. Blood arced in small droplets away from his lips, spattering the front of his shirt.

She stepped over the glass on the floor, lifting her stone over her head.

"Wait."

"Fuck yo —"

His heavy boot connected solidly with her shin. The rock slipped from her fingers, landing with her on the floorboards. He kicked at her again and connected hard against her hip. She thrashed her way out the door, her moment of triumph as gone as her weapons. Broken glass sliced her palms as she went. She felt the shards cut into her, but the pain didn't register.

I'm going to fuck you and gut you.

He appeared in the doorway, upright and dark. He stepped out into the late day shadows, toward her. His crimson face, a demon's mien, as ruined as a damned thing.

She tried to scream, but only a frail whimper escaped her throat. She gasped, "No, please." She kept pushing away, but he took another step and closed the distance. He dropped to his knees and straddled her, his blood dripping onto her face. She tried to bat at him, but he knocked her hands away and reached for her throat. His fingers were cold and strong, and it wasn't long before her vision started to darken.

Nelle reached up between his arms to claw at him again, but she was so weak. Her fingers traced down his intact cheek almost tenderly. She croaked out as much of his name as she could. "Mac . . ."

Confusion clouded his face. His clear eye focused and then rolled again. She felt his fingers loosen for a second. She took a gasp of air and said, "Please." They tightened again. But it was enough. She'd gotten a breath. The cool air filling her throat and lungs brought the moment into clarity and a flood of things ran through her head as she tried to find the words that would buy her more life. A second. Half a minute. Anything, but not to die. She wanted to beg, but couldn't think of one thing to say that would make him want to stop killing her. She wondered how many women he'd murdered. She thought about the one in his trunk. That was how they did it, wasn't it? They started with their mothers and then girlfriends, wives, and finally strangers.

Which dead woman was she?

Not the last. Not while his wife was still alive.

He blinked rapidly as if he was trying to clear his vision. Clear his mind. His face shifted from disconcerted to sad to panicked, like a mask made of swiftly flowing water until it settled on hate again. The moment had passed. So had his confusion. He knew who she was. And he'd come to kill her.

She raked his good eye with the hand that had caressed his cheek a moment before and shoved with her nails. He shrieked and leaned away from her. She tried to claw at him again, but he knocked her arm away. She bucked up with her hips and he lost balance, pitching forward. He braced himself against the ground with an arm. She thrust her hand down between his legs. His jeans were stretched tight and she couldn't get a good hold. But the grip she did get was enough. She squeezed his balls and he pitched over onto his side, moaning. She scrambled away from him. Her hand banged against something solid. She looked. It was a knife. Like something from a movie. Big and terrifying. Something that wasn't made for cutting twine or opening packages from Amazon. This was a tool made to open people. A knife made for war.

She grabbed it and scrambled on her knees toward Roarke. He'd gotten to his knees and held out a hand as if he was trying to feel for where she'd gone. She reared up and plunged the knife into him as deep as she could, hitting him between the shoulder blades. It stuck in, but not as far as she imagined it would when she swung it. Again, the force vibrated painfully up into her arms like it had before with the tire iron. He howled and fell back onto his side.

This time she held on.

She pulled the blade out and stabbed him again in the thigh. His screams echoed through the trees. She crawled closer, climbing over his legs and shoving him onto his back, straddling him like a lover. She held the knife in both hands, raised it high above her head, and drove it down.

This time, it went in deep.

The sensation felt unreal. She wrenched it out of his body and thrust again, stabbing into his chest and neck and face. He felt less real with each blow that wasn't answered with a scream, or a shout, or even a sigh. His last breath was a wet burble bubbling up through his ruined mouth.

After that, he wasn't real anymore.

And she penetrated him again and again until she was too fatigued to pull the knife out from where it stuck a last time. Where he'd once had a mouth.

And then Nelle finally found her voice.

She screamed for the rest of his life.

61

Nelle **stared at the body** lying in the dirt as the sun dipped down behind the trees, the knife sticking out of its face like a trail marker.

SPECTRE PATH

Unlike the woman in the trunk of his car, the sight of Mack's corpse didn't make her want to look away. There was comfort in seeing it, knowing he wasn't lurking in a shadow or a corner of her house, waiting. He was right here and hadn't moved in maybe forty minutes or more. No longer a person, he was a thing. An it. A body and nothing more.

She'd made him that.

If she turned away, though, things seemed as if they might be less certain. She felt afraid not to stare at his corpse for fear it'd begin crawling after her, hungry and insatiable.

She didn't know how long it had been since she'd stopped killing him. Long enough it was getting dark. And while he was undeniably dead, she wanted to be far away from him when the sun finally set. Before the deep darkness of wooded places embraced her and her imagination brought him back to life.

She tried to stand, but her ankle and heel wouldn't bear her weight. She would have to crawl out of the woods. That was fine. Crawling was better than being carried out. She pushed up onto her hands and knees and began to make her way down the hill, trying to ignore the pain of rocks and roots pressing into her knees and cut palms. Mud and forest debris stuck to her bloody hands. When she got around to the side of the cabin, she stopped and looked back over her shoulder, certain that Malcolm Roarke would be standing there, looming over her with that big knife, his face restored to maniac fluid unpredictability. He wasn't following. He was dead — still, she looked back to be certain. Something felt unfinished. She crawled back over to him and dug into his pants pockets, finding his keys and cell phone. Her phone was still in the cellar.

The cellar. Evan *is in the cellar.*

Fresh tears swelled in her eyes. She wiped them away angrily and pushed back at the impulse to cry. *I won't cry until I know. And I won't do it next to you, motherfucker.* She spit in what had been the dead man's face and woke his phone to call for help. The signal bar was low, but she was not entirely out of range. She dialed and waited. After a moment, a woman answered. Her voice crackled and broke up, and Nelle only understood what she said because she knew what she'd been expecting the dispatcher to say. "Nine one one, what's your emergency?" She tried to speak, but her throat was dry, and her voice failed. She coughed and tried again. The woman on the other end asked something, but Nelle couldn't understand. The sound was too broken up. Then there was silence. She looked at the phone. The call had dropped. She dialed again and a different person — a man this time — answered. But the conversation was the same. She tried to speak, telling the dispatcher that she needed an ambulance to go to her house because her husband was hurt badly. When she finished begging for help, the silence told her, again, the call had dropped. She gritted her teeth and clenched her fists in frustration.

It's just a call! One goddamn call! I just need this. One. Fucking. Thing.

She looked at the phone as if it was a collaborator with its owner. Frustrating her on purpose so she couldn't bring help. That was ridiculous, but Nelle couldn't help feeling like she wanted to smash the thing against a rock for its bond to a corpse when it should be helping her.

There'll be a signal in the parking lot. There's definitely a signal at home.

She stuffed Roarke's phone and his keys into her waistband and crawled away.

Partway down the hillside, she found a broken branch on the side of the path that was both sturdy-looking and long enough to use as a makeshift crutch. Her hands and knees were aching and raw from moving over the rough terrain. She pulled the branch out of the brush, stuck the narrow end in the dirt and with a little struggle, got up onto her good foot. She'd been running on adrenaline and fear for an entire day, and now that the danger had passed, exhaustion was catching up to her. She couldn't rest yet. Danger *hadn't* passed. Though the active threat was gone (*He* is *gone, right?* she thought as she looked over her shoulder again), Evan needed help. She put her weight on the stick and tried a step. The jagged end was painful under her arm, but it was better than crawling. She could manage this. She was *walking* out of the woods, alive. She was walking home.

To Evan.

How long ago had she left him in the cellar? Minutes? Hours? She felt like she existed outside of time, as if it had stopped and she was living in the space of a single second that dragged out for eternity. No time. There was no time to lose. She tried to move faster, but had to be careful not to fall and hurt herself worse than she already was. It would be no good to try to walk out of the woods and break her leg. So, it was slow going. Slow and steady might not win the race, but it was the only way to finish.

The sun continued to sink as she too went down. The shadows grew longer until they were swallowed by the monolithic darkness cast by the hillside. It grew darker, and colder, and the path became harder to see. And then she emerged from the trees at the trailhead behind the welcome center. Her first instinct was to return to it and try to make the call to the authorities she'd wanted to make there first of all. Instead, she turned toward the red car parked in the lot. Home was a mile away, and it would take her too long to get there on the path, especially in the state she was in.

Throwing her support branch in the back seat, she opened the car door and brushed as much of the shattered glass out into the gravel as she could before climbing in. She shut the door and pulled the keys out of her pants. She stared at the fob for a bit, wondering what to do with it. There was no key prong; it was just a remote. Near her thumb, the word PANIC, in red capital letters stared up at her like a command. Yes. Panic was what she felt she was about to do.

Not yet. Get home first.

The car had a keyless ignition. She searched for the start button on the dash. The button that opened the trunk reminded her of what was less than six feet behind her. Sticky red and still and soft like a lover. She found the ignition and pushed it. The engine rumbled to life. The way the whole thing vibrated around her, made her feel powerful in a way she wasn't outside of it. It was a beast she controlled. It had to do what she said, take her anywhere she wanted to go, and, if she desired it, run down whatever stood in her way. Sitting in it, she felt protected and safe for the first time since early that morning.

It wasn't *her* power, though. It was borrowed — stolen — and she couldn't keep it.

She put the car in gear and pulled out of the lot toward home. It was hard to work the brake with her hurt foot, but she managed because she had to. It didn't require as much from her as standing did. But, boy, did it hurt. She pushed through the pain and pulled onto the highway. The car roared and complained as she struggled to shift from first to second, and then to third. She hadn't driven a stick shift in years, but it came back to her.

Before she realized it, she was slowing to turn into her driveway. Time had collapsed in the other direction — no longer an eternal single pinpoint second, but slipping away in leaps of minutes that passed like breaths. She pulled around to the side of the house beside the black Range Rover parked in front of their cars. Her guts cramped as she remembered the *other* men who'd come to kill her and her husband.

Nelle got out and hobbled on her crutch for the front door. She paused, her hand floating by the door handle.

Had either one of them survived? Were they waiting?

She pulled Roarke's phone out of her pocket and looked at the bright display: four bars. As good a signal as they ever got in their house. She thought about hitting redial. Speaking to the 911 dispatcher again, telling whoever answered that her husband needed an ambulance. They both needed help. She hesitated.

She limped around the side of the house toward the back. When she rounded the corner, she saw the red bulkhead door sticking up, dark as dried blood, a faint light spilling out from inside. The thought of going down into the cellar was paralytic. Roarke wasn't down there, she reminded herself. She'd left him in the woods.

But the other two.

Dead. She'd killed one of them. Watched him die. And heard the other one get shot.

I heard Roarke get shot too. Saw his face.

Her panic told her to leave, call the police and let them deal with it.

Evan was in the cellar. He needed help. He needed *her.*

Dead. Those men are dead. And Evan is alive, and he needs help.

She had to go down into the dark and be with her husband. She had to find him and hold him while help came. She had to be strong, because he needed her and she needed him every bit as much, and this was what they did. They leaned on each other in difficult times because there wasn't anyone else in their lives who held them as well.

She stumbled around the steel doors to the lip of the concrete steps and sat on the top one, descending into the dark hole on her behind, like a child, repeating to herself, "Please be alive. Please, please be alive." Trying to *become* strong, but feeling as fragile as glass right before it breaks.

XIII

◆

THE CELLAR

No

Nononononononononono

Oh please please please no, she whispered

but no one answered

XIV

◆

COSTS

63

FIFTEEN WEEKS AFTER CLOSING

Tony gave Nelle a slight nod, and she pushed the button that sent the casket gliding slowly into the crematory retort. She watched a flame ignite underneath as the bottom of the box met the heat inside, and then a brighter flash when the lacquer caught. The feeling of heat on her face made her want to blink and look away, but she kept her eyes open and trained on the flames. She watched the casket slide the rest of the way in and the steel door come sliding down slowly behind it, cutting her off from the heat and her husband's remains. Evan would have scoffed at the extravagance of the casket she'd picked out. He'd have said, "Why pay for something like that? I'll never know I'm in it." But *she* knew. She wanted him to have something nice. An extravagance that in their past lives they never would've been able to afford. Like a nice car. Or a house. Tony had tried to tell her she didn't have to pay for it, but she didn't want to take advantage of him after he'd been so good to her the last few weeks. And she wanted to do this thing. She *needed* to buy this thing. In the end, Tony agreed to charge her his wholesale cost, but no more. She paid him and was pretty sure he just turned around and sent the money to some charity. That was Tony Tremblay. He was a good man.

Evan had been a good man. He was kind and funny and a good lover. And if she'd ever felt a feeling, he knew what it was just by looking at her. He *got* her in a way no one else she'd ever met had. She'd wanted to have children with him, and he was excited to be a father someday. But they hadn't worked that out yet. There was always time, they'd said. But there wasn't always time. There was only the time you had and not a second longer, no matter how much you wanted there to be more.

"Let me take care of the rest," Tony said. He put a light hand on her arm. It was meant to be reassuring. She let him touch her, though the feeling of another person's hand on her made her stomach tense and her breath quicken just a little. A little dose of adrenaline coursed through her, and she wanted to jerk her arm away and take a step—or a hundred—back. She stood there and tried not to show how terrified just a little innocent touch made her feel.

She thought about her friends waiting in the lobby. *Their* friends. They'd wanted to come into the crematory "witnessing room" with her, offering their strength to buttress her own, but Nelle asked them to wait outside. Part of it was that she felt that this moment was hers; she wanted it for herself. A quiet moment to say goodbye to her husband. Part of it was guilt. Guilt over his death. Guilt over everything.

If she and Evan hadn't moved out to the suburbs. If she'd never met him in the first place. If she'd moved out of state after high school and traveled like she'd dreamt of doing, how differently would things have turned out for everyone? Evan would be alive; that much was certain.

If she and Evan hadn't bought the house, someone else would've, and they'd be burning *their* dead. Perhaps there would be even more funerals to attend than only one. Of course, there were more than one. The woman from the courthouse and her daughter. Samantha's parents, the woman in the trunk, Siobhan. They were dead too. But they weren't *her* dead. She hadn't killed them. Still, there was a guilty voice in her heart that told her all the choices she'd made in her life had brought her to this moment, and all those people who'd gotten hurt had been pulled along in her wake.

Whether or not it was rational, it was in her. In those boxes of philosophy notes in the cellar—in her essays on Simone de Beauvoir. "I am the very face of that misery..." She was responsible. For everything. Even if she wasn't.

Evan too, though he was gone.

If they hadn't stolen the money...

She thought about the men she'd fed into this very crematory oven. She felt less guilt for what she'd done to them. They got what they deserved.

She'd dragged their bodies out to the shed and locked them in. It had been so hard; they were so heavy and she'd been hurt and tired, but she'd done it. She cleaned up the mess where the one had been shot upstairs. Wiped Roarke's blood off the leather sofa and the hardwood floors. Picking up after the one in the cellar had been easier. She'd given him a heart attack. No blood. She found their guns and stuck them in the back of the Range Rover and then parked that in the neighborhood across the highway before ambling home to call for help.

The dispatcher on the phone had exuded a practiced composure as he spoke that upset her. She was afraid and panicked because the world had split apart and she was barely hanging on, dangling over an abyss, and she wanted him to be upset along with her too. But the man on the telephone was calm. He told her in his neutral voice, help was on the way. He told her to stay strong. *Stay.* A barking laugh had escaped her mouth at that, like a soul departing. *How do you remain something that you never were to begin with?*

And then the hospital. A stream of doctors and nurses and detectives came to see her. They'd visited her with questions, and she answered them carefully. The painkillers the doctors prescribed her made her feel fuzzy, but she told her story. About the cellar, the phones, and leaving the message, and about getting free and the struggle and running away. She said that she ran and hid in a cabin in the woods that she knew from the hikes she liked to take from time to time and waited, and that when he found her, she killed him. She told them all of it.

Almost.

She didn't talk about the ruined girl in the cellar. In the yard. Among the trees. Who often stood in the corner of her hospital room.

Everyone believed her, though the detectives always seemed on the edge of wanting more. As if some missing detail of her story was a gap that needed to be filled. But the detectives who came to visit her were kind. Detectives Lirvin and Freschi. They treated her with respect, and when they found the letter from her mother and the locket in Malcolm Roarke's apartment, they brought them back to her. One of them — the woman, Stacey now — said the DA wanted it, but she'd told him the perp was dead; the Commonwealth could live with *pictures* of the necklace. Nelle thanked the woman through her tears and took the gift. Holding the necklace, she realized she and her mother had something new in common now. Since her stepdad had died, they were both widows.

Widow. She was too young to be one. Of course, no one was too young to lose. She was living proof. Her and the woman in the car trunk. Stacey told her that woman's name was Siobhan McKinley. She'd been a friend of Samantha's. From the news, Nelle learned that Mack killed Donna DaSilva, a courthouse employee, and her daughter, Joanne, too. He'd killed his ex in-laws, and the cops said that if Nelle hadn't killed him, he would've kept going: they'd found a cache of weapons and explosives at the Darnielles' house. He'd been staging from there. Her heart sank. First, she felt grateful Juanita and Colin hadn't been home, then she wondered what would've happened if she'd been able to break that patio glass door and get inside. Would she have gotten her hands on one of those guns and been able to confront him? Would she have been able to reach Evan sooner and save *him* if she had?

She doubted it.

By the time she was released from the hospital, she'd expected the Range Rover to have been towed away and for a fresh set of detectives to come knocking, or worse. But it was still right where she'd parked it, untouched. She drove it back to her house, loaded the men's bodies inside, and brought them to work, where she burned them in the middle of the night. All of her problems, gone with the breeze at the top of a chimney. She'd taken their "cremains," ashes and unburnt bone fragments, and scattered them in the brush behind the house. One good rain, and the Russians were the same earth as everything else back there. Their car she left in long term parking at the airport, and took the Logan Express shuttle bus back to Ripton, and a cab home from there.

She watched the news. Roarke showed up often. He was a big deal. They talked about his start as a high school athlete, destined for college ball until he was sidelined by injury. His interests, his passion for building, and the failed home remodeling business were fodder for the think pieces analyzing the mind of a gunman. So we can know the signs better and try to prevent the next mass killer from emerging, optimists agreed. Nelle was a realist. She knew what those endless prosopographical pieces were really for.

Roarke's ex-wife gave interviews and wept for her parents and her friend and all the horrors her former husband had wrought. Nelle declined to be interviewed, but they seemed more than happy to talk to Samantha. After all, she'd lost so much more than anyone else. And she had no reservations about being the public face of the tragedy. The *other* woman who'd escaped Malcolm Roarke's rampage. The national media ran with the story. Experts came crawling out of obscurity to analyze why he'd done what he had, trying to understand *him* and his motivations. Some sympathized, talking about how unfairly men are treated in the family court system and how abandonment of affection is a terrible form of abuse that can turn good men bad. They called him by his nickname, Mack, and implied Samantha's culpability in driving him to violence. Whatever the perspective, his name seemed to be spoken ten times for every single utterance of Donna DaSilva; her daughter, Joanne; Siobhan McKinley; or the Zamyatins. The newscasters mused that the list of his victims would've been longer, but Samantha's boyfriend had stolen her away to Vermont to propose over the holiday. The news called him the fiancé. They tried to spin the end of the story as the triumph of beginnings over endings. Love over hate. Showed the two of them sitting with a little red dog on their front porch like a happy family. But Nelle knew Samantha's engagement would always be the anniversary of "the Ripton Rampage." It was no way to start a life together. Nelle wished her well, but she suspected their future would be full of angry ghosts.

Eventually, the coverage died down as a different national news story took center stage, and people's attentions shifted back to Washington and Pyongyang and Hollywood and wherever the next body count was waiting to be tallied.

Tony touched her shoulder and brought Nelle out of her trance. "Do you want to go wait with your friends?" he asked. Nelle shook her head and said, "I'll be out in the garden. I think I need a few minutes by myself." Tony was right. She didn't want to do any of the rest of what it would take to finish. It wasn't anything she ever wanted to do again. She was done with the dead, and had told Tony she quit. He took the news like he took everything else, in stride and with grace. She didn't know what she'd do without him or this job. It wasn't the money—she had more of that than she could spend. It was the stability. The job, his support, were something fixed to hold on to. She figured she was going to find out, though. She left him to finish the job of reducing the love of her life to ashes.

The garden outside was shady and cool. A breeze swept through, raising gooseflesh on her arms. She ignored the chill and fingered her great-gran's necklace. The pictures inside replaced with her and Evan. She felt overcome with rage and despair, and slumped on the bench and thought that there was nothing left for her. Her friends told her anytime she needed to talk, they were there for her. But she didn't reach out. She didn't tell them that for days after, she went back to where she'd left Roarke's body, regretting telling the police where it was. She went back to that cabin and imagined him lying there in the ivy behind it, purpling, with bugs beginning to lay eggs in his corpse, and she fell down and cried and screamed and thought that she should have buried him somewhere in the forest where he'd never be found because eventually the police would release his body to next of kin, and he didn't deserve anyone to mourn him. That was too good for him. If there was a single person in the world who would mourn Malcolm Roarke, even accidentally, or show sympathy or care at his disposal, she wanted to stand in the way of it. He didn't get to have a ritual. He didn't deserve to be lowered into the ground while his mother wept or a sibling said a prayer. "Closure" be damned. He deserved what he got when Nelle ruined him. And what she wanted to give him was an anonymous cremation in the middle of the night without a word of grief or regret, just like the other two. And after she burned him, she wanted to scatter him in a dumpster behind a strip mall somewhere to spend eternity with the rest of the world's trash. Because that was exactly what he was.

She didn't say any of that to her friends, because those were her private thoughts and her lasting regrets. The passing days only served to give her a chance to reflect on the choices she'd made in her desperation, and regret and self-doubt swelled.

Fresh tears stung her eyes, and she sat and cried heavy, sobbing gasps of despair. When she found herself too exhausted to cry anymore, she wiped her eyes and sat up. She heard the door behind her open and footsteps crunch across the gravel path. Her spine stiffened. Tony stood over her shoulder but didn't try to touch her this time. He said, "Can I get you anything?"

"No. I'm okay," she lied. She stood and said, "I think . . . I should go home." It wasn't home anymore. Yet having fought for it, she wasn't ready to let go. Not yet. It was all she had left of her husband.

He looked scared. Not of her. *For* her. "There's no rush, Nelle. If you need something, I can get it for you. Don't punish yourself."

She laughed and thought, *You can't tell me what to do.* Instead, she said, "Thank you, Tony. Maybe you're right. I'm going to go. Can you let my friends know I'll get in touch with them later?" Knowing she probably wouldn't. She walked out of the garden to the parking lot and drove in silence to her house in Ripton.

The police tape that had denied her entry for days was gone. She let herself inside and stood in the front room for a long moment, listening, hoping deep down she'd hear the familiar sounds of her husband in the kitchen, knives and pans and glasses clanking as he got a start on dinner. She hoped to hear from behind the wall, "Bar's open!" But there was nothing. No smells of sautéing mushrooms or chorizo, no clank of the wineglass he sipped from while chopping peppers. And worst of all, no music.

She shut the door behind her. The alarm system chirped, and she felt a swell of panic rise in her. An unborn scream, pregnant in her throat. She swallowed it and locked the door. Nelle hung her car keys on the hook beside it and wandered through the kitchen into the living room.

Her phone pinged, and she saw a new text from her mother.

Are you okay?
Need me to come over?

She knew she should reply, but didn't know what to say. She wrote back,

No. It's ok. I need some time alone.
I'll come by tomorrow after I check on Inês.
I love you.

I love you.

She silenced her phone and dropped it on the sofa. She knelt down in front of the shelves Evan had filled first before they'd unpacked anything else. She pulled out his favorite record and fit it over the spindle.

She lowered the needle and listened to the warm, serene guitar strum a soft bossa nova rhythm. He'd said it reminded him of his parents when he was young, watching his father Joãozinho play the guitar while his mother danced in their living room.

Every time she thought she had no more crying left in her, fresh tears filled her eyes.

She set the album jacket on the floor and curled up next to it, closing her eyes and listening. She lay there in a lonely house much too big for a single person and whispered to herself, "No darkness. Only light."

Acknowledgments

To start, I owe considerable gratitude to my agent, Howard Morhaim. He read this manuscript many more times in its nascency than anyone should reasonably be expected to, and his insights into the story were essential to it being what it is. In that same vein, my editor, Jaime Levine, is the other of my collaborators who believed in this story and its characters and helped me find exactly the right way to tell the tale. She got exactly what I wanted to do and was instrumental in bringing out the best of this book. Thank you, Jaime!

Thank you, Frank Raymond Michaels, for answering my questions about computer tech and security. Despite his efforts to educate me, any mistakes or inaccuracies herein are mine alone. Thanks to my friend Lyndsey Emery for the insight into the experience and practice of medical pathologists. Talking to you was one of my favorite (and weirdest) moments of research into this book, for sure! Also, thank you to Alison Courchesne for directing me toward the episode of Malcolm Gladwell's *Revisionist History* podcast describing the idea of "pulling the goalie" when I told her I was writing a home invasion thriller (Season 3, Episode 7, "12 Rules for Life," for anyone who's interested). Now I can finally watch the movie!

Also, a very special thank you to Katya Heldwein for helping me construct and transliterate Russian phrases she is much too polite to ever say aloud. That was such an entertaining way to spend an afternoon.

I am fortunate to have a large community of literary friends, colleagues, and influences who stand at the ready to give me love, inspiration, and support. Among them are Paul Tremblay, Christopher Golden, James A. Moore, Brian Keene, Errick Nunnally, Christopher Irvin, K. L. Pereira, Josh Malerman, Thomas Sniegoski, Hillary Monahan, Dana Cameron, John McIlveen, Tony Tremblay, Izzy Lee, Joe Lansdale, Jennifer McMahon, and Andrew Vachss. Thank you all for your friendship and guidance.

My son is the constant star in my sky. Thank you, L., for always having a hug ready and offering to play Halo with me. You're the best kid what ever was in the whole history of kids! No, you cannot have the last slice of cold pizza; it's mine.

Finally, as always, I owe the most gratitude to my wife, Heather, for her unwavering affection, especially while I wrote a book set in a simulacrum of our house, endangering characters reflective of ourselves. It seemed like a good idea at the time, but put me in some pretty bleak places coming out of my office daily after work. Your patience and love are the sun and the moon to me. You're my rescuer and best friend. Always.

I miss you, Dallas.

Sleep well. You earned your rest.